MORE . . .

"Coonts does a remarkable job of capturing the mood of clashing cultures in *Hong Kong*." —*Publishers Weekly*

"Filled with action, intrigue, and humanity."
—*San Jose Mercury News*

CUBA

"Enough Tomahawk missiles, stealth bombers, and staccato action to satisfy [Coonts's] most demanding fans."
—*USA Today*

"[A] gripping and intelligent thriller."
—*Publishers Weekly* (starred review)

"Perhaps the best of Stephen Coonts's six novels about modern warfare." —*Austin American-Statesman*

"Coonts delivers some of his best gung-ho suspense writing yet." —*Kirkus Reviews*

"Dramatic, diverting action...Coonts delivers." —*Booklist*

FORTUNES OF WAR

"*Fortunes of War* is crammed with action, suspense, and characters with more than the usual one dimension found in these books." —*USA Today*

STEPHEN COONTS'

DEEP BLACK:

CONSPIRACY

Written by Stephen Coonts and Jim DeFelice

St. Martin's Paperbacks

This is a work of fiction. All of the characters, organizations, and events portrayed in this novel are either products of the author's imagination or are used fictitiously.

STEPHEN COONTS' DEEP BLACK: CONSPIRACY

Copyright © 2008 by Stephen Coonts.
Excerpt from *The Assassin* copyright © 2008 by Stephen Coonts.

ISBN: 0-312-93700-8
EAN: 978-0-312-93700-3

Printed in the United States of America

St. Martin's Paperbacks edition / June 2008

St. Martin's Paperbacks are published by St. Martin's Press, 175 Fifth Avenue, New York, NY 10010.

10 9 8 7 6 5 4 3 2 1

AUTHORS' NOTE

The National Security Agency, Central Intelligence Agency, Space Agency, Federal Bureau of Investigation, National Security Council, and Marines are, of course, real. While based on an actual organization affiliated with the NSA and CIA, Desk Three and all of the people associated with it in this book are fiction. The technology depicted here either exists or is being developed.

Some liberties have been taken in describing actual places and procedures to facilitate the telling of the tale. Some details regarding the President's security have been omitted and other fictionalized in the interests of actual security.

1

EVEN THROUGH THE scope, the black circle at the center of the target looked tiny. The shooter tried to remember everything the rifle instructor had told him, held his body steady, checked his breath, eased his finger against the trigger.

He didn't have to be perfect. He just had to be decent.

The Remington barked. The bullet missed the center of the target, hitting the white space just beyond.

Again, the shooter told himself. Better this time. Better.

The shot sailed high, to the outer ring.

I can do better, thought the shooter. He took a long breath, then slipped his left hand ever so slightly forward. He imagined that the center of the target was not a black circle a hundred yards away but a man's head.

This time, the bullet hit the mark.

The shooter tried again, once more imagining that he was firing at a person. His shot sailed a bit to the left but still managed to find the black disk. So did the next.

"You're getting much better," said his instructor as he paused to reload.

"I think I've found the key," said the shooter. He grinned.

The instructor waited a moment to hear what he might think that was, but the student had no intention of explaining. He had registered for the rifle class not merely under false pretenses—unlike the other students, he had no intention of ever going deer hunting—but also using a false name and ID.

"Well, very good," said the instructor finally. "Keep at it."

"I will," said the shooter, beginning to reload.

PINE PLAINS LOOKED like a picture-perfect town, a throwback nineteenth-century village, complete with striped awnings over the main street storefronts and white picket fences on the side streets. The center of town was dominated by a freshly painted three-story bank building—Stissing National, which had so far resisted overtures to join the megabanks that dominated the region. The drugstore to its right could make the same claim, with an old-fashioned soda fountain clearly visible through the sparkling plate glass at the front of the store. And the hardware store demonstrated that it was *still* just a hardware store, not a fancy home decorating center, by displaying a full run of lawnmowers and assorted shovels and rakes on its half of the sidewalk. Neither the machines nor the tools were chained or otherwise secured, the store owner confident that no one would walk away with them.

Secret Service Special Agent Jerry Forester turned his big Ford off Main Street, heading down Meadow Avenue. He gazed past the row of wood-sided houses toward the field beyond them. It was late spring, and though the field had been cleared, it had not yet been planted, the owner timing his crop to meet the needs of a processor, who would already have contracted for the result.

Meadow Avenue ended at a set of train tracks. Forester took a right, passing the ruins of an old whistle-stop as he headed back in the direction of the state highway. The houses that lined the road were bigger than those packed into the tight streets at the town center; they had larger lawns and longer driveways. But the newest was probably more than forty years old, built before whirlpool tubs and two-story entryways became fashionable. The sugar maples in their yards had stout trunks and were generous with their shade.

Forester lingered at an intersection, considering getting out of the car and going for a walk. But then he realized if he did, Pine Plains' idyllic character would quickly fade. He'd see the beer cans tossed onto the long lawns by bored teenagers over the weekend and notice graffiti on the sides of the Main Street buildings, including the five-fingered star that proved even rural America wasn't immune to the awesome coolness of outlaw gangs. The torn shingles on the church and the rust stains from the broken gutter would be difficult to miss. The man sitting in the window seat at Kay's Breakfast Nook would have a wild expression and the vague smell of hospital antiseptic in his clothes.

Step inside some of the houses and the last bits of the illusion would quickly melt away. Forester had no illusions about human evils and how widespread they were. Even if he hadn't grown up in a town exactly like Pine Plains, he'd spent the last twenty-three years working for the Secret Service, a job that permitted no naïveté. He knew the foibles of the powerful as well as the delusions of the powerless.

And the knowledge choked him.

Best to leave it like this, he thought. Best to leave the image intact, even as the snarling dog of cynicism, of apathy and black despair, growled at his neck. He was in a hole and he was not getting out. The drive he'd taken to cheer himself up had done the opposite. There was no fooling himself, no fooling the cloud that clung to him every moment of every day.

Forester's cell phone buzzed. He pulled it from his pocket.

"Forester."

"Jerry, where are you?"

"Running a little late."

"Wait until you see the nightgown I'm wearing. How long before you get here?"

"Half hour."

"Oh, pooh. I'm going down to the bar."

"In the gown?"

"I might."

"Call up room service. I'll put the pedal to the metal."

"You better."

As Forester switched off the phone, he noticed a police cruiser growing in his rearview mirror. He glanced down at his speedometer; he was doing just over sixty. The state had a law against driving with a cell phone and required seat belts to be buckled, but it was too late to do anything about either; the bubblegum lights erupted red. He hit his blinker and pulled off the side of the road before reaching for his Service ID.

AMANDA RAUCI TOOK another sip from the wine and glanced at her watch. It was nearly half past seven.

Where the hell is Jerry? she thought to herself, putting the glass down. He should have met her at least two hours ago. Even if he'd gotten lost, it shouldn't have taken him this long to get here.

And Jerry Forester never got lost.

Maybe his rotten bitch of a soon-to-be ex-wife had called him with some new bullshit. She was always torturing him with something, even though they were getting a divorce and hadn't lived together for nearly a year. Amanda couldn't understand why he even took the bitch's calls, since inevitably they ended with her screaming at him.

Actually, Amanda could. Forester wanted custody of his two sons, or at least some connection with them. The bitch was doing her damnedest to keep it to a minimum.

Amanda caught a glimpse of herself in the hotel room's full-length mirror. The nightgown, which had seemed so sexy when she'd put it on earlier, looked a little silly, even sad. She decided to change into her street clothes. When she was dressed, she picked up her cell phone and called Forester again. The call, her third in the past hour or so, went to voice mail like the others.

"Hey, where are you?" she asked. "Meet me in the bar, OK? And hurry up. I'm hungry."

IN THE HALF hour she waited at the bar, Amanda turned down two different offers of drinks. With her hunger getting the better of her, she asked the bartender for a menu, then gave Forester another call. Once again she got his voice mail. She didn't bother leaving a message.

The baked sole in vermouth was very good, but Amanda left most of it. Too many people were staring at her, calculating whether they might relieve her loneliness.

This wasn't like Forester, not at all.

Amanda went back to her room, half-expecting—hoping— that the light on the phone would be blinking, indicating she had a message. But it wasn't.

Amanda started to dial the number for his office, thinking he might have checked in. She stopped before the call went through. Their relationship was a secret, and besides, by now there would be no one to check in with. It was going on eight o'clock.

Amanda went to the desk in the corner of the room and picked up the phone. Gerald Forester had not checked into the hotel; he didn't even have a reservation, according to the clerk. This didn't necessarily bother Amanda—the hotel wasn't that busy, and maybe Jerry had always intended on staying with her anyway.

Maybe. Ordinarily, though, he reserved his own room, since the Service paid.

A phone book sat at the edge of the desktop. She pulled it over and leafed through the yellow pages, caught between her instincts to act and the uncertainty of what to do. Then the investigator in her took over; she flipped to the hospital listings and began making calls.

The list was quickly exhausted. No Gerald Forester had been checked in or reported to an emergency room.

The only possible reason for standing her up was that something was happening on his case. Amanda didn't know exactly what it involved—Jerry never discussed what he was working on. But she did know that he hadn't planned on doing any real work until tomorrow.

Amanda called the desk again. Had Mr. Forester checked in yet?

"No," said the clerk, annoyed. "Did you call earlier?"

Amanda put down the phone. And then, on a whim, or maybe to satisfy a growing sense of insecurity, she began dialing other hotels in the area, asking if a Gerald Forester had checked in.

Did she think he was cheating on her? It wouldn't be cheating, exactly, if they weren't married. She was worried, and insecure, and unsure. After the third call—"No guest by that name, sorry"—Amanda got up and began pacing the room.

Amanda heard a noise in the hall. She stopped, held her breath as she heard the footsteps.

Decide, she told herself. Are you mad at him for being late and not calling, or are you happy nothing is wrong and he's finally here?

Happy.

But whoever was outside didn't stop at her door. She opened it, saw another man taking out a key several rooms away.

Back inside, Amanda called the next hotel.

"Do you have a Mr. Gerald Forester there?"

"Yes, ma'am. Should I connect you to the room?"

Amanda felt as if she'd been punched in the chest. "Please."

The phone rang, but there was no answer.

THE DANBURY RAMADA was only two miles from the InterContinental, and it took less than ten minutes to get there. Amanda's heart sank when she saw Forester's car in the parking lot. She sat in her car with the engine running, literally feeling sick to her stomach.

And then her anger took over.

Who the hell was he in there with? Where did he come off calling her—*calling her*—and then standing her up?

Amanda got out and walked toward the hotel. She was angry—too angry, she thought—and she reversed course.

Why would he reserve a room in another hotel without telling her?

Maybe it was to keep their affair a secret.

Amanda passed by his car. Looking inside the passenger-side window, she saw a notebook, some pens, and the edge of a room card.

So he'd checked in earlier, without even telling her!

Forester was always locking his keys in somewhere—his car, his office, his house. To avoid embarrassment, he planted spares all over the place. When he stayed somewhere, he made sure to get two cards and left one in his car. He must have gotten up here earlier, gone out, come back—maybe to pick up someone.

Amanda ducked under the rear bumper on the passenger's side, fishing for the small metal key container Forester kept there. She took it, then slid open the top and took out the car key, only to find that he hadn't bothered to lock his car.

There was no room number on the key—but the small envelope it came in had the number in tiny script at the bottom edge.

She could surprise him if she wanted. Surprise him in bed with whatever whore he'd picked up.

Unless it was his wife. Amanda scanned the parking lot, sure for a second that his soon-to-be ex had come up here to confront him about something. But Amanda didn't see the car.

She was being ridiculous, acting like a petty bitch herself. She put the key card back and started toward her car.

He *did* owe her an explanation. Leaving her waiting at the bar for hours was rotten.

And uncharacteristic.

Why not go up there right now? If he was cheating on her, at least she would know.

Amanda realized that she hadn't replaced the spare key holder. She turned and walked back to the car. But before she got there, she changed her mind again: she was going up to his room. She opened the car door, grabbed the room key, and then walked quickly into the hotel, determined to confront him before she could change her mind.

There was no one at the front desk. She walked straight ahead toward the elevators, head down, determined.

Angry.

The elevator doors opened in slow motion. Amanda got inside, pressed the button for the fifth floor.

The doors opened in a few seconds. She found the room at the very end of the hall, took a deep breath, and knocked.

"Room service," she said curtly, her anger still sharp.

No answer.

Amanda knocked again. "Room service," she said, a little louder. "Mr. Forester?"

Nothing.

"Jerry, open the damn door."

Still nothing. Amanda slipped the card into the slot. The two lights at the top of the lock came on, both red, then green.

I shouldn't go in, she thought to herself, placing her hand on the handle. She pushed anyway.

"Jerry?" she said. The light was on. "Why are you—"

She stopped in mid-sentence. Her lover sat in the chair across from the door, a good portion of his mouth and head blown away by a bullet from the old-school .357 Magnum that sat on the floor below his open hand.

CHARLIE DEAN PULLED the strap of his bag over his shoulder and stepped out of the plane, ambling down to the concrete runway. A narrow man with thinning hair near the terminal bent toward Dean as he approached.

"Mr. Dean?"

"I'm Charlie Dean."

"Red Sleeth." The man stuck his hand out. "How are you?"

"When your girl said there would be a driver waiting, I didn't expect it to be the guide himself," said Dean.

"We're a one-man operation," replied Sleeth. "One man, one woman—the girl was my wife. I don't think she'd be offended," added Sleeth, reaching for the bag.

Dean insisted on carrying it himself. He followed Sleeth as he walked toward a parking lot on the side of the terminal.

"I'm glad you had an opening," said Dean. "I know this was kind of last-minute."

"Happy to have you. Customer who canceled will be happy, too. We refund his deposit if we find someone else to take the slot."

Sleeth's battered Ford Bronco looked a few years older than the nearby mountains. Dean paused a few feet from the vehicle and looked around. The sun had already set, but he could see the tall shadows in the distance. It was beautiful country; you stood in a parking lot and thought you were at the edge of the world.

"Never been to Montana, have you, Mr. Dean?"

"No, sir. Beautiful land." Charlie swung back to the truck.

"Yes, it is," said Sleeth. "Ready to get yourself a mountain lion?"

"Ready."

"Good. It'll be the greatest experience of your life. There's nothing as exciting as hunting a mountain lion. Everything else you've ever done will pale in comparison."

Dean knew that wasn't true but smiled anyway.

DURING THE SIXTY seconds immediately after she saw her lover's dead body, Amanda Rauci acted like the trained Secret Service agent she was. Unholstering her pistol, she checked the rest of the room and made sure there were no intruders. She then went to him, squatting just close enough to make sure he was dead.

There was no question. Blood, skull, and brain material from the gunshot's exit wound had splattered on the curtain behind him. The back of the seat and floor were covered with thick red blood.

As Amanda straightened, the restraint imposed by the Service training began to slip away. She felt many things: Shock and grief and fear. Panic. Her heart raced.

Why would he do this?

Why didn't I realize he was suicidal?

Is it my fault?

Is it really suicide? How can that be?

His eyes gaped at her, as if they were accusing her of something.

I have to get away, she thought, and for the next sixty seconds the trained Secret Service agent shared the body of a panicking, guilt-stricken woman. She backed from the room, carefully making sure not to touch anything. She took a handkerchief from her pocket, opened the door, closed the door, walked swiftly down the hall toward the elevator, then came back and ducked into the stairway instead. Amanda descended all the way to the bottom floor, where the stairwell opened to the outside. She turned and pushed the crash bar with the side of her hip, then walked around to her car.

Amanda didn't begin to cry until she was almost to her hotel. The tears slipped down her cheeks in ones and twos. Then, as she waited to turn into the parking lot, they burst from her eyes in a steady downpour.

The driver behind her laid on the horn. Startled, Amanda went straight instead of turning, accelerating and then hitting her brake to pull into the lot of a Friendly's restaurant. She left the car running but leaned her head on the wheel to weep.

Why did he kill himself? Why? Why?

Why did he have her wait for him?

Why? Why?

And why had she snuck away, as if she were guilty of something? As if she were the killer?

She couldn't leave him like that. She should call the police.

But they'd want to know why she was there. And then everyone would know why she was there. It would be one more thing that would hurt his sons.

And the police would want to know why she didn't report it in the first place. They'd want to know why she let herself in and then left. It would look like she was a murderer.

She could go back, she thought. Do it all over. No one had seen her.

She should do that for him. Not let him lie there for hours until he was found.

Amanda did her best to dry her tears. She decided she would go back, get into the room, and make the call. Everything would be more or less as it had really happened—except she wouldn't mention that she had left.

And she'd put the keys back, the room key and the car key. She'd completely forgotten about them.

Her resolve melted when she saw two police cars in front of the hotel, their red lights tearing up the night.

Now what should she do?

She looked back at the road just in time to see a policeman flagging her down. She slammed on the brake and jerked to a stop right in front of him.

Were they looking for her? Did they suspect her?

God, no one would believe her if she told the truth.

Why did you run if you had nothing to hide? You panicked? What professional law enforcement officer, what Secret Service agent, ever panics?

She hadn't panicked.

Yes. Yes, she had.

Amanda reached to roll down her window, waiting for the inevitable question, waiting for everything that would follow. Then she realized that the policeman was simply stopping traffic. There was an ambulance coming from the other direction, siren on and lights flashing.

It's too late. Much, much too late.

I should follow it in, she thought. But when the officer pointed at her and waved her on, she complied.

"SO, MR. RUBENS, you don't believe that the National Security Agency should spy on Americans?"

William Rubens took a slow breath before answering, very conscious that he was being set up.

"Our job is to provide intelligence, Senator," the NSA's deputy director said. "We have strict guidelines for gathering and disseminating information, and we follow them."

"But you believe that Americans should be spied on."

"Senator, my role is to follow the law regardless of what I believe," said Rubens. "And no, as a personal matter, I do not believe that."

Senator Gideon McSweeney smiled broadly, looking around the committee room as if he had just scored some massive point.

"And was the law followed in the so-called American Taliban case?" McSweeney asked.

"Speaking for my agency's actions, absolutely."

"Without qualification?"

"The law was absolutely followed. No qualifications."

The senator paused, looking down at the papers in front of him.

"Did you obtain subpoenas before gathering your intelligence?" McSweeney asked finally.

Rubens leaned back in the chair. Ordinarily his boss, NSA Director Admiral Devlin Brown, would be sitting in this chair, doing his best not to tell the senators what he really thought of them. But Brown had suffered a heart attack three weeks before, leaving Rubens to take the hot seat while he recovered.

"We followed the law, as always," said Rubens.

"Did you obtain subpoenas?" McSweeney asked again.

"Where necessary."

"And *where* were they necessary?"

Rubens had been instructed by the President not to be specific about the intelligence gathering in the case, which had involved a misguided young man from Detroit who had unfortunately gotten himself involved in a plot to destroy a crude oil receiving station in the Mexican Gulf.

Much of the information had come via a high-ranking al Qaeda operative who had come to the United States to make contact with sympathizers. Deep Black had implanted a bugging device in his skull; the device was still there, continuing to transmit valuable information to the NSA. Describing the subpoenas could, conceivably, lead to information about the operation itself, and Rubens had no intention of revealing anything that had not already been made public.

"I can only say, Senator, that the law was followed," Rubens said.

"A law in which there are no checks and balances, since the subpoenas are handed down in secret and need never be revealed."

"There is a system in place," said Rubens. "I can elaborate if you wish."

McSweeney had no intention of letting Rubens take up the rest of his allotted time with an explanation of how the independent but secret judicial panel did its job, an explanation that would include the fact that more than 30 percent of the requests for subpoenas were turned down and that roughly 85 percent of the subpoenas resulted in an arrest or a documented disruption of a terrorist plot. Instead, McSweeney gave a short speech that invoked everyone from Thomas Jefferson to John Sirica as he discoursed on the need to uphold basic American values in the continuing war against terrorism.

Neither Rubens nor anyone in the room could have possibly

disagreed with McSweeney, but his unspoken implication that the administration did not follow the law nettled. Rubens felt like asking if the senator thought the government should have let terrorists blow up the offshore oil port, with the subsequent loss of perhaps a third of the country's petroleum import capabilities.

But as satisfying as that might have been momentarily, it was entirely the wrong thing to do. Senator McSweeney was running for his party's presidential nomination. The purpose of his speech was not so much to make the present administration look bad—though he certainly didn't mind doing that—as it was to make him appear both concerned and informed. Appearances to the contrary, he had no personal animosity toward the NSA and in fact had supported supplemental budget allocations for the agency several times in the past. As long as Rubens allowed himself to be used as a punching bag, McSweeney would still consider himself a friend when the supplemental budget came up for a vote in a few months.

Make McSweeney look like a fool, however, and there would be no end of trouble.

Rubens pressed his thumb against his forefinger, digging the nail into the fingertip, to keep himself quiet.

"Time, Senator," said the committee aide keeping track of the allotted time.

"Of course, I hope that my remarks will not be interpreted as a criticism of the National Security Agency, which has done and continues to do an excellent job," said McSweeney quickly, throwing Rubens and the agency a bone for being a good punching bag. "I would extend that praise to you as well, Mr. Rubens. I know you to be a man of the highest personal integrity."

Somehow, the remark irritated Rubens more than anything else the senator had said.

Finally dismissed, Rubens tried hard to make his thankyous seem something other than perfunctory, rose, and walked swiftly to the door at the back of the room. The sparse audience was about evenly divided between congressional aides and media types. The latter swarmed toward the door, eager to ask follow-up questions. Unlike the senators, there was no need to accommodate the reporters, and Rubens merely waved at them with the barest hint of a smile, continuing swiftly into the hall.

"Sorry, sorry," he said, head tilted forward, his pace picking up. "Already very late. You're interested in the senators, not me."

He succeeded in distancing himself from the pack, and was so focused on getting out of the building that he nearly ran over Jed Frey as he turned the corner toward the side entrance. Frey, a short but athletic man in his late fifties, caught Rubens with both hands as he veered back in surprise.

"William, how are you?"

"Jed. I'm sorry. Are you here on business?"

"In a way. Do you have a few minutes?"

Frey was the director of the Secret Service. A lifetime government employee, he had held a number of jobs in the Treasury and State Departments after beginning as a Secret Service special agent.

"I'm due back at Fort Meade," said Rubens, referring to the NSA's headquarters, often called Crypto City.

"Perhaps I can ride with you awhile."

"Naturally," said Rubens, starting toward his car. "President still giving you fits?"

"Hmmmm," said Frey noncommittally.

Even more so than his recent predecessor, President Jeffrey Marcke seemed to delight in overruling or even ignoring the advice of the Secret Service. Marcke never saw a crowd he didn't want to plunge into, much to the dismay of his bodyguards, and liked to point out that during George Washington's day and for many presidencies afterward, anyone could walk into the executive mansion. Rubens knew of at least a dozen times when Marcke had gone places despite warnings from the Secret Service; Frey surely knew many more.

But the director did not like criticizing his boss, and changed the subject. "You spoke at the hearing without an aide?" he asked Rubens.

"I see no purpose in wasting someone else's time as well as my own."

Though Frey laughed heartily, Rubens did not mean this as a joke. In fact, he had only taken a driver rather than driving himself because he knew he could get some work done on the way.

Frey called his own driver, then joined Rubens in the backseat of Admiral Brown's Lincoln.

Rubens liked Frey; he was consistently honest and unpretentious. He also tended toward the laconic, a quality Rubens shared. In nearly every other way, however, the men were exact opposites. Frey's father had been a policeman in Detroit, and Jed had grown up in one of the city's tougher neighborhoods. The street still clung to him; though he was short and relatively thin, Frey had a way of dominating a space and did so now, shoulders squared and head pushed forward. His biceps bulged in his shirtsleeves as he folded his arms in front of his chest. The light gray hair on his forearms matched the color on his head.

"This involves one of my agents, a man named Gerald Forester. You know about him?"

Rubens shook his head.

Frey's entire body rose and fell as he took a deep breath.

"Supposedly it's suicide. But I don't buy it."

7

SENATOR MCSWEENEY DUCKED out of the committee room and began looking for his aide and driver.

"Jimmy Fingers, where the hell are you?" McSweeney's voice boomed in the hallway.

"Behind you, Senator. Watching your back. As always."

"We're late."

"Yes, sir."

James Fahey—alias Jimmy Fingers—caught up to his boss and began walking beside him. Fahey had earned his nickname as a young political aide in the state capital; a rival had claimed he had his fingers in everything. The nickname hinted of connections to the old-line Irish political machine as well as the Mob; it was meant as a slur, but Fahey took it as a compliment and somehow it stuck.

"Quick stop at the Swedish embassy, fund-raiser at Brown's Hotel, meeting at the Savoy, followed by dinner with Dr. and Mrs. Fox. Heavy rollers."

"You don't have to tell me who Dr. Fox is, Jimmy. I've been at this almost as long as you have now."

Political columnists liked to style Jimmy Fingers and his boss as the "Original Odd Couple of Politics." Born to a family of what the commentators politely termed "independent means," McSweeney had rugged good looks augmented by impeccable tailoring and lightly moussed hair. Jimmy Fingers, about the same height but far more slender, looked frumpy and wrinkled no matter how fresh or expensive his suit. His hair, thinning rapidly, made a haystack look neatly ordered. And those who said he had a face only a mother could love were being far too kind.

But the men were a matched set where it mattered—politics. Jimmy Fingers was often called the senator's hatchet man, and one writer had even declared Fingers was the "dark genius behind the throne." It was true that in local races Jimmy Fingers had generally favored tactics suited to X-Treme Boxing. But he could be subtle as well, just as McSweeney could use the knife when necessary.

Both men were equally committed to one goal: furthering McSweeney's political career. And they had shared that goal for more than twenty years, since Jimmy Fingers had taught McSweeney how to use direct mail to attack his opponent in an assembly race.

McSweeney's Secret Service bodyguard edged a little closer as they walked outside. The protection was optional, but since the campaign had received an e-mail death threat, McSweeney had opted for it.

"When's Wilson meeting me?" said McSweeney as they walked toward his car.

"He'll be upstairs at Brown's Hotel."

"Let's blow off the Swedish embassy reception," said McSweeney. "I'd like more time to talk to Wilson."

"Svorn Jenson is going to be at the embassy. He and his pals will be good for a hundred thousand in the campaign. All you have to do is smile at him and leave. He'll be thrilled."

"Oh, all right. What's Wilson going to tell me, anyway?"

"What he always does. The numbers are bad, but they're improving. He needs to justify the money you're spending on him."

"The numbers better start moving soon," said the senator. "Or he's going to have to find a real job."

"Worry about the primaries, not the polls," said Jimmy Fingers. He opened the door but didn't get in.

"Aren't you coming?" asked McSweeney.

"I have to pick up some dry cleaning before we head back to the district. I figured this would be a good time—the Swedes didn't invite me to the reception."

"You could go in my place," said McSweeney.

"Maybe next time, Senator," said Jimmy Fingers, pushing the door closed.

ONE THING GIDEON McSweeney had to give Jimmy Fingers—the guy was never wrong when it came to potential donors. Svorn Jenson's face lit up the second he saw McSweeney enter the reception; McSweeney pumped his hand, then went off to pump a few more before ducking out the side door. Even though he was in the embassy for no more than five minutes, he had made a friend—and campaign donor—for life.

Brown's Hotel, his next stop, was located in suburban Virginia, a few miles from the Beltway. McSweeney spent the ride there calling potential campaign donors. Running for President took an incredible amount of money, and raising it took an incredible amount of time, especially when you were the second or third favorite candidate in the upcoming Super Tuesday primary. Despite his upset victory in New Hampshire and his efforts since, McSweeney's campaign was faltering, and privately he felt he'd need a miracle to make it through the next month.

He was about a quarter of the way through his list of calls when they reached the hotel. McSweeney took his time getting out of the car. A knot of people gathered on the opposite sidewalk. They were gawkers rather than well-wishers; McSweeney could tell from their expressions that they didn't recognize him. That was a disappointment—his television spots had been in heavy rotation in the state for a week—but he didn't let on, waving enthusiastically and urging them to remember him in the upcoming primary.

Turning back toward the building, he began striding toward the lobby door. Each step stoked his confidence, and by the time he reached the edge of the red carpet in front of the glass, he felt invincible.

Number three? Two? No way. He was going to surprise everyone. It was New Hampshire all over again.

Something caught his attention and McSweeney turned

his head to the right. He saw a figure in black clothes standing beyond a knot of tourists.

The man had a gun.

"Get down!" yelled someone. In the next moment, McSweeney felt himself falling to the ground.

8

THERE WAS NOTHING in Frey's description of the agent's death that convinced Rubens it was anything but a suicide. The man was going through a painful divorce that promised to separate him from his children. Even Frey admitted that Forester could occasionally be moody and was most likely disappointed that he hadn't advanced rapidly up the Secret Service hierarchy, despite early promise. And while Forester had handled literally hundreds of investigations during his career, he didn't seem to have generated any enemies from them. The cases he had been working on before his death were typical ones as far as the Secret Service was concerned. The most serious involved an e-mailed death threat against a candidate for President—ironically, the candidate was Senator Mc-Sweeney, who had just finished grilling Rubens. Forester hadn't closed out the inquiry, but Frey's cursory review of the case made it appear there wasn't much there.

The state police and the local prosecuting attorney had made it clear that, as far as they were concerned, the agent had killed himself. But Frey had ordered the Service to conduct its own investigation.

"There are some interesting loose ends," said Frey. "Before he died, Jerry received some e-mails that we'd like traced to the source."

Frey reached into his jacket pocket and took out two pieces of white paper, which had printouts of the e-mails. Both e-mails had a Yahoo return address, and there was standard header information.

"The e-mail address has been falsified," said Frey. "It originated somewhere overseas. It says Vietnam, but we think that's false. We'd like to know from where, of course."

Rubens took the paper. Among the Secret Service's lesser-known duties was the investigation of identity theft, and the agency had its own array of computer experts. If they couldn't trace it, Rubens thought, the message must be suspicious.

"We don't have the e-mails that Forester sent," added Frey. "I'm afraid we don't know whether that is significant or not. He worked on the road a lot, and routinely would have 'shredded' sensitive information on his laptop. The e-mail would have been erased."

Rubens looked at the first e-mail.

Sir:

The business was a long time ago. All information long gone.

The second e-mail was much the same:

Sir:

I cannot be of assistance. Please.

"The business?" asked Rubens.

"I have no idea what it means. The e-mails seem to have come as he was investigating the threat made against Senator McSweeney. That e-mail was tracked to a library just outside Baltimore, where someone used a public-access computer. But we couldn't find a connection. Forester looked at constituents and other people who may have had a beef with the senator. Doesn't look like he found a link. He was still checking into it—he was going back to the area where McSweeney first served as assemblyman when he died."

Rubens folded the e-mails and placed them into his pocket. "Did you know the agent very well?"

"Yes, as a matter of fact. I broke him in. He was a good man."

Before Rubens could find a way to tactfully suggest that Frey's opinion might be clouding his judgment, the Secret Service director's phone buzzed.

He answered it, and immediately his face turned grim. "I'm on my way," he told his caller after listening for a few moments.

He snapped off the phone and turned to Rubens.

"We've just had a report of shots fired at Senator Mc-Sweeney. I'll need to get to my car."

9

THE TARGET MOVED at the very last moment, complicating the shot, but the shooter stayed on mission, pulling his finger steadily and smoothly against the trigger. The roar of the gun in the closed room was greater than he'd expected, but the recoil curiously less. The bullet sailed true, a perfect shot.

He had no time to think about these things, however; the entire enterprise had been carefully timed, and to make his getaway cleanly he had to leave immediately.

In the stairs on the way down, his heart double-pumped. It was a brief clutch, nothing more than a hiccup—a reminder of his age, nothing more. Rather than slowing down, he doubled his pace: he was too old to fail now. The chance to succeed would not come again.

The door slapped behind him as he made it to the street. He heard sirens the next block over. Quickly, the shooter slipped the steamer trunk with the rifle into the side door of the minivan, then slammed the door shut. The motor, started by remote control as he came down the steps, was already humming.

He fought against the instinct to press his foot too firmly on the accelerator. When he reached the corner, he stopped, signaled, then carefully pulled out into traffic.

Ten minutes later, he was on the Beltway. Only then did he give in and press the button for the radio.

The first report made his heart double-pump again.

"Senator McSweeney has been shot in Washington, D.C., just outside the Capitol Building!" said the announcer breathlessly.

The fact that the reporter had gotten the location wrong should have tipped the shooter off, but for the next few miles he drove in a kind of fugue state, believing that everything had gone wrong.

And then a different reporter came on, one who was actually at the scene.

"The senator appeared to be unhurt," said the reporter. "He was immediately taken into Brown's Hotel, where he was to be the guest of honor at a campaign fund-raiser. I was just arriving myself. Let me repeat, Senator McSweeney appears to be OK."

Thank God, thought the shooter. Thank God.

MCSWEENEY RESISTED UNTIL he realized that his bodyguard was trying to drag him into the hotel, away from the chaos and commotion on the street.

"I can do it myself," he muttered, struggling to get to his feet.

McSweeney tripped over the carpet as he came through the door and flew into the lobby, crashing against one of the hotel workers before regaining his balance. People were ducking or cowering or simply standing in dazed silence, unsure what was going on.

"Down, we're going down, through this door," said the Secret Service agent next to him. "Steps. Watch the steps."

McSweeney's lungs were gasping for air by the time he and the agent reached the bottom landing. They turned left, entered another hallway, then went into a room at the right. The Secret Service agent, face beet red, stood by the door, pistol out.

"Why are we here?" McSweeney asked the Secret Service agent.

"Please, Senator, until the situation is secure."

"Why are we in this room?"

"It'll just be a moment. It's under control."

McSweeney reached into his pocket for his phone.

"Sir, please—no communications until we're sure everything is copasetic," said the agent. "Just to be safe."

"My wife is going to be worried."

"It shouldn't take very long."

McSweeney put the phone back reluctantly. "Who shot at us?"

"I don't know, sir," said the agent. He put up his hand, then held it over his ear, obviously listening to something on his radio.

McSweeney's phone began to buzz. He checked the caller ID window on the phone and saw that it was Jimmy Fingers. McSweeney flipped it open despite the bodyguard's frown.

"I'm OK, Jimmy," he told his aide. "The fucker missed me."

"Jesus, Mary, and Joseph, thank God! Do you know the radio just said you were dead?"

"Well, I'm not."

"We'll want to get a statement out right away."

"Rumors of my death are greatly exaggerated," said McSweeney, echoing Mark Twain's famous comment.

"No, something more serious," said Jimmy Fingers, always thinking of the political ramifications. "A potential slogan. 'My work won't be stopped by a madman.' If you were in the lead, then you could joke. No, it has to be just right. We'll work it out when I get there. I'm a few minutes away."

McSweeney felt a twinge of resentment at Jimmy Fingers' tone, even as he knew from experience that Fingers' advice would prove correct.

"I'm glad you're OK, Senator," added the aide. "This will help us. You'll see."

"Help us?"

"No one tries to assassinate a loser."

THERE WAS A knock on the office door. Rubens reached for the silver security blanket and covered the desktop. It didn't matter that the desk was bare at the moment. Even *that* might mean something.

"Come in, Mr. Gallo," said Rubens.

"Johnny Bib sent me up," said Robert Gallo. One of the computer experts assigned to Desk Three's Analysis and Research section, Gallo defied the normal definition of "geek." He stood just over six feet and, while no muscle builder, certainly looked as if he could hold his own in a fight. "It's, uh, that Secret Service stuff."

"Have a seat, Robert. Tell me."

"Well, like, OK, the thing is, these e-mails really *were* sent from Vietnam," said Gallo, handing paper copies of the e-mails to Rubens. "That wasn't an alias or some sort of spoof like the Secret Service guys thought. I mean like, duh."

One of the unfortunate downsides of choosing the best people in the business, thought Rubens, was that they tended to *know* that they were the best, and thus came across as a little too arrogant for their own good. He liked Gallo; he would have to talk to him about this.

"See, everybody was probably thinking, Fake-oh, because when you look at the port information—"

"If you could move ahead to the point."

"So, OK, like, I check the phone records to see who like called. I hack into the Vietnamese phone company—"

"What exactly did you find?" asked Rubens.

"See, there were three people who had connections around the time the messages were sent. The e-mails are a couple of days apart. But I have three people. So I checked them, like, and—"

Clearly, thought Rubens, Gallo was being influenced far too much by his boss, John "Johnny Bib" Bibleria, who always followed the most circuitous route to the point.

"The thing is, all of them are on one of the CIA watch lists, right?" said Gallo. "What are the odds, huh?"

Actually, they would be very good, since only a limited number of people in Vietnam were allowed computer access, and for a variety of reasons—the fact that they were government officials, possibly dissident students, et cetera—the CIA would be interested in them. But Rubens didn't interrupt.

"So I figure let me go and check that, and I find out, like by accident, that the server, OK? We've been watching the server and, you know, traffic on it, files stored, everything, because of some CIA request three or four years ago."

Mildly interesting, thought Rubens. "What was the request about?"

"That's just it." Gallo held out his hands. That was *definitely* a Johnny Bib gesture; surely the young man had to be saved somehow. "I'm like, my clearance isn't high enough to get the info. And neither was Johnny Bib's."

Finally, the point.

"Johnny's clearance was not high enough?" asked Rubens.

"Yeah. Blew me away, too."

Rubens picked up the phone. "What was the name of the program?"

"Infinite Burn."

THE NAME DIDN'T register with the CIA's deputy director of operations.

"It's not current," Debra Collins told Rubens.

"It may be three or four years old," said Rubens.

"Hang on then."

It took Collins so long to get back to Rubens that he thought he had lost the connection.

"Bill, are you still there?" she asked when she finally got back on the line.

"Yes."

"Infinite Burn had to do with Vietnam."

"Interesting," said Rubens, though of course he already knew this. "One of my staff on Desk Three came across it earlier. He would like access to the files and it's rather urgent. It has to do with a Secret Service agent who was looking into a death threat against Senator McSweeney."

"The senator who was shot at today?"

"Yes."

Collins didn't say anything for a moment.

"Look, I have to go into a meeting," she told him finally, "but could you and I meet later to discuss this? In person?"

"Is it really necessary?"

"Infinite Burn was our code name for a plot by the Vietnamese to assassinate American leaders in revenge for the war."

12

CHARLIE DEAN TOOK a slow breath, pushing the air through his teeth as quietly as possible. He scanned both sides of the stream, then moved his eyes slowly across the canyon in front of them, looking for their prey.

"Tracks are less than an hour old," said his guide, Red Sleeth. Red pointed at the outer rim of the impression, still moist. "Dogs are real close now. You hear how they bark? It'll pick up even louder and faster as they close in. Ready?"

Dean nodded.

Sleeth rose and started following along the double track of footprints left by his two hounds. They'd been tracking this mountain lion through the Montana wilderness since early morning, after discovering a three- or four-day-old kill hidden in the brush below.

Sleeth splashed through the water to the other side of the creek, moving up the embankment into a copse of juniper. Dean followed, pushing through the calf-high grass and scrub to a small rock outcropping. A trail cut across the terrain to his left, intersecting the gray and green side of the canyon. It would be dark soon; they didn't have much time left to catch the lion today.

"This way," said Sleeth, pointing to a cut that angled downward to the left.

Dean followed, picking his way through the rocks as the guide crossed back to the north. The ground leveled out, then angled upward sharply. Dean slung his rifle over his shoulder, snugging the strap as he began climbing. He

couldn't see the dogs, but from their barks it seemed that
they were moving to the northeast.

"You kept up pretty well for an old guy," said Sleeth
when they reached the rim of the canyon.

"You think I'm old?"

"Didn't mean to insult you." Sleeth gave him a yellow-
toothed smile and pointed across the ridge. "The dogs are
running that way. I think if we can swing straight across the
side of that ridge, we may cut him off."

Ten minutes later, the dogs' barks sounded even farther
away, though Sleeth claimed they were closer.

"Snow up here just last week," said the guide as he and
Dean edged downward. "Now it's all gone or we'd have an
easier time."

"Yeah."

"Warm today."

"You figure forty degrees is warm?"

"Depends on your point of reference."

"True enough."

"Stop. Listen." Sleeth held up his hand, pointing to the
sky. "The dogs."

The dogs were barking, loudly, in short, quick yaps.

"They've treed him," explained Sleeth. "Come on!"

Dean followed the guide down into a thin copse of trees.
The dogs' excited barks bounced off the two sharp horizon-
tal walls that bookended the canyon about a quarter mile
away.

Dean started to think about the shot. A treed lion was not
particularly difficult to hit, and Dean began to feel a little
guilty, as if the dogs and the guide had given him an unfair advantage. Like any hunt, the tracking and chase were the critical elements; the finish was just the finish—necessary for
success, yet vaguely unsatisfying, especially for someone like
Dean, who had hunted humans before turning to animals.

Sleeth stopped suddenly. "Something's wrong," he told
Dean, and in the next moment he started to bring his gun up.

By then Dean had already spun to his right and dropped
to his knee. Ten yards away, the brush parted, revealing the

face and teeth of an angry lion. The big cat pressed its weight onto its front paws and sprang forward, teeth bared.

Dean fired toward the lion's head.

And missed.

He threw himself left as the animal lunged, its paw clawing his leg. Rolling on the ground, Dean bashed the butt of the rifle into the animal's side. The mountain lion's snarl filled his ears as he tried to scramble away. He felt as if he were underground, swimming in a pit of sand.

The cat rolled off to the side and Dean pushed himself to his feet. He had a round chambered. The gun was up, aimed. He fired, point-blank, this time taking the cat through the head.

A dank musk surged around him as if it were air rushing into a vacuum chamber: death's scent.

The animal shook violently, its feet vibrating.

Sleeth ran over, .357 drawn. He administered the coup de grâce to the lion, then looked over at Dean.

"You OK?" he asked.

"Yeah," said Dean.

Everything had happened so fast, he couldn't decipher it. Had he shot once or twice?

Twice—he'd missed the first time.

How, from that range?

It didn't make sense, but he *had* missed.

The dogs were howling. Dean looked toward the sound.

"The other lion is out of the tree," said Sleeth, his voice a monotone. "One of the dogs is hurt."

Dean started in that direction.

"Wait," said Sleeth, catching up. "We can't shoot the other lion. Your license only allows one kill."

"OK," said Dean, lowering his gun.

13

"OLD WARRIORS. ANCIENT grudges," declared Simon Dauber solemnly, summarizing the brief in the CIA secure conference room. Though most of his experience was in China, Dauber had been on the Southeast Asia desk long enough for Rubens to know and respect him. Those two things did not usually go hand in hand where the CIA was concerned.

"Old warriors can be quite potent," remarked Hernes Jackson. "They shouldn't be discounted."

Rubens had taken Jackson and Gallo along for the briefing. Unleashing Johnny Bib on the CIA would have been considered cruel and unusual punishment.

While Jackson's point was valid, there was a lot to back up Dauber's assessment of Infinite Burn. The CIA had developed information about the assassination plot from an agent code-named Red Diamond three years before. Diamond was a smuggler with ties to the government, a borderline undesirable whose status, naturally, made him a very interesting "catch." He had given the CIA a number of tidbits over the two years that he had been on the payroll.

Most of the information had to do with drugs that were being transported, probably by rivals, in and out of Thailand and Cambodia as well as Vietnam. That information had been extremely reliable. He'd also given up details about different military matters. In those cases, his track record wasn't quite so impeccable. He had a tendency to exaggerate, even when reporting on things like purchases of spare parts for aircraft.

Nor did the information about Infinite Burn fit in with what might be termed his usual reporting patterns. Even the CIA officer who had been running Red Diamond at the time felt it came out of left field. The officer had tried to sniff around among other sources, without finding anything.

Yet here they were, three years later, with an assassination attempt on a prominent U.S. senator—exactly as Red Diamond had predicted.

"So let's say they have all these guys go deep undercover into America, right?" said Robert Gallo, repeating one of Dauber's hypotheses. "How do they communicate with them?"

Dauber shook his head. "Don't know."

"How do they pick targets?"

"You have to remember, we didn't find much evidence beyond Red Diamond's original information. And he died a short time later. Or disappeared."

Red Diamond had fallen from a boat in Saigon Harbor and was never heard from again. The case officer believed Red Diamond had probably been shot before falling, but that was not part of the police report.

"Your source implicated Thieu Gao," said Jackson. "He's now their ambassador to the U.S."

"It's important to note that we didn't develop anything more tangible at the time than rumors," interrupted Debra Collins, who had said very little during the entire session. "We developed no other information from the government. And a program like this—one would assume it had to have approval at the very highest levels to proceed."

"Not necessarily," said Jackson. "It could be simply, as Mr. Dauber said, old soldiers working together on their own."

"That would not be the Vietnamese way," said Jack Li, another Vietnam/Asian expert.

"But it is possible."

"Whatever the assessment at the time," said Rubens, "clearly this needs to be pursued."

"I agree," said Collins.

A HALF HOUR later, Rubens and Collins sat across from each other in her office, waiting for a call back from the President's National Security Advisor, Donna Bing. Rubens didn't particularly relish talking to Bing and he sensed that Collins didn't, either.

Ironically, Bing's appointment had drawn Collins and Rubens closer together, encouraged to ally in the face of a common enemy. Briefly lovers, they had become rivals after the creation of the NSA's Desk Three—also known as Deep Black—because as a covert action unit it encroached on the CIA's traditional bailiwick. They'd also both been considered for Bing's job—Rubens, in fact, had turned it down, a decision he now deeply regretted.

Rubens hated Bing for several reasons. It wasn't just that she had cut off his access to the President, or that she tended to question everything Rubens proposed. It wasn't just that she presumed she knew the background of every possible international situation and had considered nuances no one else had, or even the fact that her assessments of the international situation tended to be about ten years out-of-date.

The thing that *most* annoyed Rubens was the tone of her voice, a nasal singsong tottering on the edge of becoming a sneer.

The voice greeted them with a perfunctory, "What is it?"

"Donna, Bill Rubens and his people have developed some information concerning Vietnam that we thought important to bring to the President's attention," said Collins. "There is an intersection with intelligence we developed about three years ago. Bill is here now."

Rubens detailed what they had found. To his great surprise, Bing's voice seemed bright, even cheery, when he finished.

"Good work. We must pursue this."

"That's why Ms. Collins and I are calling," said Rubens.

"This is a Deep Black project?"

"We hadn't quite gotten that far," said Rubens. "I don't know that there is a role for Desk Three."

"What you're talking about here is a covert attack on the American government," said Bing. "I want the best involved."

Rubens glanced over at Collins, whose agency had just been indirectly insulted.

"Take the lead," added Bing. "I'll inform the President."

And then she clicked off.

"You *really* should have taken the job, Bill," said Collins. "You made a big mistake. For all of us."

14

THE LION HAD used the commotion to jump from the tree, wrestling briefly with one of the hounds before making its escape. The dog had two long, deep cuts in his flank but was actually very lucky. He hadn't lost much blood and could easily have had his neck snapped in the confrontation.

Sleeth worked on the dog's wounds carefully, cleaning and dressing them, all the while nuzzling the animal to comfort him. The hound had belonged to Sleeth's father, who'd retired as a guide just the year before.

"Good lion hound's worth a fortune," said Sleeth, but Dean sensed that his concern for the animal had nothing to do with money. "I don't think I have to put him down. I'd hate to."

"We can make a sling and carry him out," suggested Dean.

"Be heavy carrying the lion, too."

"We can do it. If we can't, the dog's more important."

"I appreciate that," said Sleeth. "I really appreciate that."

His other dog circled as they rigged a stretcher. They took the animal up the hill to the dead lion. Sleeth had a collection of metal poles that he used to sling the dead animal for carrying. The poles were thin and Dean didn't think they'd hold the weight of the cat, which topped a hundred pounds. But the pole hardly bent at all, even when they tied the dog as well.

"If it's too heavy, let me know," said Sleeth, starting out.

Dean grunted. It *was* heavy, and the truth was, he didn't really care that much about having a trophy. But leaving the lion felt like admitting defeat—or, worse, like an admission that he was old, as Sleeth had commented earlier.

He was old. But still strong. And stubborn.

More the latter, maybe.

He could still see the lion charging at him. It was almost as if it had happened twice—once he made the shot; once he didn't. And there was a fork in reality: in one version he'd been mauled; in the other he'd emerged victorious, barely scratched.

But it had all happened together. There had been no turning point, no choice, just reaction. Everything scrunched together.

And how the hell had he missed that shot?

The sun was edging below the horizon, leaving the mountains in deep shadow. Sleeth aimed toward a dried streambed about two and a half miles away, where his wife could meet them with her pickup truck. They walked in silence, avoiding the roughest terrain, neither man admitting how heavy the double burden was.

An hour passed. By now it was fairly dark. Sleeth checked in with his wife on the radio and told her they were still about a mile away.

"If it's too heavy for you, we can come back with some help at dawn," Sleeth said to Dean.

"No, I'm all right."

They climbed for about fifteen minutes, struggling up a rocky gorge. Dean lost his footing near the top; his knee twisted out beneath him and he fell sideways, the dead cougar's fangs tapping against his face—a reproof, it seemed.

He pushed himself to his feet, shouldered the metal stick, and clambered with Sleeth up the hill. Once they reached the top, the path was easy, wide spaces between trees and a gentle slope to the creek bed where the truck waited.

"More than you bargained for, Mr. Dean?" asked Sleeth's wife as they drove back toward the Sleeth house. Sleeth was with the dog in the back.

"It was interesting."

"What do you do for a living?" she asked. A few years younger than her husband, she had a thick neck and well-defined biceps and forearms, and a face prematurely aged by the sun.

"Own some gas stations," said Dean. He'd sold the stations when he went to work for Deep Black, but of course he wasn't about to mention what he really did.

"This is a bit more interesting than your normal day's work, I'd guess," said Mrs. Sleeth.

"You'd be surprised," said Dean, propping his arm against the window of the truck.

A FEW HOURS later, the dog patched up and the mountain lion prepared for the taxidermist, Sleeth joined Dean in the living room.

"I'm refunding your money," said Sleeth, sitting down in the leather chair across from Dean.

"Why?" asked Dean.

"I almost got you killed. I was sloppy. I did a terrible job."

"Nah."

"I should have known there was another animal there. Male and female lions will hunt together when they're mating. I should have known."

Dean, no expert on mountain lions, studied the Scotch in his glass, then took a sip, savoring the Glenfiddich as it burned in his mouth.

"You were really cool up there, dealing with the cat," continued Sleeth. "A lot of guys—"

Instead of finishing his sentence, Sleeth got up and walked to the sideboard nearby, fixing himself a drink.

Dean took another sip of his Scotch.

What if he'd missed on the second shot as well?

He wouldn't be here to think about it, probably. Or maybe he would be, waiting for a medevac helicopter, eyeball dangling from its socket.

Sleeth sat back down.

"It's unusual for a lion to attack humans," he said. Maybe there was something wrong with it, or maybe it had attacked before, or maybe it saw them as rivals for its mate. Ordinarily, the cats didn't attack unless cornered, not even to protect their young. The words drifted past Dean's head.

Maybe he'd missed that first shot because Sleeth was right: he *was* getting old.

Dean's sat phone began to ring.

"I just want to check this. Excuse me," he told Sleeth. He got up, pulling the phone out as he walked to the door.

"Dean," he said outside.

"Charlie, this is Chris Farlekas. I'm afraid you're going to have to cut short your vacation. There's something urgent that we need your help on. We'll have a plane meet you at Le Havre Airport. OK?"

"What time?"

"As soon as you can get there. It'll be on the ground in half an hour."

15

"OH, HOW PRECIOUS—a onesie with a matching rattle."

Lia DeFrancesca tried very hard not to roll her eyes as the guest of honor continued to gush over her baby shower presents. The very pregnant guest happened to be Lia's best friend from high school, Tina Ricco, now Tina Ricco Kelly, well into the eighth month of pregnancy. Besides a healthy glow and a constant need to pee, Tina's condition had apparently short-circuited several parts of her brain, causing her to use the word "precious" at least twenty times an hour and to speak of herself in the plural, as in, "We just think that's adorable," and, "We'll have that drink super-sized."

Visiting Tina and her husband in their new home in North Carolina for a few days had seemed liked a good idea when Tina invited Lia. She envisioned long afternoons by the shore, sipping a cool drink from a tall glass. She might even get in a little shopping.

But the weather had turned out to be on the cool side, and Tina was generally too tired to spend more than fifteen minutes on her feet at a time. She was also too busy to go out— Lia's arrival had come in the midst of a relentless stream of relatives and other friends, who dropped by nearly around the clock to "chat" and offer encouragement. Tina had made the mistake of saying that she planned on having the baby without painkillers, and her visitors felt obligated to let her know how foolish she was. They did this with war stories about their own excruciating times in labor, stories so vivid that even Lia got sympathy pains.

Fortunately, the pains of labor were no longer the topic of choice at the shower. Unfortunately, it was replaced by nonstop horror stories of babies with colic, babies who never slept, babies who never kept food in their stomachs. The odd thing was that the stories were told in the most cheerful way imaginable, and generally capped off with words to the effect of "You'll love being a parent." Lia resorted to vodka-spiked lemonade to remain calm.

If I ever have a baby, she thought, I'm going to keep it a secret until he's eighteen.

Lia's cell phone rang just as Tina unwrapped her third Diaper Genie. She jumped up to take the call, so thankful for the diversion that she would have bought storm windows from the most obnoxious telemarketer.

"Lia, this is Chris Farlekas. Can you talk?"

"Almost," she said, walking out into the hallway.

"We need you here by eight A.M. tomorrow for a briefing. I know it's Sunday, I know you're off, but—"

"Not a problem."

"We'll book a commercial flight from Raleigh-Durham. When do you want to leave?"

A burst of high-pitched giggling cascaded down the hall.

"I'm calling a cab for the airport right now."

16

"THE ATTACK ON Senator McSweeney involved at least two people: the man with a pistol, who appears to have been a decoy, and the actual shooter, who was located in this building across the way."

The screen flashed as a picture of the office building across from the hotel appeared. Dean rolled his arms together in front of his chest, leaning back in the seat. He hadn't been able to sleep on the plane coming back from Montana, nor had there been time for anything more than a quick nap before reporting to the Desk Three operations center in the basement of OPS/2B.

A face flashed on the screen. It belonged to a man about thirty years old. He had buzz-cut chestnut hair and a moon-shaped bruise below each eye. He seemed to be in pain.

"This was the decoy," said Hernes Jackson, standing at the side of the room as he gave the briefing. "He had a pellet gun that looked like a Beretta. His name is Arthur Findley."

Jackson clicked the remote control in his hand, bringing two more pictures of Findley on the screen. In both, Findley looked heavily medicated, with a vacant gaze.

"Mr. Findley has been in and out of mental institutions for several years. His last known address was at an outpatient facility in Washington, D.C., two years ago," continued Jackson. "Since then, he's had no known address. He's apparently somewhat well-known to the homeless community. He seems to have been approached by a man who called himself John a few days ago. The man befriended him by giving him money, and eventually asked him to show up with the gun in front of the hotel."

"And he didn't have a problem with that?" asked Lia, sitting to Dean's right. She'd already been here when Dean arrived, and seemed quiet, almost contemplative. They'd barely had a chance to say hello before the briefing began.

"Mr. Findley appears to have the mental age of a five-year-old," said Jackson. "He clearly didn't understand the implications. We have a sketch of the man, based on Mr. Findley's descriptions."

A nondescript computer-generated face appeared on the screen. He was white, of average height, maybe middle-aged.

"Needless to say, the FBI has come up with no real information about this person, John. There's nothing in the Secret Service files, either."

"What about the real shooter?" asked Lia.

Jackson shook his head. "Nothing. He appears to have used a stock Remington rifle with store-bought ammunition. They have that from the bullet. The thinking is the shooter wasn't a professional. The shot was taken at eighty-five yards."

Dean grunted. On a range, eighty-five yards was nothing, not for a sniper or even a well-trained Marine. But in real life, with adrenaline flowing like beer in a biker bar, it could feel like miles.

Jackson said that the FBI was working to attempt to identify where the bullet had been purchased. But tracking ammunition wasn't easy, especially when the ammo was relatively common, and so far the efforts had proved fruitless.

"The FBI identified the office from the trajectory of the shot," continued Jackson. "There was nothing there—no spent shell, no trace of anything. All of the windows in that floor were open. The building has been vacant for about five months. No eyewitness has come forward. Two people in the area believed they saw an Asian man in the building a few days before."

"Not much of a description," said Lia.

"It may be significant," said Jackson. "Which brings me to the second half of our briefing."

"Let me preface the ambassador's brief by saying that the relationship of this incident to Special Agent Forester's death has yet to be determined," interrupted Rubens. "There may in fact be no relationship at all. The only point of connection is that Forester was tracking down threats against the senator when he died. It is that investigation that concerns us."

Jackson flashed a picture of a Secret Service agent named Gerald Forester on the screen, explaining who he was and the fact that he had died about a week before the attempt on McSweeney. While the state police and the FBI had initially concluded that McSweeney had committed suicide, the head of the Secret Service had pressed his own agency to check into other possibilities.

"The lead investigator, an agent by the name of Mandarin, has also been assigned to this case," said Jackson. "That's not necessarily a coincidence, though Mandarin is regarded as one of their top investigators."

Jackson added that Mandarin had told him that he thought Forester had killed himself because "that's where the evidence is," but that the agency wasn't going to close out the case any time soon.

"Prior to his death, Agent Forester made some inquiries by e-mail to a person in Vietnam. He wanted to talk to someone there, though it's not clear why. We don't know what he intended to ask or hoped to find out. We don't even know for sure who it was he was trying to talk to. We have narrowed down the number of possibilities to three, all of whom both have a connection to the present government and were involved somehow in the war. That's significant because Vietnam was believed to have been working on a program to assassinate American leaders three years ago."

"And that," said Ruben dryly, "is why you are here and we are involved."

Jackson continued to fill in details, noting that McSweeney had served in Vietnam, which would make him an excellent candidate for a revenge plot. He also admitted that there was considerable room for skepticism. The NSA had a "robust" system in place for intercepting and monitoring Vietnamese communications, official and otherwise, and while these were being reviewed, no information had been gathered that revealed an assassination plot.

"Also, if Agent Forester thought that the threat originated from Vietnam, he would have communicated that to his superiors," added Jackson. "And he did not."

"Maybe he didn't get the chance," said Lia.

"Possibly."

"What did McSweeney do in Vietnam?" Dean asked.

"He was a Marine officer," said Jackson. "Toward the end of the war, he served as a commanding officer with the strategic hamlet program in Quang Nam Province, outside of Da Nang."

"I know where it is," said Dean.

It was the same area where he had served. He didn't know McSweeney, though he had heard of the strategic hamlet program—a risky, typically Marine-type program that had troops live with the Vietnamese. It was a good idea or a loony idea depending on who was talking about it. They all agreed it hadn't worked.

"How do you feel about Vietnam, Charlie?" asked Rubens.

Dean shrugged. "I don't feel anything particularly."

"Very well. Then I want you and Lia to go there and find Agent Forester's contact and see if you can get him to shed light on his message." He looked at his watch. "Spend the rest of the day familiarizing yourself with Agent Forester and his investigation. Be back and ready to leave this evening."

17

THE SHOOTER HAD had a clear, easy shot from the fourth-floor window. He'd have been able to see the senator's car arrive and had a good angle as he walked up toward the door. The shooter would have been able to see the decoy as well, assuming he had walked in the middle of the sidewalk.

Charlie Dean knelt at the window, studying the view. Eighty-five yards, with traffic, people, distractions—it wasn't surprising that the shooter had missed. Forget the fact that the rifle and ammunition were off-the-shelf: adrenaline would have been the shooter's real enemy. How many people could even learn to control their breath under stress? It wasn't easy. The instructors told Charlie he had a knack for it, but he didn't think it was easy.

And yet the setup seemed perfect. The shot was clear; there was no trace of a bullet, no trace of anyone in the room.

That argued that the shooter was, if not a professional, someone who took extreme care, who'd thought about the setup a great deal.

"What did he use to steady the gun?" Dean said, stepping back. "If he didn't shoot from the window ledge, what did he use? Did he have a tripod? No way he took an offhand shot."

"He puts something on the radiator there," said Lia, pointing. "Takes it with him when he's gone."

"Nobody sees him."

Dean went back to the window and stared down. Maybe the guy was a pro, but one out of practice, a man who hadn't killed in a long time. Someone like himself, who knew the theory but had lost the steps, who got too excited when the moment came. Who'd missed—just as Dean had when the lion charged.

"Charlie Dean, Charlie Dean—what are you thinking?" Lia asked.

"I don't know," said Dean as he rose.

He scanned the block, looking for anything that might have distracted the shooter. Then Dean did the same thing in the room. It was a high-ceilinged, empty office; the linoleum on the floor was stained but swept clean, the walls bare except for shadows where photos had once hung.

"So?" asked Lia.

"Let's go see what the Secret Service people have to say."

18

"LET ME PUT it this way," Brian Wilson told Senator Mc-Sweeney as he began the slide show on his laptop. "If it weren't for the possibility of collateral damage, I'd say you should get shot at every week. You've gained four to five points in the polls in every state. The metrics are definitely trending in your direction."

Jimmy Fingers rolled his eyes. Though in his early thirties, Wilson looked as if he were still a college kid, and dressed the part. He constantly sprinkled terms like "metrics" and "coefficients" into his talk. Jimmy Fingers wasn't so old-fashioned that he would ever allow a candidate to seek office without a pollster, even if he was only running for dogcatcher. Still, Jimmy resented the tendency to reduce everything to numbers, and thought they were way overvalued.

What did people *think* of McSweeney? That was what was important, after all. Did they think he was lucky to be alive? Or did they think he was special enough that the assassin's bullet had missed because of fate or God's hand?

The answer meant a world of difference. But of course Wilson didn't even ask the question.

"There are a few days left to make an impression for Super Tuesday. With all the publicity about the assassination attempt, I'd like to shoot a spot emphasizing your war record," suggested Brian Carouth, the campaign's media consultant, after the pollster wrapped up. "I think it will play very well."

"No. We don't need to do that," said McSweeney. "The spots we're using have done just fine."

"A little more biography—" suggested Carouth.

"Issues are what's important," said McSweeney. "My health plan, immigration, taxes. That's what we pound."

"Now, Senator, as we all know, people vote for the man, not the white paper," said Wilson. He glanced at Jimmy Fingers, probably expecting him to help, but Jimmy said nothing. "And a war record is a big plus. It says a lot about a man's character."

"The Vietnam War is not the negative it once was," added Carouth. "That's ancient history."

"There's no need to bring up my military record," said McSweeney. "We'll leave it alone."

Jimmy Fingers recognized from McSweeney's tone that he would not change his mind on the matter, even as Wilson continued pushing the ads. It was refreshing to see the consultant strike out so decisively, thought Jimmy Fingers.

Truth be told, Jimmy Fingers actually agreed with Wilson. But since when was truth an important ingredient in a political campaign?

19

LIA FLICKED THROUGH the notebook. Most preschoolers had handwriting neater than Forester's. Nor were his notes particularly informative or complete. An entire page would be devoted to a time—10:30, say—that appeared to be for an appointment, though neither a date nor a place was recorded. The words "Pine Plains" were written at the top of the last page. At the bottom of the page, were numbers and one word: "84, Parkway, 44, 82."

"Is this some sort of code?" Lia asked, passing the sheets to Dean.

John Mandarin, the Secret Service special agent in charge of both the McSweeney investigation and the inquiry into Forester's death, frowned.

"We think those are directions. Interstate 84, Taconic Parkway, U.S. Route 44, and State Route 82. It would be how to get to Pine Plains."

"But he didn't go to Pine Plains," said Dean. "He went to Danbury."

"Nearest approved hotel," said Mandarin. "He would've gone first thing the next morning. Had an appointment with the police chief there."

"Is this the last notebook?" asked Lia.

"It's the only notebook. Far as we know."

Mandarin was the classic Secret Service agent. He was average height, weight, and build. While his last name indicated that there were Chinese ancestors somewhere in his family's past, his face mixed Asian and European characteristics so well that it would have been impossible to place him in any genetic pool without a DNA test. He wore a brown suit, a white shirt that appeared to be graying around the collar, black shoes and socks. His accent was as bland as a midwestern television announcer's, and when he spoke he kept his hands perfectly still. In total, Mandarin was a veritable Zelig who could fade into even the most convoluted background.

"Can we see another of Agent Forester's notebooks?" asked Lia. "Something to compare it to?"

"I have to tell you, we really don't see much of a connection between Forester's death and the McSweeney assassination," said Mandarin. "State police called Forester's death a suicide. FBI looked at it and they agreed."

"What do you think?" Dean asked.

"Officially, the matter is still open. But unofficially . . ." He shook his head.

"Our angle is the e-mails," said Dean.

"Yeah, I know. Another wild-goose chase."

Something about the way Dean stared at the Secret Service agent reminded Lia she loved him. It was an intrusive, unwelcome thought—a distraction when she should be working—but it was difficult to banish.

Mandarin went to a nearby file cabinet to see what he could find. He returned with two pouchlike folders. Besides typed reports and disks, there were stenographers' notebooks filled with notes.

Lia checked the pads. If anything, there was even less detail in them.

"Are you positive this is the only notebook he used for this case?" Lia asked, pointing to the one Dean still had in his hand.

"He never did anything in Pine Plains," said Mandarin. "Killed himself first. Believe me, we've gone through his things. It wasn't in the room, or at his house. Lousy business," added the agent. "His wife seemed to be a bitch, but he's got kids, you know? He wanted custody, and she wouldn't budge. Probably why he pulled the plug."

Mandarin pressed his lips together, then looked at the

floor. He had the air of a man who would trade half a year's salary to get another assignment.

"Can we have a copy of the notebook?" Lia asked.

"Yeah, I guess. Take a couple of days. You'll have to fill out a form and then—"

Lia snatched the notebook from Dean's hand and started toward the copy machine.

"What are you doing?" asked Mandarin.

"Filling out the paperwork," she said, pulling up the machine's cover to begin copying.

20

AMANDA RAUCI GOT up from the couch and walked to the kitchen. Her eyes had finally stopped burning, but her head still felt as if it were filled with straw. Her whole body did.

The bottle of Tanqueray had only a finger's worth of gin left in the bottom.

God, she thought, did I drink all that?

Jerry, Jerry, Jerry.

Amanda rubbed her forehead, then poured the last of the gin into her glass. She hadn't gone out of the apartment since coming back after discovering Forester's body. She hadn't even gone to the funeral.

She couldn't have trusted herself. She was sure his ex-wife had driven him to this.

Amanda drained the glass in a gulp. Then she went to the window in her living room and pushed it open. The air smelled damp, as if it was going to rain soon. A motorcycle revved in the distance. As it passed, she heard the soft chatter of some children walking on the trail that ran behind her condo.

Why would Jerry kill himself?

He wouldn't. She knew in her gut that he wouldn't. There was just no way—no possible way—that he would kill himself.

Maybe if he didn't think he'd see his boys.

But he'd never do this to them. Never.

Or to her.

But what other explanation was there?

A fresh wave of self-pity swept over her. Even though she knew that's what it was, even though she hated the emotion more than anything, it left her helpless. She stared blankly out the window, eyes unfocused.

"He didn't kill himself," she said finally. "He didn't."

Amanda pushed the window closed. If she'd said those words once, she'd said them a thousand times in the past week and a half.

Amanda's vacation had a few more days to run; then she'd be back at work. She had to pull herself together before then. She had to stop drinking.

"I'll try another shower," she told herself. "And then make a plan."

21

LIA LET DEAN ask the questions. Mrs. Forester seemed to respond better to him. She was almost flirting, in fact.

Mrs. Forester readily admitted that she and her husband had been in the process of getting a divorce. Nor did she hide the fact that they hadn't gotten along for several years.

"Does it make sense to you that he killed himself?" asked Dean. They were all sitting in the small dining room, around a battered, colonial-style dinette set.

She picked a nonexistent piece of lint from her sweater before answering. "No, Mr. Dean, it doesn't."

"What do you think happened?"

"I don't know. I suppose he did kill himself. But honestly, it wouldn't have been over the divorce. Jerry wasn't emotional like that. We didn't get along, and this was the logical next step. Divorce, not suicide."

"Was he concerned about custody or money?"

"He was always concerned about money. As for custody, he could care less about the boys."

"When will they be home?" Dean asked.

"I'd prefer if you left them alone," said Mrs. Forester. "I'd greatly prefer it."

"All right," said Dean.

The boys' impressions—and their mother's, for that matter—weren't what he and Lia had come for. Still, she found it interesting that no one thought Special Agent Forester was the sort of man who would take his own life. She glanced at the photographs on the wall next to the buffet. They were old family shots; Agent Forester was in several. He looked happy enough.

So did his wife.

If he had died the day after the photos were taken, would she have seemed more affected by it? Would she be crying instead of waving her hand dismissively?

"One thing that we would like to do," said Dean, getting to the point, "is look at the hard drives on the computers in your house. We're hoping there might be some information there that would help us."

"If you're looking for a suicide note, you won't—"

"Actually, we're interested in seeing if there might have been a connection to a case that we don't know about," said Lia. "We just have to rule everything out."

Mrs. Forester sighed. "You know, I've spoken to investigators twice already."

"We understand. But we need to dot every *i*," said Dean. His voice seemed more soothing than normal; Lia couldn't tell if he was consciously making an effort to be nice or reacted that way to damsels in distress.

Not that Mrs. Forester appeared in distress.

"My sons need the computers for their homework," she told Lia and Dean.

"We don't need to take the computers," said Dean. "If you have an Internet connection, the whole process can be done in a few minutes."

Mrs. Forester frowned, then studied Dean's face. Obviously, she liked something she saw there, because finally she said OK and got up from the chair.

"My son Gerald got his computer from his father, so it's probably the one you should check first," said Mrs. Forester.

Lia felt a twinge of anger when their hostess touched Dean's hand as she showed them toward the short flight of stairs to the split level's top floor. She knew that was foolish— if anything, Dean should use the attraction to help them get what they wanted. But still she felt jealous.

The house had been built in the early 1970s. The wood floors were scuffed and yellowed, and there were other signs of age, like painted-over gouges on the baseboards and fixtures that had gone out of style decades before. But it was clean and well kept; even the boys' bedrooms were well-ordered. To judge from the pennants and photographs on the wall, the fifteen-year-old was a fan of the Nationals and the Washington Redskins. A pair of tickets to an upcoming NASCAR event were tacked to the edge of the shelf over the computer monitor.

Lia wondered if the boy had been planning to go with his father.

"Is there a password?" Dean asked as the computer booted.

"No. Do we need one?"

"Nah. I don't use one, either," said Dean.

Mrs. Forester leaned close to Dean, her hand resting on his shoulder. Lia stepped around to the other side, watching as Dean brought up the Web browser and signed onto a special page set up by the Art Room. Within a few seconds, the techies back at the NSA were dumping the contents of the computer's hard drive into their own computers.

"Did your husband leave any papers behind when he moved out?" Lia asked Mrs. Forester.

"Just our finances. Nothing to do with work."

"Could I look at them?"

"My finances?" Mrs. Forester straightened. "Why?"

"Maybe there's something there."

"I really don't feel like having you snoop through my personal records."

"Are you hiding something?"

Mrs. Forester's lower lip quivered as she suppressed her anger. Lia held her stare.

"You don't have to show us anything you don't want to," interrupted Dean.

Shut up, Charlie, thought Lia to herself.

"Thank you," said Mrs. Forester.

"It might be useful," said Lia. "Knowing about money issues that might have driven—"

"There were no money issues in our marriage," said Mrs. Forester frostily. "Jerry was the issue. And you won't find that in our checkbook. When it came to providing, he did an adequate job."

"Did your husband like to travel a lot?" asked Dean.

"Just for work."

"Did he ever go to Vietnam?" asked Lia.

Mrs. Forester made a face and shook her head.

"You're sure?"

"I think I'd remember something like that."

"Did he know anyone who was Vietnamese?"

"I haven't a clue."

"Was his father in the Vietnam War?" Lia asked.

"Not that I know."

"Could we see the other computers?" asked Dean, rising.

Mrs. Forester's tone immediately softened. "There's only one more. In my bedroom."

"Let's take a look then."

"WHY'D YOU GET nasty?" Dean asked as soon as they were outside on the driveway.

"I wasn't nasty."

"You were a little rough, asking for her finances."

"Maybe there's something in there."

"The Secret Service and the FBI would have checked that out."

"Why are you making excuses for her?"

"I'm not."

"You're going pretty easy on her."

"Her husband just died."

"She didn't seem that broken up about it. My guess—"

Dean cut her off by putting his hand in front of her, physically stopping her a few yards from the street. A teenager had stopped on the sidewalk nearby. He looked like a much younger version of Gerald Forester.

Dean nodded in the boy's direction, then began walking again. Lia stared to follow.

"Hey, are you here about my dad?" asked the boy. His voice mixed bravado with anger; he was partly challenging them, and partly pleading for information.

"We were just checking up on a few things," said Dean. "He didn't kill himself."

The young man held his arms straight down, fists clenched. For a moment Lia thought that he was going to leap at Dean and pummel him.

"We'd like to prove you're right," said Dean. "Can you think of anything that would help us?"

The question seemed to catch the kid in the stomach, a punch that grabbed his breath.

Lia misinterpreted the reaction, thinking he had something he'd been wanting to point out but hadn't until now. Before she realized that he was only trying to hide his grief, she asked if he knew of anyone who had threatened his dad. Tears began rolling from the corners of the young man's eyes. He pressed his lips together so tightly they turned white. Then he bent his head forward and walked past them, his pace growing brisker until he reached the house.

22

AGENT FORESTER'S COMPUTERS were plain vanilla PCs running Windows XP, home version, and they were filled with the sorts of things one might find on perhaps 85 percent of the home computers in the United States—a word-processing program, a Web surfer, home finances software, and an assortment of soft porn.

The fact that the porn had been deleted made no difference to NSA computer expert Robert Gallo, whose computer tools allowed him not only to view the images but also to reconstruct "missing" parts of the files. More important, his software allowed him to search the files for encrypted messages.

He found none.

"Porn wasn't even that interesting," he told Johnny Bib. "Better stuff on MySpace."

"Who's having the affair?" asked Johnny, pointing at one of the text blocks on Gallo's machine.

"Huh?"

"The instant message."

Gallo moused over to the screen and brought up the files. The instant messages had been left from a cache several weeks before.

> *U awake?*
> Goin' to bed. Jealous?
> *Need to use yr computr tomorrw*
> OK

Hw's yr Frnch?
Francois?

"Oh yeah. Account ID got ripped out when the file was deleted, but it's gotta be the kid, no?"

Johnny Bib picked up one of the printouts, leafed through, and showed it to Gallo. "Takes Spanish."

"Yeah, so that's why he's asking about the girl's French. If it's a girl."

Johnny Bib leaned over Gallo's screen. "It's from computer one."

"Yeah, but the kid used both. You think it's important?"

Johnny Bib answered by staring at Gallo, opening his eyes as wide as they could go, and then crossing them.

"I guess that's a 'duh,'" said the analyst. He selected a software tool that constructed a "session profile" and used it to determine when the computer had been used and what else it had been used for during the IM session. There were plenty of gaps, as the tool relied primarily on cookies, saved and deleted files, and other bits of deleterious. Nonetheless, it showed that at roughly the same time the instant message had been saved, the checkbook program was running.

"All right. Probably Agent Forester," Gallo said. "But why would anyone need French?"

"Ha!" said Johnny Bib. "Find out who was on the other end. And see what else you can recover."

THIN AS IT WAS, the fact that Forester had been having an affair with another Secret Service agent was the first real evidence against the suicide that Rubens had seen. Men who were having affairs, especially with younger women, did not kill themselves.

In his opinion. A prejudice, surely.

Rubens dismissed Johnny Bib and placed a call to Jed Frey. The Secret Service director was not in his office, but his voice mail gave the number of his cell phone. Rubens punched the number in. Frey answered immediately.

"Jed, this is Bill Rubens. I have some additional information about Agent Forester I wanted to share. It's somewhat sensitive."

"Shoot."

"Gerald Forester was having an affair with another member of the Service. We've recovered several suggestive IMs they sent."

"IMs?"

"Instant messages. Her name is Amanda Rauci. I wonder if that's come up."

"It hasn't," said Frey.

"I'd like to have someone talk to her," said Rubens.

"Fine. We'll tell her to be available."

"It occurs to me that she might be a target herself," said Rubens. "If Agent Forester's death wasn't a suicide."

Forester didn't answer.

"Jed?"

"You're right," said Frey. His voice sounded as if he were coming from quite a distance away. He was thinking about Forester, Rubens guessed. "We'll protect her."

There were two things that interested Rubens. One was his admittedly optimistic thought that someone who was having an affair wouldn't kill himself, assuming the affair was still continuing. And the second was the fact that French was often used in Vietnam.

Rubens called down to the Art Room and told Marie Telach that he had changed his mind about the assignment for Vietnam. He wanted Lia to talk to Amanda Rauci.

"I believe she may have an easier time connecting with her than Ambassador Jackson," said Rubens. "Though he, too, can go along."

"Lia is supposed to be going to Vietnam with Charlie."

"Have Tommy Karr meet him there instead."

"He is on vacation."

"I'm sure Mr. Karr will understand."

23

KJARTAN "TOMMY" MAGNOR-KARR reached across the table and poured the last of the wine into his girlfriend's glass.

"Are you trying to get me drunk, mister?" said Deidre Clancy.

"Nah. Just tipsy."

Deidre smiled at him. Tommy Karr realized he was the one who was tipsy, though not on the wine.

"So tomorrow, we go to Disneyland Paris?" he said, picking up his glass.

"You came all the way to Paris to go to Disneyland?"

"I came all the way to Paris to see you," said Karr. "Everything else is bonus."

"You flatterer."

Deidre told him in French that he was a sweet-talking foreigner whom she knew she must be careful of; Karr's limited French allowed him to pick out every third word—the good ones, of course.

"How about the Louvre tomorrow?" she asked in English. "With a picnic lunch in the Luxembourg Gardens?"

"Disney Thursday?"

"Disney Thursday."

"Deal."

As the word left Karr's mouth, his sat phone began to vibrate.

"Uh-oh," he said.

Deidre heard the buzzing. "I don't suppose you could not answer it," she said.

"I could ignore it. But then they'd send someone to chase me down. Which might be kinda fun."

"You better answer it," said Deidre.

Karr took the phone from his pocket and slid up the antenna.

"O'Brien's Real Italian Delicatessen," he said. "Mao Zedong speaking."

"Tommy, it's always fun to hear your voice," said Marie Telach. "Can you talk freely?"

"Hey, Mom. Not really."

"Good. I know you're on vacation, but Mr. Rubens needs you to cut it short."

"Gee, that sucks," said Karr. He looked over at Deidre, who already wore a disappointed frown. "Right away?"

"Yes. We need you to meet Charlie in Tokyo tomorrow night."

"Tomorrow? Do I have a choice?"

"Yes, as a matter of fact you do. Would you prefer to fly on Aeroflot or Air France?"

24

AMANDA RAUCI CLUTCHED her fingers together, trying to stave off the urge to put another mint Life Saver in her mouth. They were a dead giveaway that she had been drinking in the middle of the day.

Bloodshot eyes weren't exactly camouflage, either, but there was nothing she could do about those.

"The director will see you now," said the secretary.

Amanda nodded, and rose from her seat. Despite her earlier resolution, she reached into her bag and took out a mint, popping it into her mouth before entering Frey's office.

"Please sit down," said Frey.

The icy tone told her everything. She forced a smile to her face as she pushed one of the modernistic seats up close to the director's desk. The chair felt uncomfortable, oversized; Amanda's feet didn't reach the floor. She bit the candy she'd just put in her mouth, swallowing the tiny pieces in a single gulp.

"I can't believe you would hinder an investigation by withholding important information," said Frey. "I can't believe it."

Amanda said nothing.

"Why? Why didn't you say anything? Surely you knew Jerry was dead."

"What was there to say?"

"When did you last see him?" Frey asked.

"A few nights before he died."

"During your vacation?"

"Before my vacation started."

"Was he depressed?"

Amanda shook her head.

"Why didn't you say anything?" asked Frey again. "Didn't you think it was relevant?"

Because if she said anything, then it would be real. Then he would be gone, really, utterly, truly gone. And she was gone as well.

"Where were you the night Jerry died?"

"I was at a hotel, waiting for him."

"Waiting for him? Where?"

"A few miles from . . . I guess . . . where . . ."

She had to stop to control the sobs. How much was she going to tell Frey? Everything? Or just part?

Part. Whatever she could get out before despair took over.

"We spoke," Amanda said. "He told me to wait. I was in the bar awhile. I was there, I guess, when he—"

Sobs erupted from her chest so violently that she shook and couldn't continue.

Frey offered no sympathy. "That's it?"

She nodded. Clearly if she told him she'd been there— God, if she told him she'd been there, he'd have her charged with murder.

"You still have vacation days left?" asked the director.

Amanda formed her fingers into fists, then ground them into her cheeks to stop the tears and sobs. "Yes," she managed.

"Then take them. Hand in your credentials, and your weapon. Leave them here."

"I'm suspended?"

"What do you think?"

25

LIA AND DEAN stopped at a small family-style restaurant not far from the Foresters' house for an early dinner. Lia immediately regretted it. The restroom was filthy, in her experience never a good sign. But Dean had already ordered for both of them by the time she got to the table.

"You really think you know what I want?" she asked him.

"Turkey wrap."

"Maybe I wanted a hamburger."

"That would be a first."

It wasn't so much that he was right as the fact that he was smug about it—quietly smug, of course—that annoyed her.

"I felt bad for the kid," said Dean.

"Yeah."

"I'd hate to see that happen to my son."

"What son?"

"If I had one."

Lia, confused, said nothing until the waitress came with their drinks—seltzer for Dean, iced tea for her.

"You knew I wanted iced tea, too, huh?"

Dean nodded.

"I'm that predictable?"

"Only about food."

"Do you have a son, Charlie Dean?"

Dean stared at her. The words had blurted from her mouth, almost of their own volition. She'd stopped being Lia DeFrancesca, Desk Three op. She was just . . . herself.

"I don't have any children," said Dean. "You know that."

"Yeah."

"What I meant was, when I *have* kids, I wouldn't want them to think I killed myself."

Lia didn't hear the rest of what Dean said. *When I have kids. When.*

With her?

Was that his plan? Was it her plan? Did she want kids? After her week at Tina's, children were even further than usual from Lia's thoughts.

But did she want kids?

The question was too much to think about right now. Lia forced her attention back to what Dean was saying. She'd missed the transition, but he was talking about Mrs. Forester.

"Maybe she's right," said Dean. "He might have told people at the Secret Service that he wanted custody of the kids, but that might have been bull."

"Why do you say that?" Lia asked.

"Because of what he did. Because if he really loved the kids, he wouldn't have killed himself."

"I don't think it was suicide," said Lia. "And neither does Rubens—that's why we're going to Vietnam. Whoever tried to kill McSweeney killed Forester first."

Dean didn't say anything, which usually meant he disagreed.

"I doubt she bought those NASCAR tickets," said Lia. "He must've loved the kids."

"Taking somebody to a car race doesn't mean you love them," said Dean.

"How would you know?"

Dean frowned—then changed the subject. "How was your friend?"

"Still pregnant. How was your hunting?"

"OK. I missed."

"You *missed*?"

"The lion came out of the brush at less than ten yards. I had a point-blank shot. I missed."

"It surprised you."

"Yeah."

"Then what happened?"

"It jumped on me. I rolled around. Finally I shot it."

"Charlie."

He shrugged. "I don't know why the hell I missed."

The waitress came over with the food. The turkey wrap was excellent, though Lia was loath to admit it.

"Let's say you're right and Forester was killed and it's all related," Dean told her, returning to their mission. "Why kill him? What did he know? The Secret Service had no information. If they had, they would have prevented the assassination attempt."

"That's what we have to find out. Duh."

"What if there's nothing there?"

"Won't be the first time," said Lia, digging into her sandwich.

DESK THREE OPERATIONS Personnel Director Kevin Montblanc met them as they stepped off the elevator near the Art Room about an hour later.

"Uh-oh," said Lia. "What's wrong?"

Montblanc laughed. His moustache helped make him look a bit like a walrus, dressed in a soft sport coat cut in a way that made him look like an English gentleman from the 1920s.

"Do I always signify a problem?" Montblanc asked.

"Always," said Lia.

"There's been an assignment change is all. Charlie, you're to meet with Ms. Telach as planned. Lia, you're going to work with the Secret Service and FBI. Mr. Rubens wishes to speak with you himself. He's in his office."

"I'm not going to Vietnam with Charlie?"

"Afraid not."

"OK."

Lia turned to Dean, sorry now that she hadn't continued the conversation they'd started and then aborted in the restaurant about kids. Foolishly she'd thought they'd have plenty of time to talk about it.

She wanted to tell Dean that she would miss him, and to

take care of himself, and to miss her—but she felt awkward in front of Montblanc.

"See you around, Charlie."

"Yeah," said Dean.

She spent the entire trip up to Rubens's office trying to decipher the meaning of that "yeah," before concluding it meant nothing more than "yes."

MARIE TELACH WENT over the mission with Dean in a small conference room on the secure level of the Desk Three operational center. The room was spartan; there was no massive video screen, no high-tech sound system. The furniture looked a half step above what one might find on sale at Wal-Mart. Small laptop-like computers sat on the table, permanently connected to each other and the Deep Black computer system via a thick, shielded cable. The room was soundproof and, like the entire level, incapable of being bugged.

Or as Rubens would put it, not *yet* capable of being bugged. No security system was impenetrable; defeating it was simply a question of devoting resources, creativity, and time.

"Your cover will be as a salesman for agricultural machines. An agricultural exposition is being held in Ho Chi Minh City and we've arranged for credentials for you. There'll be a packet of background and technical material in your briefcase. Tommy Karr will meet you in Tokyo," continued Telach. "From there we've arranged for you to fly to Thailand, and then take another plane to Ho Chi Minh City. A driver will meet you at the airport."

"You mean Saigon, right?" said Dean.

Marie smiled. Dean didn't know how old she was, but he guessed she was too young to have experienced Vietnam firsthand. It was just history to her, or worse, legend.

And to him? Only a dim memory. Something that had happened to someone else, to a young Marine not even old enough to drink. In fact, he'd lied about his real age to get into the Corps.

Not the last lie he'd ever told, but the last one he felt reasonably good about.

"The driver will be a local, someone businessmen use," said Telach. "He'll speak at least some English, but of course we'll be able to help you with our own translator here. Please leave your communications systems on so we can do that. The CIA will vet the driver, but obviously he won't be working for us. Be careful what you say."

Dean nodded.

"Kelly Tang is the CIA officer assigned to help you. She's covered as a Commerce employee, and she'll be at the expo. She'll be arranging different receptions and maybe a luncheon where you may be able to meet one if not more of the contacts. That's still a little loose."

A picture of a woman in her early twenties appeared on the screen.

"This is Tang. Look for her at the reception the first night. The CIA is trying to dig up some information on Infinite Burn as well," added Telach, referring to the Vietnamese assassination program. "We're all sharing information. So far, they don't have anything. And for the most part, they're skeptical."

"So am I," said Dean.

"Good." Telach continued, detailing how the CIA and local embassy people could be contacted. Tang would make available local agents—foreigners who worked for the CIA—if Dean needed help.

"There are three people you'll have to contact. We don't have an enormous amount of information on most of them, so you'll have to gather some of it on the run. We do have some recent photos for two of them, and an old wartime shot of the third. They were all connected with the war, but whether that's significant or not we don't know."

A Vietnamese man a little older than Dean appeared on the computer panel.

"This is Cam Tre Luc. He's a mid-level official with the interior ministry. He has some responsibility for the state police, though we're not precisely sure what his role is. I would expect that he's the number-one candidate, simply because he's in the right position to know about a plan like this, but he's going to be the trickiest one to contact."

Dean read the biographical notes. Cam Tre Luc had been fifteen in 1968. According to the Army intelligence records, he supplied troop estimates and alerts when units were moving. His information had been rated as "often reliable"—excellent, under the circumstances.

"He could easily have been a double agent," said Dean. "Supplying our guys with just enough information to keep them happy, while he sucked them dry for the other side."

"That's true for all of them," said Telach. She tapped her keyboard. "This is Thao Duong. He was a low-level member of the South government who was rehabilitated following the war. He now has a job in one of their commerce agencies, helping facilitate international business. You should be able to meet during the convention. Last but not least is this man, Phuc Dinh. He was a provincial official for the Vietcong who was on the American CIA payroll. He now works for one of the Vietnamese semi-official agencies that govern and facilitate travel in the country. He lives in Quang Nam Province. We don't have a recent photo. We've constructed a computer-assisted aging shot to show what he might look like, but you know how that goes."

According to the computer rendering, Phuc Dinh was a bald man, roughly Charlie's age, with a dagger-shaped scar on his cheek and a scowl on his face. The outline of his face was fuzzy, as if the computer wanted to emphasize the image was guesswork rather than reality.

"Do you have more information on them?" Dean asked.

"A little. You can click on those tabs and bring up their entire dossiers. There are files from the war. As you'd imagine, they're pretty sparse."

Dean put his finger on the touch pad at the base of the keyboard, paging back to Tre Cam Luc. The CIA's wartime dossier consisted of a physical description, some notes about his position and the reliability of his information—three on a scale of five—and a very old photo. When he was finished reading, Dean slid his finger down on the touch pad, hesitated for a moment before selecting the next panel.

Phuc Dinh. DOB 12/4/45. Born, Quang Nam Province.
Communist Party member since at least 1960.
??Leader/lieut of VC cell in Quang nam-Da Nong
province, near Laos border.

Ht. 5–3 wt. 114 pnds . . .
brn, brn
Identifying marks—scar right cheek

Contact lost Feb 23, 1971

A small black-and-white photo accompanied the half page of text.

Dean had seen the photo before—more than thirty years before, when he had been assigned to kill Phuc Dinh.

An assignment Dean had successfully completed.

"You OK, Charlie?" asked Telach. "You look like you've seen a ghost."

"I'm fine," said Dean. "When's my plane?"

27

THE FACT THAT Forester had a girlfriend erased some of the sympathy Lia had felt for him, even as it added more evidence to her suspicion that he hadn't committed suicide.

"Very possibly, this woman will have additional information," Rubens told Lia as he briefed her in his office. "Or some insight into the situation. I'd like you to speak to her and—"

"I know the drill," she said. "You don't have to connect the dots."

Rubens frowned and began lecturing her on the "need for decorum" when dealing with "sister agencies."

"Ambassador Jackson will assist you in speaking to Ms. Rauci, and then deal with the Washington people," said Rubens. "I'd like you to work in the field, see what you can find. If Forester was murdered, his killer may lead us back to the conspirators."

"Peachy."

"We want you to look for computers Forester might have used to send e-mail when he went to Pine Plains. Check the hotel where he was found. There is a business center there."

Lia found her thoughts wandering, first to the Forester family, then to Charlie Dean and what he had said about kids, then to Rubens himself.

Rubens was, by all accounts, independently wealthy. He was also consumed by his job, often working around the clock and sometimes spending several days in a row at the NSA complex. Overseeing Desk Three was just a small part of his duties. It was no wonder then that while fortyish—she had no idea what his actual age was, though she guessed he was younger than he seemed—he appeared to have no life outside of the Agency. No wife, no child.

Lia didn't *really* know that, did she? He didn't wear a wedding ring, but many men didn't. She didn't see any family photos on his walls, only fancy paintings.

"Excuse me a second," she interrupted. "Do you have a child?"

Rubens, though undoubtedly used to her impertinence by now, blinked twice.

"Because I'm wondering," continued Lia, "if you were fighting for custody, and you didn't get it, would it be enough to kill yourself?"

"Assuredly not. But I hardly think I am a representative sample, Lia. Keep an open mind—draw no conclusions."

"Yeah, yeah, I know all that."

Rubens frowned, then resumed his lecture on how to behave.

28

THERE WERE SEVERAL reasons Dean remembered the mission to kill Phuc Dinh. The first was the oddness of the first name—though it was common enough in Vietnam, the obscenity it sounded like in English was not easily forgotten.

The second was the comparative uniqueness of the mission. "Hunter-kills"—assignments to kill a specific person—while not rare for scout snipers in Vietnam, were relatively infrequent; even though Dean was considered good at them, he racked up only a handful during a year's tour. Most often, he and other snipers worked with Marine units during patrols or sweeps, striking North Vietnamese Army units operating in the area.

Even as a hunter-kill, the assignment was unique. It was on the Laos border, and the man giving the assignment went out of his way to specify that Phuc Dinh was a priority target "to the exclusion of all others." Which meant don't waste your time shooting anybody else until this SOB is toast.

But for Dean, the assignment stood out for one reason far beyond all the others: it was on this mission that he had lost his best friend in the world, John Longbow.

Dean had met Corporal John Longbow in Scout Sniper School. Unlike Dean, who'd gotten the assignment directly out of boot camp, Longbow had already been to Vietnam before volunteering to become a sniper. Everyone in Scout Sniper School was a standout Marine. Longbow was a standout among the standouts.

At first, the instructors tried to push Longbow harder because he was the oldest, but it quickly became clear that he pushed himself harder than even the toughest taskmaster could. By the end of the first week, the sergeant in charge of the unit was relying on Longbow as a fourth instructor.

Despite all this—or maybe because of it—the other trainees in the unit shied away from him, especially in the few hours they had "off duty" following training. The corporal never said much, and many interpreted his silence as a kind of arrogance. And working with him on the range could be a little demoralizing—he was *so* precise, *so* controlled, so perfect, that anyone who measured himself against Longbow inevitably came up short.

Force Recon shared the camp with Scout Sniper School, and there was occasionally some bad blood between the two units. From the snipers' point of view, the Force Recon trainees were always looking for a fight, trying to prove that *they* were the real Marines and that everyone else in the service was an embarrassment. They called snipers' rifle boxes diaper bags; the put-downs increased exponentially in vulgarity from there.

One night Longbow had just made the chow line when four or five Force Recon show-offs began making fun of him, calling him Tonto and asking if he'd gotten his red face from lipstick. Longbow, who was somewhat touchy about his Indian heritage, ignored them at first, but this only egged them on more. Dean walked into the mess hall to find Longbow surrounded. Not knowing exactly what was going on— but already disliking the other unit for its habit of bragging and abusing the snipers—Dean double-timed to Longbow's side. The corporal glanced over his shoulder, saw Dean, then turned back and stared at the other men.

"Oh, whoa, it's the evil eye," cracked one of the Force Recon trainees. "I'm feeling weak. Weak."

He fell to the floor. The others convulsed in laughter.

For a moment, Dean wasn't sure what was going to happen. Or rather, he was *sure* Longbow was going to kick the

Marine on the ground in the face and after that wasn't sure what would happen. Dean figured, though, that he would be backing up his fellow platoon member.

Instead, Longbow stared for a second longer, then turned away. It was a good thing, too—a captain had seen what was going on from the far side of the mess hall and was on his way over. Had there been a fight, all of the men would undoubtedly have been kicked out of their respective schools.

Dean and Longbow ate together in silence. They never spoke of the incident again. But from that point on, Longbow helped Dean whenever he could, offering him different bits of advice on the range and helping him master some of the finer points of the shooting art, such as compensating for winds above 10 miles an hour.

They were assigned to the same unit in Vietnam—not much of a surprise, since about two-thirds of the school's graduates were sent there. After requalification at Da Nang, Dean, Longbow, and four other men they'd trained with joined a unit in an area known as "Arizona Territory." Their assignments varied, taking them to the Laos border and back, generally to work with Marine companies on sweeps or at forward camps where at night the enemy was so close you could smell the fish he'd had for dinner.

The origin of the nickname Arizona was in some doubt. Some Marines thought it was an apt comparison of the highly dangerous area to the Arizona of the lawless Old West. Others thought it came from the parched pieces of landscape, scorched by Agent Orange. In any event, the nickname was not a compliment.

Usually the snipers went out in two-man teams, especially when they were working alongside other Marine units conducting patrols or attacking an enemy-held area. At first, the new men were teamed up with more experienced snipers; before long, they were the experienced hands and others the newbies. Dean and Longbow only worked together on CID missions, and then only very important ones for which they were hand-selected by their CO.

"CID" stood for "Counter Intelligence Department"; the organization was actually a CIA group that ran special operations in the area, often using Marine snipers to get things done. A CID mission could involve gathering intelligence, or it could target a special VC soldier or official for assassination. The mission against Phuc Dinh was the latter.

"PHUC DINH LIVES in a village about three miles from the border," John Rogers told Dean and Longbow. The CIA officer had commandeered their commander's tent to brief the mission. Rogers had only been in the region for a few months, but that must have seemed like forever to him; he bucked up his facade of courage with gin, and the stink sat heavy on him even at 0800.

"There's a series of tunnels in this canyon here," said Rogers, pointing at the map. He sat in a canvas-backed field chair; Dean and Longbow were across from him on the captain's rack. "They used to hole up in them on their way south until we got wise to them. Now they go much further west, over the border."

Dean stared at the grid map. Experience had shown the relationship between such maps and the real world was often tenuous. Villages were often misnamed and in some cases a considerable distance from where they were supposed to be. More important, maps could never tell you the most important thing—where the enemy was.

"Phuc Dinh goes across the valley into Laos every week to ten days to make contact with units on the Ho Chi Minh Trail. He travels at night. Your best bet at catching him alone is on one of those nights.

"Dinh is your target, to the exclusion of any others."

Dean glanced over at Longbow. The sniper was staring intently at the back of the captain's tent, zoning in the distance. Dean guessed Longbow was thinking of the mission.

Rogers rose to leave.

"Can we go into Laos to get him?" Dean asked Rogers.

"Technically, no." Rogers picked up the small briefcase

he'd brought with him. "Send a message back that the red hawk has died."

THE MISSION BRIEF did not include the reason that Phuc Dinh was to be shot. It was obvious that he must be some sort of important VC official, though that alone probably wasn't enough to arouse CID's wrath. But reasons were irrelevant to Dean and Longbow; Phuc Dinh was the enemy, and that was all the reason they needed to kill anyone.

The two snipers rode with a Marine company making a sweep about ten miles south of Phuc Dinh's village; the unit ran into trouble as soon as their helicopters landed and Dean and Longbow spent nearly five days with them, the first three within spitting distance of the landing zone. Dean and Longbow didn't much mind the time itself, since they weren't sure when Phuc Dinh would be moving, but the delay cost them valuable supplies, most notably about half of the ammo for Longbow's bolt rifle, a Remington 700. Dean, acting as Longbow's spotter, though ordinarily a team leader himself, carried an M14 with a starlight scope.

Finally, the unit managed to extricate itself and got under way. When Dean and Longbow split off from the others, they were just under six miles from Phuc Dinh's village. The jungle was so thick there that it took a whole day to walk three miles toward it. Then, just as they were settling down for the night, they caught a strong odor of fish on the wind.

A VC unit was moving through the area, possibly stalking the Marines Dean and Longbow had just left. The smell came from the food the Vietcong ate and meant they were incredibly close, perhaps only a dozen feet away.

To the Vietcong, Americans smelled like soap, and probably the only thing that saved Dean and Longbow was the fact that they had been in the bush long enough for the grime to overwhelm any lingering Ivory scent. The Vietcong passed them right by.

There was only one problem. The enemy guerillas were moving in the direction of the unit Dean and Longbow had left. The snipers didn't have a radio. In those days, effective radios were bulky and had to be carried on your back. They were also in short supply. So there was no way of alerting the other unit short of sneaking back and telling them.

Dean and Longbow discussed what to do. Their orders had priority, clearly—"exclusion of any others" was supposed to cover a situation like this—but they couldn't leave their fellow Marines to be blindsided. Dean and Longbow circled to the southwest, stalking the stalkers.

Four hours later, the Vietnamese unit reached the flank of the main unit. Dean, looking through the starlight scope of his M14, saw one of the Vietcong rise to throw hand grenades and begin the attack. He put a three-round burst into the man's head. The grenade detonated, and the firefight was on. The guerillas lost the element of surprise and quickly withdrew. Dean and Longbow had to retreat as well, barely escaping the crossfire. The detour had cost them not only several hours but also more ammo and water.

"VILLAGE HAS FIVE huts," said Dean, looking at it through his field glasses. "Five huts. Shit."

"You sure this is the place? Supposed to be four or five times that."

He pulled out his map again. While it could be difficult to correlate points, in this case the location seemed fairly obvious—the village was located at the mouth of a bend in a small creek, which corresponded with the map. There were other geographic marks as well, including the road and the valley three miles to the west.

EVEN SO, THEY took another day making sure, circling across to the valley and back, even moving to the edge of a second village two miles to the south. This village was also considerably smaller than the map and briefing had indicated, and in the end Dean concluded that the information, like so much intelligence they were given, was simply wrong.

So they went ahead and set up an ambush. There were at least four different paths from the village into the valley, but the sharp cliffs on the east side of the valley meant there were only two passes across, and both lay within a half mile of each other. The snipers had their choice of three positions to fire from, all between five and six hundred yards. They settled on a good spot in the middle, not because of the range—even the M14 could handle that distance—but because a fifty-foot sheer drop made a surprise attack from the rear unlikely.

Twenty-four hours passed without them spotting anyone. While their position was shaded, the heat kept increasing and both men stripped to their skivvies to try to keep cool. Conserving water was difficult in the heat. It was the dry season, and a particularly parched stretch at that; moisture of any kind was hard to find. From about dusk to midnight— the time they figured Phuc Dinh was most likely to be traveling—they both stood watch. During the other twenty hours or so they took turns resting—it wasn't sleep really, more a fitful sitting in a nook of the rocks.

By the fourth day, they were both down to their final canteen of water. Refilling the others was not a problem— they'd spotted a shallow spring-fed brook about a mile away on the way in—but it was, of course, dangerous, since only one person could go and there was no way the other could cover him while watching the trail.

Dean, as second man on the team, should have been the one to go. But Longbow overruled him.

"I need to stretch my legs," he told Dean, taking the M14. "Don't break my gun."

Some men believed it was bad luck and worse to let anyone else touch your gun. Longbow didn't; Dean had fired his rifle before.

Still, Dean did think about it as he watched his companion climb up and then down the hill. There didn't figure to be any action while Longbow was gone, though. It was still daytime.

Dean made sure he had the bolt rifle sighted properly, then picked up the binoculars and resumed watching the trail. He stared through the glasses for more than a half hour without blinking. He could see a lot more with the binoculars than he could with his sniper's scope, but he was always conscious that they, too, were limited. The world the binoculars showed was carved into precise circles, and the real world was not.

About an hour after Longbow left, a cone-shaped hat poked over the hill in the distance. Within a few seconds it was joined by a second, then a third and a fourth. Four men were moving across the trail toward Dean. They weren't "ordinary" villagers, either—all carried AK-47s.

Dean scanned them carefully. Phuc Dinh was not among them. Dean let them pass.

Not more than five minutes later, another villager appeared. It was Phuc Dinh.

Dean knew it was. He saw Phuc Dinh's face, and the scar. And he was moving quickly, confidently. Probably the four men who had passed first were a security team, making sure the path was clear.

Phuc Dinh had a pistol in his belt but no other weapon. Dean stared through the scope of the bolt rifle, steadying his breathing. Phuc Dinh's head moved toward the crosshairs. The wind was 3 miles an hour.

Just as Dean's finger started to pressure the trigger, shots rang out up the trail behind him. The shots were from an AK-47—years later, Dean would still remember the distinctive stutter the 7.62mm bullets made as they left the barrel, the sound partly echoing against the rocks, partly muffled by the jungle.

There was no way that the shots could have warned Phuc Dinh in time. Dean was already pressing the trigger. And yet for some reason Phuc Dinh had already begun to dive away.

Maybe Dean rushed the shot. Maybe the wind kicked up incredibly. Maybe the fact that the weapon wasn't his—even though he'd fired it before—messed him up. Maybe Phuc Dinh had seen a flash of light from Dean's scope, or realized he was vulnerable, or just had an itch to move. Maybe this was just the one time out of ten thousand that a sniper missed a shot.

In any event, Dean's shot went wide left, hitting Phuc

Dinh's arm rather than his chest as he fell or threw himself off the side of the trail.

Dean immediately corrected and took another shot. He struck the only part of Phuc Dinh that was exposed, his right leg. As that shot hit home, Phuc Dinh bounced farther down, completely out of Dean's view.

In the meantime, the automatic-weapons fire behind Dean continued. The gunfire wasn't meant as a warning, and it wasn't being fired at Dean. The men had obviously come across Longbow.

Dean ignored the other gunfire. His job was to take out Phuc Dinh. Only when that was done could Dean help his friend. Dean climbed up out of his "hide" or sniper's nest and began circling to the west across the ridge for a shot. He had to go about ten yards before he could see into the spot where Phuc Dinh had dropped.

He wasn't there.

Dean took a long, slow breath. The important thing, he told himself, was not to make a mistake. He knew he'd gotten Phuc Dinh in the leg and, while that wasn't fatal, it would slow him considerably. Most likely he'd moved back down the trail into the jungle. All Dean had to do was track him.

As Dean started down the rocks, he heard the gunfire in the distance intensify.

There was no question that he had to stay with his target until he was dead. Longbow would have done the same. The fact that the Vietnamese were firing so many shots was a good thing; it meant that they probably didn't have a real target, and they were giving their positions away besides.

And yet Dean did feel a tug as he moved down the hillside, low to the ground, snaking toward the edge of the jungle, hunting his prey.

It couldn't have taken Dean more than five minutes to get to a spot in the trail that he calculated would have been far enough behind Phuc Dinh that he could cut him off. But after Dean reached it, he spotted a few drops of blood, making it clear that the target had already slipped by.

Dean began to follow the trail, aware that he might be the hunted rather than the hunter. After about two hundred yards, he realized he wasn't seeing the blood anymore. He stopped, listening, but heard nothing. He moved into the brush and began paralleling the trail.

By now the sun was almost directly overhead, and while the trees provided shade, the heat steamed through him. He was thirsty. Dean told himself that Phuc Dinh had to be tiring as well and that, wounded, he'd be slower and less careful. Dean pushed on. He stopped every few yards, listening. Finally he heard a sound—brush moving—and he froze.

At first, Dean wasn't exactly sure where the sound came from. Then he heard something else, which helped him locate it thirty feet to his left. He snaked through the vegetation, moving toward the sound as quietly as he could.

The thick leaves were more effective than a smoke screen. Men could pass within a few feet of each other and not be seen. Hearing was more important, though the jungle filtered that as well, mixing in the sounds of animals and the natural rustle of the wind as a screen.

Finally, Dean spotted something that didn't look like vegetation about ten yards away. He wasn't sure if it was a man, let alone whether it was Phuc Dinh.

Dean moved forward so slowly it was as if he were only leaning in that direction. The gun was at his hip, ready to fire. The gray shape became the side of a chest. Something above it moved.

Eyes.

Dean fired.

The bullet punched a quarter-sized hole through Phuc Dinh's chest. In the sparse second it took Dean to chamber another bullet, life had ebbed from the VC commander; he fell straight back, collapsing against the trunk of a tree.

Dean's heart beat three times before he reached the body. A pistol lay next to Phuc Dinh; his mouth gaped open. There was no question he was dead.

Dean, like all scout snipers at the time, carried a small

Instamatic camera to record kills. He pulled it from his belt pouch and took two pictures. Then he took the VC officer's pistol, slid it into his waistband, and went to find out what had happened to Longbow.

29

WHEN NATIONAL SECURITY Advisor Donna Bing asked Rubens to convene a joint briefing session on the Vietnamese Assassin Plot, as she called it, Rubens tried to demur, telling her he thought it was premature. But she had insisted, and so late that evening he and Ambassador Jackson trekked down to Washington via Admiral Brown's helicopter to meet with representatives of the CIA, FBI, and Secret Service to, as Jackson put it, sing for their supper.

It was easy to see how much credence the various agencies placed in the theory by how high-ranking their representatives at the meeting were. Collins was there for the CIA; the initial information was theirs and she had turf to protect. But Frey had sent one of his deputies and a mid-level member of the investigative task force on the McSweeney investigation. Rubens didn't even know the FBI officials representing the bureau.

He understood the skepticism. His agency's review of Vietnamese intercepts found nothing that indicated a plot existed.

"Of course they would be careful about it," said Bing briskly. She badgered the other agencies for opposing theories—a disgruntled constituent was preferred by both the FBI and Secret Service, though he had yet to be identified—and then disparaged them. For once, she dropped her belligerent attitude toward Rubens and actually seemed—not *nice*, exactly, but human.

Rubens saw why when she summed up the session.

"Looking at this from the macro level, it makes utter sense," Bing declared. "The ultimate players here are the Chinese. They've helped the Vietnamese set it in motion—I would be looking for that connection in the intercepts."

Rubens was hardly a fan of China. But if there was still scant evidence that the assassination plot had been backed by the Vietnamese, then there was even less—as in nil—that the Chinese had a hand in it. He exchanged a glance with Jackson, who, diplomat that he was, returned only a hint of a smile.

"Was there something else, Bill?" asked Bing.

"I would only emphasize that we have yet to develop hard information about Vietnam's involvement, let alone China's."

Disappointment fluttered across Bing's face. But she quickly banished it, saying, "Well, then we have to keep working. Unfortunately, this is the sort of development where I would expect future attacks to bear us out."

She rose, dismissing them.

"Thank you, ladies and gentlemen. I'm sure the President will be pleased."

"Interesting theory," said Jackson on the helicopter home.

"That's one word for it."

"Sometimes it's useful to know why the wind is blowing at your back."

"In Donna Bing's case, it nearly always signifies there is a hurricane seeking to overtake you," replied Rubens.

30

BY NOW, THE rifle fire in the distance had stopped. Dean decided it was worth the risk to save time by taking the trail, doubling back to the sniping position to make sure Longbow hadn't returned. When Dean saw the nest was empty, he went back down, circling away from the trail and then paralleling it as he slowly worked toward the spot where Longbow would have gone for water.

It took Dean nearly an hour to find the first body. He couldn't be positive, but he guessed from the clothes that it belonged to one of the men he'd let go past him on the trail. Even in death, the man clutched his AK-47 so tightly Dean had to use a knife to pry it from the man's hands. Dean took two magazines from the guerilla's body, tucking them into his pockets before continuing across the ridge.

While the vegetation here was sparse, there were still plenty of places to hide, and Dean had to stop every few minutes to search the terrain and listen for movement. The impulse to rush to his friend's aid felt like a dog growling at his side, nudging him forward. But moving too quickly could get Dean killed, and he struggled to keep his emotions and adrenaline in check.

It took a good twenty minutes to find the second man. He lay a hundred and fifty yards from the first, curled in a fetal position, huddled around his gun. The top part of his head had been split open by one of the M14's bullets, revealing an oozing black mass where his scalp and forehead had been. Though hardened to death, Dean had to turn away as he searched the body for ammo and anything else that might be useful.

A third Vietnamese guerilla had died a few yards away. He was a small man, barely five feet, and thin; his chest and back were pockmarked with bullets. It had taken six to put him down for good.

Dean found Longbow next.

Longbow's bush hat had been blown off during the battle, and it lay like a discarded rag in the pebbles near the water hole. The soldier lay on his side a yard and a half away, the M14 leaning against his body, as if it had been propped there.

Dean bent down on one knee, looking at his friend's face, hoping that he would be breathing, not believing what he knew was true. Longbow stared back at Dean, his expression twisting pain and bewilderment together.

Was he asking where Dean was when he needed him?

A shot ricocheted across the nearby rocks and into the water. Dean threw himself flat, smacking his rib on the butt of the AK-47 he'd been holding. He rolled right as another shot ripped through the ground nearby. Dean pulled the automatic rifle up and fired off a burst before jumping to his feet and running in search of cover.

There was no answering fire, but he knew he hadn't hit his enemy. The guerilla was firing from behind a large clump of jungle grass and rocks about fifty yards away. Dean decided that his best bet was retreating downhill, then circling back to flank the guerilla from the slope of the nearby ridge. The hardest part was the first twenty feet—under heavy fire, Dean climbed up the side of a large boulder, squeezed through a tumble of rocks, then crawled through a cluster of brush. His enemy emptied his rifle in the few seconds it took for Dean to reach safety.

Nearly fifteen minutes later, Dean reached a point where he could look down on the guerilla's position. It was empty. Bent grass showed the way he had gone.

By now tired, hungry, and thirsty, Dean considered whether it might not be better to let the man go. Probably it was, but logic didn't rule Dean that day. He slipped down the rocks and moved as quietly as he could into the thick vegetation.

He nearly tripped over the guerilla, who'd collapsed only a few yards from the grass where he'd fired from earlier. He was wounded but still alive.

Dean saw the man's body heave right before he fired point-blank into the bastard's head.

"ARE YOU AWAKE?"

Dean opened his right eye warily. The man sitting next to him on the plane smiled awkwardly. A stewardess stood behind him.

"Are you awake?" she repeated.

"Yeah," said Dean, straightening.

"We're about to serve breakfast."

"Sure."

He rubbed his eyes, then accepted a cup of coffee. The stewardess passed him a plate of French toast.

"I find it impossible to sleep on a plane," said the man next to him. "Even in first class."

"I usually don't sleep that well myself," said Dean. He cut up the wedges of bread, wondering when he had fallen asleep. He drained his cup of coffee and asked for another, trying to purge his memory of the look on Longbow's face.

31

TOMMY KARR SAW Dean as soon as he came out of the customs area on the first floor of Narita Airport in Tokyo. Karr watched the crowd, making sure Dean wasn't being trailed by anyone. Satisfied, Karr circled around outside and found Dean waiting at the taxi stand.

"You're on the wrong line," Karr told Dean.

"Do I know you?"

"I hope so." Karr winked at him, then nodded with his head, leading Dean back into the terminal.

"I thought we were staying over," said Dean.

"We are. There's a courtesy van from the hotel."

"Wouldn't we rather take the cab?"

"And blow our expense account?"

Karr led Dean around to the minivan, which he had used earlier to get here. The driver hopped from the cab as soon as he saw them coming, greeting Karr with a loud "hello" and taking Dean's bag.

"Loves country music," said Karr, climbing in through the sliding door. "How'd the sales go?"

"Not bad," said Dean, not missing a beat.

"Make quota?"

"Just barely."

Karr kept up the sales banter all the way to the hotel. Dean, though he played along, seemed even more somber than usual.

"Somber" wasn't the right word, exactly. "Contemplative," maybe. Or just "taciturn." Guys who didn't talk much always seemed like they were thinking about something. Karr wasn't sure whether that was true or not. Dean always denied he was thinking about anything, so how would you know?

Dean got a room two floors above Tommy's. They scanned it for bugs, then turned on a white-noise generator so they could talk.

"So how was your flight?" Karr asked Dean.

"Long."

"Where are we going?"

"They didn't tell you?"

"Telach said you'd brief me."

"Vietnam."

"What are we going to do, get a do-over on the war?"

Dean frowned. He wasn't much for Karr's jokes, which struck Karr as more fun than if he had been.

"Let's go get something to eat," Karr told him. "And worry about it later."

"Yeah, all right."

"There's this sushi place downstairs that looks really good."

"I'm not eating anything that hasn't been cooked," said Dean.

"Where's your sense of adventure?"

THEY ENDED UP in a restaurant several blocks away, circling around and splitting up at one point to make sure they weren't being followed. Dean knew the precautions were overkill—no one had any reason to be following them at this point—but he didn't object when Karr suggested them. He let Tommy be Tommy, cracking sardonic jokes in the restaurant and making funny faces at the emotionless waitstaff, trying to get them to laugh. He was in many ways just a big kid—a very, very big kid—and Dean knew that Karr had a tendency to deal with stress by pretending to be the class clown. He was one of those guys who would probably be telling jokes in the helicopter as it touched down in a hot LZ.

Better than puking, Dean thought.

Personally, he found it better to be quiet.

Maybe the mission was a "do-over" in a sense. Phuc Dinh—how could he have missed him?

He hadn't. Phuc Dinh was definitely dead. And it had definitely been him—the photo was positively ID'd when Dean got back to camp. The scar cinched it.

Better to be quiet before battle, Dean thought. Quiet your mind as well as your mouth—he tried to push the memory of Longbow and Phuc Dinh away, focusing on the here and now of the Tokyo restaurant.

"What do you think this is?" Karr asked, holding up a piece of sashimi.

"Fish."

"Sure, but what kind? Sea urgent, you think?"

"Urchin."

Karr winked, then swallowed the food whole. "Definitely urgent."

Dean couldn't help himself; he cracked a smile and raised his hand to signal the waiter for another beer.

"How was your vay-kay?" Karr asked.

"If you mean vacation, it was fine."

"Bag any mooses?"

"I was hunting mountain lions."

"Get any?"

"One. Almost bit off my head before I brought it down."

Karr thought it was a joke and smiled. "Why do you like hunting, Charlie? What's the attraction?"

The waiter came over with Dean's Sapporo. He took a sip, and then answered Karr's question by asking if he had ever gone hunting himself.

"Only for girls," said Karr. Then he laughed so loud everyone around them turned to see what was so funny.

AMANDA LOOKED AT the clock on her stove. She was supposed to meet with a member of the Agency's human-resources staff to discuss her "official status" in an hour.

Or was it a member of Internal Investigations? Amanda couldn't remember; she'd been too far gone when she took the phone call, and in fact could barely read her handwritten note showing the person's office number.

It didn't matter. Amanda wasn't going to keep the appointment.

Not because she was drunk. She was sober, as her pounding head and dry mouth reminded her.

Amanda had decided to leave town, though where she was going she wasn't sure. There was no reason to hang around. The Service would surely fire her. It wasn't fair, but that was the way it was going to be. She could tell from the way Frey had looked at her the other afternoon; he wanted her gone. And he would get what he wanted.

She didn't care. She didn't care about anything.

She cared about Jerry Forester, but he was gone. She was mad at him and sad for him, devastated and angry at the same time.

How could he do this to her? And to his boys. To his older son.

She had more questions for Jerry—many—but they would never be answered. The only way to deal with them was to get far away from them. If she didn't, the questions would consume her.

As would the booze.

The smell of Lysol and vomit stung her nose in the bathroom. She'd spent nearly two hours cleaning the place, and still the scent of half-digested gin clung to the ceramic tile. She pushed at the window, though it was already open as far as it would go.

The doorbell rang. Her first thought was that it was someone from the Service, coming for her because she'd missed her appointment. But that was impossible—she hadn't missed it yet. And they wouldn't bother to fetch her.

Amanda went to the front door and peered through the tiny peephole. A short Asian woman and a much older man stood in the foyer. The woman reached to the bell again.

"What is it?" said Amanda.

"Ms. Rauci?"

Amanda hesitated. If they knew her name they weren't Mormons or someone else she could easily send away.

"We're with the federal marshals' service, Ms. Rauci," said the woman. She held up a government identification card. "We need to talk to you."

Marshals?

"Why?"

"It's about Gerald Forester," said the woman.

Well, of course it was. Amanda turned the dead bolt but left the chain on the door, opening it a crack.

"What do you want?" she asked.

"This isn't a good place to talk," said the woman.

"I'm due at work in an hour."

"This shouldn't take long."

The woman's face was hard; Amanda realized she wasn't going to be put off.

"It would be more comfortable for all of us inside," said the man.

Even if Amanda hadn't known and practiced most of the games a two-person investigation team would play, she would have pegged the older man as the good guy a mile away. He seemed to have cultivated a grandfatherly look to help him with his interviews.

She slid off the chain and took a step back.

"I'm Lia DeFrancesca. This is Hernes Jackson."

"Hi." Amanda remained in the hall.

"Maybe if we sat in the living room or kitchen?" suggested Jackson.

Amanda led them to the kitchen.

"You have a bag packed," said Lia. "Coming or going?"

"Coming," lied Amanda. She felt her lip quiver, and longed for a drink. "Thirsty? I'll make some coffee."

"No thank you," said Lia. Jackson shook his head.

The two officers pulled out chairs but didn't sit down. Neither did Amanda.

"We were interested in knowing if Agent Forester ever discussed cases with you," said Lia.

"That would be against the rules."

"True," said Jackson. "But sometimes things are said anyway. It's not going to be held against him, I assure you."

"He's dead. How can you hold anything against him?" said Amanda.

"Did he?"

Amanda shook her head. "Jerry wasn't like that. He . . ."

The tears began flowing. She couldn't help it. She ran to the bathroom and buried her face in a towel.

LIA GLANCED AT Jackson. She had spent the entire ride to Amanda Rauci's house exhorting herself to keep an open mind. But seeing Amanda convinced Lia once again that there was no way this was suicide. Amanda wasn't beautiful; she was a bit on the plump side, and though she was only in her early thirties her face was already showing the signs of age. But still, it was impossible for Lia to believe that someone would walk out on both his kids and a girlfriend, especially one who obviously loved him.

"Maybe you should see if she's all right," Jackson suggested.

"Yeah."

Lia went down the hall. The apartment smelled as if it were a hospital.

"Ms. Rauci? Amanda?"

"What?"

The sharp bite of her voice, stronger than Lia had expected, took her by surprise. "Hey, look, I know this sucks," she told Amanda.

"Do you? Do you really know how it feels?"

The truth was, Lia didn't, not really, not firsthand. She'd been very lucky—Charlie Dean had come close to being killed on a mission but always survived.

"There were a couple of things about this that don't make sense," said Lia. "I don't think it happened exactly the way everyone says it did. So, maybe, we can figure it out?"

The door opened abruptly. Amanda, red faced, stared at her.

"Why are you interested?" said Amanda. "Who are you really with? I know you're not federal marshals."

"I told you, we're working with the marshals' office, helping out."

"Who are you really?"

Lia could be harder than anyone, and yet she felt real sympathy for the woman. Rubens hadn't told her and Jackson to lie, exactly, and Lia decided that Amanda was more likely to cooperate if she told the truth.

Even if it was in a roundabout way.

"We're with the NSA, on loan to the marshals service, which is helping with the investigation," she said. "We're trying to track down an e-mail your husband—your boyfriend—received. It may indicate that an assassination plot had an overseas origin. That's why we're here. That's what we're interested in."

Either the explanation or Lia's unconscious mistake about the nature of the relationship—calling Forester Amanda's husband—softened her.

"Let's go back into the kitchen," she told Lia. "Or the living room. That's better."

Lia took Amanda's elbow, clutching it gently as they walked down the hall. She suddenly felt like the host, rather than the uninvited guest.

"Do you want something?" Lia asked. "Coffee? Or something stronger?"

"Tea," said Amanda. "There's a kettle. Just tea."

TALKING ABOUT HIM was a catharsis. The words rushed from Amanda's mouth, thoughts and emotions flowing that she had never even known she'd had. The two NSA agents, the hard Asian woman and the kindly grandfather, sat and listened. Amanda still wasn't entirely sure why they were here, what they were really after—what Lia had told her made some sense but lacked enough real details to convince her. But once she had started to talk about Jerry, it didn't matter.

Finally, the man, Jackson, interrupted her. "Did he say why he was investigating in Connecticut?"

"It wasn't Connecticut. That was where we—where he—could get a hotel. The investigation was over in New York, a few miles away. We—I went up there to meet him. We were going to meet. But—"

The tears overwhelmed her for a moment. She thought of the nightgown she'd worn. She'd already thrown it out.

"He decided to stay in another hotel. I don't know why. I thought he was coming to the hotel I was at. He called me and then, well, he said he would be there and didn't come. I thought he stood me up. Well, I guess he did."

She bent over, sobbing until there was nothing left.

If they asked now whether she'd seen him dead, if they'd even hinted that they knew there was more to the story, she would tell them. She couldn't hold back. She felt like a balloon that had been popped and left exhausted on the floor.

But they didn't know to ask.

"The e-mail we were interested in," said Lia, "came from Vietnam. Does that ring any bells?"

"Vietnam?"

"Did Forester know anyone there?"

"No."

"Did he ever go there?"

"Not that I know," Amanda told them. "Did one of his investigations involve a Vietnamese national?"

"Not as far as anyone knows," said Lia.

"He did ask you if you spoke French," said Jackson.

Frey had already asked Amanda about the instant messages; now she realized why.

"I speak some. He never told me about a case," repeated Amanda. "Maybe it did have something to do with one, but he never explained. If he was thinking about it, he changed his mind."

"Really?" asked Jackson, his tone disbelieving.

Amanda shook her head. "He didn't discuss his cases. Not Jerry."

They were silent for a few moments. Amanda's breath wheezed against her teeth and lips.

"He didn't use his work computer to send the e-mails we've been looking at," said Lia. "Would you happen to know—would he have used yours?"

"Mine?"

"A personal one?"

"I don't have a home computer," said Amanda. "I haven't had one for a year."

"What do you use for browsing the Web?"

"I don't. I—sometimes I use the computer at work. To shop. But I don't need one. Just the work one. And the Service has that."

They were silent again. Amanda felt guilty that she had never gotten the old computer fixed or replaced. Maybe if she had . . .

Ridiculous. But she couldn't get rid of the thought. If one thing had been different somewhere, her lover might still be alive.

"You said that he didn't discuss specific cases with you," said Jackson. "And not this case."

Amanda nodded.

"But I would imagine you'd know how he usually went about working on cases?"

"What do you mean?"

"He used stenographic notebooks," said Lia. "We only found one in this case, and that had been back in his office, not with him when he died. Would that be unusual?"

Amanda thought of the notebooks he used, brown steno pads, which he often folded over so he could carry them in his back pocket.

Had she seen one that evening in the room?

No. He often kept them in the car—he had a habit of tucking them away as soon as he got in.

Where?

In the back, under the seat.

Maybe they'd already found the notebooks and were trying to trick her somehow. Did they know about Jerry's *other* habits, his paranoia about being locked out of anywhere? Did they know about the extra key he kept under the bumper—a key she still had?

Or the room key?

Was this a trick?

It would be a classic investigative maneuver: curry sympathy, extract as much information "softly" as they could, then begin pressing her.

Did they think she killed him?

God, they must. It was all a setup.

"He did take notes in a steno pad," Amanda said calmly. "Do you think—you're asking me this because he didn't kill himself?"

"Do *you* think he killed himself?" asked Jackson.

"No." Amanda knew she shouldn't say anything—she should be quiet, silent—but the words blurted from her mouth. "I can't believe he'd do it. His boys, especially the older one. This will destroy them."

"He is taking it hard," said Lia.

So they'd been there. It was a trap.

"Is there anyone you know of who would want to kill him?" asked Jackson.

Amanda turned toward him. Jackson might be old, but he was the vicious one, the classic wolf in lamb's clothing.

Amanda shook her head. "Have you looked into his cases?"

"The Service hasn't found any that stood out," said Lia. "They're still reviewing them, but they seem to have no real leads."

"Maybe you have a different opinion," said Jackson.

"No." Amanda rose. "I'm sorry, I'm supposed to be at work. I really have to leave. I have to go."

The two NSA officers exchanged a glance, then rose.

"Here's a number you can reach us at," said Jackson, producing a card.

"Do you have a card, too?" Amanda asked Lia.

"I don't. You could just call that number and ask for me. Lia."

"Just Lia?"

"They'll know who you're looking for."

SHE SEEMED EXTREMELY uneasy," said Jackson when they reached the car.

"Her boyfriend just died," said Lia.

"When I was in the State Department," said Jackson, "some supervisors would put pressure on employees who were having affairs. Does that still go on?"

Lia felt her face flush. "No."

She could never imagine Charlie killing himself—but if he died, and the circumstances were arranged so that it appeared as if it were a suicide, how would she feel? How would she act? Would people think that their affair—not exactly a secret—had somehow caused his death?

Especially if it was a suicide. Everyone would be thinking that Amanda Rauci somehow drove Forester to kill himself. First the wife, then the girlfriend; it was all too much for him.

"I guess she's just upset," said Jackson. "It is painful to lose a lover."

AMANDA LEFT THE building a few minutes after the NSA people. She thought that they might be watching her, and so she acted as nonchalant as she could, backing slowly from her space and heading on the highway exactly as if she were going to headquarters.

Were they following her? Amanda took an exit to get some gas, watching carefully. She'd been trained to spot surveillance teams and didn't see any of the usual giveaways, but the one thing that experience had impressed on her was that you could never be sure enough that you weren't being followed. She decided against running an aggressive driving pattern to flush out anyone following her; doing that would tip them off to the fact that she knew she was being followed.

Her best course was to act naturally—go into the office, sit through whatever crap she was supposed to sit through, then leave. She'd pretend to do some shopping, slip away then.

But what if she was arrested when she went to the office?

Arrested? For what?

Murder?

No way. No.

What if someone had seen her at the hotel? What if she'd left some print or DNA somewhere? Even a tear might give her away.

The NSA wouldn't be involved then. It would be FBI agents.

Maybe they'd simply lied. A weird lie to throw her off.

She'd already spoken to the FBI agents, dumb jerks who weren't anywhere near as thorough as the NSA people. Or maybe that was the game plan—she'd never be on her guard with the NSA people, right? Because they were spies, interested in foreign intrigue, not simple murder.

What the hell had Jerry been working on?

So was there another notebook? If so, maybe something in there would tell her what had happened.

Only if someone else had killed him.

They thought that was possible, though. Otherwise they wouldn't have come to see her.

Assuming they were telling the truth.

Amanda was so consumed in her thoughts that she missed the exit for her office. As she passed she instinctively slapped on the brake, then pulled onto the shoulder. She slapped the wheel angrily.

She was acting like an inept jerk. Paranoid and distraught.

She should be able to keep her head clear. She was a federal agent, trained to stay calm in an emergency. What if she'd been on an assignment? What if she'd been guarding someone?

But that was exactly the point. In that case, she'd have a script to follow. In that case, she'd be removed from the situation, distant. It would be easy. She wouldn't know anything, or anyone, but her job.

Amanda took a pair of very long breaths. She got back into traffic, and headed toward the next exit.

I'll dump the car at a Metro stop, she decided. I'll find that notebook. Because if they do think it's murder, then sooner or later they're going to accuse me.

It's what I would do if I were following the script.

33

WHEN DEAN ARRIVED in Vietnam the first time, he hadn't been prepared for the heat. It hit him with his first step off the plane. He was soaked in sweat by the time he stepped onto the tarmac. He felt as if he'd stepped into the mouth of a whale.

He wasn't quite prepared for it now, either.

The 757 had parked a good distance from the terminal, leaving the passengers to walk down a set of portable steps to a nearby bus. It had just rained, and there were large, shallow puddles on the cement apron. Dean glanced to his right and caught sight of a row of old hangar buildings, brown half-pipes made of corrugated metal. Thirty-some years before, the buildings had housed U.S. Air Force fighter-bombers; now they looked like overgrown gardening sheds.

"I thought this was the dry season," said Tommy, picking up the pace toward the squat, open-mouthed bus nearby. The door was where the hood would be on a truck.

"Dry means less than a monsoon," said Dean. The air steamed with the recent rain, though by Vietnamese standards the seventy-seven-degree temperature was mild.

"Bring back memories?" asked Karr, sliding into a seat.

"Not really."

"That's good. Warn me if you feel a flashback coming on."

Dean had actually been to the Saigon airport only once, to pick up someone. It had been nighttime and from Dean's perspective the airport consisted only of security check-points and a big, poorly illuminated building. So rather than seeming familiar or even nostalgic, the airport to him now seemed blandly generic, as if it could be anywhere in Asia. The large hall where the passport control was located reminded him of the airport in Istanbul, Turkey, where he had been a few months before: somewhat modern, somewhat utilitarian, a place where a crowd could be counted on not to loiter.

The customs line was only a dozen people long. A Vietnamese woman in front of Dean slipped a twenty-dollar bill into her passport. The clerk took it without comment, studied her documents, then waved her through.

There was no reaction from the clerk when Dean presented his American passport; he flipped through it quickly, then handed it back.

"Have a good day," said the man, reaching for Karr's documents behind Dean.

"Hello, Charlie. How does it feel to be back in Vietnam?" asked Jeff Rockman, the runner back in the Art Room. He was speaking to Dean through the Deep Black communications system, partly embedded in Dean's skull.

"Fine," said Dean, turning around to wait for Karr.

"We're in their video security system," said Rockman. "Smile—you're looking right at the camera."

Dean scowled instead. The Art Room regularly "invaded" computer-controlled video security systems to keep tabs on operatives during a mission. Ironically, the more sophisticated the system, the easier it was for the Desk Three hackers to penetrate. This system, which transmitted its images not only to the local security office but also to an interior ministry monitor in Ho Chi Minh City, was about as secure as a child's piggy bank.

Karr joined him and they walked down the steps to the baggage claim area.

"A woman bribed the passport guy with twenty bucks," said Dean, talking to the Art Room though he pretended to be speaking to Karr. "What was that about?"

"Commonly done," answered Thu De Nghiem, the Art Room's Vietnamese interpreter and an expert on the local culture. "It's a holdover from the past. A lot of returning Vietnamese will include 'tips' in their passports, though it brings them nothing. You will find a lot of petty corruption in the country. It's pathetic really. A tip worth a few cents at most can get you very far."

"I'll remember that."

Karr led the way to the luggage carousels, where their suitcases had yet to appear. As they joined the small knot of people milling around the conveyor belts, Dean spotted two men in suits watching tourists from the far end of the hall. A maintenance worker mopped up the spotless floor just to their right.

"Your bags are being searched in the room behind the belt," said Rockman. "Shouldn't be long."

"I hope they don't steal my razor," said Karr. "I really need a shave."

A half hour later, reunited with their luggage, Dean and Karr passed through the customs area without being stopped for an official inspection. Just past the door, a row of people crowded against a waist-high temporary metal fence, searching for the faces of relatives. The line extended out toward the main hall of the reception area, overflowing outside.

"I'm guessing that's our driver," said Karr, pointing at a silver-haired man near the door. He held a cardboard sign with the words "Car/Bean" on it.

"Kin chow," said Karr, sticking out his hand.

"Xin chào," said Dean, correcting his pronunciation. The words for "hello" sounded like "seen chaw" to an American. The rhythm and tone—a flat, slightly drawn-out singsong—were as important as the sound of the consonants. *"Tôi tên là Charlie."*

"And I'm Tommy," said Karr, shaking the driver's hand.

"Very nice to meet you," said the driver. "I am Lu. You speak Vietnamese?"

"I know a few phrases," said Dean. *"Rất vui đuoc gặp anh.* I am very pleased to be able to meet you."

Lu answered in Vietnamese that he, too, was happy to meet Dean and welcome him to his country.

"The car is outside," he added in English. "I will take you to the hotel."

"How about a drive around the city first?" asked Karr.

"You want scenic road?"

The juxtaposition of "scenic" and Vietnam seemed highly ironic to Dean, and yet as they drove to the hotel he realized that the country was indeed beautiful. Even the developing outskirts of Saigon, which looked a lot like the smaller cities of China, with cranes and bulldozers scraping the earth, had plenty of lush greenery to set off the yellow machines and the buildings they passed.

The city itself looked almost nothing like the Saigon Dean had visited as a Marine. New high-rises were sprinkled among the colonial-style buildings that had completely dominated then. Instead of casting shadows on the older, smaller buildings, the high-rises seemed to light them up, pulling them out of the past.

Motorbikes flooded around the car as it circled a city square marked by a fountain and leafy green trees. Dean noticed a family of four clinging to an older bike, a three-year-old leaning precariously toward the ground.

"The New World Hotel," said Lu as they pulled up. "You enjoy it very much."

Built in 1995, the New World was one of the city's finer hotels. Located not far from the Tao Dan Culture Center and Lelai Park, it towered over the downtown area, pushing the lesser buildings in its shadow toward the murky Saigon River. Sleek marble panels lined the hotel's glass-enclosed atrium, and the lobby looked as luxurious and modern as any Dean had seen.

Karr whistled as they took it all in.

"We better get some serious sales to justify this bill, huh, Charlie?"

Lu helped them with their bags, then gave them a card to call if they needed a driver again.

They checked out their rooms, which were next to each other on one of the executive floors. Karr examined the rooms for bugs while Dean planted some of their own, positioning dime-sized video cameras so the Art Room could see not only their rooms but also the hallway, elevator, and stairs. The bugs sent their signals to a booster unit the size of a paperback book, which he placed on the interior window ledge of his room. The small case looked like a battery waiting to be recharged.

Their rooms secure, Dean and Karr ambled out of the hotel and began what looked like a haphazard walking tour of the area. They spent a few minutes oohing and aahing, "doing the tourist thing," as Karr put it—checking out the general area to make sure they were familiar with possible escape routes.

Then they became more serious. They rented motorbikes from four different shops, stashing them at different parking areas so they would have them if necessary. Dean rented a car as well, though in Saigon, cars tended to stand out and were not as useful as the more ubiquitous motorbikes.

Karr, meanwhile, made a visit to a small notions shop several blocks from the hotel, emerging with a pair of large suitcases. Inside the cases were weapons and other equipment pre-positioned in the country. The weapons included an assortment of pistols and a specially designed assault gun called the A2; its boxy magazine held ninety-nine caseless 4.92mm bullets, which could be fired in three-round bursts—or all at once, which would take a little more than ten seconds.

"See anything familiar yet, Charlie?" asked Karr, when they hooked up again. He had already stashed some of the gear in a locker at the bus station and now filled the trunk of the rental car with the rest.

"No."

Dean glanced around. The Saigon streets were very different from what he remembered. Even allowing for the fact that he had only been here briefly, very long ago, the place bore almost no resemblance to anything he remembered. He tried to scrub away the obvious anachronisms of his memory—the drab green military vehicles, the rock music that occasionally blared from the most unexpected places, strategically placed sandbags and gun emplacements. There were just too many things to add—tall skyscrapers, a multitude of motorbikes, billboards that, except for their Vietnamese characters, could have been sitting over an LA freeway.

"Feels like I've never been here before," said Dean, though that wasn't 100 percent true.

AFTER SPREADING BACKUP gear around the city, they found a spot to park the car where it wouldn't be disturbed and went back to the hotel.

"You think you'll be all right at the reception on your own?" Karr asked Dean as they got into the elevator.

"You think you'll be all right breaking into the ministry on your own?"

"I'm not breaking in, Charlie. I'm visiting. After hours." Karr smiled. "There's a difference."

34

A SMILING WOMAN in a long red dress approached Dean shortly after he entered the reception in the Ben Thanh Hall on the second floor of the hotel. She looked Asian but was taller and younger than most of the women Dean had seen in the hotel so far.

"You must be Mr. Dean," said the woman. "Kelly Tang. I'm with the U.S. Department of Commerce."

"Nice to meet you."

"Just get in?" asked the covered CIA officer.

"This morning."

Tang asked him about his flight, glancing to the right at two men who had come in just behind him. She cut him off as he answered, excusing herself and then going over to speak to them.

It was a pretty clever move, Dean thought, designed to show anyone watching that she wasn't really interested in him.

Or maybe not. Maybe she really wasn't interested. It was sometimes hard to read the CIA people they worked with.

Dean walked over to the bar and ordered a seltzer. A Japanese businessman standing nearby pretended to do a double take when the drink was delivered.

"No alcohol?" asked the man in English.

"I'm afraid it will make me fall asleep," said Dean.

"You are the first American I have ever met who did not drink. What do you do?"

"I sell farm equipment for Barhm Manufacturing."

"Barhm? In Minnesota?"

"Yes," said Dean.

"You are my competitor," said the man, who stepped backward slightly and then bowed, as if they were two sumo wrestlers facing off. "Toshio Kurokawa. I with Kaito."

"Pleased to meet you," said Dean, lowering his head.

"You have a very good machine, RD-743."

"The rice cultivator," said Rockman from the Art Room. "Kaito's rival model is AG-7. They outsell you about twelve to one in the States."

"Thanks for the compliment," Dean told Kurokawa.

"Say something about his machine, Charlie," prompted Rockman. "To show your bona fides."

That was the problem with the Art Room. They were world-class kibitzers, always trying to tell you what to do. The last thing Dean wanted to do was talk shop. Rockman might have all the facts and figures at his fingertips, but there was no way to finesse the nuances. A really skilled bull artist might be able to get away with it, but Dean had never considered himself very good at lying. The best thing to do, he thought, was simply change the subject.

He turned and pointed vaguely across the room, singling out no one in particular. "Is that man from the agricultural ministry?"

Kurokawa squinted across the room. "Yes," he said finally, but Dean got the impression that he was just being agreeable and didn't want to admit he had no idea whom Dean meant.

"Have you been in Vietnam before?" Dean asked Kurokawa.

"Many times."

"This is my first visit," said Dean.

"An interesting place to do business."

"So I've been told."

Dean saw Tang approaching out of the corner of his eye. He asked Kurokawa what part of the country he liked best. The Japanese businessman said diplomatically that all parts of the country were interesting.

A waiter with a tray of American-style appetizers appeared,

relieving Dean of the onerous task of making meaningless conversation. Kurokawa took a small barbecue-flavored piece of chicken and a fried dumpling.

"Mr. Dean, I'm sorry to have left you. I hope you don't think I was rude," said Tang. She brushed a lock of her shoulder-length hair from her face as she spoke. Tang had a rounded face on a slim body, as if she were the product of a genetic mismatch. But she smiled easily, and the vivacious energy that emanated from her made her attractive.

"This is Mr. Kurokawa," said Dean, introducing his drinking partner. "He's with Kaito. My very successful competitor."

The Japanese salesman bowed.

"There's someone I would like you to meet, Mr. Dean," said Tang. "He can be very useful to your company as you do business in Vietnam."

They left Kurokawa and went across the room to a short, narrow-faced Vietnamese bureaucrat.

Thao Duong, the first of Dean's three contacts.

"Mr. Duong, I would like you to meet my friend Charles Dean," said Tang, allowing a hint of formality into her voice. "His company makes a very good rice cultivator, which could help you increase your yields."

"This would be very good," said Duong. He had a plate of appetizers in his hand; it was heaped high with food.

Tang drifted away. Dean, struggling with small talk, told Duong his company was very interested in doing business. The Vietnamese official merely nodded and continued to stuff his face. He was very thin, and Dean wondered if he didn't get a chance to eat regularly.

"I haven't been in Vietnam since the war," said Dean. "A great deal has changed."

"Yes," agreed Duong.

"I spent a lot of time in Quang Nam Province," said Dean. "Has it been built up a great deal now?"

Duong shook his head. "Not much. The industry is concentrated here. Factories."

Duong looked around the hall. He seemed nervous, as if he thought someone was watching him.

A good sign or a bad sign? Tang hadn't been told exactly what they were up to, so there was no way that Duong knew, either—unless, of course, he was the man Forester had contacted. In that case, Duong would probably think it was more than a coincidence that he had been invited here and that he was now being approached.

"I think we might have a mutual acquaintance," said Dean, deciding there was no reason to beat around the bush. "Jerry Forester."

Duong shook his head immediately.

"I thought you might have spoken with him recently by e-mail."

Duong said nothing.

"I thought maybe you had something you'd like to say to him."

"Excuse me," said Duong, and without saying anything else, he turned and walked toward the door, not even stopping to put his half-empty plate down.

35

LIVING AND WORKING in a communist country under a dictatorship had certain severe disadvantages for citizens, but it did make some things easier for spies. Case in point: official-looking documents were rarely questioned, as long as they had official-looking signatures.

The papers Tommy Karr had directing him to appear in the office of the deputy chief of trade on the third floor of the interior ministry were signed and stamped in three places. The guard at the front door squinted at each stamp, then opened the door and waved Karr inside.

The man at the desk proved suspicious. Noting that it was after hours, he decided to call the deputy chief's office.

His vigilance earned him a severe tongue-lashing from the deputy chief's "assistant"—aka Thu De Nghiem, who answered the phone after the call was routed to him by the Art Room's hackers. Red-faced, the security officer personally escorted Karr to the elevator, even leaning inside and pushing the button for the third floor.

"What'd you say to him?" Karr asked the Art Room as the elevator started upward.

"He asked why the deputy chief was working late," Rockman told him. "Thu told him to save his questions for his performance review."

"That'll fix him."

"Once you're out of the elevator, the stairs should be the second door on the right."

"Feel blind without video surveillance cameras, huh?" said Karr.

"They would help."

"Makes it easier for me," said Karr, who didn't have to worry about the guard following him upstairs through the monitors. He did, of course, have to make sure he got off on the right floor, which was why he headed for the stairs as soon as he got there. Thao Duong's office was on the fifth floor.

"Just plant plenty of video bugs as you go, OK?"

"Sure will. How's the one downstairs?"

"Guard's still there."

"Fire code violation," said Karr when he found the door locked. He bent down to examine the lock. "Wafer tumbler lock," he announced. He reached into his lock pick kit for a diamond pick.

"Tommy, we have a shadow from one of those offices down the hall on the right," said Rockman. "Someone's coming."

Karr had already heard the footsteps and straightened.

"Who are you?" asked the man in Vietnamese.

The Art Room translator gave Karr the Vietnamese words to reply, but the op had already decided on a better strategy.

"'Scuse me," he said. "I wonder if you could direct me to Mr. Hoa's office? I seem to have gotten lost. I'm supposed to be there like five minutes ago."

"Who are you?" repeated the man, again in Vietnamese.

"See, I have this paper."

Karr took out the paper he had used to get into the building.

The man was unimpressed. "Mr. Hoa has gone home," he told Karr. "Leave."

"I'm sorry, I don't understand Vietnamese," said Karr, though what the man was saying would have been clear even without Thu De Nghiem explaining it in his ear.

"Tommy, get out of there," said Telach.

"Go!" said the man, using English this time. "Go!"

"I don't want to get in trouble," said Karr.

"You come back tomorrow," said the Vietnamese man, switching back to his native tongue. "Go."

"You gotta give me back my paper."

Karr reached for it. The man shook his head.

"Just go, Tommy," said Telach.

Karr placed his hand on the Vietnamese official's shoulder. He was a good foot taller than the man, and probably weighed twice as much.

"I get my paper back now," Karr said. "Or I throw you out the window at the end of the hall over there."

"You need that translated, Tommy?" asked the Art Room translator.

"He understood perfectly," said Karr under his breath, walking back to the elevator with the paper in his hand.

36

WHILE THE DEEP Black operatives were conducting what might be called a point attack on the Vietnamese, Robert Gallo was in charge of a broader effort, one that took place over several battlefields, all of them electronic.

The NSA routinely monitored transmissions from several countries, collecting literally mountains of data every day. There was so much, in fact, that much of it was never inspected by a human. Even the automated programs that looked for things like key words or "hot" e-mail routes couldn't inspect every single message.

Once the Deep Black mission was initiated, a team of analysts specifically assigned to Desk Three began culling through the data. Their efforts were still primarily guided by automated programs, which helped them analyze the information in a variety of ways. Not even the most optimistic member of the team expected to find a specific message that said "kill this person." What they hoped to spot was a sequence of communications that indicated some sort of conspiracy—transfers of money, communications that did not fit an "ordinary" diplomatic pattern, and that sort of thing.

Gallo was assigned to work with those analysts, looking to see if there were systems that were not being tapped and which deserved to be. When the analysts developed a theory that an assassination team might be a private enterprise only partly supported, if at all, by the government, they gave him a list of servers being used by Vietnamese businesses. He began penetrating them, using "bots" or automated programs, in this case similar to viruses, to get the servers to give up information about themselves.

Angela DiGiacomo helped him handle the bots, which had a tendency to get "lost"—though bots were rarely tripped up by security protocols, errors in programming on the host's end occasionally scuttled them. DiGiacomo was very good at debugging the systems, figuring out where the problems lay, and adapting the programs to work around them without being detected.

She was also extremely attractive. Gallo found himself stealing glances at her breasts as she complained about the inept coding of a Chinese gateway that had been giving her all sorts of hassles.

"What do you think I should do?" Angela asked him.

Gallo felt his palms starting to sweat. What he *wanted* her to do had nothing to do with work.

"Fix it for them?" he stuttered finally.

She rolled her eyes and went back to work.

37

HAVING FAILED TO get in through the front door, Karr resorted to Plan B—the back door.

Or more precisely, the back basement door, which was not only locked but also connected to a burglar alarm system.

Neither problem was insurmountable. The same pick that would have opened the door to the stairs worked equally well on the basement lock. The alarm system employed a magnetic sensor that would set off an alert as soon as the magnet was removed or the circuit broken. There were a number of ways around this; the easiest—in this case—was by using a second magnet and a metal shim.

The difficulty came from the fact that the building's rear door could be seen from several restaurants and storefronts across the street. So to prepare his way, Karr had to first find a way to become invisible.

A large truck had been parked just up the street. Too bad it hadn't been parked about ten yards to the south, thought Karr; then it would easily block the view.

Well, that wasn't *really* a problem, was it?

Within a few minutes Karr had jumped the truck and moved it behind the building. The view of the door now cut off, Karr went to work. He used his handheld PDA as a gauss-meter, locating the alarm system's magnet sensor mounted in the threshold. Though it was an unusual spot, it was not difficult to defeat; Karr slid a small neodymium-iron-boron magnet into place as he pushed open the door. A wadded

Vietnamese newspaper kept the spring-loaded door ajar, giving him an easier escape route if needed.

The door opened into the bottom floor of the stairwell Karr had been trying to enter earlier. Karr put on his night glasses and started climbing.

"Tommy, Marie thinks you ought to wait until Dean comes over to back you up," said Rockman. "Shouldn't be too long now."

"Great idea," said Karr, continuing up the steps.

"I thought you were going to wait."

"I didn't say I would wait. I said it was a good idea."

Karr moved as quickly and as quietly as he could up the steps. He stopped when he reached the fifth floor, double-checking to make sure there was no alarm on the door.

"Clear or not clear?" he asked Rockman.

"We don't have video."

"I'm looking for a bet," said Karr. He got down to his knees and slid a small video bug beneath the door.

"Clear," said the runner in a resigned voice.

The door was locked, and once more Karr had to break out the pick.

"Guess they never have fires in Vietnam, huh?" He slipped the pick in, pushed up gently, then stepped into the darkened hallway.

Thao Duong's office was near the end of the hallway. Surprisingly large, it had a simple metal desk and a comfortable chair, but no other furniture, not even a bookshelf or a place for a visitor to sit. Papers were stacked along the left wall, some as high as Karr's waist.

"Single computer on the desk," Karr told the Art Room as he checked the sole drawer. It contained only two pens. "PC. No network card that I see."

"Wireless network?" asked Rockman.

"Not sure." Karr took out his PDA and tapped the screen, bringing up a simple wireless detection program. The dialog button on the screen remained brown—no wireless signal. "Nada."

Karr inserted a small electronic dongle into one of the computer's USB ports at the rear, then booted the computer. Karr's dongle, about the size of a lipstick, allowed him to bypass the computer's normal operating system, making it easier to upload its contents to the Art Room. As the machine came to life, he took a wire from his pocket and inserted one end into a second USB port, then connected it to his sat phone. When that was done, he went over to the papers.

"This is all Vietnamese to me," he told Rockman, removing his PDA from his pocket. He slipped a camera attachment on it and began beaming images of the stacked pages to the Art Room.

"Agricultural reports," said Thu De Nghiem.

After a couple of stacks, Karr realized that each pile represented a different province. The stacks contained an assortment of agricultural information dating back six or seven years.

Not exactly what he'd hoped to find.

"How's that download coming?" he asked Rockman.

"We're about halfway done."

Karr sat down in front of the desk, considering where he should plant the audio bug he'd brought. Given the lack of furniture, the most logical place was in the computer, but that also meant it would be the most likely place anyone would look for it.

Under the pile of papers?

Hard to tell when they might be moved.

There was a thermostat on the wall.

Karr decided there was no sense being too cute and decided to simply stick the bug under the desk. Since he was already sitting on the floor, he leaned back and crawled under. But as he started to put the bug in place he saw a large envelope taped to the bottom of the desk in his way.

"What have we here?" he said, pocketing the bug. He undid the tape and took the envelope down.

"Tommy—Thao Duong is walking toward the building."

"No shit? My building?"

"Get out of there."

"You finished with the download?"

"No."

"Then what's your hurry?"

Karr undid the clasp on the envelope. There were newspaper clippings inside, and a small key, the sort that would be used for a locker.

Karr took out his video bug and scanned the key.

"You got all this?" he asked Rockman.

"Of course we got it," said Rockman. "Get out of there, Tommy. Out. He's in the lobby."

Karr put the key back in the envelope and returned it to its hiding spot.

"Done with the download?" he asked, climbing back to his feet.

"We're done—go. Go!"

Karr turned off the computer and pulled his gear away, trotting to the door. As he was about to open it, he realized he'd forgotten to plant his bug. Necessity being the mother of invention, he decided the top of the doorjamb was a perfect place not only for an audio bug but for a video one as well.

"Pictures with the words," he told the Art Room, starting to turn the doorknob.

"The elevator is opening on your floor," hissed Rockman. "It's Thao Duong. Get out of there."

"Great advice," said Karr, taking his hand off the knob and stepping back into the room.

38

ONCE HE MADE contact with the Vietnamese official, Dean's job at the reception was over. He had to stay to maintain his cover, however, so he did his best to make small talk with the Vietnamese agricultural officials, bureaucrats, and other foreign salesmen at the gathering. Never good at mingling, Dean found it even more perplexing with the accented English that was used as the common tongue. The "conversations" generally consisted of vague questions answered by nods and half smiles.

He avoided Tang. It was a good bet that at least some of the Vietnamese suspected she was CIA, though he noticed that didn't stop them from talking to her. She may not have been extraordinarily pretty, but she was one of the few women and by far the youngest at the gathering, and that definitely worked in her favor.

"You were here during the war?" a bespectacled Vietnamese man asked Dean just as he was getting ready to leave.

"Yes," said Dean.

"Where?"

"Quang Nam Province, mostly."

"You were a Marine, then," said the man. It was a reasonable guess; for much of the war the Marines had been the primary American force in Quang Nam, with a large base at Da Nang.

"Yes, I was." Dean looked at him more closely. The man had brown splotch marks on his face and wrinkle marks at the corners of his eyes, half-hidden by the glasses. He was a few years older than Dean. Though thin, he had broad shoulders and a substantial chest; if he were a tree he would be an oak.

"I was with the Army of the Republic of Vietnam," said the man. He made no effort to lower his voice, though he was referring to the South Vietnamese Army—in theory an enemy of the present government. "A lieutenant and then a captain."

"I see."

"We worked with Marines. Very good fighters. Loyal."

"Thank you."

Curiosity roused, Dean asked the man how he came to be part of the present government.

"I was not a spy or a traitor," the former Army officer told Dean. "I've been rehabilitated. Connections help."

"Charlie, Tommy's in trouble," said Rockman in his ear. "We need you to back him up now."

Dean made a show of glancing at his watch.

"I have to make a phone call back to one of my accounts at home," he told the former ARVN soldier. "I'm sorry to have to leave."

"My card," said the man, reaching into his pocket. "If you have some free time, call me."

"I'll try," said Dean, taking the card, though he knew it was doubtful he'd use it. "I'd like that."

39

EVEN A MAN half Tommy Karr's size could not have found a place to hide in Thao Duong's office. So Karr found one outside the office—he opened one of the windows directly behind the desk.

The ledge was all of four inches thick, but Karr didn't have much choice. He pushed the window down behind him, then began making his way to the next window, gripping the gaps in the bricks as firmly as he could.

The light in the office came on just as Karr reached to the window of the next room. He pulled himself across, then felt his right toe start to slip on the greasy stone ledge.

This way, this way, he told himself, trying to balance his momentum forward. He did a little slide step and pinched his fingers tighter, pushing himself close to the window. His left foot sailed out over the pavement and his hand lost its grip. Just in time he grabbed the upper part of the window, rattling the jamb but keeping himself on the ledge.

"Tommy, are you all right?" asked Rockman. "Where are you?"

"Getting some air. What do you see with that video bug I left in the office?"

"Just sitting at his desk. We'll tell you when he's gone."

"What's he doing?" Karr asked.

"Working. He went to the pile and took a report out."

"Come on. You're telling me he's a dedicated bureaucrat?"

"I'm just the messenger. Wait a second—he's reaching for that envelope you found."

"You ID the key?"

"Looks like the type used in a firebox or trunk. Do you think you can follow him when he leaves the building?"

"If I can grow wings in the next five minutes, I'll be happy to," said Karr. "Where's Dean?"

"He's on his way. But he's never going to get there in time. Looks like Thao's getting ready to go—he put the envelope back."

Karr tried opening the window, but it was locked from the inside. Breaking it would make too much noise while Thao Duon was next door, but if Karr waited until he left, it would probably be too late.

Karr glanced toward the ground and then back at the building, trying to see if it might be possible to climb down. There was decorative brickwork at the corner that he could use as a ladder, but that meant going past three more double sets of windows. He was bound to slip sooner or later.

How about going up? There was only one floor between him and the flat roof. A row of bricks ran just above the windows, a decorative bump-out thick enough to grab on to. He wrapped his fingers around the bricks and pulled himself up as if doing a reverse chin-up. He put his right boot against the window casing for more leverage. He started to pull himself up, then realized it wasn't going to work; the window ledge above the row of bricks was too far away to reach. But it was too late; he couldn't get his feet down without risking a fall.

A SHORT LINE of taxis waited at the curb of the hotel. Dean got in the first one, and with the aid of the Art Room translator gave the driver an address a half block from the office building where Karr was. It was less than four miles away, and there was very little traffic on the streets at night, but Dean found himself bouncing his foot up and down on the floor in the backseat, anxious to get there.

"Wait for me here," he told the driver when they were about a block from the destination. Dean threw a twenty-dollar American bill on the front seat and bolted from the cab.

"Tommy's around the back of the building," Rockman told him. "Thao Duong is still in his office. We want you to trail him if you can."

"Tommy, can you hear me?"

"He's on the window ledge," said Rockman.

"Connect us."

The op-to-op mode on the communications gear could be activated either by the operatives themselves or by the Art Room. Dean heard Karr's heavy breathing and asked if he was OK.

"Uh, yeah," grunted Karr. "Just busy."

"I'll be there in a second," said Dean, starting to run.

IF HE WAS going to fall anyway, Karr decided it would be better existentially to fall while going up rather than down. He gritted his teeth and jerked his right leg upward, swinging it up and over the ledge above him—and into the window glass, which shattered above him. He pushed up with his hands, curled what he could of his foot inside the building, and then for a moment hung suspended in mid-air.

"Hang on!" yelled Dean in Karr's ear.

"Oh yeah."

Upside down, Karr struggled to get a grip on the side of the window. He was now draped halfway in and halfway out, part of him inside the room and the larger part out. Blood rushed to his head. His face swam in sweat.

Karr had just enough of his calf inside the window to leverage himself upward. The rest of the glass broke and fell into his lap as he pulled himself up. Hands bleeding, he managed to maneuver himself around into a seated position.

Shouldn't have done that, he told himself. It was OK to be negative once he'd succeeded.

Something smacked the side of his face. He looked up but couldn't figure out what it was. All he could see in his night glasses was a black blur.

"Grab the rope," said Charlie Dean. "It's by your head."

"Where are you?"

"Grab the damn rope before you fall," said Dean. "I'm on

the roof. I don't know if this rig is going to hold long enough to pull you up."

"Nah, I'm OK," said Karr. "Is there a door up there?"

"Yeah, but—"

"I'll meet you on the sixth floor," he said, slipping inside.

40

SINCE THE ASSASSINATION attempt, reporters always began interviews with Senator McSweeney by expressing concern for his continued well-being. Some were sincere, some sounded sincere; few were both. McSweeney played a private game with himself, trying to predict beforehand the sort of expression he would receive. In this case, the reporter had the bad taste to suggest that getting shot at had helped McSweeney tremendously in the polls.

"I wouldn't recommend it," said McSweeney tartly.

The reporter was correct; McSweeney had vaulted from also-ran to the odds-on favorite not only for Super Tuesday but also in the round of primaries the following Thursday and Tuesday. If the trend continued, he would wrap up the party nomination within a month.

The pollster worried that it was just a temporary bump. Jimmy Fingers pointed out that as long as "temporary" got them through Tuesday, it might as well be permanent. Sympathy vote or not, McSweeney's aide added, the effect had helped Reagan during his first term when Hinckley tried to kill him. "It gave him space for his first-term agenda. This time, it's going to get you elected."

McSweeney preferred to think that people would vote for him based on his record. But if they pulled the lever because he had the good sense to duck when someone shot at him, so be it.

"Why do you want to be President?" asked the reporter from the *Times-Union,* starting the interview with a softball question.

McSweeney rubbed his chin with his thumb and forefinger, an old trick to make it look as if he were giving the question serious thought. In fact, he had a ready answer, a stock rehash of sound bites he knew would play well no matter how the reporter sliced and diced them in his story.

"It's time to tap the full potential of the people. The President is the only person—the only real national leader—who can do that effectively."

McSweeney continued, citing John F. Kennedy, talking about the contributions and attitude of the World War II generation, and laying out a program that all but the most cynical hack would applaud.

"But why, *really*?" said the reporter when McSweeney finished.

The question threw McSweeney. It wasn't the words so much as the tone of familiarity. The reporter sounded like a friend who had detected a false note in a casual comment and wasn't going to stand for bull.

Why did he want to be President?

Power, prestige. The ability to do what he wanted to do without being stopped.

The guarantee that he would be included in history books.

Who didn't want to be President, damn it?

"I'm not sure I understand what you mean," said McSweeney.

"Inside," said the reporter. "Why do you want to be President?"

McSweeney began recycling his earlier answer. But he got only two sentences out of his mouth before the reporter said, "Ah, come on, Senator. Why do you really want to be in the White House? Ego? The babes?"

Someone other than McSweeney might have answered the reporter's poor attempt at a joke with a humorous joke of his own, cementing a favorable relationship for the rest of the campaign. Most of the others would have said something ridiculously stupid *meant* as a joke, but so inept that it would end up burying them when quoted.

McSweeney found a third way—he simply didn't answer.

"Wanting to make America a better place, help us live up to our potential, can seem corny," he told the reporter. "But that's what I'm about. And it's funny, I've always been absurdly idealistic, even as a nine-year-old. My mom has an essay I wrote on how I wanted to be President and how I was going to help the environment and improve schools."

"Really? You have it?"

"She has it. Call her. Between you and me, my spelling was probably atrocious. I still have trouble. Thank God for spell-check."

41

"HE'S COMING OUT of the building," said Rockman as Dean met Karr in the stairwell. "He's turning right."

"You really lost your calling, Rockman," said Karr as they clambered down to the basement. "You'd be great doing play-by-play."

"Very funny. He's crossing the street. He doesn't seem to have a car nearby," added Rockman. "We'll lose him in a minute."

Propelled by the need to rescue Karr, Dean had had no trouble running up the stairs. Going down, though, was a different story. He felt winded, and every step jabbed at his legs. The calf muscle in his right leg cramped while his hamstrings pulled taut.

"I have a cab waiting about a block to the west," grunted Dean, losing ground to Karr, who jogged down the steps two or three at a time. The younger man's pants were red with blood, but it didn't seem to slow him down.

"I got something better than a cab," Karr told Dean, hitting the landing and turning toward the door. "Come on."

By the time Dean caught up with him outside, Karr had hopped into the truck behind the building. The truck's motor coughed to life as Dean pitched himself into the seat.

"Just turn left on that street behind you," said Rockman.

"Got it," said Karr. He threw the truck into reverse, swerved into the intersection backward, and squealed the tires as he changed direction. The truck tottered sideways, then picked up steam.

"Keep us in one piece," said Dean, still out of breath.

"Oh yeah!" said Karr. It was more a battle cry than an acknowledgment; the truck continued to accelerate.

Dean slapped his hand on the dashboard as Karr barely avoided hitting a parked car at the next corner. The truck tilted on its left wheels as he veered through the intersection; Dean braced himself, waiting for the crash.

"That's him up there, getting onto the Honda *ôm*. Damn," said Karr.

The Honda *ôm*—the generic name for a motorbike used as a taxi and common in the city—was headed in the wrong direction. By the time Karr found a place to turn around, it was nowhere in sight.

"Rockman, get us directions to Thao Duong's apartment," Dean said. Then he turned to Karr. "Let's swap places."

"Why? Don't trust my driving?"

"Your leg's bleeding," Dean answered.

"Ah, just a scratch."

"Well, let's give it a chance to heal."

"You don't trust my driving," said Karr.

"No, I don't."

Karr chuckled, and pressed harder on the gas.

THAO DUONG LIVED a few blocks away. Even from the outside, it seemed obvious he hadn't taken the cab there; the place was dark. Dean left Karr in the truck and went up the fire escape. The window to the kitchen was open; Dean lifted it and slipped inside. Ten minutes later he was back in the truck, having planted two audio bugs in the flat and a tracking bug on the bicycle Thao kept in the hallway.

"Gotta be our guy," said Karr as they returned the truck. "Whatever you said to him at the reception spooked him."

"Maybe," said Dean. "But if he is, how do we get him to talk?"

"You turn on the charm," said Karr. "But before that, we ought to find out what he's got locked away."

"Yeah," said Dean.

A light-colored sedan passed on a nearby street. The car

looked like an unmarked police car, though he caught only a glimpse. They waited a few minutes, then slipped from the truck and began walking in the direction to the hotel.

"You don't think Thao Duong's our guy?" asked Karr.

"Seems too easy."

"Easy?"

"First guy we check?"

"Odds are only one out of three," said Karr. "Just as likely to be number one as number three."

"The one thing I know about Vietnam," said Dean, "is that nothing's easy. And nothing's what it seems."

"That's two things," said Karr. "You can't fool me, Charlie. I was once a mathematician."

42

THE MARSHALS' SERVICE credentials didn't impress the state troopers in Danbury, Connecticut, nor were they shy about letting Lia know that they'd been over the same ground with both the Secret Service and the FBI, ad infinitum. But one of the investigators was recently divorced, a little lonely, and obviously bored—a combination that made getting him to give her a complete tour of the crime scene and an in-depth review of the case child's play.

The only downside was that he wanted to take her to lunch as well. Not particularly hungry—and in no need of a shadow as she checked out the computers in the hotel for messages Forester might have sent—Lia let him down as gently as possible, feigning a headache. But he didn't really get the message until she told him she had to call her boyfriend.

"Oh," said the investigator. "Maybe another time."

"Wait," said Lia as he headed for his car.

When he turned around, she could see the hope in his eyes. She felt like a heel.

"Was there a notebook in the car?" she asked. "One of Forester's notebooks seems to be missing."

"Notebook? No."

"Oh."

"Sorry."

"It's OK."

"Another time."

"Sure."

Lia drove back to the hotel where Forester had killed himself, thinking about Charlie Dean the whole time. She wished she'd gone to Vietnam with him—or that he was here with her. She thought of calling him, or asking the Art Room to connect them, but Vietnam was eleven hours ahead time-wise; he'd be sleeping.

The hotel advertised that it "catered to businesspeople" by offering a "dedicated business center." The business center turned out to consist of a fax machine and copier, along with two computers connected to the Internet. The person supervising the center was also assigned to clean up the nearby eating area and help at the front desk, and left Lia alone soon after showing her the room. Lia slipped a specially designed "dongle" into one of the computer's USB ports, then had the Art Room read off the contents of the hard drive via the Internet. She repeated the process a few minutes later with the second computer.

"Did you get it all?" she asked Marie Telach, taking out her sat phone and pretending to use it.

"Another minute. When you're done, check out the hotel where Amanda Rauci stayed. Maybe he was there."

"She says he never made it."

"Check it out anyway," said Telach, her tone implying that Lia was somehow slacking off.

"Wild-goose chases are us," replied Lia.

THE OTHER HOTEL was set back farther from the road, up a twisting driveway that made it feel more secluded—it looked exactly like the sort of place someone would pick for an affair, Lia thought. The lobby was located at the side of an atrium, and the place had a less rushed, more luxurious feel than the other hotel. The business center here had a full-time employee and six computers, three of which were occupied when Lia came in. There was also a wireless network, allowing individuals to connect to the Internet via their laptops.

"Room number?" asked the room's supervisor.

"I haven't checked in yet," said Lia.

"I'm sorry, the computers are only for guests."

"Well I'm *going* to register," said Lia.

"Come back when you do."

Lia left the room and walked back to the atrium, where she took out her sat phone, pretending to use it while she spoke to Telach.

"You want me to flash the credentials and ask if I can look at the computers?" Lia asked. "Or should I just rent a room?"

"Rent a room," said Telach.

"Sorry," said the desk clerk when Lia got there. "We're booked solid. It's a busy week. Two weddings, and the biker festival. You here for the Harleys?"

"Just looking after a friend," said Lia.

"Maybe at one of our sister hotels."

"But my mom really wants me to register here," said Lia. "Right, Mom?"

The clerk gave Lia an odd look.

"Sometimes I talk to my mom in my head," Lia explained.

"Tell her to check the central reservations system now," said Telach. "Looks like one of the bikers just got a flat tire."

43

DEAN WOKE UP in the middle of the night, not knowing where he was. He stared at the ceiling, waiting for his memory to come back. It took only a few seconds, and yet those few seconds seemed enormously long. He sank into them, unsettled, his disorientation extending.

Finally he realized he was in Vietnam. Dean remained on his back, still staring into the gray light above him.

How strange was it to come around in a circle?

It wasn't as if Vietnam or the things he did here haunted him. From time to time he'd remember things, missions as a sniper, old buddies, songs that he'd first heard here, but Vietnam never obsessed him, never burned viciously in his brain the way it did for many others. Vietnam to Charlie Dean was a place and time in the past, not the present. Its demons had been real enough, but they had no afterlife to haunt him.

Except for Phuc Dinh.

Dean sat upright in the bed, then slipped his feet over the side to the floor, one by one.

He *had* made that kill. He'd taken a photograph to prove it. So why wasn't it in the file?

There were a million possible reasons, starting with the fact that what he'd seen at Crypto City wasn't the file, just a copy of some things that were in it.

Or might have been. He had no real idea. He didn't know what happened behind the scenes or above him. He knew only what the CIA people and the Marines who dealt with them wanted him to know.

AFTER HE'D KILLED the last VC guerilla on the trail, Dean had gone back to his friend's body. There was no way Dean was leaving Longbow behind. Dean hoisted Longbow onto his back and began trekking up the trail into the jungle. He couldn't have expressed the emotions he was feeling. Grief and anger, guilt—everything was tangled together.

The original plan called for Dean and Longbow to either hook up with the unit they had swung into the area with, or, missing them, trek about twenty miles southeast to a small observation post held by another Marine unit.

Twenty miles in the Vietnamese heat was a good, long hike, even if you weren't carrying a body. Dean didn't think about the distance at first, trudging slowly but steadily, using the path for long stretches before tucking into the jungle and making sure he wasn't followed. Twice, he lost his way and found himself almost back where he started. By nightfall, he reckoned his destination was still fifteen miles away.

Dean knew he was going no farther with Longbow's body. What had once been his friend was now a decrepit bag of gases and ill-smelling remains. And Dean himself was so exhausted he could barely carry himself. His only option was to leave Longbow where he could find him and come back with help.

Dean had no shovel. The best he could do for his friend was hide him in the brush. Dean marked several trees, and in the morning took two measurements to the trail so he could be certain of the location. Tears streamed down his face as he headed in the direction of the Marine camp. It was the first and last time he ever cried in Vietnam, and one of the very few times he was moved to tears in his life. They were tears of shame, for in his heart he felt that he had failed his friend by abandoning his remains.

Four or five hours later, too exhausted to go on, Dean stopped for the rest of the night. He crawled under a large tree about a hundred yards from the trail and slept fitfully.

An hour before dawn, he woke and began walking again. When he reached a road about a mile and a half later, he collapsed by its side.

Within a few minutes, he heard American voices nearby. Dean shook his head and feet, rocked back and forth, made sure he was awake. The voices continued.

"Hey," he said finally. "Hey, are you guys Marines?"

The silence that followed convinced him he'd imagined the voices.

"Damn," he muttered.

"Where are you?" came a voice back.

Dean got to his knees. "Are you Marines?"

"Who are you?"

"Dean. I'm a sniper. What unit are you in?"

It turned out to be the company they'd come up with. The men were waiting for a helicopter, due any minute.

Dean told the commander where he'd left Longbow's body. Four Marines were sent up the trail immediately—Dean was too wasted, though they had to hold him back—but couldn't find him.

"We'll be back to get him," said the captain. "I'll bring a platoon—I'll bring the damn division if I have to."

That captain was as good as his word, rallying a sizeable search force, but Longbow's body was never found.

DEAN ROSE AND began pacing back and forth in the large hotel room.

If he didn't shoot Phuc Dinh, who had he killed?

And if Phuc Dinh was alive, was Longbow?

They were both dead. Dean was sure of it. Sure of Longbow, and sure of Phuc Dinh. But in the gray stillness of the hotel room, Dean wondered if he was the shadow and they were the ones living and breathing.

44

THE ART ROOM didn't turn up anything interesting on the other computers. Though it was already after three, Lia decided she would go over to Pine Plains and see if she could talk to the police chief there. His dispatcher said he would be in the office until five and after that would be available at home.

"It's jess around the corner," the dispatcher added. "You can walk."

Forty-five minutes later, Lia drove down the main street of the small town, gazing at the one- and two-story clapboard buildings as she searched for the police station. The town reminded her a great deal of the Connecticut village where she'd grown up. A sleepy farming community for most of its existence, it had recently been overrun with weekenders from New York City, who found the two-and-a-half-hour drive a worthwhile trade-off for relatively cheap real estate and the illusion of a simpler life, so long as that simpler life included Starbucks and a pricey dress shop tucked into a side block behind the bookstore.

Old-timers had made one of two choices: cash in on the newcomers by catering to their whims or slink back and mutter about them behind the closed ranks of old friends. Lia's hometown had negotiated a similar clash twenty years earlier; the result was an ambiguous and somewhat uneasy truce, where the old-timers held on to the low-level political and business positions and the transplanted city people ruled everything else.

Lia's mother and father had feet in both camps, and

regarded the transition with mixed feelings. It was not always easy to predict their views, however. As she parked behind the village hall, Lia thought of her father, ostensibly a member of the old-timers' camp, with eight generations in the local graveyard. He viewed the local police chief, whose family had been in town since the mid-1800s, with twice as much skepticism as he would have shown a newcomer.

Pine Plains' police chief was about the age of Lia's father, but there the resemblance ended. Tall and still fairly trim, Christopher Ball had a narrow face set off by a graying brush cut and a tight-lipped smile. He greeted her with a crusher of a handshake.

"I'm with the marshals' service," said Lia breezily, showing him the credentials. "I'm following up on the Forester case."

"So my dispatcher said. I don't recall the case."

"Agent Forester. The Secret Service agent who killed himself in Danbury?"

"Oh, OK. Sure."

"Did he speak to you the day he died?"

"No. He was supposed to show up the next day. We had an appointment. I stayed in the office waiting. Had to have a part-timer come in to do my road patrol because of it."

"Did he tell you what he was looking into?"

"Not at all." Ball pushed his chair back and got up. "Service agents out of Danbury told me about it the day after. Or maybe it was Poughkeepsie."

Ball stared at her. His rising was evidently intended to signal that they were done talking, though Lia didn't budge.

"So you knew nothing about the threat against Senator McSweeney?"

"I have no idea why your man thought that someone from Pine Plains was involved. I'd've been happy to investigate anyone—happy to do it still."

"When Agent Forester came to talk to you, did he have a notebook with him?"

Something flicked in Ball's eyes. "He never came to talk to me." Ball took another step, reaching the edge of the desk.

"Something wrong, Chief?" Lia asked.

Ball frowned. "It's getting toward dinner."

"Thanks, but I'm not hungry."

His frown turned into a full-blown scowl.

"Senator McSweeney has a house near here, doesn't he?" asked Lia.

"That's up in Columbia County. Forty-five minutes—an hour, if you drive the speed limit. Most don't."

"You deal with him a lot?"

"Are you trying to investigate me, miss?"

"Do you need to be investigated?"

"Get the hell out of my office."

"Gladly," said Lia.

"WHY'D YOU ANTAGONIZE him?" Telach demanded when Lia reached the car.

"Something about him doesn't jibe," said Lia.

She pulled out the booster unit for the audio fly she had left in the office and activated it. Lia looked around, trying to decide where to leave the unit. The fly couldn't transmit very far on its own.

"He's just a macho ass," said Telach. "Unfortunately, that's not against the law."

"I planted a bug. Are you picking it up?"

"A bug? I didn't authorize you to plant a listening device, Lia."

"Since when do I have to ask?"

"Stand by," said Telach abruptly.

45

CHIEF BALL KEPT his wrath and tongue in check as he contemplated the arrogant federal agent whom he'd just dismissed. Teeth clenched, he stomped out of the village hall, down the white wooden steps, and around the back to the path that led to Maple Avenue, where he lived with his wife.

The federal people had egos the size of the Lincoln Memorial. The younger they were, the more full of themselves they were. And the women were the worst.

Ball waved at his neighbor, who was ushering his two sons to Little League practice. Ball had to be nice to Marco, because the shortcut was on Marco's property.

Actually, Ball decided, he didn't have to be nice to anyone. He made up for it by scowling at Scott Salotti, who was mowing his lawn next door.

So they were still interested in Forester, were they? They couldn't just take "no" for an answer and move on?

"Hi, honey," said his wife from the kitchen when he came in the front door. "Dinner's ready."

Ball didn't bother answering. He went up to the bedroom and changed out of his uniform.

"Your beer's on the table," his wife said when he came into the kitchen. She rose on her tiptoes and kissed him on his cheek. "Something wrong?"

"Just the usual."

"Village board talking about cutting back the part-timers' hours again?"

"Nothing specific." Ball took a swig of the beer, Miller Lite. "I'm going out after dinner."

"But we were going to watch *Survivor* together."

"Another time."

A pout appeared on his wife's face. But it dissipated quickly, as they always did.

46

RUBENS WAS SO angry he pounded his desk. He barely kept himself from shouting. "Lia left a bug in the police chief's office because he was rude to her?"

"You know Lia," said Telach, frowning uncomfortably.

"It's one thing for her to trash-talk someone and quite another to leave a bug in his office."

"Well, she did both."

"We're not overseas, Marie. We can't be leaving audio devices in people's offices—*especially* the police."

"I didn't tell her to. But—"

"There's a but?"

"The operatives are trained to work a certain way. That's what she's doing. If she were in Vietnam—"

"She's not in Vietnam. Why did she even bother?"

"It's just standard procedure. She's not used to working in the U.S."

As angry as he was, Rubens realized that Telach was right. The Deep Black operatives had been trained to operate overseas, under very dangerous conditions, where the rules of engagement—what could or couldn't be done under different circumstances—were much looser. Listening in to other people's conversations was something they did all the time. America was a very different environment, and the ops and support team had not been trained to operate in it.

Admittedly, the lines could be difficult to discern. Examining the contents of a public-access computer was OK, because it was by definition open to the public and there was no expectation of privacy, the same as walking down the street. But a computer in a home was different; Desk Three needed permission to access it.

My fault, thought Rubens. Ultimately, my fault. I haven't properly prepared my people.

What would Senator McSweeney and his committee say to that?

"Disable the bug immediately," Rubens told Telach. "Lia is not to place any more surveillance devices without my explicit approval. If she has a problem with that, have her talk to me."

"Yes, Chief."

47

TOMMY KARR HAD cut a good jagged line into the bottom of his calf. It wasn't deep, but it was definitely artistic, looking like a bolt from a Scandinavian lightning god.

Which suited Karr just fine. He cleaned it up and re-dressed it as soon as he woke, pronounced it patched, then went down to the hotel's breakfast lounge, where he found Charlie Dean drinking coffee at a table tucked between plastic fronds.

"You're limping," said Dean.

"Scandinavian, actually." Karr smiled, then went over to the coffee urn at the side of the room. While he was gone, a waiter came over to take his order; Karr found the man standing idly by the table when he returned.

"You can get the next one," said Karr, sitting down.

"You sleep all right?" asked Dean.

Karr nearly choked on the coffee. "Whoa—high-test." Coffee in Asia tended to be as weak as tea; this was the exception. He felt a caffeine shock rush through his body. "Really gets ya goin', huh, Charlie?"

"I guess."

"I slept OK," said Karr, getting back to Dean's question. "How about yourself?"

"Like a lamb."

"I always wondered about that," said Karr. "How do lambs really sleep? They look all cuddly and all, but do we really know that they're sleeping soundly? Maybe they have nightmares about wolves."

"Could be." Dean sipped his coffee. "What do you think about swapping assignments? Your leg seems pretty bad."

"Nah. I'm fine."

"You're limping."

"Chafing from the bandages." Karr held up his cup. "Ready for a refill," he said to the waiter, who was across the room.

"Tommy, is your leg really bad?" asked Marie Telach, who'd been listening in over the com system. Unlike Dean and Lia, Karr almost never turned the system off.

"See, now ya got Mom worried," Karr told Dean. "I'm fine," he added, speaking to the Art Room. "What's the latest on Thao Duong?"

"Still sleeping in his apartment. He got back about three hours after you left."

"What do you figure he was doing?"

"I believe that's your job to find out," said Telach.

"Must be getting toward the end of the shift," Karr told Dean.

"He's stirring," interrupted Sandy Chafetz, their runner. "Tommy, your subject is getting up."

"Boy, and I was just about ready to see what they had for breakfast."

"I'll go," offered Dean.

"Nah. Coffee's got my heart racing anyway. Got to do something to work it off." Karr got up. "Check in with you later."

48

AMANDA RAUCI HAD no trouble finding the state police impound lot; she simply located the police barracks and then cruised the junkyards and service stations in the area until she saw a lot with two Ford Crown Victorias parked near the fence. The Fords, unmarked police cars put out to pasture, stood guard before a small array of wrecks, a Mustang confiscated from a drug dealer, and Gerald Forester's Impala, conveniently located not far from the fence.

It was only just past five, but Amanda decided the place looked deserted enough that she could hop the chain-link fence from the back and not be noticed. But she hadn't counted on the two large German shepherds, who bounded up on the other side of the fence as she approached.

Amanda backed away.

A supermarket about a mile and a half away was having a sale on hamburger meat; she bought four pounds. But as she checked out, she worried that it wouldn't be enough of a diversion. She needed something to put them out, not just fill them up.

Amanda found a diner with a phone booth nearby. Setting the tattered phone book on the narrow metal ledge beneath the phone, she began calling vets until she found one willing to give her a mild tranquilizer to calm her dog's motion sickness.

The office was several miles away, and Amanda got lost twice before she found it. By then it was just a few minutes before closing, and when she went in, the night assistant was walking toward the door with his keys in his hand, ready to lock up. She felt a flutter of panic but quickly pushed it away.

"I called a little while ago about my dog," she said. "The pills?"

"Uh, pills?"

"Acepromazine," said Amanda. "It's for motion sickness, right?"

While generally given for motion sickness, acepromazine was actually a tranquilizer; it mainly calmed dogs down so they could make a long trip. But though the woman Amanda had spoken to on the phone had seemed easygoing and said getting the pills would be no problem, the kid now was suspicious.

"You were supposed to come earlier," he said.

"I came as quickly as I could."

"Well, where's your dog?"

"I couldn't take him in the car, right? He throws up." Amanda tried to smile. "The nurse said there would be no problem."

"That was just Sandy. She's not like a nurse or anything. Not even an assistant."

The young man frowned. Amanda tried smiling again.

"I know it's late."

"Let me see if they left you anything," said the kid finally.

He turned around and went back toward the front desk. As two or three dogs being boarded started barking in the back, the vet's assistant stooped under the front counter and retrieved a yellow Post-it.

"Um, what was your name again?" he asked, squinting at the note.

"Rauci."

"They couldn't find the file."

He showed her the note. It explained that they couldn't find the file and that the young man—Dave—was not to give her the pills without it.

Amanda noticed that the boy was staring at her chest. She wondered if she could somehow seduce him into giving her the tranquilizers.

"We haven't been in in ages," she said, taking a step toward him.

"See, usually, if they know you pretty well, it's not a problem," said the boy. "But I think Sandy got you confused with someone else."

"I think I've gotten pills from the doctor before."

"Could you spell your name."

"*R-a-u-c-i.* Maybe they looked under *R-o-s-s-i.* A lot of people think that's the only way to spell it."

"Oh, that's a funny way to spell it," said the young man, turning toward the filing cabinets.

"It's not funny if it's your name."

The young man blushed. "I just meant, uh, she might have gotten it wrong."

"No offense," said Amanda, thinking she was making progress.

She stepped around the counter and joined the vet's assistant at the lateral files. She'd never been very good at flirting, let alone seduction. She wished she'd been wearing a skirt.

Amanda touched the kid's hand. His face reddened. But before she could go any further, his cell phone began playing "Take Me Out to the Ball Game."

"Go ahead; you can answer the call," she told him, stepping back. "I'm not really in a rush."

"Just my girlfriend."

"It's OK."

The young man grabbed the phone from his belt and stepped a few feet away. Amanda followed, eying the large set of keys on the counter. But he was too close for her to grab them.

"Do you mind if I use the restroom?" As she spoke, she touched his neck; he nearly jumped.

"Yeah, go ahead. Down the hall that way."

Amanda decided she would just leave the window to the restroom open, then come back later and sneak in. She stepped inside quickly. It took only a second for her to undo the lock at the window.

She looked but couldn't find wiring for an alarm.

The dogs being boarded began barking in their pens down the hallway as soon as she stepped from the restroom. Glancing toward the front, she walked quickly into the kennel area. There was a glass-faced cabinet near the door, stocked with medicines and things like bandages and sutures. The cabinet was locked, but she guessed that there would be a spare key somewhere in one of the offices.

The young man was still on the phone when she came back, talking plaintively to whoever was on the other line. Amanda walked quickly around the counter, hoping that the drugs had been left somewhere nearby. But she didn't see them. So she bent over the files, looking for another name she could appropriate.

"Look, I still have somebody here. I'll call you back, all right?" said the young man. "No. I have to call you back."

"Problems?" Amanda asked when the young man came around the counter.

"Really, like, you shouldn't be back here."

"I'm sorry, I was just going to help. I was thinking that the name might actually be under my ex-husband's. We, uh, had a falling-out. Divorce, you know."

The kid smirked. "Yeah, I know how that goes."

"You're married?"

"No way."

"Try Anthony Stevens."

The young man retrieved the folder.

"The black Lab?"

"Fifer."

Still kneeling in front of the cabinet, the young man examined the folder. Amanda put her hand on his shoulder.

Was it too much? she wondered.

Apparently not. The young man got up.

"All right," said the young man. "Hold on."

He retreated to an office directly off the reception area, then returned with a bag and a small receipt tape.

"Here you go. How do you want to pay?" he asked.

"You could just send us a bill," she said.

The young man frowned.

"Or I could pay in cash," she volunteered, anxious now that she was so close to finally getting the pills.

"Great."

But as she opened up her wallet, she realized she had only five dollars left.

If she used the credit card, anyone looking for her would be able to trace her to the area.

If she couldn't talk him into billing her, could she just come back and break in? Glancing over at the keys on the counter, she saw there was a small alarm key on the chain. Breaking in would be too risky.

"I guess I don't have that cash. If you could bill—"

The young man pointed at a sign on the side of the counter: "All bills must be paid at visit."

"A check or a credit card will do," said the kid.

"All right," said Amanda, taking out her credit card.

AFTER ALL THE effort it took to get the tranquilizers, drugging the dogs was anticlimactic. The animals went straight for the hamburger, whimpering and begging, tails wagging, as she bent near the fence. They might have looked ferocious from a distance, but they were friendly enough if you gave them food. Within an hour, both animals lay down near the fence and drifted off to sleep.

Amanda used the spare key she'd taken the night of Forester's death to open the door. She doused the interior light, then poked around with her hand under the passenger-side seat. A single stenographer's notebook was folded up in the cushion between the springs.

Amanda stopped at a McDonald's restaurant two miles down the road, bought herself a vanilla shake, and slid into one of the back booths to read the notebook. Her heart was pounding so loudly it nearly drowned out the giggles of the teenage girls huddled over a cell phone two booths away.

The first page was blank. The second page had part of a case number and two telephone numbers.

The notes started on the third page. The handwriting was hurried, abbreviated.

As she read, Amanda heard her dead lover's voice in her head.

> *Phne—nthing.*
> *Call list—??*

The threat had been made by e-mail, but as a matter of routine, Forester had suggested that the office monitor or record all calls. He'd also asked the phone company for a "call list"—in this case, a record of phone calls that had been received by the number, probably over the past two months. Amanda couldn't tell exactly what the note meant—was he reminding himself to check the call list, indicating that he should look into it further, or simply recording someone else's confusion?

The next pages had office hours and contact numbers for the senator's campaign and Senate offices; Amanda guessed that Forester wrote them down so he'd have them while he was on the road.

Then came a note that read: "Mar 24 call."

March 24? That was at least a month before the threat had been received.

Ten or twelve blank pages separated that section from a fresh set of notes, written with a different pen.

Amanda skipped through ten or eleven blank pages, then found another.

> *Reginald Gordon*
> *Athens, GA*

There was a phone number and an address. At the side of the page were tick marks—Amanda knew that was Forester's way of counting how many times he'd tried calling a phone number without connecting.

There were dates and times on the next page—this must be from the conversation with Gordon, Amanda thought.

> *Nvr called.*
> *No.*

No threat.
Called in Jan for help only—one Marine to another. News story was bull. Blowing off steam.

Senator staff said couldn't help. Never talked to him. Rfused.
Not fair, no.
—seems still mad.

A different pen:

No records USMC.
ID body???
Resurfaced. Quiet.

The next page was headed by a carefully penciled notation: "FROM MEMORY":

Check records strategic hamlets
Da Nang 1971–72
Three people would have known
Best source—Vietnamese Phuc Dinn (sp??)—tried to have assassinated. Knw he's still alive because spke to him. Will he tell??

Then, on the last page of the notebook with any writing, the contact information for the police chief of Pine Plains.

49

THE TRUTH WAS, Dean didn't much feel like play-acting at the convention. But that was his job, and so after he finished breakfast he went down to the lobby and took a taxi to Saigon's new convention center about ten minutes away. The restlessness that had kept him awake half the night had settled into a background buzz; he told himself that he had a job to do, and that if he concentrated on that, everything else would fall into place.

Dean made sure the government officials who were working near the front of the hall saw him, and even took a few business cards from some of the display booths. By 9:45 he'd walked around the convention hall twice. He headed toward one of the business centers, figuring he would find an inconspicuous place where he could check in with Karr and the Art Room, when he was intercepted by Kelly Tang, the CIA officer helping on the case.

"Mr. Dean, how are sales going?" said Tang, a cheerful den mother checking on one of her charges.

"Not bad."

"Why don't you have a cup of coffee with me? Come on. Vietnamese coffee is very good, if you know where to go."

Dean followed her outside of the meeting hall proper to a large area of tables and chairs. While she went for the coffee, he took out some brochures and papers from his briefcase, as if he were checking to make sure he had enough material for a sales call. He wanted anyone who noticed him to think he was what he claimed to be, a salesman.

"Think you'll sell me a rice harvester?" she asked, returning with two cups.

"I can get you a special deal," he said, pushing the papers back into his briefcase.

"You want to talk to Cam Tre Luc?" she said casually, stirring sugar into her cup.

"Yes."

"A man will meet you at the Plum American Restaurant near the IDC Office Tower at noon. He uses the name Lo."

"How will I know him?"

"He'll find you. He'll have a card just like this," she said, producing a business card.

Dean nodded.

"He's going to want money," added the CIA agent. "A thousand, just for setting up the contact."

"A thousand U.S.?"

She shrugged apologetically. "A couple of other people turned me down."

"Problem?"

"Not really. Cam Tre Luc is a tough and important person in a ministry that few Vietnamese want to anger."

"Why do you think I'm going to make him mad?"

Tang smiled and changed the subject. "Did you and Thao Duong get along?"

"We're working on our relationship."

"Very good. Have you sold anything at the convention?"

"Not yet. This is really just a scouting mission," he said loudly. "We plan to make a push next year. But if anyone does want to buy, then of course I'm prepared. The Japanese are difficult competitors, but we'll hang in there."

"Please let me know if I can help your company in any way," said Tang, rising and sticking out her hand.

"I will."

"Best of luck with the sales."

50

THE WINDOW AT the agricultural ministry that Karr had broken the night before had already been patched by a piece of cardboard. If there had been an inquiry, neither Desk Three's phone taps nor the bugs in Thao Duong's office had picked it up.

Whatever had disturbed Thao Duong the night before was not bothering him now, at least not outwardly; the Art Room translator told Karr that the Vietnamese bureaucrat was going through papers studiously, at times muttering the equivalent of "OK" or "Yes" to himself but saying nothing else.

The scan of his computer hadn't revealed anything more interesting than an unexpected increase in the rice harvest. The experts had decided that the key Karr had photographed definitely fit into a lockbox of some sort, but they had no clue about where that box might be.

Growing bored, Karr walked to his motorbike, parked in a cluster in front of a café a block away.

"Sandy, I think I'm going to shoot over to Thao Duong's apartment and have another look around," Karr told his runner. "I'd like to see if he hid the strongbox somewhere nearby."

"We didn't see it on the video bugs you guys planted last night."

"I don't think he brought it in. Maybe there's a place behind his apartment house. Let me know if he leaves his desk."

It was only six blocks to Duong's apartment house. Karr cruised past the front of the building, then drove around the back and into the alley where they'd gone in the night before. The alley looked even narrower than it had in the dark. Beyond the fence at the back was a row of dilapidated shanties. When he'd seen them last night, he'd thought they were unoccupied. Now he saw enough laundry hanging amid them to clothe a small army.

There were no good hiding places in the alley, and the dirt behind the building hadn't been disturbed. If Duong had retrieved a strongbox last night, he hadn't hidden it here.

Karr rode his motorbike out of the alley and around the block, cruising around a man pulling a small cart of wares. He started to turn right at the next block, then realized he was going the wrong way down a one-way street. He veered into a U-turn and found himself in the middle of a flood of motorbikes, which zagged every which way trying to avoid him. Horns and curses filled the air.

"Jeez, this is as bad as Boston," said Karr.

"Subject is moving, Tommy," said Chafetz. "Heading for the elevator."

"Ah, very good. On my way."

51

DEAN GOT TO the restaurant a half hour early, planting video bugs on the ladderlike streetlight posts outside. Waiting for someone to get him a table inside, he slipped a video bug under a light sconce at the front of the dining room. A waiter came and showed Dean to a table against the far wall; he could see the entire room and couldn't have picked a better vantage.

"OK, Charlie, we're getting good feeds all around," said Chafetz in his ear. "You ready?"

"Sure."

"We have some additional background on your Mr. Lo," the runner added. "Real low-level dirtbag. He served some time in a state prison for running prostitutes, but the sentence was outrageously short—a week. His name is connected to a number of businesses in the Saigon area. Our DEA has a file on him for possible drug smuggling. A real Boy Scout."

"I'll try and remember my knots."

A few minutes later, a man in his late twenties wearing a silk shirt, crisply tailored blue jeans, and slicked-back hair under a backward baseball cap entered the café, trailed by three men wearing American-style caps, T-shirts that fell to their knees, and jeans as sharp as their boss's.

The man spotted Dean and sauntered over.

"Here on business?" The man's smile revealed a gold filling in his front tooth. Besides six or seven gold chains and a halter that read: "BD Ass," his jewelry included a set of silver-plated knuckles.

"I'm waiting for a Mr. Lo," said Dean, pushing the business card across the table.

Lo grinned. He pulled out the nearest chair, turning it backward before sitting down. The men who had come in with him stood nearby.

"You have money?" asked Lo.

"What for?" said Dean.

"I have a hip-hop act that needs studio time. Many interests."

"I'll bet."

"You know what hip-hop is? You're an old man." Lo laughed. "Are you sure you know what you're getting into, grayhair?"

"That is Lo, in case there's any doubt," said Chafetz. "Computer matched the face."

"I was told that Mr. Lo would have a business card similar to this one." Dean tapped the card.

Lo glanced at it. "That's nice."

"So where's Cam Tre Luc?" said Dean. It was obvious Lo wasn't producing his card.

"Oh, Mr. Luc is a very important person. You won't find him here."

Dean remained silent, waiting for Lo to explain what the arrangement would be. The supposed hip-hop impresario leaned forward in his chair, then turned his head slowly to each side, an exaggerated gesture to see if anyone else was listening in.

Dean thought Lo was disappointed to see that no one was.

"You pay me and I tell you where to find Mr. Luc," Lo told him.

"No."

Lo looked shocked. He pulled back in the chair, then abruptly rose and started away.

"What are you doing, Charlie?" asked Rockman in Dean's ear.

Dean reached for his cup of tea and took a small sip, watching as Lo and his entourage left the café. The Vietnamese man struck Dean as the worst combination of American "gangsta" clichés, aping copies of copies that he saw on smuggled MTV tapes.

Which didn't mean he wasn't dangerous, Dean reminded himself a half hour later when he left the café. He walked up the block and turned to the right, just in time to be confronted by one of Lo's companions. Dean spun around immediately, catching a would-be ambusher with a hard elbow to the mid-section. As the man rebounded off the ground, Dean grabbed the pipe he had in his hand and struck the other man in the kneecaps.

Lo and the third member of his "posse" stood a few feet away, next to the corner of the building. Dean whipped the pipe at his remaining bodyguard, then threw Lo up against the wall, pinning him there with his .45.

"I'm still looking for Cam Tre Luc," Dean told Lo. "Here's what we're going to do. I'll let you go now without a new breathing hole in your neck. You arrange for me to meet Luc. I meet him, then I'll pay you five hundred American."

"Deal was one thousand," said Lo.

"That's right. But I'm taking five hundred back for my troubles. Like you said, I'm not as young as I used to be. I'm going to need some Bengay when I go home."

"Saigon Rouge, midnight. He will be with Miss Madonna. Five hundred cash," added Lo as Dean released him. "You pay at the desk when you come in."

"That's a whorehouse," said Chafetz in Dean's ear as he walked away.

"Well, I didn't figure I'd be meeting him in a church," said Dean, flagging down a passing Honda *ôm*.

52

KARR SPOTTED THAO Duong as he came out of his building. Duong turned to the left and began walking in the general direction of the port area near the mouth of the Saigon River.

"I'm going to tag him," Karr decided, telling the Art Room that he was going to get close enough to put a disposable tracking bug on Duong's clothes. Karr drove down the street, then pulled his bike up onto the sidewalk to park. From the side pouch of his backpack he removed one of the filmlike personal tracking bugs, carefully peeling the back off so that it would stick to its subject.

Though his white shirt and white cap were hardly unusual on the Saigon streets, Thao Duong was easy to spot as he approached. He walked with a nervous hop, and held his hands down stiffly at his sides, as if they were a boat's oars trailing in the water.

Unlike the street, which was packed solid with motorbikes and the occasional bus or taxi, the sidewalks were fairly clear, and Karr had no trouble timing his approach. Sidestepping a row of bikes parked against a building at the corner, he lumbered into Thao Duong just before the intersection, sending him sprawling to the ground. Karr scooped the thin man to his feet, planting the clear bug on the back of his hat at the same time.

"Sorry, pardner," Karr said cheerfully. "Very sorry." He repeated the translator's apology in Vietnamese.

Thao Duong's face had turned white. For a moment, Karr thought he was going to have a heart attack. But he sped forward, skip-walking across the intersection just as the light turned.

"Working?" Karr asked the Art Room.

"Yes," said Chafetz. "He's crossing the street about halfway down the block."

"Must have a suicide wish," said Karr as the motorbikes whizzed by.

ABOUT FIFTEEN MINUTES later, Thao Duong entered a three-story office building within sight of the port. The building looked as if it dated to the early 1950s, and its stucco exterior looked as if it hadn't been painted since then.

"Which side of the building?" Karr asked the Art Room.

"North side," said Sandy Chafetz. "We're not sure what floor, second or third."

Karr took what looked like an expensive tourist camera from his backpack and began fiddling with the lens. The camera contained a miniaturized boom mike that could pick up vibrations on window glass, but it had to be aimed at the proper window.

"How's this?" he asked, aiming the device at the top floor. The feed was sent back to the Art Room via the booster in his pack.

"Nothing. Try the next room," said Chafetz after two minutes.

Karr aimed the "camera" at the next window.

"Two women talking. Next window," said Chafetz.

It took three more windows before Karr found the proper room. By that time, it appeared that Thao Duong's conversation was nearly over; he was telling someone how disappointed he was.

"It's a dispute about money. The other guy seems to be holding him up for more than they bargained for," explained Thu De Nghiem, the Art Room translator. "And he wants payment by the end of the day."

"Don't they always?"

"Thao Duong is coming out of the building," said Rockman. "In a hurry."

A white-haired Vietnamese dockworker was staring at Karr's camera when he turned around.

"Take my picture?" Karr asked the man. Before he could object, Karr had clicked the "camera" off and thrust it into the man's hands. "You look through the viewer, see? Then press the button on the top."

The man gave Karr a confused look, then did as he was told, aiming it in the general direction of the blond American giant who had just accosted him. As soon as he pressed the phony shutter button, Karr came toward him.

"Didn't work," said the man in Vietnamese. "No click."

"Thanks, Pop," said Karr, grabbing the camera.

"No click. No click."

"He's telling you that the camera didn't work," said Thu De Nghiem in the Art Room.

"No, well, then I'll have to get it checked out."

"You want the words in Vietnamese?" Thu De Nghiem asked.

"No," said Karr. "But tell me how to ask him where there's a good restaurant. My stomach's growling."

"THE OFFICE THAO Duong visited in Saigon belongs to a company called Asia Free Trade Shipping," Marie Telach told Rubens. "As the name implies, they arrange shipping from the port. Furniture, mostly. Some leather goods."

"Have you found a link to Infinite Burn?" asked Rubens, staring at the screen at the front of the Art Room. It showed a feed from the front of Thao Duong's building. Thao Duong was back inside in his office, having returned there after visiting the Asia Free Trade Shipping office.

"Nothing obvious. But the company does have connections in the U.S.," said Telach. "And the man Duong met wanted more money. Maybe for a second attempt?"

Rubens put the fingers of his hands together, each tip pushing against its opposite. Good intelligence was often a matter of making good guesses; the trick was knowing when a guess was good.

"Nothing else?"

"We're looking."

"Stay on Duong. Arrange to intercept any international calls Asia Free Trade makes. Put together a call list, a transaction scan—find out everything there is to know about anything remotely connected to either Duong or that company."

DEAN CAUGHT UP with Karr just after Thao Duong had begun to move again, this time walking in the opposite direction from the waterfront. At first they thought he was going back to his apartment, but about a block away he veered right and began zigzagging through a series of small alleys.

"Thinks he's being followed," said Dean. "We better hang back for a while."

"He's going to take one of those taxi bikes," predicted Karr. "Come on. I have a motorbike around the corner."

"You think I'm getting on the bike with you?"

"It's either that or walk," said Karr.

"I'd rather walk," insisted Dean.

Karr obviously thought he was joking, because he started to grin. Dean relented when Sandy Chafetz told them that Thao Duong had apparently found a Honda *ôm,* since he was heading north at a good clip.

They followed Thao Duong to the north side of the city. Dean kept his eyes closed the whole way.

"He's in a bus station," Chafetz told them when they were about a block away. "Odds are the key he had last night fits a locker there."

"Not much of a bet," said Karr. He pulled off the street into a small loading area at the side of the station. "You feel like driving for a while, Charlie?"

"You follow him. I feel like stretching my legs."

"What are you going to do?"

"See what else is in his locker."

THE TRACKING DATA from the Art Room was good enough to locate a person to within a meter and a half. That still left Karr nine feet of lockers to check. Each door was just over a foot square, and they were stacked six high.

"Can you give me a little help here?" he asked Chafetz.

"Your guess is as good as ours."

Karr reached into his pack and pulled out his night glasses, hoping that the infrared lenses would pick up a temperature difference in the locker that had been recently opened.

It didn't.

He glanced around the waiting room, hoping there might be a video camera trained on the locker area. But there were none.

There were forty-eight lockers. He'd start in the middle, and work his way outward. He'd check two or three at a time, then go away, make sure he wasn't being watched, and take two or three more.

Not ideal, but the best solution under the circumstances. He'd plant video bugs so the Art Room could watch his back.

Should've let Charlie take this one, he thought to himself as he scouted out the best places to put the bugs.

DEAN FOLLOWED THAO Duong back to his office, circled the block, then found a café nearby to hang out. The place dated from the days when the French ruled Vietnam; its facade, woodwork, and furniture were all modeled on a Parisian café. Dean wondered if the familiarity had provided any comfort to the French diplomats and soldiers watching the last vestiges of their empire slip away in the late forties and early fifties.

A half hour later, Chafetz told him a young man had just walked into Thao Duong's office and received an envelope.

"Follow the messenger and see where he goes," the runner told Dean. "The locator bug is still working on Thao

Duong, so we'll know if he leaves the building. This looks more interesting."

Dean left a few dollars—American—to pay for his coffee, then went to get his motorbike. As the young man who'd made the pickup came out of the building, a blue motorbike pulled in front and stopped. The kid hopped on and sped away.

Dean managed to get close enough to read part of the license plate for Rockman. But the bike's driver knew the city far better than Dean, and was considerably more aggressive in traffic; within four or five blocks Dean had to concede he'd lost him. Dean headed to the riverfront area and with Chafetz's help found the Asia Free Trade Shipping building, but there was no trace of the messenger there, either.

"SHE'S ASKING WHAT you're doing," the translator told Karr as he opened another locker.

"Does she work here?" Karr asked.

"I don't think so. See, most—"

"Tell me how to ask that in Vietnamese."

Thu De Nghiem gave him the words. Karr repeated them to the woman as best he could. He also continued to work the lock with his pick. The others—he was now on number thirteen—had been easy; this one seemed to be gummed up with something.

The woman's tone became more high-pitched. Karr prodded his tool in the lock, then finally heard a click.

He turned to the woman. "My key always sticks," he told her in English, though by now he was reasonably certain she didn't speak it.

"She says she's going to report you to the authorities," said Thu De Nghiem. "She thinks you're a thief."

"I *am* a thief," said Karr brightly. "How old you figure she is? Sixty?"

"Younger," said Nghiem, who was looking at a feed from Karr's bug.

Karr opened the locker and saw a large manila envelope, similar to the one he had found beneath Thao Duong's desk. He gave it a big smile and took it with him to a nearby seat.

The woman followed; her harangue continued uninterrupted.

"You remind me of my mother," Karr told her.

She kept right on talking.

"Yo, Thu," Karr said to the translator. "This lady reminds me of my mother. What are the words?"

"For what?"

"You . . . remind me . . . of . . . Mom."

Clearly perplexed, Thu De Nghiem translated the sentence. Karr repeated the words loudly and correctly enough to stop the woman's rant. He then proceeded to spin a story in English and mispronounced Vietnamese about how he had returned to Saigon to find his mother, who had come to the States, given birth to him, then abandoned him and returned home to Saigon.

"You look very much like the picture Dad has on the bureau back home," Karr declared, in first English and then Vietnamese. "Are you my mom?"

The woman mumbled something, then fled.

"Did I get the accent wrong?" Karr asked the translator.

"She thinks you're a nut," said Nghiem. "I promise you, she'll be bringing back the police."

Karr laughed and peeked into the envelope.

"Wow," he said.

"Mr. Karr, do you have a problem?" asked Rubens, coming on the line.

"No problem at all," said Karr. He pulled out his PDA and popped the camera attachment on. Then he held it inside the envelope far enough to get a picture of the bundles of hundred-dollar bills sitting there. "No, I have no problem at all. At least none that a hundred thousand bucks can't solve."

55

THAO DUONG'S HARD drive, downloaded by Tommy Karr to the Art Room the previous evening, contained an unremarkable assortment of agricultural reports and bureaucratic memos, each laboriously worked over: Robert Gallo, who was in charge of examining the drive, found at least nine drafts of most of the reports.

There was one file, however, different from all the rest. Not only were there no other versions; it was encrypted, albeit in a simple encryption performed by the word processor that had created the file. Gallo used a software tool to "break" the encryption. The result was a solid block of numbers, which Gallo at first assumed was another encryption. He applied a range of software tools to try to parse the block without getting anything that the translator could recognize. Giving up, he forwarded the file to the cryptology section; the people working there had better tools and worked with encryptions all the time, unlike him. He also posted it on an internal intranet "blog" or continually updating log used by the Deep Black team to communicate their progress and problems. A few minutes later, Johnny Bib turned up in Gallo's office, hovering over his shoulder.

"Call home," said Johnny.

"Huh?"

"Ding-a-ling," said Johnny Bib.

Gallo couldn't figure out what he meant.

And then he did.

"They're phone numbers?"

"*Ha!!!!*"

RUBENS RUBBED HIS eyes, trying to clear away some of the fatigue making them blur.

"There are contacts in New York, Washington, LA, all cities where the senator has been," Gallo told him. "None of these numbers are red sheeted. FBI has nothing on them, and neither does the CIA. If there's a network there, we have zero data on it."

Money and a network of connections in most major American cities—this looked a hell of a lot like what they were looking for, Rubens realized.

"Have you built call lists for these numbers?" Rubens asked.

"Didn't want to do that without your OK. 'Cause it's, like, in the States."

"Go ahead and do so," Rubens told him. "I'll forward this information to Ambassador Jackson and see if we can get additional information from the FBI. Keep me informed."

56

THE TRACKING BUG Karr had placed on Thao Duong ran out of juice a little past six, while Thao Duong was on his way back to his apartment. Dean and Karr decided there was no use planting another; Thao Duong was likely to get changed when he got home anyway. They trailed him to his house and waited outside until half past eight. The Art Room reported that he was watching television; Dean and Karr decided to knock off for dinner before checking out Saigon Rouge. They stopped in a noodle place; pots of boiling water and noodles were brought to the table, along with an assortment of vegetables and meat that they were supposed to toss in the water to cook.

"Do-it-yourself soup," said Karr, enthusiastically tossing in everything from his side dish. "I'll take anything you don't want."

Dean found himself brooding while he waited for the noodles to cool. He missed Lia. It had nothing to do with the mission; he just wanted to talk to her, to feel her bumping up against him.

"You hit the red-light district when you were in the war, Charlie?" asked Karr.

"I was only in Saigon once, for a really short time."

"Not just *this* red-light district," said Karr, spooning up some broth to taste. "Any red-light district."

Dean knew what he meant, but instead of answering, he stared at Karr.

"Good stuff," said Karr.

"Isn't it hot?"

"Steaming."

"I did go to a cathouse once," said Dean.

"Cathouse?"

"That's what we called them," explained Dean apologetically. "It was my eighteenth birthday—my *real* eighteenth birthday. Some of the guys arranged it for me."

"Pop your cherry, huh? Great present."

"They thought so."

Dean hadn't been a virgin; the other men made that assumption because he didn't have a girlfriend back home, never talked about getting laid, and was consistently shy around women, a trait that afflicted him to this day.

Between his shyness and the girl's limited English, the encounter had been awkward. The only part that he remembered now came after it was over—he was shy, but not *that* shy—she'd given him a soft kiss and then left the bamboo-and-rice-paper-sided room.

"You ever been to a prostitute, Tommy?" he asked Karr.

"Nope."

Karr looked up from his soup. Then his face slowly turned red. "Is that part of the plan?"

UNLIKE THE "CLUBS" that catered to tourists in Saigon's business and trendy downtown areas, Saigon Rouge catered to Vietnamese. It was located on the edge of District 4, a tightly packed shantytown slum.

Even the most committed party member would lose his illusions about communism and workers' paradises here. Knots of old people dressed in rags congregated in front of tumble-down tin-faced huts, soaking up what little breeze the night air provided. The area was one of the poorest places in Asia, and, by extension, the world.

But on the street where Saigon Rouge stood, a half-dozen Mercedeses idled in the night, their drivers watching the sidewalks warily from air-conditioned cabins. Most of the drivers were armed with the latest submachine guns or automatic rifles, though the majority of District 4's denizens knew better than to attack or harass the men who owned the cars. Justice in the Socialist Republic of Vietnam could be quite severe, especially here.

A kind of demilitarized zone had grown up around Saigon Rouge, making possible a thriving black market. The block was a thriving locus for drug smugglers, who found it convenient to locate near a ready pool of cheap labor. It was also the headquarters for several other illegitimate and semi-illegitimate businesses, for whom operating beyond the eye of local authorities had certain advantages.

There was, for example, a man who traded in tiger parts, shipping them surreptitiously to various Asian and, on occasion, Western countries. He owned a narrow two-story building directly across from Saigon Rouge. The bottom floor of his building was stacked with an assortment of antique junk. The top floor was completely vacant, which made it a convenient vantage point for observing the brothel.

"You have guards on both ends of the hallway on the third floor," said Rockman, who'd taken over as their runner in the Art Room. A Global Hawk Unmanned Aerial Vehicle—a robot aircraft carrying ground-penetrating radar that had been "tuned" to look inside the building—was orbiting overhead, supplying real-time intelligence on the building and surrounding area. The aircraft's gear was sensitive enough to discern human beings as they moved in the hallway.

"The hall is z-shaped," added Rockman. "The guards can't see each other, or the room itself."

"Does that door on the top connect to the back stairwell?" asked Karr.

"Yes," said Rockman. "Looks like the guard sits in front of the door. Has a chair there and everything. Once you get the video bugs in the lobby, we'll be able to ID the subject when he comes in. Then we'll follow him up to the second or third floor, wherever he goes."

Karr turned to Dean. "Ready?"

Dean nodded.

"Sometimes a man's gotta do what a man's gotta do," Karr said, preparing to give his body to science.

DEAN KEPT HIS finger against the rifle's laser button as he watched from the window, ready to flip it on. His glasses would show him precisely where the A2's bullets would hit if he fired. But that wouldn't necessarily save Tommy Karr if things went bad.

"He's coming around the side of the building right now," said Rockman from the Art Room.

Besides the Global Hawk's images, low-light video was being provided by a small unmanned aircraft nicknamed the Crow; Dean and Karr had launched it from the roof of the building when they'd arrived. The Crow's image was being displayed on the screen of Karr's PDA, which he'd left on the floor near the window for Dean, but Dean found the image distracting, and it was much easier to rely on Rockman as his long-range eyes and ears.

Karr sauntered into view, a big blond American walking like he owned the world. Dean tensed as a black sedan pulled onto the block; he raised the boxy assault gun, ready to fire. The rear door of the car opened. A single, diminutive figure got out. It was a middle-aged woman, who crossed the street in front of Karr and went into the building. Karr let her get ahead of him and paused for a moment to look around, as if worried that someone might see him. Then he spun toward the entrance.

"Here goes nothin'," said Karr cheerfully, ducking inside.

THE WOMAN WHO sat on the couch that dominated the entry hall at Saigon Rouge didn't know what to make of the tall blond American who crowded her doorway. She did, however, know what to do with the two hundred-dollar bills he took from his pocket.

"You are American?" said in English.

"Norwegian," Karr replied. And then, in halting and poorly accented Vietnamese, he told her that he had heard from certain friends that Saigon Rouge was the only place to visit when in town.

"You speak Vietnamese?" she answered.

"Just a little," he told her. "Mom taught me."

"Your mother, Joe?"

"She came from Lam Dong Province."

This baffled the woman even more; Karr had zero Vietnamese features, and Lam Dong was not known for producing giants. But she had seen many strange things in her years as a madam, and questionable parentage was hardly unusual, let alone relevant in the face of a fee several times over the normal charge.

"No guns inside," she told him, holding out her hand.

"Now how do you know I have a gun?"

"Everyone have gun. We search."

A squat bodyguard dressed in a brown Vietnamese suit came out from the other side of the flowered screen opposite the couch. Karr took his Beretta from his belt and handed it over, then dropped to his knee and took the small Walther from its holster above his right ankle.

"I get it back, right?" he said, handing the gun to the madam.

"You get back, yes. Search him, please."

The man found Karr's Walther TPH pocket pistol on his left ankle. The bodyguard smiled triumphantly and rose—missing the other Walther on Karr's right ankle. Barely five inches long by three inches high, the tiny gun fired .22-caliber bullets, but it was better than nothing.

"Must've forgotten about that one," said Karr as the madam took the weapon.

"No joke, honey," said the madam. She hesitated, then waved her bodyguard back to his hiding spot. "You follow me, and no tricks."

"You're the one with the tricks."

"Very funny, Joe. Norwegian has a good sense of humor."

She led Karr through a beaded doorway to what in a normal house might be a parlor, though here it would have been more accurately called a bullpen. The woman who had preceded

Karr into the building was just leaving with a much taller red-headed girl wearing a silk kimono that reached to the top of her thong strap. Four other girls lounged on the couches, wearing Western-style lingerie. It was just going on eleven; business wouldn't pick up for another hour or so, which was when Cam Tre Luc was expected.

"Who?" said the woman, gesturing. "You make a pick."

"So hard to decide," said Karr, glancing around.

"You want Miss Madonna," Rockman reminded him.

Karr knew who he wanted, but he didn't want to make it too obvious. He also wanted to give himself time to plant a video bug here. He'd slapped one apiece on the frames to the doors as he'd come through but thought he needed at least two in this room to cover it adequately.

Two women got up from the couch and walked over toward him in a languid, dreamy dance, hoping to help him make up his mind.

"Cute," purred one of the girls. The other began blowing in his ear.

"Decisions, decisions," said Karr.

There was a small bust of Ho Chi Minh in the corner. The vantage was perfect, but there was no place to put the bug where it wouldn't be obvious. Karr decided he would have to settle for the underside of the table.

"Come with me, Joe," said one of the prostitutes, running her hand down his side. She wore an oversized yellow camisole that fell just far enough below her waist to make it clear that was all she had on.

"Whoooph," said Karr. "Getting hot in here. Say—can I have a drink?"

"Tommy, don't drink anything," hissed Rockman. "It may be doped."

The second girl, who wore a long strapless gown, began rubbing Karr's other side. He slid between them, angling for the couch near the table where he wanted to plant the bug.

This was an invitation for the other girls to join in. They *were* girls—Karr doubted any of them were older than fifteen.

The madam went to a secretary-style desk at the side of

the room and revealed a small bar. Karr snaked his hand
around the girl with the strapless gown and slid the bug under
the end table. She naturally interpreted this to mean that he
was interested in her, and ran her hand up and down his thigh.

"What you drink, Joe?" asked the girl in the camisole,
pouting because she seemed to be losing out.

"Water," said Karr.

"Water?" asked the madam. "You need vodka. It will
make you loose. You are too tight now. High-strung."

"Oh, is that what you call it?"

The girls giggled. The one in a see-through pink chemise
got up and began doing a dance in front of him, wiggling her
breasts.

"I was told there was a girl named Miss Madonna," said
Karr. "Is she here?"

"Miss Madonna?" The madam made a face as if she did
not know who he was talking about, then shook her head.

"She was the best, I heard," said Karr. "I came all the way
to Saigon to see her."

The girls began rubbing him frantically, hoping to get
him to change his mind. Karr kept his gaze on the madam.

"Very expensive," she told him.

"Two hundred not enough?" asked Karr, reaching back
into his pocket for the bills.

"Five hundred."

"I think two is more than enough."

"Three-fifty."

"I have three." Karr removed the bills from his pocket.
"All I have."

Another frown. "Fifteen minute," said the woman.

"Thirty."

"Twenty."

"Deal." Karr pushed himself up from the couch—which
wasn't easy. "Sorry, ladies. Another time, I'm sure."

"KARR'S ON HIS way up," Rockman told Dean. "They're taking
him to see Madonna. All right, he's in—the room, I mean."

"I figured that out," said Dean.

"Miss Madonna has the suite at the back of the third floor. There's a window on the alley. No fire escape."

Somehow, Dean didn't think the code enforcement people would care. He turned his attention back to the street, watching as a light-colored Toyota Land Cruiser pulled up near the whorehouse. Two men dressed in black jumped out from the back, scanned the street, then tapped on the truck's roof.

"Hey, Rockman, what kind of vehicle does Cam Tre Luc have?"

"Yeah, we see that, too," said Rockman. He cursed—it looked like their subject was more than an hour early. "We'll check the image when he comes into the hallway to be definite, but that looks like him."

57

THE VIETNAM NATIONAL phone company had an admirable security system designed to prevent computer break-ins. It was so admirable, in fact, that Gallo had studied the system it was modeled on as a sophomore in college.

If he recalled correctly, the class mid-term required students to demonstrate all six ways of breaking into the system without being detected.

Gallo had shown there were actually eight.

After he broke into the system, Gallo obtained a list of every phone call Thao Duong had made in the past two years. Gallo then obtained lists of everyone those people had called—and everyone whom they had called. He then took the American numbers—Canadian, Mexican, and Caribbean as well as U.S.—and requested call lists on them. Ironically, though these requests were filled voluntarily by the phone companies, they took the longest—several hours rather than the ten or fifteen minutes it would have taken Gallo to get them by breaking in.

Bureaucracy.

Gallo shared the information with the other analysts, who used it in a number of ways. One created a chart showing Thao Duong's "friend network"—acquaintances whom he regularly spoke to—and looked for interesting individuals. Another focused on finding banks and financial institutions active in the list, and began tracing transactions that Thao Duong might be involved in. Another compared the phone numbers against intercept lists, looking for people whom the NSA or other agencies were already monitoring.

Two facts emerged from the analysis: Friends of Thao Duong had made wire transfers totaling over one hundred thousand dollars within the last week. Another set of friends had connections with the shipping industry, and with China.

The one thing that did not show up was connections to government officials outside of the agricultural ministry. As omissions were often more important than inclusions, this was noted as well.

Gallo also used a tool that compared the network of connections he had compiled to other known organizations, including al Qaeda. The tool tested how similar this network was to different profiles—in other words, did it look like a terror organization or a Girl Scout troop?

The tool worked on the theory that groups with the same goal tended to work in the same way. To use a very simple example, the members of a bowling league would tend to meet once or twice a week at a specific location within driving distance of their homes. They would generally purchase certain specific items—bowling shoes and bowling balls, for example. Most would fit a specific demographic, and would group themselves with others of an even tighter demographic on their team—the under-30 league, or the under-40 league, for example.

Rarely could the tool definitively identify what a network was organized to do. It didn't in this case, though some form of international commerce or trade was suggested. Its real value was suggesting other areas of inquiry. According to the tool, there should be more bank transfers as yet undetected. It also suggested that, based on the call patterns, Thao Duong was an important member of the network, but not the top person. Several other individuals—or nodes, as the program called them—were highlighted for in-depth investigation. Beyond looking for criminal and public records pertaining to them, the analysts would look at financial records, transaction lists such as credit card charges, and anything else they could find. Gallo handed off the list to the analysts, asking that they compile profiles. Several were in America.

Within two or three minutes of sending the request via e-mail, he got a phone call from Segio Nakami, the number two on the Desk Three analytic team. Almost the exact opposite of Johnny Bib, Nakami was considered eccentric at the Agency because he wasn't eccentric.

"Robert, you're asking for profiles?" said Nakami.

"Yeah, I got this thing going for Rubens in Vietnam."

"There are Americans on the list."

"Yeah?"

"What are you looking for?"

Gallo explained what he was doing.

"Did you fill out the papers?" asked Nakami when he finished. By "papers," Nakami meant legal requests; the forms were actually done electronically.

"I thought, like, I didn't have to because Rubens said go."

"No, you have to fill them out."

"Um, it's going to like take two hours."

"Are you on real time?" asked Nakami.

He meant, was Gallo supporting a mission, where the information was needed right away or in "real time"? Except that Nakami didn't mean that all, because he knew very well that Gallo wasn't down in the Art Room.

"No," said Gallo.

"I'm sure Mr. Rubens didn't want you to bypass procedure," said Nakami. "Let me know if there's a problem."

Stinking lawyers, thought Gallo, reaching to bring up the proper screen.

58

"BOTTOM LINE, FORESTER was a burnout. He was never going anywhere in the Service. His wife was giving him the boot. And he had this personality—he'd just basically given up on things. The only exception to that was his girlfriend, and frankly, that seems like it was pretty one-sided." Special Agent John Mandarin leaned back on the park bench in front of the Danbury town hall, where Lia had arranged to meet him. "That's why he killed himself."

"So you think I'm wasting my time checking into Forester's death," said Lia, recapping in a sentence what Mandarin had taken five minutes to explain.

"Look, it's not my time, so I can't tell you what to do," said Mandarin. "But off the record, I think the director—"

Mandarin stopped mid-sentence. Lia followed his glance toward two young women walking across the street.

"They're underage," snapped Lia.

"Just looking," said Mandarin lamely. "The thing is, it was pretty obviously a suicide. Staging that—it's real easy in the movies, OK? But in real life, those things happen a certain way. When I was a policeman for a while I saw two of them. Which is a lot. And I'm not the only one who thinks that. The FBI came over as soon as the state police figured out the guy was a federal agent. There was no jurisdictional backbiting here, no finger-pointing. We were called and we came. Believe me, if there had been any sign of anything other than suicide, somebody would have seen it."

"So if it's all so obvious, why isn't the case officially closed?"

"You mean why is the director still asking questions?" Mandarin smiled. "I think the director was kind of shook by it. Frey was Forester's first boss, showing him the ropes. Or supposed to. I think he felt guilty about it."

Mandarin shook his head. He had a slightly older woman in his sights now, good-looking, with tight, expensive jeans. Lia resisted the urge to elbow him in the ribs.

"Frey had a reputation as a real hard-ass," said the Secret Service agent finally. "That's how he got to where he is now. He came down hard on people. Too hard, probably. He stuck a couple of things in Forester's file early on. Little things, but, you know, anyone looking at them sees whose initials are at the top there, and they're going to figure that this guy is not on the chosen list, if you know what I mean."

"Frey held him back?"

"No. Not on purpose. He probably thought he was doing him a favor." Mandarin laughed. "I worked with Frey when he was one of us. Yeah, I'm that old." He laughed again, even harder. "Very, very, very competent guy. The guy you want watching your back, believe me. The President can trust him. But tough on the help. Kicked me in the butt more than once."

"The state police report noted the chain wasn't locked on the door."

"Ehhh. Not a biggie."

"There were no prints on the doorknob, which seems strange," Lia pointed out. "Not even Forester's."

Mandarin held his hand out in front of him. "Door was a handle type. I go to open it, I push down, odds are I don't leave a print. Spring brings it back behind me. Everybody obsessed with forensics, but a lot of times in the real world things don't follow a script."

Mandarin leaned back on the bench, stretching.

"I'm only holding the case open because not all the reports have come back yet. I'm not pushing for them to come back," he added, giving her a sideways glance. "Because I have better things to do, if you get my drift."

"I don't."

"I'm in a no-win position. The big boss wants me to find that it wasn't suicide. Everybody else in the world tells me it was." Mandarin shook his head. "I'm sorry. He killed himself. I don't like to think of it myself, but that's the bottom line."

"Even if it was a suicide," said Lia, "he's our only connection to Vietnam."

"I guess. I don't buy the whole overseas-conspiracy thing."

"Why not?"

"For one thing, the shooter missed. A government goes to the kind of lengths you're talking about here, they're going to pick someone who doesn't miss."

"Everybody misses once in a while."

"Maybe."

"What do you think happened?"

"Really pissed-off constituent decides to do the senator in. Hired a crazy to help. Or maybe he's a crazy himself."

"So why can't you find him?"

"It's not as easy as you think." Mandarin got up. "Listen, I gotta get going. I have to find something for my son's birthday. Then I have to get up to Albany because McSweeney's due there. You're welcome to join us if you want, OK? Or if you want more help here, let us know. But I think you're spinning your wheels here."

"How old is he?"

"Who, my kid? Thirteen. Good kid, but a tough age."

"Forester had a son around that old," said Lia.

"Yeah, I know."

"Would you commit suicide knowing how it would affect your son?"

"I'm not Forester."

59

MADONNA WAS A blonde—not natural of course, though all her parts matched. She was older than the girls who had been downstairs. She wore a tight-fitted vinyl bodice and leather boots over fishnet stockings, apparently imitating one of the singer's many incarnations, though the resemblance was distant at best. Karr couldn't tell if the subdued belligerence she met him with was part of her act.

"Who are you?" she said, almost angrily.

"Just a guy."

"Just a guy." She picked up a cigarette pack from the nightstand next to the bed and knocked one out. "What do you want?"

"The obvious," said Karr.

She smirked. Karr scooped the lighter from the table and lit it, holding the flame for her. Madonna hesitated, then leaned in. She took a long drag and blew the smoke in his face.

"You like that, huh, Joe?" she said.

"Name's not Joe. And no, not really."

"Strip."

"You first."

Madonna took a long puff from her cigarette. "All right," she said.

Karr sat down on the bed, watching as the hooker unbuttoned her top. Her breasts sprang free with the last button, round oranges each topped by a pert red cherry. She raised her boot and put it on Karr's leg.

"Lick it," she said.

"I don't think so."

Miss Madonna pretended to pout. Karr took hold of the boot and helped her pull her foot free. He did the same with the second, then got up and brought the shoes to the side of the room. As he straightened them, he positioned a video fly on the wall just under the window.

The prostitute threw one of her stockings at him as he turned back around. He caught it, and waited for the second. But instead of tossing it, Miss Madonna dropped it on the floor. She rose, then tugged at the zipper of the vinyl girdle she was wearing. The garment fell away, revealing a white lace thong.

"Tommy, Cam Tre Luc is in the building," said Rockman in Karr's ear.

"And we were just getting to the good part."

Miss Madonna gave him a quizzical stare.

"Well, don't stop," Karr told her.

She pushed her arms back and let her vest slide off her shoulders. Then she paused, taking another drag from her cigarette.

"The madam's on her way up in a frenzy," warned Rockman.

"Mmmmmm," said Karr, as Miss Madonna hooked her thumbs into the panty's thin strings.

Before she could get any further, the madam's strident voice was heard in the hallway.

"Mister, mister, big mistake. You go quick. Right now, quick."

"His bodyguards are right behind him, Tommy," said Rockman. "Get out of there."

"Charlie, I'll talk to him," said Karr.

"No, I'm on my way over," said Dean. "Hang out there and back me up."

The madam burst into the room. "You go," she told Karr.

"Right now?"

"Get dressed quick," the madam told Madonna, adding something in Vietnamese that prodded the whore into motion.

The madam grabbed Karr's arm.

"Come with me," she told him, tugging him out the door

and then pushing him down the hallway toward the back stairs. One of her bodyguards trailed silently behind.

Cam Tre Luc, meanwhile, was diverted at the top of the opposite stairs by a girl from another room who sensed trouble. Though out of view, Karr could hear her attempt at seduction and Cam Tre Luc's protests.

"Where are we going?" Karr asked the madam as they reached the stairs.

"You done."

"I didn't get my money's worth."

"No charge. Full refund. Come back tomorrow."

"How about a substitute?" he asked as she pushed him into the stairway. "Someone who doesn't smoke."

DEAN CIRCLED AROUND the back of the building and came out in the alley directly across from Saigon Rouge. Cam Tre Luc had left a single bodyguard in his SUV; according to the Art Room, one of his men was in the "reception" area and another had gone up to the third floor, waiting discreetly by the stairs while his boss conducted his business.

The original game plan called for Dean to go down the block to a four-story building next to the Saigon Rouge. He'd climb the fire escape, get on the roof, jump down to Saigon Rouge, and then go down the stairs. The guard there would be disposed of with a shot of fast-acting anesthesia; Dean would then have a clear path to the room. While Karr was supposed to be back in the other building watching him, Dean decided there was no reason it wouldn't work with him inside the whorehouse.

"Tommy's in a room on the second floor," said Rockman as Dean pulled down the fire escape and began climbing up the side of the building. "He convinced the madam he'd take someone else."

"What's Cam Tre Luc doing?"

"What do you think?"

CAM TRE LUC was not a fool. He knew that someone had been with his whore before he arrived, and he did not like it. Even though he had come earlier than normal, he expected that the girl would be ready and available—and alone. He paid considerable money for her attention and he was, after all, an important member of the government.

But achieving his position had required considerable discipline. Cam Tre Luc realized that things had to be dealt with at the proper time, and in the proper order; placing emotions above rational thought doomed one to failure. His first priority was to be pleasured; he would deal with Miss Pu, the proprietor of Saigon Rouge, when that was accomplished.

Cam Tre Luc had first visited prostitutes during the American War, when he was still a young man. He was in fact married at the time, but his wife was a world away across the border in North Vietnam. While seeing prostitutes was frowned on by his superiors, Cam Tre Luc had had no difficulty justifying it to them—when living among the corrupt, one must wear their clothes.

Justifying it to himself would have been more difficult, so he did not bother doing so.

Things were now considerably different. His superiors, much higher now in government, would certainly not be as understanding—but there was no need for them to be, as he had more than enough information on any of them to do significant harm should they use this against him. As for his wife, she was here in Ho Chi Minh City. But their years of separation had conditioned her to accept completely their separate lives. If she knew that he visited prostitutes—he suspected she might—she did not say.

Miss Madonna slipped her hands around his chest from behind and began unbuttoning his shirt. He began to breathe more quickly—which was unusual. Generally the stroke of her fingers relaxed him.

Perhaps he was becoming too old for this.

THE ROOF DOOR was bolted from the inside, and to open it Dean had to use a super-magnet tool that he carried in his vest. Unhooking the latch to get the rod to slide required a bit of body English, and Dean lost a good three or four minutes before he could get the rod far enough off the stop to allow the door to open.

He leaned in far enough to see that the coast was clear and there was enough light so that he wouldn't need his glasses, then hunched back to get ready. He unzipped the small pouch at his belly and took out what looked like an oversized gardening glove. The glove was actually a hypodermic device, studded with needles that would feed a quick-acting synthetic opiate loaded into a bladder stored in the palm. While it was easier than using a regular doctor's needle, the device required Dean to get extremely close to his victim. It was also highly preferable to inject the drug into the neck area and hold on for a good five seconds. All of which meant getting up close and personal with a very unhappy person.

Glove on his right hand, Dean tucked his pistol into his belt and slipped down the stairs. The guard stood just inside the open doorway; Dean could see his shadow as he tiptoed down.

The man who'd taught Dean how to use the "doping glove" was a former Special Forces soldier. He'd made it look easy, pulling his subject back with one arm held around the neck while clamping the open area near the throat with the glove. Dean, however, worried that in the frenzy he'd accidentally hit himself with one of the needles, and so he improvised: he stepped from the doorway, grabbed the body-guard's ponytail, and yanked him sideways. As he did, he jabbed his gloved hand at the man. Dean missed the body-guard's throat, getting his face instead. He held on as the sur-prised Vietnamese man struggled and attempted to scream. Dean took two hard punches to the chest before a third missed badly and told him that the drug had begun to do its job. He dragged his victim away from the door, making sure to leave him on his side so that if he vomited—unfortunately, a common side effect of the drug—he wouldn't drown in his own puke.

"First door on your right," said Rockman. "Go!"

No shit, thought Dean. He could have done without the runner's encouragement.

Dean pulled the pistol from his belt, took a breath, then walked quickly to the door of the room. He pushed through the beads and saw Cam Tre Luc lying on the bed, his face between the legs of a blond whore.

"Cam Tre Luc?" said Dean.

"Who the hell are you?"

"I'm sorry. I came for a friend—Gerald Forester. He's hoping you have information for him."

"You have no business here," Cam Tre Luc told the man, staring into his eyes. "Out."

They stared at each other for several long seconds.

"Charlie, Madonna has a pistol behind her back," warned Rockman.

Dean ignored the girl. Though obviously angry, Cam Tre Luc looked pathetic, naked from the waist down; his legs were spindly and his butt creased with sagging fat.

"Forester needs your help," Dean told him. He reached into his pocket for a card. "Call this number." He dropped the card on the bed. "I didn't want to approach you at your house or office. No one else knows. Don't, lady," Dean added, pointing his pistol at the prostitute as she slipped out of bed. "I know you have a gun. I'm not here to hurt anybody."

Cam Tre Luc continued to glare at him.

There was a shout in the hall.

"The phone number," said Dean, pointing at the card. "We can make it worth your while."

Miss Madonna started to scream.

"Time to go, Charlie," said Rockman.

"I'm on my way," said Dean, backing out of the room.

CAM TRE LUC felt himself tremble with rage and embarrassment and—worst of all—impotence. Who did this American think he was?

Cam Tre Luc had no idea who this Forester was, nor would he have helped a Westerner under any circumstances. But in this case—in this case he would have revenge for his humiliation.

"Give me that gun," he told Miss Madonna. "Then get my pants."

DEAN HAD REACHED the stairs by the time Rockman warned him that Cam Tre Luc's guard was coming down the hallway. With his first step downward, Dean lost his footing. He shoved his hand in the direction of the railing and grabbed it for a moment, temporarily steadying himself. But the railing then gave way and Dean shot forward, pirouetting down six or seven steps to the landing on the second floor.

It sounded as if everyone in the whorehouse was shouting. Rockman and the interpreter in the Art Room were both talking at once. A gunshot cracked in the far distance. Wood splintered near Dean's head. Someone was shooting at him, the bullets flying just a few feet away. For some reason, the sound was different than bullets usually sounded, more brittle, less real.

Dean started to crawl around the landing to the next run of steps. Suddenly the stairway exploded with a loud crash. A brutal flash of light blinded him. Dean began to choke. Then he felt himself fall or fly—he couldn't tell the difference.

A voice came out of the swirl below him.

"Hang on, partner," said Tommy Karr, who'd hoisted Dean to his shoulder. "One more flight to go."

AS KARR REACHED the alley behind Saigon Rouge he dropped the second small tear gas grenade he had in his hand, then turned toward the motorbikes they'd stashed earlier.

"Let me down," growled Dean from Karr's shoulder.

"I was hoping you'd say that," answered Karr, but he didn't let go of Dean until they reached the bikes. There were shouts now all along the block, and Karr could hear the sounds of engines starting and people running. No one was in the alley, however; confusion was still on their side.

Dean stood woozily, putting his hand against the wall for balance.

"Get on my bike. Come on," Karr told him, tilting it to the side.

"I'll take my own."

"Suit yourself," said Karr, kick-starting his to life.

Dean got on the other bike woozily.

"You OK, Charlie?"

"Yeah." His bike purred to life.

Someone appeared in the alley behind them, yelling at them to halt.

"I'm going to throw a flash-bang," said Karr, grabbing at his belt. "Go. I'll meet you back at the hotel."

As Dean thundered off, the person who'd yelled at them—one of Cam Tre Luc's bodyguards—began shooting. A bullet bounced off the wall opposite Karr, spraying pieces of clay from the brick. Karr tossed the flash-bang grenade over his shoulder and then hit the gas, hunkering down as the grenade exploded behind him.

The grenade was enough of a diversion to keep the bodyguard from following, but either one of his bullets or the shrapnel from them punctured Karr's rear tire. He didn't notice until he hit the main street and tried to turn; by then the air had run out completely and the rubber shell was so mangled that it whipped off with a screech a cat might make if its skin was pulled from its body. Karr felt the bike shifting abruptly to its side. He tried to let it fall beneath him, hoping to walk away from the wipeout just as he would have done as a teenager on his uncle's farm a few years before. But Karr's foot caught on the frame of the bike; knocked off balance, he spun around and landed on his back in the middle of the street.

Karr jumped to his feet just in time to narrowly miss being run over by a bus. He tried chasing it down to hop on the back, but it was moving too fast and there were no good handholds besides.

"Hey, Charlie," he said, continuing down the block. "I need a lift."

"He's circling back for you," said Rockman. "Run to the north."

"Which way is north?" said Karr.

"Take the next left. Bodyguards have gone back to the building," added Rockman. "Cam Tre Luc is really angry."

"Guess he's not the guy we're looking for, huh?"

"I wouldn't be too sure about that, Mr. Karr," said Rubens from the Art Room. "Let's give it some time and see what develops. For now, please get as far away from the area as possible."

"Good idea, boss," said Karr, hearing Dean's bike approaching in the distance.

61

MARIE TELACH TURNED to Rubens.

"We'll have Cam Tre Luc's voice patterns analyzed," she said. "But I'd say his surprise seemed fairly genuine. I don't think he was the one communicating with Forester."

"No," said Rubens. He folded his arms.

"Is it worth sending anyone north to check on the last possibility?" asked Telach. "Thao Duong looks like he's got to be involved."

Thao Duong was involved in *something*, thought Rubens. That much was clear.

"He's positioned perfectly to funnel money from the government to the people in America," continued Telach. "He speaks with people in different American cities."

"True," admitted Rubens. "But how would Forester have found him? And why would he think he'd talk?"

"Because a source here told him he would. Or he knew something about his background."

"Yes," said Rubens vaguely. He wasn't convinced. "What's the third man's name?"

"Phuc Dinh. A minor government official in the area near Da Nang," said Telach.

"Have Charlie contact him. Mr. Karr can continue watching Thao Duong. Have him keep his distance. Let's give the intercepts a few days and see what they turn up."

RUBENS WAS JUST picking up the phone to call Collins at the CIA and update her when National Security Advisor Donna

Bing called wanting to know what the status of the "Vietnam thing" was. He gave her a brief rundown.

"So this Thao Duong is in the middle of it," said Bing, her excitement obvious. "Can you get him to talk?"

"I'm not sure that he is in the middle of it," said Rubens. "I'm not even sure there is anything for him to be in the middle of."

"No need to be so circumspect, Bill. You're not talking to the Senate. I suggest we pick him up and talk to him."

"I believe I'd need a little more information before I went ahead and *picked him up*," said Rubens. "We'll require a finding."

A "finding" was an order based on specific intelligence, approved by the NSC and signed by the President directing Desk Three to take a certain action. Activities that had the potential of causing extreme international trouble—like forcibly kidnapping an official of a foreign government in his home country in a nonemergency situation—could only be carried out pursuant to a finding. It usually took at least two meetings of the NSC before one was prepared.

"Don't worry about the finding," Bing told him. "I'll arrange that. Are you in a position to bring him back?"

"Certainly if he volunteers to come back, we can accommodate him," said Rubens.

"That's not what we're talking about."

"I can have a full team in place seventy-two hours after the finding," said Rubens.

"Get it in place now."

Rubens hung up. Was Bing being overly aggressive because she wanted to prove her theory about Vietnam and the Chinese? Or was he being more cautious than warranted?

Rubens couldn't be sure. The one thing he did know was this: for a man who prided himself on being logical and unemotional under pressure, he felt a great deal of foreboding every time he spoke to Donna Bing on the phone.

62

"LO IS COMPLAINING that you stiffed him," Kelly Tang told Dean early the morning after the adventures at Saigon Rouge. They'd arranged to meet for breakfast at Saolo, a cafe near his hotel. "He wants five thousand U.S. from me."

"I would have paid if I saw him," Dean told her. "And I only owe him five hundred, not five thousand."

"You should pay him. If you don't, I'll have to, just to shut him up."

"I will," said Dean. "Eventually."

Tang folded her arms. "It's not easy developing people, especially people like Lo. They're a necessary evil."

Dean slipped his hand into his pocket and retrieved the envelope with Lo's five hundred dollars. "So pay him."

Tang frowned. "It's not counterfeit, I hope. He'll know the difference."

"It's not counterfeit."

Tang took the money and slipped it into the waistband of her pants.

"I need another favor," said Dean.

"What?"

"I need to get to Quang Nam," Dean told her. "I need a driver I can trust."

"Quang Nam?"

"It's a province near the DMZ."

"I know where Quang Nam is," said Tang curtly. "And there is no more DMZ. The war ended a long time ago."

"Sorry."

"A driver? Why don't you fly to Da Nang?"

"I prefer to drive."

The real reason was that the airports were always watched and Dean didn't want to be seen traveling around any more than necessary. Besides, he'd need a vehicle once he was in Quang Nam.

"You can come if you want," added Dean. "I'm going to Tam Ky."

"I can't. I'm sorry, I have too much to do here. I'll find you a driver, though. Trustworthy. To a point."

Dean started to interrupt, but she continued, explaining what she meant.

"We're in Vietnam. No one is completely trustworthy. Not even yourself. Don't worry. She's nothing like Lo."

"She?"

"You have a problem with women?"

Dean shook his head.

"You won't be able to use your same cover," Tang told him. "You'll have to say you're an aid worker. It will arouse less suspicion. With her. She doesn't like conglomerates. It'll be easier."

"OK."

"How soon do you want to leave?"

"As soon as possible. Today would be good."

Tang frowned. "I'll do the best I can. No guarantees."

Dean took a sip of tea, then nibbled on the sugared pastry he'd ordered blind off the menu. It was made of very thin layers of what he thought was phyllo dough and enough sugary syrup to send a dentist's entire family to college. Karr would have loved it; Dean found it far too sweet but was too hungry not to eat.

"I heard there was some excitement in District Four last night," said Tang.

"Oh?"

"There were some explosions in a house of ill repute. The police were even called."

"Don't know anything about it."

"I'll bet."

Tang smiled, then reached across the table and put her hand down on his.

"You'll be careful?" she said.

"Sure."

"I like you, Mr. Dean. You're old-school." Tang patted his hand, then got up. "Check your phone messages in about an hour."

Dean thought about the soft tap of Tang's hand as he walked back to his hotel.

"ARE YOU COMING for me, Charlie?"

Dean blinked his eyes open. He'd dozed off.

"Charlie?"

It was Longbow, calling him. He was in the sniper nest, waiting for Phuc Dinh.

A dream. It's a dream.

"Charlie? Are you coming? Charlie?"

The air began popping with gunfire.

Charlie?

"YOUR DRIVER IS downstairs," said Rockman, talking to Dean via the Deep Black com system. "Charlie—are you awake?"

The phone rang. Dean jerked upright in the bed. He'd lain back to rest and drifted off.

He'd seen Longbow in his dream. And Phuc Dinh. They were both alive.

Nonsense.

"Answer the phone, Charlie," said Rockman. "Are you there?"

"I'm here, Rockman." Dean picked it up. "Yes?"

"Mr. Dean?"

"I'm Charles Dean."

"You need someone to take you to Quang Nam?"

"Yes."

"I'm in the lobby."

"I'll be there in five minutes."

LIA PACED AROUND the hotel room, unable to sleep though it was going on 1:00 A.M. After meeting with Mandarin, she'd spent the day and much of the night with an FBI agent who was checking on three different disgruntled constituents of McSweeney's, in and around New York City and Westchester. The only thing she'd learned was that FBI agents had a particularly poor sense of direction.

More and more, the whole thing seemed like a wild-goose chase.

Then again, what Deep Black assignment hadn't?

Maybe tomorrow would be better. Lia had an appointment with the doctor who'd examined Forester's body the night he was found.

She sank into the chair at the side of the room and flipped on the television. The volume blared, even though she had her finger on mute.

The person in the next room banged on the wall.

"Sorry," Lia said, turning it down.

Lia trolled through the channels. There was nothing on that interested her. She left it playing and went to the window, staring out at the stars, thinking of Charlie Dean.

Vietnam was eleven hours ahead—it'd be around noon.

"Hope you're doing better than I am, Charlie," she whispered to the night.

ORIGINALLY, JIMMY FINGERS thought of it the way he thought of any grand election strategy: a story for the voters. It had an arc and a hero. It also had a set end point, which they'd reached.

But like all good campaign strategies, this one had been overtaken by events. It had succeeded incredibly. Yet there were also signs of problems. Not only were Secret Service people everywhere; now there were FBI agents and U.S. marshals and for all he knew CIA officers combing through the files and shaking the trees for suspects. With that many people involved, someone was bound to stumble onto something that would upset the overall campaign. They might begin focusing on the wrong things. He could easily lose control of the narrative.

"Another Scotch?" asked the bartender, pointing at Jimmy's glass.

There was a shout and applause from the other room, where several hundred campaign workers had gathered to watch television coverage of the primary results. Senator McSweeney, upstairs taking a shower, would be down in an hour to declare an unprecedented victory in the Super Tuesday polls. With the exception of Arkansas, where he'd taken a close second to the state's favorite-son candidate, McSweeney had swept.

It was all due to the assassination attempt. Not so much because it had made McSweeney seem sympathetic as well as important, but because it had given people a chance to listen to his message. So maybe the senator had been right after all—maybe sticking with the issue spots at a time when there was plenty of "soft" news about his personality was the right thing to do.

He'd mention that, Jimmy thought, glancing up at the television screen to see that the media had just put Florida in the McSweeney column. Jimmy Fingers lifted his Scotch in a toast to the state and its electoral votes.

Jimmy Fingers' phone buzzed. He pulled it from his pocket, knowing it was McSweeney.

"So?" asked the senator. "What do you say?"

"Have a quick drink and come on down," said Jimmy Fingers. "I'd invite you to join me at the bar, but I'm not sure you'd make it through the crowd."

"I'm coming down right now," said McSweeney. "Meet me backstage."

"You got it." Jimmy Fingers snapped the phone closed and downed his drink before getting off the stool.

Yes, the story definitely needed a new direction, just to keep it going.

65

QUI LAI CHU was not what Dean expected. For one thing, she was considerably older—his age, he guessed, though it showed mostly at the corners of her eyes. She was also taller than most Vietnamese. It turned out that she had a French mother—a fact Rockman supplied as Dean followed her to her car, a two-year-old immaculately white Hyundai parked in front of the hotel.

"Grandfather was in the French diplomatic corps. Mother married a Vietnamese—well, that's obvious from the name, huh?"

Dean grunted.

Qui took two quick steps and opened the rear door of the car.

It felt odd, having a woman open the door for him.

"I thought I'd sit in the front with you," said Dean. "If that's OK."

"Your bag?"

"I'll just keep it with me. It's not a problem." Among other things, Dean had his Colt in it, and preferred to keep it close.

Qui bent her head slightly, indicating that she understood, and went around to the other side of the car. She moved with a grace that seemed to take possession of the space around her.

"Where in Quang Nam are we going?" she asked when she got behind the wheel.

"The capital. Tam Ky."

"One thousand American. You pay for gas and meals," she said. "And lodging. We won't be able to go and come back in the same day, unless you have very little business."

"My business may take several days," Dean told her.

She bent her head again. "Two hundred for each additional day."

"Do you want to be paid in advance?" Dean asked.

"I trust you for when we get back, or I wouldn't be here. The weapon that you have in your bag—you won't need it."

"I hope not," said Dean.

"Vietnam is safer than you think, Mr. Dean. I'm surprised that your superiors at the International Fund allow you to travel with a weapon."

"I don't tell them everything."

Qui put her key in the ignition and started the car. She pulled out smoothly into the stream of motorbikes, blending with them as she wended toward the highway.

"Saigon is very different from when you were here during the war, is it not, Mr. Dean?" she asked.

"How do you know I was here during the war?"

"A guess. You look at the city in a certain way. I have seen this before."

"I was here during the war," said Dean. "In Saigon for a few days. Most of my time was in Quang Nam."

"You were in the Army?"

"Marines."

"Ahh," said Qui, as if this explained everything.

"What did you do during the war?" Dean asked.

Qui's lip curled with a smile, but it faded before she spoke. "The war lasted a long time, Mr. Dean."

"You can call me Charlie."

"It was a long war, Mr. Dean. It began before I was born. I grew old well before it was over."

Qui didn't elaborate. Dean turned his attention to the scenery. The factories, office buildings, and apartments gave way to stretches of green. Houses poked out from behind the foliage in the distance, as if they were playing a child's game of hide-and-seek. The trucks that passed from the other direction were mostly Japanese made, though here and there Dean was surprised by a Mack dump truck and a GMC Jimmy, among others. A half hour out of Saigon, Dean spotted an old American tank left from the war sitting off the road. Though surrounded by weeds, the tank appeared freshly painted, its olive green skin glistening in the sun.

Dean kept his cover story ready, expecting Qui to ask about it. His preparation wasn't necessary, however; she seemed to have no interest in small talk, let alone quizzing him about his bona fides. He wondered why Tang told him he needed a new cover until they passed a large piece of bulldozed land off the highway in the Central Highlands, more than two hours after setting out. Qui muttered something loudly to herself as they passed, then realized Dean had heard her.

"They tear down everything," she said. *"Pourri,"* she added, beginning a riff in very profane French about corrupt corporations and equally corrupt government officials raping the land. She spoke far too quickly for Dean's very limited French, but the depth of her feeling was clear.

"Without the curses, she said, 'Corporations and politicians suck,'" Rockman told him.

"I guess I didn't catch too much of that," Dean told her. "But you're angry about the bulldozers?"

Qui smirked. "It's a beautiful country."

"It is."

"You're only just realizing that?"

Dean stared at her, noticing again the lines around the corners of her eyes. They looked softer now.

"I didn't appreciate beauty the first time I was here," he told her.

"Do you now?"

"As I got older, I started to see things differently."

There was a knot of traffic ahead. Without answering him, or even making a sign that she had heard, Qui turned her full attention to the car, maneuvering to pass.

Dean stared out the passenger-side window. A man plowed a field with an ox-drawn plow, struggling to overturn the earth. Smoke curled in the distance, a small brush fire set to remove debris.

The scene was both common and familiar. His brain plucked a similar one at random from its memory—an image from a helicopter, a flight out to Khe Sahn early in his tour here, when he was still being tested.

When he was still fresh meat.

"You're here to assuage your guilt," said Qui.

"How's that?" Dean asked.

"You're a do-gooder. Most do-gooders, if they're not young, are making up for something. You're making up for the war, aren't you?"

"I don't think so," Dean answered without thinking. Belatedly, he realized he should have said she was right—it fit with his cover.

"It's all right," said Qui. She turned and smiled at him. "I'm a bit of a do-gooder myself."

66

TOMMY KARR TOOK a sip of the white liquid, swished it around in his mouth, then swallowed.

"Good?" asked the old man who had offered it to him.

"Good's a relative concept," squeaked Karr. The liquid tasted like digested coconut mixed with rubbing alcohol.

"You want?"

"I'll take a Coke, I think."

The man gave Karr a small bottle of the cola. Karr held out a ten-thousand-dong note for the man. A look of disappointment spread across the vendor's face.

"No American?"

"How much American?"

"Ten dollar."

"For a Coke? I want soda, not cocaine."

The old man didn't understand.

"One dollar," said Karr, reaching into his pocket.

"Five dollar."

"Then I pay in Vietnamese."

"Two."

"Tommy, Thao Duong is leaving his office," warned Rockman from the Art Room. "He told his supervisor he's going for lunch."

"Here, take the soda back." Karr thrust it into his hand.

"OK, Joe. One dollar."

"Next time!" said Karr over his shoulder as he jogged for the bike.

"Fifty cent!" sputtered the old man. "Dime! You pay dime!"

KARR REACHED THE front of the office building just as Thao Duong came out. The Vietnamese official turned left, heading in the opposite direction. Karr turned at the corner, then spun into a U-turn, barely missing two bicyclists and another motorcycle.

"Don't get into a traffic accident," hissed Rockman.

"You know, Rockman, you take all the fun out of this job," said Karr.

As he joined the flow of traffic on the main street, Karr saw Thao Duong walking about a block ahead. He was headed down in the direction of the port, just like yesterday. Karr drove ahead four blocks, pulled up on the sidewalk, and parked. Then he leaned back against the side of the building, waiting for Thao Duong to catch up.

Karr was still waiting ten minutes later.

"Tommy, what's going on?" asked Marie Telach.

"Must've gotten waylaid somewhere," said Karr, starting up the street in search of Thao Duong.

"All right, it's not a crisis if you lose him," said the Art Room supervisor. "He may be trying to spot you."

"Gee, thanks, Mom. Hadn't thought of that," said Karr.

Karr checked the storefronts along the street as nonchalantly as he could. When he reached the block where he had spotted Thao Duong earlier, Karr turned right down the cross street. There were a dozen noodle shops lined up on both sides of the block. He guessed that Thao Duong was inside one, having an early dinner, but most were located in the basements of the buildings and it would have been difficult to spot him without being seen himself.

"What's the situation, Tommy?" asked Telach.

"Must be having lunch somewhere down this block," said Karr. "No way to find out without exposing myself."

"Hang back then."

Karr felt his stomach growl. He was debating whether he

might not go into the noodle places anyway when he spotted someone who looked like Thao Duong coming up from one of the shops near the end of the block. Karr slapped a video bug on the light pole near him, then walked up the street.

"That him?" he asked the Art Room.

"That's him," said Rockman.

"You see where he came out of?"

"He was already walking when the bug turned on. Why? You think he met someone there?"

"No, I'm starting to get hungry and I was hoping for a recommendation."

67

IT WAS STARTING to get dark by the time Dean and Qui reached Pleiku, a city in the Central Highlands roughly three-fourths of the way to Tam Ky. The streets were unlit, but Qui had no trouble navigating, driving down a small side street and stopping in front of a two-story stone building whose facade was covered with moss. Dean felt a surge of adrenaline as he got out of the car; they'd been driving so long that he was glad to have his feet on the pavement again. He took his bag and walked into the house behind Qui, muscles tensing, ready for action.

An older man in dark blue denim pants and shirt greeted them inside a small foyer. The man knew Qui, though he had not been expecting her. When Qui told him in Vietnamese that they needed two rooms for the night, he led them inside to a small room that was used as both a living room and office.

"You're going to have to pay, Charlie," Rockman reminded him. "That's the custom. It's cash up front."

Dean bristled at Rockman's interference but said nothing. The fee for both rooms came to ten dollars.

"His wife will make us something to eat," Qui told Dean as they walked toward their rooms. "There's a terrace in the back. It will be pleasant there."

"I'll see you there," Dean told her.

DURING THE WAR, an American base known as Camp Holloway had been located just outside Pleiku, on the site of an old French air base. Helicopter transports and gunships, light observation and ground-support airplanes used the base. It had been attacked by Vietcong many times. The nearby city had suffered greatly; much of Pleiku had been burned during the North's final offensive after the Americans left.

"He's offering to take you to the old base tomorrow," Qui told Dean, translating the old man's offer of a tour. The hotel proprietor clearly thought Dean was a visiting veteran who had fought here and wanted to see what had become of the place.

"No, thanks," Dean said. "I'd like to get to Quang Nam as quickly as possible."

Even before Qui translated, the old man's disappointment was clear. He told her that Dean was not a man with much curiosity or interest in the world. Qui softened his assessment when she translated it for him.

"You're not very nostalgic," she told Dean.

"I guess I'm not."

"Did you serve near here?"

Dean shook his head.

"Of course not," said Qui, remembering what he had told her earlier. "You were a Marine. You would have been near Da Nang or Khe Sahn, or up in Quang Nam. Where we're going."

Marines had served in other places throughout the country, but Dean didn't correct her. She was, after all, right on the crucial point.

"Is that why you're going back?" she asked.

"It's a coincidence."

"Really?" she asked, but she let it drop.

The old man began talking about how much better things were when he was young. It wasn't clear from what he said exactly what was better or why—except that he was younger. Dean listened to him describing the countryside and the villages. There was no running water and no electricity. The villagers sold fresh fruit to people in the city, and got prices good enough to live on.

"We had a great festival for Vu Lan Bôn," said the old

man. "From many, many miles, people would gather to honor their ancestors."

"What kind of holiday is that?" Dean asked.

"It's Buddhist. Bôn. The fifteenth day of the seventh month. For ancestors who have gone to the Holy Land," said Qui.

"The hungry ghosts," added the old man's wife. "If you do not feed your dead, they wander the world, hungry."

It was the living who wandered if the dead were not peacefully at rest, Dean thought to himself, but he said nothing.

68

THAO DUONG WENT home after eating. Karr followed, keeping his distance as the Art Room had directed earlier. Shortly after he sat down at the café a block away, Marie Telach came on the line with new instructions.

"Tommy, we want to be in a position to pick up Thao Duong if necessary. You're going to have to find a way to get a tracking bug on him."

"Aw, man."

"I don't think it will be impossible. I was thinking you could plant one of the horseshoe bugs in his shoe. We've done that in heels before. We saw on one of the surveillance shots that he wears thick Western-style dress shoes."

"Nah, that's not what I was complaining about. It'll be easy. But I was just about to order some food," Karr said, getting up. "Now I have to get back to work."

"Didn't you just eat?"

"Snacks from street vendors don't count," said Karr.

He found a shoe repairman whose shop was still open a few blocks away. Considering the language barrier—even with the translator talking in Karr's ear, he struggled to get the tones right—he thought he did fairly well to buy an entire shoe repair set for fifty bucks. The cobbler even had his apprentice shine Karr's shoes as part of the deal.

He was wearing sneakers, so it wasn't much of a shine. Still, the thought was there.

Karr hoped that Thao Duong would veg out in front of the television and call it an early night; he'd break into the apartment and doctor the Vietnamese bureaucrat's shoes once he was sleeping. But around eight o'clock, Thao Duong put on his things and went downstairs to his own motorbike.

Karr had already bugged the bike, so he let Thao Duong stay about two blocks ahead. It wasn't long before Karr realized where they were going—the same red-light district that Cam Tre Luc had visited the night before.

"Ten bucks he's headed to Saigon Rouge," said Rockman. "I had a hunch these guys were connected."

"Where's my ten bucks?" said Karr as Thao Duong passed by the street where Saigon Rouge was.

"He'll come back," said Rockman. "Don't get too close."

Karr turned to parallel Thao Duong as he drove deeper in District 4. Finally Rockman reported that Thao Duong had stopped a few blocks away.

The buildings in the area Karr drove through were mostly one-story shacks, a patchwork of mismatched metal and discarded wood. Men clustered in the shade of the streetlights, eying the large motorcycle driver suspiciously.

Thao Duong had stopped on a block with large buildings, five- and six-story warehouses made of crumbling cement. Karr spotted the bike in front of a narrow five-story building whose bottom-floor windows were covered with pieces of cardboard boxes and whose upper windows were empty. He circled the block. A chain-link fence topped with barbed wire set off a tiny junkyard immediately behind the building. As soon as Karr stopped, a trio of large dogs ran at him, smashing into the fence as they yapped.

"Guess I'll wait somewhere else," he told the dogs, revving the bike and driving away.

"Thao Dung's bike is moving," Rockman said.

"You sure?"

"Bike's moving. I don't know if he's on it."

"Yeah, around here, it could easily have been stolen," said Karr. He zipped around the block, but rather than following Thao Duong, he cruised slowly in front of the building where he had been, pulled a U-turn at the end of the block, and came back.

"Tommy, what are you doing?" asked Rockman.

"We can always find the bike," explained Karr.

He pulled his bike up on the curb, and cruised slowly down the sidewalk to the front of the building. Though uneven, the cement was in far better shape than the nearby structures. Karr stopped next to a telephone pole, casually steadying himself there with his left hand—and planting two video bugs at the same time.

A fireplug of a man came out of the building, yelling at Karr in Vietnamese. Karr waved at the man, then gunned the bike away.

"Are you interested in knowing what he said?" asked the translator in the Art Room.

"I'm thinking it had something to do with my ancestry," laughed Karr.

"Good guess."

"Thao Duong's bike is back at his apartment," said Rockman. "It was him—he's inside. OK, we're listening to him."

"You have any information on that building?" Karr asked.

"Negative."

"See what you can dig up for me. I'll check it out later, once the genealogist goes to sleep."

By the time Karr got to Thao Duong's apartment, Thao Duong had already gone upstairs and was watching a Vietnamese soap opera. Karr cruised the neighborhood, making sure he hadn't been followed, then found a restaurant several blocks away where he could get something to eat while waiting for Thao Duong to go to bed.

Three plates of Vietnamese barbecue ribs, two dishes of steamy noodles with shrimp, and a whole chicken later, Thao Duong was still awake and watching television.

"Didn't anyone ever tell him that stuff rots your mind?" Karr told Rockman when he gave him the update.

"Guess you'll just have to chill."

"Yeah. Good thing I saved room for dessert."

69

THE DOCTOR WHO had examined Forester was one of three part-time coroners, all paid a modest retainer by the county to be on call. Full-time, he was a general practitioner, and his days were very full—or at least his office was when Lia went to see him. Even so, he squeezed her in between two appointments without her having to read more than one of the issues of *Glamour* magazine piled in the waiting room.

"Do you get a lot of gunshot wounds up here?" Lia asked, after the doctor had reviewed the basics of the autopsy report.

"I know what you're getting at." He smiled, but there was an edge to his voice. "Small-town guy, looks at a homicide maybe once or twice a year, if that. Right? Part-time guy. How's he supposed to know what he's looking at, right?"

"It crossed my mind."

"Admittedly, we don't have many homicides here. Which is why the coroners are part-time."

He reached down and pulled a file from the bottom drawer of his desk, opened it, and slid a photo forward. It showed what the bullet had done to the back of Forester's head. Lia had seen a black-and-white copy; it looked more gruesome in color.

"I have seen that sort of thing before," said the doctor. "A lot, actually. I worked in trauma medicine in New York City for about five years after my internship. I have to tell you, this is a textbook case."

Lia leafed through the rest of the photos the doctor had.

Most hadn't been included in the formal report, though nothing in them jumped out at her.

"The Secret Service has copies of the report," said the doctor. "They had their own doctors look at the body, of course."

"Isn't it true, though, that you can't tell whether it was suicide from the wounds?" Lia asked. "Someone could have held the gun to his mouth."

"Technically, you're right. But his mouth was closed around the barrel, the direction of the bullet was exactly as you'd expect if he were holding it himself, there were no signs that he was being held down or that he'd been in a fight."

"He'd had some drinks."

"Sure. His blood alcohol content was oh-point-one-one. Legally intoxicated if he were driving, but not stumbling-down drunk. He wouldn't have been unconscious. The pathology report on the organs was handled by the state police initially. They all came back negative. There weren't any signs of drug abuse, no pills at the scene. Really does look like a suicide. I've seen a couple like this. Very ugly."

Lia put the report and photos back in the folder. Staging a death to make it look like suicide wasn't impossible, and despite what the doctor said, she still had her doubts that he was expert enough to pick it up. But the police had said the same thing.

So was she resisting? Because she knew a little about Forester?

"Depression is a funny thing," said the doctor, finally finished sending the files. "We look for logic, but sometimes it's not there." He rose. "I know people have a hard time with suicides. Accepting it. But I think it's pretty clear that's what happened in this case."

70

THAO DUONG'S BEDROOM floor was filled with dust. Tommy Karr's nose started twitching as soon as he got down on all fours and began creeping toward the side of the bed, where the Vietnamese bureaucrat had dropped his shoes. Karr stopped twice to suppress sneezes, pinching his nose closed and holding his breath.

The second time he stopped, he felt something run over the back of his thigh.

A mouse? Or a very large centipede?

Karr clamped his hand over his mouth, leaned forward as quietly as he could, and grabbed Thao Duong's left shoe. Then Karr sat back and rolled onto his side, doing a modified sidestroke to the door. Karr got to his feet in the next room but kept holding his breath until he was outside on the fire escape. As soon as he had closed the window behind him, he began coughing and gasping for air at the same time.

"Tommy, are you OK?" asked Marie Telach from the Art Room.

"Just need some chicken soup," he told her.

"Jeez, aren't you full yet?" asked Rockman.

Karr checked his pants and shirt, making sure that he wasn't covered with insects. Then he went to work on Thao Duong's shoe. The heel was easily removed, but there was a problem—it was so worn that not even the slim transmitter would fit inside. Karr settled for placing two of the much smaller temporary trackers, which not only had a much more limited range but also would send signals for at best twelve to sixteen hours.

Karr ransacked his brain and examined the feed from the surveillance bugs, trying to think of an alternative hiding spot, but Thao Duong's relatively bare existence made it impossible. He didn't use a briefcase or a mobile phone. Karr would have to return the following night to replace the bugs.

And maybe the dust. He pulled off his shirt, planning to use it to clean the floor so it wouldn't be obvious from his marks in the soot that someone had come in.

"All right," he told Rockman finally. "I'm going back into the apartment. Hopefully I won't sneeze."

Thao Duong had begun to snore loudly. Karr's nose began to itch as soon as he tiptoed across the threshold. He slid the shoe into place, then began dusting.

A centipede scurried under Thao Duong's bed as Karr backed out of the room.

At least it wasn't a rat, Karr thought to himself, retreating from the house.

THERE WERE PLENTY of rats in the building Thao Duong had visited earlier, including a pair with two legs who were sleeping in the front vestibule, pistols in their laps.

Karr could see both men from the landing of the second-floor hallway where he climbed in through the side window. He positioned a video bug so Rockman could keep an eye on them, then moved down two steps and lowered a video bug from a telescoping wand to examine the rest of the first floor.

The open, loftlike space was crowded with sewing machines and large, empty shelves and bobbins where fabric and thread had been stored.

It was also well populated with vermin, who were running laps between the refuse.

Karr went back up the stairs and slipped over to the doorway to the second floor. If there had ever been a door here, it was long gone, as were the hinges and any other trace. This room, too, was open, though there were no machines—only wall-to-wall bodies.

Karr tacked a video bug on the wall, then tiptoed to the nearest figure, huddled fetuslike on the bare wood floor. The man wore only a pair of shorts. His chest moved in and out fitfully; except for that, there was no sign he was alive. Near him were three children, also each wearing only one piece of clothing, each with a hand wrapped over another's shoulder.

"Must be a hundred people here," whispered Karr.

"We count one hundred and two," said Rockman.

Karr backed out quietly, then crept up the steps to the third floor. The space appeared to be totally abandoned; overturned chairs sat under a thick layer of dust in the middle of the floor. With his nose starting to revolt, Karr went up to the fourth and last floor. This, too, was empty; large pieces of the ceiling hung down, and here and there he caught glimpses of the moonlight shining through the cracks.

"I can't imagine that place was a whorehouse," Karr told Rockman, placing another video bug near the doorway.

"Just a flophouse," said Thu De Nghiem. Then the translator added bitterly, "Uncle Ho's legacy."

"So what was our guy doing here before, you think?" Rockman asked.

"Maybe he's going to take some of that rice he tracks for the government and give it to these people," said the translator.

"Somehow I doubt that," said Karr. He slipped back down the steps toward the window he had used to get in. Just as he reached the landing, Rockman warned Karr that one of the people in the room on the second floor had woken.

"Sitting up," said Rockman, his voice stopping Karr mid-step.

He was only about six feet from the window, but he'd have to pass in front of the doorway to get there. Karr leaned back against the wall.

"Another person, two more, awake," reported Rockman. "Kids. They're coming to the door."

Karr climbed back up the stairs, his back against the wall. He reached the third-floor landing just as three girls, roughly ten years old, came out of the room and went down the steps.

"Going out into the back," said Rockman.

"Probably to relieve themselves," added the translator.

"Tommy, the guards are moving," said Rockman.

Karr went back down to the second floor, opened the window, and began climbing down. As he did, he heard an angry shout from inside. He jumped to the ground; rolling to his feet, he grabbed his gun, ready.

But the guards weren't coming for him.

One of the girls started to scream.

"Get out of there, Tommy!" said Rockman. "Go!"

ONCE THE PAPERWORK cleared, Gallo began probing comput-ers overseas to see if he could snag anything interesting. He sent e-mails to computers owned by people he could track down; the e-mails contained what were essentially viruses that would help him ferret out his prey. It was a bit like fish-ing without bait, however; it might be hours before the e-mail was even opened.

Bored, he considered going home and getting some sleep—for about five seconds. Instead, he went to the lounge, got two Red Bulls, and came back and started looking through the in-house blog to see what the analysts had found in the data he'd help them compile.

Two things stood out. One, a lot of the people whom he had tracked down in the States didn't exist—their names didn't match the Social Security numbers on their bank accounts.

And two, their bank accounts were as empty as his was.

"Their bank accounts look like mine," Gallo told the empty lab. "They're all scraping by."

It was a definite pattern, but what did it mean?

Gallo did what he always did when he couldn't figure something out—he lay down on the floor and stared at the ceiling.

Maybe they just used cash.

Sure. If they had it.

So many people without money, though?

So many Vietnamese people.

Actually, most of the names didn't look Vietnamese; they were Chinese: Chan, Wang.

There were ethnic Chinese in Vietnam. A lot of them.

Why would you need so many people in a network to assassinate someone?

Well, they weren't real people. Or they were real, but their Social Security numbers were fake.

"Oh!" shouted Gallo, jumping up from the floor.

72

TOMMY KARR WAS a dedicated professional, personally chosen by William Rubens as a Desk Three op for his athletic abilities, intelligence, and good judgment under incredible pressure. Karr had disarmed a bomb under fire while dangling from the Eiffel Tower and captured a killer while sick with a life-threatening designer virus.

But Tommy Karr had one serious weakness: he could not ignore a cry for help from a little girl.

He made it to the backyard just as one of the two thugs was about to smack the girl a third time. Launching himself in the air, Karr put 280-some pounds into the man's back, crushing two of the man's vertebrae as he hammered him into the ground. For good measure, Karr broke the man's jaw and cheekbone with a hard right before jumping to his feet.

The man's companion let go of the girl and pulled out a pistol. Karr never saw the weapon—he'd already set himself into motion, bowling into his enemy before the man could click off the safety and take aim. The gun fell to the ground, as did the Vietnamese thug. Karr kicked his face soccer-style, snapping something in the man's neck.

"Tommy, what the hell is going on?" demanded Rockman.

Karr ignored the runner. He scooped up the fallen gun and went to the three girls, who were standing a few feet away. They stared at him in amazement, tears frozen on their cheeks by awe.

"Hey, ladies, are you all right?" asked Karr. He dropped

down to his knees, bringing his six-eight frame a little closer to their size.

"Yi," said one of the girls, her voice very low. She pointed at Karr. "Yi."

"Yeah. That's what it is," answered Karr. "Yi." He smiled and nodded his head. "Yi."

The other girls' mouths opened even wider. The tallest girl said something Karr couldn't understand; the others answered excitedly.

"Yi," they started to chant. "Yi."

"What's that mean?" Karr asked the translator in the Art Room.

"Haven't a clue. Those girls are speaking Chinese."

One of the girls started speaking in a soft voice. Karr nodded and smiled, hoping to encourage her. At the same time he glanced toward the thugs in the corner, making sure they were still out cold.

"Hey, Rockman, can you get someone to figure out what they're saying?"

"Stand by."

"Yi," said Karr. He pointed at them. "Yi."

The little girls laughed and pointed back. "Yi."

"Well, it's fun, whatever it is," said Karr. He started walking toward the corner of the building.

"Yi?" the tallest girl called after him. *"Nee chü nar?"*

"She wants to know where you are going," said a new translator, coming onto the Deep Black communications line. Her sweet voice reminded Karr of his girlfriend's. "Is she calling you Yi?"

"I guess."

"Hou Yi?"

"Huh?"

The translator gave him a phrase, which Karr repeated. This elicited a flood of sentences from the older girl.

"They think you are the Divine Archer Yi," explained the translator. "A mythological hero. Among other things, he shot down the sun."

"There's something I've never done."

"They want to know if you will take them to the boat," added the translator.

"Boat? What kind of boat?"

"America?" asked one of the girls.

"You want to go to America?" Karr asked in English.

Before the translator could give him the words, Rubens cut into the line.

"Mr. Karr, I think what you are dealing with here are refugees who are hoping to escape to America," said Rubens. "I believe we may find that Thao Duong is a snakehead, not an assassin. A snakehead," added Rubens dryly, anticipating Karr's next question, "is a person who illegally smuggles immigrants overseas."

73

RUBENS TURNED AWAY from the Art Room's main screen, sour and disappointed. He'd devoted an enormous amount of resources to discovering an illegal immigrant operation.

And that was all they had to show for an operation that had included a rather large number of intercepts, data searches, and field operations.

Dean hadn't spoken to Phuc Dinh yet; perhaps that would yield something definitive. But Infinite Burn seemed less than likely.

It could be very cleverly disguised and hidden, surely.

Robert Gallo rushed into the Art Room, breathlessly shouting Rubens' name.

"Mr. Gallo, what can I do for you?"

"Thao Duong is a people smuggler," said Gallo. "I've been analyzing his network and—"

"The term is 'snakehead,' " said Rubens. "Good work, Mr. Gallo. Ms. Telach, prepare a dossier of the pertinent information for the Immigration Service and FBI. And then get some sleep please. You, too, Mr. Gallo," Rubens added. "And by that I mean in a proper bed, at home, not on the floor of your lab."

GALLO RETURNED TO his lab to find Angela DiGiacomo beaming at him. He was feeling pretty confident after talking to Rubens—almost enough to ask for a date.

But she spoke first.

"You got something!" she said. "Another threatening e-mail to McSweeney."

"No shit?"

Gallo pulled out his seat and hunkered in front of the computer. Angela put her hand on his shoulder.

Not bad, he thought.

"Can you track it?" she asked.

"Maybe." He stared at the screen. "Probably," he said. His fingers started to fly around the keyboard.

Five minutes later, Gallo looked up from the computer and realized that Angela had left. He cursed silently to himself, then went back to work.

DRIVING BACK TO her hotel after speaking to the doctor, Lia wondered why she was so convinced that Forester hadn't killed himself. Was it the kid? Amanda Rauci? Or the fact that a Secret Service agent was supposed to be tough enough to stand up to standard strains and stresses, like a marriage gone bad?

Maybe Lia just didn't like the idea that someone could feel so bad he would want to kill himself. She'd fought so hard to live that she couldn't imagine the other side of things.

Her sat phone rang. It was Chris Farlekas, the relief Art Room supervisor. Lia, as she often did, had "forgotten" to turn her com system back on after lunch.

But he wasn't calling to scold her.

"We have something," Farlekas told her. "It's another e-mailed threat. We know where it came from. Ambassador Jackson is informing the Secret Service and FBI liaisons, but you may want to tell Mandarin about it yourself."

Farlekas explained the circumstances. The house was just north of Poughkeepsie, not far from the Taconic State Parkway or Pine Plains—but not close enough, Lia thought, to be the target of Forester's investigation.

"Go with them when they investigate," Farlekas added. "We can analyze the computer a lot quicker than their people can."

AT EIGHT STORIES high, Tam Ky's municipal building not only towered over the town but also dominated the jungle beyond, its white body standing like a ghost before a dark castle. From the distance, the building made the city seem larger than it truly was, the eye and brain adding bulk to the blocks around it out of a sense of proportion.

"I don't want you to get insulted," Dean told Qui as they parked. "But when we go in, I'm going to talk to him alone."

"I'm not insulted." Qui took the key from the ignition and opened her door.

There were more bicycles and motorbikes here than there were in Saigon, and many fewer cars. A large open square paved with pinkish brown stones sat before the municipal building at the center of town. Dean couldn't remember being in Tam Ky during the war, but he was sure it wouldn't have looked like this—bright and shining in the sun, the facades of the nearby buildings showing off new paint, the tree leaves so green they almost looked fake.

There were no guards, and no receptionist in the lobby as they entered. The floors and walls were polished stone.

"Second floor," Rockman told Dean. "Near the back."

Dean passed the information on to his interpreter, who simply assumed that Dean knew where the person was he'd come to meet. They walked up a wide flight of stairs at the side of the lobby, passing a large mural of Uncle Ho Chi Minh.

The office corridors were much less elaborate than the public area below. The carpet was well-worn and the hallways narrow. The doors to many of the offices were open, revealing mazelike interior passages and tiny cubicles separated by carpet-faced partitions. Dean didn't see more than two or three people as he passed.

Dean and Qui entered the second door from the end, turning until they found a woman sitting at a small desk.

"I'm here to see Phuc Dinh," Dean said in English. Qui translated.

"You have an appointment?" The young woman, who looked barely out of her teens, used English.

"No. But we have a mutual friend."

Dean meant Forester, but he thought of Longbow instead.

"Mr. Dinh is out this morning. We expect him back after lunch."

"Our friend's name is Forester," said Dean. "I'll be back after lunch."

He leaned against her desk, slipping an audio bug into place.

DEAN BOUGHT QUI lunch at a café a few blocks away. While the translator went to the restroom, Dean took out his satellite phone and pretended to be talking on it as he talked to the Art Room. He'd left a booster unit in the car, but it was a little out of range; the two bugs he'd planted at the office building were sending garbled signals.

"You're going to have to leave a booster much closer," said Rockman.

"All right, I'll do it as soon as I get rid of Qui."

"Do you think you'll be able to tap the building phone network?" Rockman asked.

"I'm not sure," said Dean. "There were no guards in the lobby. There looked like there was a door at the other side of the staircase. But anyone could come right down and see me."

"You could say you were lost."

Dean looked up and saw Qui returning.

"Yeah, well, I'll make sure to update you tonight," Dean said into the phone. "Take it easy."

Qui gave him a soft smile as she sat. "Reporting in?"

"Yeah."

"Did you know Phuc Dinh during the war, Mr. Dean?"

"No, I didn't."

"I know you're not here for your job, Mr. Dean. Not for the International Fund, at any rate."

"What would I be here for, if not that?"

"Your conscience would be my bet."

A waiter approached. Dean let Qui order two large bottles of water, and then meals.

"Do you remember the people you killed?" she asked when the waiter retreated.

"Some I remember," Dean told Qui honestly. "Every one of them wanted to kill me."

"I'm sure."

"What side were you on during the war?"

The waiter appeared with their water before Qui could answer. She waited until he was gone.

"The proper answer today in Vietnam, Mr. Dean, is that we were all on the same side. The proper answer is that we all fought for liberation in our own way."

"And what was your answer during the war?"

Qui sipped her water. She was a beautiful woman, Dean realized, too old to be pretty, but age had given her a presence that a younger woman could never emulate. She looked up at him and caught him staring; something flashed in her eyes—anger, maybe, or resentment—and then she looked down.

Dean, too, changed the direction of his gaze, turning his head and looking across the street. Two girls were jumping rope in front of a small shop across from the café. One wore a matched top and pants in pink; the other had Western-style jeans, complete with sequins down the side. They were laughing and singing a counting song as they skipped over the rope.

"Many times I have driven men who came to the country as a kind of penance as well as curiosity," said Qui. "I think it odd, apologizing for necessity."

"Maybe that's not what they're apologizing for."

"Maybe not."

"I won't need you to come back with me," Dean told Qui. "You can take the rest of the afternoon off. I'll see you for dinner."

She nodded slightly.

Neither of them spoke as they ate. Dean wanted to ask her about the country—ask what it was like now, and what it had been like when she was growing up. He felt an urge to ask a lot of questions, not just of her, but of everyone in the country: if the North had been defeated, would things have been better? But he couldn't.

AFTER LUNCH, DEAN took a seemingly aimless walk around town. He spotted a Dumpster behind the municipal building that would serve as a perfect hiding spot for the signal booster; pretending to toss out a bag he'd found in the road, he slid the device under the Dumpster.

"Much better, Charlie," said Rockman. "Thanks."

Dean took another walk. When he returned to the municipal building, he walked inside, strode to the steps at the back, and quickly opened the door to the basement. He couldn't find a light switch; he took out his key chain and used the small LED light he kept on it to guide him down the steps.

"Network interface is going to be somewhere in the western side of the basement," said Rockman, who'd been studying an aerial photo of the building. "At least it ought to be."

The only things in the basement were metal stanchions helping to support the floor, and miscellaneous utilities. Dean found the telephone network access boxes and the small computer they fed in the far corner of the basement. He took what looked like two large pens from his pocket, unscrewed the tops from them, and then put them together. Then he took a thick wire from his pocket and connected one end to the tops of the pens. Standing on his tiptoes, he slid the pen onto the block ledge where the telephone trunk wire came into the building. To finish off, he wrapped what looked like a Velcro strap around the trunk line and connected it to the wire he'd inserted into the pens.

Dean's device was a listening system that used the phone

line to send its data back to the Art Room. The device allowed the NSA to hear internal intercom calls, and made it easier to pick up regular calls as well.

Dean had one worrisome moment as he came up the steps. He had planted a pair of video bugs so the Art Room could warn him that someone was approaching, but the coverage left a blind spot on the second-story stairs right near the hallway entrance. As he came up out of the basement, turning to go up the main staircase, a young man confronted him, asking in angry Vietnamese what he had been doing.

The translator told Dean how to say that he was lost in Vietnamese, but Dean knew it would be considerably more effective to simply use English.

"Mr. Phuc Dinh? I can't find his office," said Dean. "Where is it?"

"Do you think we have offices in the basement?" demanded the man in Vietnamese.

Dean held up his hands. He took a piece of paper with Phuc Dinh's name on it from his pocket.

"Dinh," he told the man. "Phuc Dinh."

"You are an ignorant American," said the man in Vietnamese. Then he added in English, "Upstairs."

"He's still watching you, Charlie," warned Rockman as Dean went up the steps.

As long as he focused on his immediate tasks—moving the booster, bugging the phones, appearing nonthreatening to the suspicious worker—Dean was fine. The moment he reached Phuc Dinh's office, however, Dean hesitated, remembering Longbow, remembering the shot he'd taken some thirty-five years before.

How cruel was fate to bring him together with this man?

"Charlie, is something wrong?" asked Rockman.

Dean answered by knocking on the doorjamb, then going in to speak to the woman at the desk.

It was a different, older woman.

"I came earlier and left a message for Mr. Dinh," he told her in English. The woman didn't seem to understand and so he repeated the words the translator gave him in Vietnamese.

"What is this about?" asked the secretary.

"I'm not sure I should discuss Mr. Dinh's business with you," said Dean, carefully repeating the translator's words. He got the tone wrong at the end, and had to repeat it before the secretary understood.

She frowned, then got up from her desk and went to find Dinh.

There were photos on the wall—a ceremony with Phuc Dinh in a Vietnamese-style suit receiving a certificate, a parade, Phuc Dinh in a row of other men . . .

And one, much older, showing Phuc Dinh standing next to the charred wreckage of a Huey, smiling.

Anger surged over Dean, like the wave of a tsunami. It was the most useless emotion, a deadly emotion for anyone, most especially a sniper. To succeed, a sniper had to operate without anger. He could live with fear, he could live with sadness, but he could not operate with anger. When he stalked his enemy, he had to be emotionless, his movement and perception incorruptible by hate or lust. When he pushed against the trigger he had to be stone-cold steady, empty of anything that would blur his aim.

"He will see you," said the secretary, returning. "For a moment."

Dean tried not to think of Longbow as he walked to Phuc Dinh's office.

The man Charles Dean had killed sat behind a small metal desk, surrounded by paper. His hair was thinner, his face a little plumper, but his scar was the same, his eyes were the same, his nose and mouth precisely as Dean remembered. Dinh was a ghost rising from the past, a dead man who had not died.

"I am Phuc Dinh," he said in perfect English. "Who are you?"

"Charles Dean." Dean forced the words from his mouth. "Can we go somewhere and talk?"

"What about?"

"A mutual friend."

Dinh started to scowl.

"Gerald Forester," said Dean. "I believe you may have exchanged some e-mail with him."

"I don't think so."

I could kill him easily, Dean thought. I could drop to my knee, grab the gun at my ankle, shoot him. It would be done in three seconds.

"Forester was murdered," Dean said. "This won't go away."

Dean stared at Phuc Dinh, expecting that he would deny knowing Forester and tell him to leave. But to Dean's great surprise, he rose.

"Come with me," Phuc Dinh told him.

"He's telling his secretary he'll be back in a few hours," said the translator.

"Home run, Charlie," said Rockman. "Home run."

76

NONE OF THE houses in the subdivision looked any smaller than four thousand square feet, and if there was a single blade of grass out of place on any of the lawns, Lia couldn't see it through the high-powered night vision glasses.

"This doesn't look too good," she told Mandarin.

"Yeah. But you never know." Mandarin cruised past Meadowview Court, slowing to get a view of the front yard. It was a little before 5:00 A.M.; even the early birds hadn't gotten up yet.

"They have a wireless network without any security," said Lia. She held up her handheld computer; the screen showed that she had just successfully signed on. "Anybody could have used the network."

"Probably. Doesn't explain the gun questions and the chat rooms, though."

"I bet there's a teenage boy inside," said Lia. "One who plays basketball and is thinking he'd like to hunt."

She'd seen a basketball net and was guessing the rest.

"Maybe," admitted Mandarin. He jabbed his thumb toward the roof of the car. The helicopters delivering the tactical team were nearly overhead. "We'll know in a few minutes."

TWENTY FEDERAL AGENTS, backed up by six state troopers and their cars, had been assigned to raid the Hennemman residence, the origin of the latest e-mail threat—a vow to "finish what's been started"—against Senator McSweeney. The government had been granted a search warrant to seize the

Hennemmans' computers and other papers and material possibly related to the threat. The evidence was not just the e-mailed threat but also inquiries from a computer on the same home network in several public forums about weapons, rifles in particular.

Two members of a special DEA team took down the door; Mandarin and Lia came in right behind them. Within ninety seconds, the house had been searched and the three occupants of the house found themselves pinned in their beds by agents.

Lia helped secure the basement—nothing more threatening there than a dehumidifier—then came upstairs to find Mandarin holding his credentials out to Mrs. Hennemman, explaining what they were doing there. Her husband lay next to her, blinking up as if he wasn't sure whether this was part of a dream or not.

"Where are the computers?" Mandarin asked.

There were four in the house, including one that was packed away in a box.

"We want our lawyer," said Mrs. Hennemman belatedly.

"Give him a call," said Mandarin, handing her his cell phone. "We'll be downstairs."

"Do you know whether your wireless network is secure?" Lia asked.

"What's that?" said Mrs. Hennemman.

77

PHUC DINH LED Dean to a restaurant two blocks from the municipal building. He nodded at the maître d' as they entered, and walked straight to the back, taking a large table set with eight places. Within moments, two waiters appeared and whisked the extra places away.

"You will have a drink?" Phuc Dinh asked Dean.

"Water, please."

Phuc Dinh ordered two bottles, along with a pot of tea.

"It was a long time ago," he told Dean. "My memory may be faulty."

The comment disoriented Dean. He was confused, and for a moment he thought Phuc Dinh was talking about *his* mission, though that was impossible.

"I had not thought of the money for many years, or think that it was relevant," added Phuc Dinh. He stopped speaking as the waiter approached.

"What money?" asked Rockman in Dean's head.

Dean ignored the runner, trying not to show anything to Phuc Dinh, playing out the original bluff as if Forester had told him everything. He was a sniper again, a scout moving silently through the jungle, distractions and emotion in check.

"The war was a long time ago," prompted Dean as the waiter left. "There were other things to think of."

"The money was lost," said Phuc Dinh. "It never arrived at the hamlet."

"The hamlet was Phu Loc Two, wasn't it?" asked Dean. It

was a guess, but a good one—that was the village where he had stalked Phuc Dinh.

"Yes. Ordinarily a courier would arrive on the tenth of the month. He would bury the money beneath a rock on a trail about three miles out of town."

"The trail to Laos," said Dean.

Phuc Dinh nodded. "And then one month, it did not arrive."

"Which month?"

"September 1971."

Dean sipped some of the tea. The restaurant was not air-conditioned, and the temperature must have been well into the eighties, but despite the heat, it felt refreshing.

"There were complaints and threats from some of the leaders in the area," Phuc Dinh said. "A rebellion. I sent a message and requested that the liaison come and explain what had happened, but he would not come. I heard later that he was killed by a rocket attack."

"What was his name?"

"Greenfield." Phuc Dinh looked up at the wall behind Dean, as if reading the answer off it. "He called himself Green. But that wasn't his first name."

"Was he a soldier?"

"No. Soldiers—Marines—were used as the couriers. But Green was a civilian—CIA, I assume."

"Was his name Green*feld*?" asked Dean.

"Maybe."

"Jack Greenfeld was a CIA officer who worked in this area. He ran a number of programs," said Dean, who wanted the Art Room to know the background. "He worked in that area. Then he was killed by a rocket attack. He was replaced by a man named Rogers."

"You're familiar with the area?" said Phuc Dinh.

"Just some of the history."

"Maybe it is the same person. Green. I don't know what the arrangements were on the American side," said Phuc Dinh. "Only that payments were distributed to different elders."

"We're researching this, Charlie," said Rockman. "Keep him talking. What does this have to do with Forester?"

Dean had already guessed the answer to Rockman's question.

"What happened after the money stopped?" Dean asked Phuc Dinh.

Instead of answering, the Vietnamese official looked back at Dean. Their eyes met and held each other for a moment.

"Did you serve during the war, Mr. Dean?" Phuc Dinh asked.

"I did."

"Then you understand." Phuc Dinh refilled his teacup. "One had always to cut his own path."

"So when the money stopped, you began working with the VC?"

"One works with whomever one can."

Dean suspected that Phuc Dinh had been working with the Vietcong long before the payments stopped; double-dealing was common. But it could have been that he changed sides then. By now it was irrelevant anyway.

"Did you know a man named McSweeney?" Dean asked. "He would have been a captain. He was with the strategic hamlet program."

Phuc Dinh stared at the wall once more. "The name is not familiar," he said finally.

"Did you have any contact with the strategic hamlet program? Before the payments stopped?"

"The couriers were Marines. Maybe they were that program?"

"Did any Marines live with you in your village?"

"You say you are familiar with the history of the area. Would Marines have lasted long in that village?"

Phuc Dinh gave him the names of the provincial leaders who benefited from the payoffs. The list was long, though the sums Phuc Dinh mentioned were relatively small—for the most part, a few hundred went to each. Still, that would have represented considerable money in Vietnam.

It probably bought a lot of AK-47s and rockets, Dean thought bitterly.

Obviously, someone decided that the money the village

leaders were getting would be more useful in his pocket. Was it the Vietcong, the South Vietnamese, or someone else?

Forester must have thought it was connected to McSweeney somehow.

Maybe he suspected McSweeney.

Or maybe McSweeney knew who did it, and was in danger because of that. Maybe the fact that he was targeted had nothing to do with his running for President.

"That's all I know," said Phuc Dinh.

"Do you have the e-mail Forester sent you?" Dean asked.

He shook his head.

"How did he find you?"

"I am not sure. I am not a famous man." He broke into a grin for the first time since they'd met. "Maybe he met someone with a long memory. He claimed to have found my name in a government directory."

"Is that possible?"

"Yes. I have contact with foreign banks. I have visited Beijing—I am in the directories. But how he knew to look, that I do not know. He asked if I knew anything about missing money. He named the date the payment should have arrived. That was all. I will not come to your country," Phuc Dinh added. "I cannot help you more than this."

Dean took a sip of tea, savoring the liquid in his mouth as if it were expensive Scotch.

"What did you do during the war, Mr. Dean?" asked Phuc Dinh.

"I was a Marine," Dean said. "I served in this province."

"It was not a good place to be a soldier."

"I'd imagine it was much more difficult to be a civilian."

"Impossible, I would say."

"There was an ambush near your village, Phu Loc Two," said Dean. "You were targeted. Some reports said you were killed."

A faint smile appeared on Phuc Dinh's face, then faded into something close to sadness, and then blank stoicism. He scratched his ear but said nothing.

"How did you escape?" Dean asked. "Weren't you shot?"

"Another man went in my place. We used many tricks of deception at the time, to confuse spies who might be watching."

"The dead man wasn't you?"

Phuc Dinh shook his head.

"But he had a scar like yours."

"When the money did not arrive, that was a sign," said Phuc Dinh, ignoring Dean's comment. "From that point on, we were on our guard. The ambush was a few months later, but we were still watching."

"There was a photo in a file," said Dean. "The man had a scar like yours."

Phuc Dinh pointed to it.

"Yes, like that," said Dean.

"A time such as that brings us to the lowest point of our existence."

"Charlie, ask him about money transfers," Rockman interrupted. "Ask him if he had any access to bank records."

Dean ignored the runner, staring instead at Phuc Dinh. He wasn't a ghost, not in the literal sense. And yet he was in every other way. He had come to Dean from the past, conjuring up an entire world that Dean had passed through years ago, an unsettled world that continued to haunt him, much as he denied it.

Dean, too, was a ghost, haunting Phuc Dinh's world, though the former VC official didn't know it.

"I lost a friend on that mission," said Dean softly. "A good friend."

"I lost many friends during the war as well." Phuc Dinh lowered his head. "The man who went in my place that day was my brother. The scars you noticed were burns from a French vicar for stealing his food when we were five and six. He used the same poker to mark us both."

78

"DIDN'T KNOW YOU were a gun nut!"

Startled, Jimmy Fingers turned to his right and saw Sam Iollo, one of the capitol police supervisors, standing nearby.

"I hope I'm not a nut," said Jimmy Fingers.

"What is that little peashooter you got there?" asked Iollo, pointing at Jimmy Fingers' pistol.

Jimmy held out a Colt Detective Special, a .38-caliber two-inch snubby. Though old, the weapon was in showroom shape, its blued finish gleaming and the wood bright and polished.

"Pretty," said Iollo. "What, you don't trust us protecting you?"

"Of course I trust you," said Jimmy Fingers.

"Hey, just busting on you there, Counselor." Iollo seemed to think that everyone who worked for a senator was a lawyer. He gave Jimmy Fingers a serious look. "Can you shoot a rifle?"

For a brief moment, Jimmy Fingers was filled with fear. Surely this wasn't an idle question, nor an idle meeting.

"Of course I can use a rifle," he told Iollo.

"Maybe you'll want to come out to the annual turkey shoot then. Good food, and the competition's fun. If you're as good with a rifle as you are with that pistol, you might take yourself home a bird."

"Maybe I will. Let me know when it's coming up."

Jimmy Fingers started to leave, but Iollo held out his hand to stop him.

"Tell me the truth now—you think he's going to be President?" Iollo asked.

"Without a doubt."

"He is looking real good. Be careful no one shoots at him again, though. Next time, they may not miss."

"Yes," said Jimmy Fingers grimly, before walking away.

DEAN PUSHED BACK in the chair as Phuc Dinh rose.

"I have enjoyed our meeting," Phuc Dinh said perfunctorily, his tone suggesting the opposite.

"Thank you," Dean told him. "I appreciate your time. And your honesty."

Once more, a faint hint of a smile appeared on Phuc Dinh's face, only to dissolve. As Dean watched him walk toward the door, it occurred to him that it would be an easy thing to shoot him, completing the mission he had been assigned thirty-five years before.

But Phuc Dinh had not caused Longbow's death any more than Dean had.

Meeting his Vietnamese enemy reminded Dean not of the war but of how much had changed in the intervening years. As a sniper, he'd seen Vietnam, the world, as black-and-white. Now he saw only colors, infinite colors. He knew his job and his duty, and would perform both. But he no longer had the luxury the teenager had of looking at targets through a crosshaired scope. What he saw was weighted with the time he'd come through, the miles he'd walked.

The ghosts he'd shared space with, haunted by and, in turn, haunting.

"IT WAS A CIA program. The Marines were involved because they were in the area," Hernes Jackson told Rubens. "I have to say that there wasn't much online from the CIA. I found nearly everything I needed from the Department of Defense. I've made appointments to look at the paper records as well. Possibly that will reveal more."

Jackson explained that the CIA had sent "support" payments to loyal village elders during the war. The payments were essentially bribes, and there were few checks and balances in the program. The CIA worked with local military units to arrange and protect couriers; depending on the sector, Army Special Forces, Marines, and even SEALs had been involved. In the area of Phu Loc 2, the CIA worked with Marines attached to the strategic hamlet program.

In the case cited by Phuc Dinh, one set of payments totaling $250,000 had gone missing during the last year of the war. This had happened after the man who had been coordinating the payments—Greenfeld, as Dean had said—was killed in a rocket attack on a Marine camp he'd been visiting. Three payments were missed in the interim, making the amount carried by the new courier extra large and probably extra tempting.

A South Vietnamese officer acted as the courier, with two Marines assigned as his escort to Phu Loc 2. There was an ambush. The Marines and the South Vietnamese officer were separated. Neither the money nor the South Vietnamese officer was ever seen again.

"The Marines just let him run off?" said Rubens.

"No," said Jackson. "There was an ambush. They came under heavy attack. According to the Marines, he was obliterated by a mortar. They ended up calling for an air evac."

The guards were Marine Sergeant Bob Malinowski and Marine Sergeant Robert Tolong.

"Malinowski was wounded in the ambush and died back in the field hospital, or en route," said Jackson. "One of the reports says that Tolong was wounded as well, but if so the wounds were minor, because he rejoined his unit immediately afterward. The CIA wanted to talk to Sergeant Tolong, apparently because he was the last American to see the cash. I am reading a bit between the lines."

"Perfectly logical assumption," said Rubens. "Go on."

Before the CIA could debrief him, Tolong volunteered to go on a patrol, checking on a hamlet team that had missed its call-in the day before. The unit was attacked in the afternoon of their first day out, a few miles west of Tam Ky. Tolong and another man named Reginald Gordon were separated from the main group. The firefight continued well into the night. In the morning, the fighting resumed when some helicopters approached, and it wasn't until late afternoon that they were extricated. Gordon and Tolong were among the missing.

"About ten days later, Sergeant Gordon showed up at the base camp of a unit about thirty miles to the west," continued Jackson. "Tolong, he said, had been seriously wounded and died a few days after the ambush. He'd buried him, but wasn't sure where. The Marines sent two different patrols into the area, but never found him."

"Did the CIA find the money?" asked Rubens.

"Doesn't appear so. As I said, I'll have to look through their paper records to be sure," said Jackson. "The men were assigned to the courier job by a Captain McSweeney. His name was on some of the reports, including two about the ambush."

"Senator McSweeney."

"Apparently. One other thing I found interesting," added Jackson. "Reading between the lines, it seems that the CIA later concluded that the courier had been set up by one of the village leaders, who was working with the Vietcong. The leader was Phuc Dinh."

"Why would he have the courier ambushed before he got the money?" asked Rubens.

"It would make sense if the South Vietnamese officer didn't really die, but escaped during the attack," said Jackson. "In any event, the CIA apparently tried to get a little revenge by assassinating him. According to one of the Marine Corps reports, they succeeded."

"So I surmised from the transcript of Mr. Dean's interview with Mr. Dinh."

"Did the interview note that the assassin was a Marine scout sniper named Charles Dean?"

81

RUBENS WAS STILL considering exactly how to summarize the situation for Bing when she returned his call.

"This is Dr. Bing. You have an update on the Vietnam project?"

"Thao Duong is part of a people-smuggling network," said Rubens. "There is no Vietnamese assassination plot."

"There's no assassination plot or he's not part of it?"

The bite in Bing's voice annoyed Rubens. He reached for his cup of cinnamon herbal tea—part of his never-ending campaign to cut back on caffeine—and took a long sip before replying.

"The only evidence that we had of a possible plot involves dated CIA data, and circumstantial evidence we developed related to Thao Duong. Upon further analysis, that evidence now fits better with the hypothesis that he was part of a people-smuggling operation originating in China. We were wrong, initially," added Rubens—even though he had cautioned about jumping to conclusions all along. "We have now given the material a very thorough review, and there is nothing substantial there."

"There was an attempt on a senator's life, Billy. If that isn't evidence enough for you, what is?"

Rubens winced. He hated being called Billy.

"I realize that you want to take a harder stand toward Vietnam," said Rubens as evenly as he could. "But I have to tell you that we have no intelligence linking them to the attempt on the senator's life."

"Then you're not working hard enough," said Bing, abruptly hanging up.

82

FINISHED BRIEFING RUBENS, Ambassador Jackson returned to his desk in the research and analysis section, planning on taking care of some odds and ends before checking back in with the FBI and Secret Service. While he'd been up with Rubens, the Pentagon had answered Jackson's request for contact information regarding the members of Tolong's unit. Among the information was an address and phone number for Reginald Gordon, the last man who had seen Tolong alive.

Jackson called the phone number, only to find it had been disconnected. That wasn't particularly surprising—the Defense Department data was many years old. Next, Jackson entered the name and last known address into a commercial database used by private investigators and others trying to track down people. Within a few minutes, he had an address and phone number in Atlanta.

This phone, too, had been disconnected.

Jackson then did what a layman might do when looking for information about someone—he Googled Gordon.

The screen came back quickly. All of the top hits were from newspapers.

Reginald Gordon had jumped from a hotel window in Washington a week before.

83

MOST TIMES, DEALING with small-town police departments was very easy. The Secret Service had a long-standing aura because of its role protecting the President; unlike the FBI or DEA, its image had not been tarnished by scandal. The locals also tended to be less suspicious that the Service might be crowding in on their territory, and as a general rule the police chiefs and lieutenants Amanda Rauci met with on various cases went out of their way to be cooperative and helpful.

The Pine Plains chief was a notable exception. She'd tried making an appointment to see him first thing in the morning, but he'd been "unavailable" until three in the afternoon. Then he'd kept her waiting nearly forty-five minutes while he was "tied up on patrol"—she suspected this meant shooting the breeze at the local coffee shop. When he finally came into the backroom suite of the village hall, which served as the local police station, he put on a sour puss as soon as he saw her. He answered her questions in a barely audible monotone.

"Never showed."

"Did you speak to Agent Forester on the phone?" Amanda asked.

"Nope."

"Did anyone in your department talk to him?"

"Maybe Dispatch." Chief Ball bellowed for his dispatcher, "Steph! Get in here!"

The white-haired woman who'd been manning the phone

and radio in the front room appeared at the door. She glanced at Amanda and gave her a reassuring look, as if to say, *His bark is worse than his bite.*

Amanda didn't believe it.

"That federal guy—Secret Service," said Chief Ball. "He ever show up that day?"

"You mean the one checking on the man who passed away?"

"*No.* The one that killed himself."

"He died before he came, didn't he?"

"Did you talk to him?"

"Just to make the appointment."

Ball looked back at Amanda, a satisfied expression on his face.

"Did he say what it was about?" Amanda asked.

"Wanted to talk to the chief."

"Agent Forester sometimes had a habit of looking over a place before he interviewed someone," said Amanda. "He might have done that the night before he died."

"Couldn't prove it by me," snapped the chief. He looked over at his dispatcher.

"I never met him."

"Other questions?" Chief Ball's voice strongly implied the answer was, No.

"I have a lot of questions," answered Amanda. She turned to the dispatcher. "But not for you, ma'am."

The dispatcher gave Amanda the same bark-is-worse smile, then left.

"You have no idea what he might have been working on?" asked Amanda.

"Well, sure, I know now. It had to do with threats against Gideon McSweeney. I didn't know then. And I doubt anybody in my town made those threats."

Amanda opened her purse and took out Forester's notebook. "He had spoken to a man named Gordon who lives in Georgia," she told the chief. "There was another man, I believe named Dinn, whom he was interested in."

"Dim?"

"Dinn. I don't know how it's spelled."

"Never heard of it."

"There don't seem to be any in the phone book."

"See?"

Amanda glanced down at the page in Forester's note-book, where he had circled the name and question marks in the middle of the page:

> *Gordon?*
> *Chief?*

"Is it possible he wanted to talk to you about Gordon?"

"Last name or first name?"

"Last name."

"Don't know any Gordons. None in the phone book, right?"

"I thought maybe it might be unlisted."

"Nah. Now we got two Gordons as first name, that I can think of. There's Gordon Hirt, the high school principal?"

"I don't know. Was he a Marine?"

"Might have been. I'm not sure. Don't know much about him. Respected. Beard. Lives down in Stanford. Here three and a half years." The chief leaned back in his chair and put his feet up on his desk. "And then there's a Gordon Clegg. I doubt it was him. He's like ninety-three and lives in Annabel Shepherd's old-age home. She takes old people in. Has a li-cense from the state. Gordon used to be sharp as a tack, but he had a stroke a few months ago. Not so good now."

"What if Gordon was a last name?" Amanda asked. "Or if it were something near that?"

"Well. That's a little different. Like Gordon. Hmmm. This isn't that big a town. I think I know just about everybody, but sometimes you can be surprised." Chief Ball stared at the ceiling, clicking through a mental Rolodex. "Goddard—we have a Pete Goddard. Retired newspaper guy, tried to make a killing off his uncle's horse farm. Bit of a jerk. Caught him speeding once and he managed to talk himself into a ticket. Usually, if you're a local, I'll let ya go. Unless you're a jerk."

"Do you have an address?"

"Stephanie?"

POLICE CHIEF CHRIS Ball fixed his hat on his head as he strode toward his car.

Thank God for dumb blondes—or brunettes as the case might be. She had the whole damn thing in her hands and she still couldn't figure it out.

One of the other 10 million *federales* working on the case would, though. Eventually. They had enough stinking people poking their noses in the woodpile.

"Hello, Chief. Nice day, isn't it?"

The chief glanced over and saw the town librarian, Joyce Dalton, walking her dog. Good-looking woman, that.

Too young for him, and married, and reading constantly, being a librarian, he would bet, but good-looking anyway.

"Mrs. Dalton. Beautiful day. Taking time off?"

"My day off. I thought I would work in my garden."

"Nice day for it. You take care now."

"I will, Chief."

Ball got into his car, trying to decide whether the dumb brunette would go to the high school first or out toward Pete Goddard's run-down horse farm.

84

THE LEAD OFFICER on Gordon's suicide case had a photographic memory, and described the scene to Hernes Jackson in vivid detail.

Too vivid, thought Jackson; he started getting queasy about halfway through.

Gordon had jumped from the twenty-third floor.

"As far as the room goes, it was locked, with no signs of forced entry, no disturbance. Gordon's suitcase was still packed and in the corner," said the detective, a middle-aged African-American named Drew Popkin.

Jackson listened as the detective described the rest of his investigation. They were standing on the pavement of a driveway a few feet from where the body had been found. According to Popkin, there were no eyewitnesses to the jump. In fact, Gordon had probably been on the ground at least fifteen minutes before somebody found him.

"Guy making a delivery for a florist. Heck of a shock."

"I'll bet," said Jackson.

The building dated from the late nineteenth century and retained much of its architectural charm. Unlike many modern hotels, its windows could be opened, though only after removing a lock and a grate that made it next to impossible to accidentally fall. Popkin had found a screwdriver and several small box wrenches in the room, along with the hardware that had been removed.

"If he came with tools, then he must have been planning on killing himself," said Jackson.

"Looks like it."

"But why here?"

"Damned if I know. Doesn't make sense that he'd want to commit suicide at all," added Popkin. "Owns a lot of land outside Atlanta. I talked with some people there; they were very shocked."

"Maybe he was sick."

"Checked into that. Doctor said he was in good health, no signs of depression."

"Why was he in Washington?"

"Don't know. He'd had some dealings with the Army Corps of Engineers, trying to get them to sign off on a project of his. But that all ended earlier this year. If he was setting up another appointment, he didn't get around to it. Didn't talk with his congressman, either. I checked."

GORDON OWNED SEVERAL hundred acres in suburban Georgia, outside of Atlanta, which had once belonged to the federal government. He wanted to develop part of it into a shopping center, but the parcel had been declared federally protected wetlands. He'd asked the Army Corps of Engineers, which had made the designation in the first place, to change it.

"We tried to explain to him that it wasn't really a discretionary designation," the man who had met with Gordon told Jackson. "He was very adamant, and persistent. He even tried to get members of Congress to convince us. But of course, we don't make that designation. We did the report on the property when it was designated because it was owned by the government. That was it. We had no other connection."

"He had his congressman call?"

"And three senators. I guess he's well connected."

"Three?"

"That we heard from. Stenis and Archer from Georgia, and McSweeney."

"McSweeney's from New York, isn't he?"

"Knew him somehow."

* * *

SINCE HE WAS in town anyway, Jackson decided that he would stop at Amanda Rauci's condo and ask her if Forester had mentioned anything about Gordon. Jackson got to her home just before five; no one answered when he rang the bell.

Back in his car, he realized she would probably be back at work by now, so he called her work number. The call was immediately forwarded to her superior.

"She's on suspension," said the man after Jackson explained who he was. "She missed a meeting with our personnel people the other day. We're looking for her, actually. One of the hairs found on Forester's clothes looks like it was hers, and we'd like to ask her about it."

85

LIA HEARD ABOUT the hair sample from Mandarin at roughly the same time Jackson did. She was packing in her hotel room, getting ready to go back to Crypto City. Now that the Vietnam connection appeared to be a bust, Rubens had ordered her home.

"So Amanda Rauci was with Forester when he killed himself?" Lia asked Mandarin when he told her about the hair.

"Whoa, hold on," said Mandarin. "A strand or two of hair could *easily* have been on his clothes without her being there. They were having an affair, remember?"

"I remember."

"No way she killed him. No way."

Lia thought of Amanda Rauci the day she and Jackson had spoken to her. Could she have killed her lover?

No.

What if he'd told her he was going back to his wife?

Lia didn't think so even then.

"I was hoping you might do me a favor," said Mandarin.

"What's that?"

"She used her credit card at an animal hospital and veterinary clinic a few miles from Danbury on the New York and Connecticut border the other day. We want to check it out in person, but most of my people have already left with McSweeney. The soonest I can get someone up there will be late tomorrow afternoon."

"Animal hospital? Did she have a pet?"

"No idea. We're wondering why she's up here in the first place. It may be a glitch—possibly she made the charge when she was here with Forester and they only put it through now. But I'd like to check it sooner rather than later."

"Sure, I'll do it," said Lia.

"Good. I'll fax you a copy of the transaction."

IT WAS GOING on six o'clock when Lia finally got to the animal hospital. The only one left in the office was a pimple-faced geek who started breathing hard as soon as she walked in the door.

Which really annoyed her, though she tried to ignore it.

"I'm looking for a woman named Amanda Rauci, who may have been in here yesterday," Lia told him after she flashed her federal marshal credentials. "She hasn't been seen since then. She's a Secret Service agent, and we're worried about her."

"Secret Service?"

"That's right."

"She was a Secret Service agent. Wow. Wow."

"Let's make sure we have the right person," said Lia, taking out her PDA. She tapped on a program and brought up a photo of Amanda Rauci. "Is this her?"

The young man reached for the handheld computer.

"We look with our eyes," Lia told him. "Only I touch my computer."

"Oh yeah, that's Ms. Rauci. She came in right about now. I was just about to close. Rauci is her divorced name, though. She has another name."

"What was it?"

"Hold on; let me think. It would be on the chart. That oughta be in the replace pile." The kid went over to a large wire basket and began sorting through the files.

"What sort of pet did she have?" Lia asked.

"Dog. She needed something because she was going on a trip and it barfed in the car."

"Lovely," said Lia.

THE NAME AMANDA had given the vet's assistant was Stevens, but the woman at the house had never heard of her. A check by the Desk Three people found no link, either.

"Probably she was driving north and her dog started giving her trouble," suggested Rockman. "She stopped off and got something for him at a place she'd seen when she was there with Forester."

"Why is that the only transaction she's had in the past week?" Lia asked.

It had started to rain lightly. She flipped her windshield wipers on and pulled out of the driveway, starting back in the direction of Danbury.

"Maybe she doesn't use the card that much because she prefers cash," said Rockman.

"Or maybe she's out of cash," said Lia, answering her own question. "And this was important enough to risk using the card for."

"You're assuming she's running away," said Telach.

"Or doesn't want to be found," said Lia.

"My dog was the same way," said Rockman. "Carsick."

"You have a dog?"

"Had to give him away because of work. I'm not home much. Not fair to the dog."

Good point, thought Lia. She didn't remember Rauci having a dog.

Did Forester have a dog? Lia couldn't remember seeing one at his ex-wife's house.

"Rockman, see if you can find out if Forester had a dog. Maybe he had a house or something up here and she's feeding it," said Lia. "I'm going to get something to eat."

Lia spotted a restaurant on the other side of the road, but it was too late to stop. She pulled off the side of the road into a short dirt driveway. As she started to back up to turn around, she realized she was at the entrance to a junkyard. There were wrecked cars nearby, and a chain-link fence. A black Doberman pinscher bared its teeth as she began her three-point turn.

"Oh!" she said out loud, realizing why Amanda had bought the dog medicine.

86

DEAN HAD JUST gotten out of bed when the sat phone buzzed
with a call from the Art Room. He held the phone to his ear
and lay back down. The mattress was so thin he could feel
the knots in the rope that held it up.

"Charlie, we want you to check on a Dr. Vuong who
works in town," said Marie Telach. "He's the doctor who was
present when the body of a Sergeant Tolong was exhumed a
few years ago. See what details you can get from him."

"You think he'd tell me if they found money?" asked Dean.

"Let's just cover the bases, Charlie. Stand by for directions to Dr. Vuong's office."

QUI WAS ALREADY waiting in the breakfast room when Dean
came down.

"I have a change in plans," he told her. "I want to speak to
one of the doctors here. He assisted when a Marine was dis-
interred a few years ago and sent back to the States. I want to
talk to him about it. It shouldn't take long. We'll leave after
that."

"Would you like me to come?"

"This is another case where I think you'd be better off
waiting outside."

"Who do you really work for, Mr. Dean?"

"I'm a do-gooder, just like you."

She smiled faintly.

"Let's have some breakfast," Dean told her. "Come on."

87

AMANDA RAUCI MOUSED up to the file command, clearing the history file so that the Web sites she had visited would be erased. She got back to the main browser screen just as the librarian arrived, intending to scold Amanda for going over the library's half-hour-use allotment for a second time that evening.

"Now, miss—" said the librarian, finger raised as if she were about to wag it at a wayward child.

"I'm done," announced Amanda, jumping from the computer.

"We do have rules, you know."

"Yup."

"And there *are* people waiting."

The librarian had obviously rehearsed her speech for a long time, because she was still sputtering as Amanda left the building.

Three hours of Web surfing had provided several interesting tidbits of information, though not necessarily what Amanda had hoped to find. Her access to her work files and the Service's computers in general had been cut off, which wasn't particularly surprising. She'd made several attempts to guess Forester's password without any luck; she couldn't tell whether his account, too, had been frozen or she was just guessing poorly. It was probably the former, though she wished now that she had tried earlier.

Amanda suspected that neither Pete Goddard nor Gordon Hirt had had anything to do with Forester's investigation.

The police chief had been *too* casual about mentioning their names, she thought; it was a misdirection play if ever she'd seen one.

Her time on the Internet seemed to confirm that. Peter Goddard, the "retired" journalist, was an author of several books on European history; two had been on the best-seller list. According to the profiles of him she'd read—one in the *New York Times*, another in an industry magazine—he spent about half of the year traveling in Europe, where he researched his material. He generally spent spring and the fall there, which meant he'd be there right now.

While Gordon Hirt had only been principal of the high school for a few years, he'd been vice principal of an even larger school two towns away for over fifteen years, according to a recent profile in the area daily. He also happened to be a committeeman in McSweeney's political party. Neither man looked to be a good candidate to have made a death threat against anyone.

Chief Ball, on the other hand, was definitely up to something. Maybe it was just that he didn't like women in law enforcement, but Amanda decided to check his background anyway. She did a general Google search, then paid for an online credit and lien report—once again using her credit card, though at least this time, pinning down her physical location would be hard.

The chief had decent credit and no criminal convictions. Two years before, he had celebrated his thirtieth year as police chief. The online edition of the local newspaper featured several out-of-focus pictures of his party, along with the mayor's comments about how lucky Pine Plains was to have him, yada, yada yada.

How had he come to Pine Plains? The article didn't say. The article claimed he was fifty-two, but the data in the credit report had him at fifty-nine.

Maybe the reporter had made an error, or maybe the chief was simply vain. The story mentioned that he had served in the military and been a part-timer before becoming one of the force's two full-time patrolmen. His first big case had involved a shoot-out with a bank robbery suspect; Patrolman Ball had bravely confronted the man and ended up shooting him dead, after a state trooper was wounded. That apparently was Ball's ticket to becoming chief, though the newspaper didn't actually say that.

Most police officers, most Secret Service agents for that matter, never fired their guns in anger, let alone shot down a murderer in a do-or-die situation. It seemed incongruous to her—here was a man who had proved his worth in battle, as it were, and yet he had chosen to stay in a small town his entire life. Was the moment of heroism an anomaly? Was the story inflated? But there must be *some* truth to it.

She remembered Jerry Forester brooding about his career. If only he'd been on a detail where he could prove his worth, if only he'd had a chance when he was younger . . .

What would he have done with it?

The library closed at seven. Amanda went out to her car, not sure what to do next. She wanted a drink desperately but knew she didn't dare. One sip and she would fall deeper into the hole she was trying to climb out of. It was too dangerous even to stop at a restaurant that served liquor or beer. She headed toward the Burger King she'd seen up the road.

A police car passed as she pulled in. Amanda didn't think much of it until she came out of the drive-thru line and found the car waiting for her. Chief Ball was sitting in the driver's seat. She rolled down the passenger-side window of her car.

"Hey, were you looking for a notebook?" asked the chief.

"A notebook?"

"One of the investigators mentioned that they were interested in a notebook," he told her. "Some kids found one off the road on County Highway Nineteen. Stenographer-type pad. Got tire marks, and it's dirty as hell. There are notes in it. Can't make most of them out. You want it?"

"Absolutely," said Amanda, though she'd been caught off guard.

"All right—well, then, follow me to the station. Unless you want to eat your dinner first."

"No, it's OK."

Amanda waited for him to pull ahead. So they *did* know there was another notebook. Maybe she should just keep going, not take it—but then the police chief would call whoever it was who had asked about it and casually mention that she'd been there.

So? What was she running from? Not the Service. From despair. There wasn't anything that they could do to her that they hadn't already done—obviously, her career there was over, at least in a meaningful sense.

Maybe Pine Plains could use a female police officer, she thought to herself as she pulled into the back of the parking lot.

She laughed. As she got out of the car, she realized it was the first time she'd laughed since her lover's death.

MINUTES AFTER AMANDA Rauci used her credit card, a copy of the transaction was forwarded to the Secret Service and, from them, to Desk Three, where it showed up in Robert Gallo's e-mail queue.

The transaction showed the card had been used to pay the American Credit Ch*k Company. American Credit Ch*k was an Internet company whose Web site boasted that it could provide instant credit information over the Internet on any American. While the claims were slightly overblown, the information was in fact fairly complete and very quick, as Gallo found out by ordering his own credit report. It even noted that he just paid off the loan on his Jetta a month before. Gallo recorded the entire query and transaction so he could see how the program worked.

"They keep a record of the transaction request," Gallo told Johnny Bib, pointing to the screen where the program's scripts and data were displayed. "They set up an account, so you have a full history and everything else. But they don't keep track of where the request came from. We'd have to look at their server records. Take me about ten minutes to get in there. Maybe fifteen. Once I'm in, it's a snap."

"Go through channels," said Johnny Bib.

Gallo hung his head.

"Johnny, it'll take at least until morning for anybody at the credit-checking place to say, 'Cool, go ahead,' " he explained.

"Try the right way first," said Johnny Bib, bouncing out of the room.

THE PROPERTY OWNER was waiting with his two dogs by the gate of the impound lot when Lia and the trooper drove up. The German shepherds, while big and mangy, were friendly; they began licking and nuzzling Lia as soon as she got out of the car.

"Nice dogs," said Lia. "Have they been drugged in the last twenty-four hours?"

"Drugged? My dogs? These are good dogs," said the man, glancing over at the plainclothes trooper. "Who would drug them?"

"Nothing unusual?" the trooper asked.

The man shrugged. "What's unusual?"

Lia and the trooper walked over to the car. The lot was illuminated by a single floodlight back by the gate, and they needed the trooper's flashlight to see inside the car.

"Still locked," said the state trooper, trying the doors.

"She could have relocked the door." Lia glanced around the lot. "This isn't the most secure place in the world."

"We've kept impound cars here for twenty years," said the owner. "Never have a problem."

"You keep all crime scene cars here?" asked Lia.

"Wasn't a crime scene," said the trooper.

"Yeah, they keep crime scene cars here," said the man. "That blue sedan over there—that was confiscated on a drug bust."

"It's OK, Max," said the trooper.

"She probably had a key," said Lia.

"Maybe," said the trooper. He ran his light across the door near the window.

"Can we look inside?"

"Sure. That's why I brought the key."

Lia waited for the trooper to open the door. The car had been locked when it was found after Forester's death. The contents had been removed before the car was brought here.

"Did you do a full crime scene work-up on it?" Lia asked.

"It's not a crime scene," said the trooper.

"She must have wanted something inside the car. Otherwise why come here?"

"I can't argue with you, but I don't know what it would be. We took the contents and gave them to the Secret Service. Service came and looked at the car themselves. Unless there's a hidden compartment somewhere."

"Maybe there is."

The trooper shrugged. "You can search it, too."

Lia slipped into the driver's seat, and began looking around the interior of the car. As the trooper said, everything that had been inside had been removed, including the owner's manual in the glove compartment.

So what did Amanda want? A receipt or something tucked somewhere no one else might see?

Why would that be valuable?

Maybe it would show she and Forester were together . . . that she killed him.

Impossible.

"There's a notebook that seems to be missing," said Lia.

"Everything we found in the car, we turned over. There's a list and photos."

"Did you take apart the seats and the linings and things?" Lia asked.

The trooper frowned. "You know, not for nothing but, this case is pretty cut-and-dried. The guy killed himself."

"So why did Amanda Rauci come here?" asked Lia. "Maybe she was looking for his notebook, too," she added, answering her own question as they walked back toward the gate. "Maybe she doesn't think it's a suicide and she wants to figure out who did it."

Lia got down on her hands and knees, outside of the car. It wasn't easy to see up under the seat, and so she fished with her hand.

"Can we take the seats out to look inside?" she asked.

The trooper turned to the owner, who sighed, then went off for a set of tools. Two hours later, they were certain that nothing was hidden there.

"I have to tell you, it really, really looks like a suicide," said the trooper as he and Lia walked toward the gate.

"So everybody says."

"If it's not, then what is it?" asked the trooper.

Lia stopped to pet the dogs, unable to think of an answer.

90

"IF THIS TURNS out to be useful to you in any way, I would appreciate a mention to my mayor," Chief Ball told Amanda Rauci when she got out of her car. He'd been careful to make sure he parked at the front, blocking the view of the vehicle at the back. Once he turned off the outside floodlight, her car would be invisible.

"Come on—that door there takes us direct to my office," he said. "A letter from your director—that would be gold. You wouldn't believe the sort of small-town politics I have to deal with. They wanted to cut my part-time budget in half this year. Basically, that would eliminate coverage five nights a week. We hit on a compromise, but I still go without two nights a week. That's kind of classified, if you know what I mean. Don't want the bad guys finding out."

"Sure."

The sarcasm in her voice was impossible to miss. But that was fine, Ball thought—she was buying the act, completely off guard.

"You have no idea the kinds of things we put up with in a small town," Ball told her. "It looks peaceful, but believe me. If we weren't here, watch out."

The chief pulled his keys off his belt and unlocked the door. He kept talking, playing the local-yokel angle to the hilt.

"I get asked to fix traffic tickets all the time. I mean, well, in some cases what are you going to do, right? You can use your best judgment if it's something out of the ordinary. You look at the driving record and you figure, well, all right, just one mistake and what the heck. Why screw up the guy's insurance rates, you know? Especially if he's just a working guy like you. But some of the things I've been asked to do—I have to draw the line. That's why I have trouble with the politics. A letter from your boss in my file, that's something that will count, though. They'll read it at the village board meeting, see; the local Jimmy Olsen cub reporter will mention it; people will know. It'll help the department. Not me. I've been here so long they can't touch me. It's the department this will help."

He opened the door and flipped on the lights. The budget cuts he was complaining about were real, and in this case were a good thing—he didn't have to worry about a night man, because there wasn't one on tonight. But the town assessor occasionally came back to the village hall to work after he put his kids to sleep. That gave Ball about sixty minutes to get the job done.

Sooner was always better than later.

"So, do you think you can help me there?" Ball asked as Amanda stepped inside. "You don't have to reveal anything to me. I know you guys have to follow your own procedures and whatnot. I respect that."

"If the notebook is helpful, I'll certainly ask my boss to say something about it," offered Amanda.

"Thanks. It's right there on the desk. Excuse me a second—just going to hit the boys' room out front. Hey, want coffee or anything?"

"No thanks."

AS SOON AS she saw the notebook, Amanda was glad she'd come. It wasn't anything like the ones Forester used; true, it was a stenographer's notebook, but it had a slick cover, which he wouldn't have liked, because it couldn't be written on and was too flimsy.

She reached into her purse and took out the real notebook. She'd show it to Ball, explain why this one was wrong. There'd be no reason for him to call anyone else.

Amanda flipped the real notebook open, looking for a page of handwriting that would be easy to compare. As she did, she noticed a page with some impressions on it in the middle of the book—writing maybe, from another page that had been so carefully removed that she hadn't noticed it before.

She held it to the light, trying to see what it said. When that didn't work, she reached over and took a pencil from the holder on Chief Ball's desk.

She could tell right away that this wasn't just a page of notes; there were too many words. It was a letter—a short, terrible letter that Gerald Forester had started to write to his sons.

> Guys:
>
> I can't explain how I feel, like rocks have covered me, rocks that follow me everywhere like live animals, pushing me down. I hate them. I hate everything. I can't stand it any more. I hate what I have to do.
> And I'm sorry. So sorry.

Amanda Rauci felt a tear well at the side of her eye. She put the notebook down on the desk and took a tissue from her purse.

BALL WATCHED FROM the corner of his eye as Amanda put down the notebook and picked up her bag.

Was she going to leave? Was she getting a gun?

He couldn't seem to get himself to act. He knew what he had to do, but he didn't want to. Or rather, he didn't want it to be necessary to do.

Do it now!

The paralysis that had held him still finally melted away. He reached into his pocket and took out the wire.

Quickly, quickly!

Chief Ball hadn't strangled anyone in more than thirty years. The key to success was surprise, especially in this case, since Amanda Rauci was presumably trained in self-defense tactics. She was sitting, though, and unsuspecting. He waited to strike until she put the tissue down and her hands were in her lap.

His wrists swept forward and then up and back in a graceful, easy, instant motion. From there, it was all strength and weight.

Rauci reached back, trying first to grab his arms. The chair slipped down; she lost her footing. Ball pulled his hands farther apart and kept his feet braced. He felt her weight, pulling against him. Something erupted inside him, a black energy that flooded his arms.

Killing someone with a wire was personal. Even if you had the advantage, the tables could be turned right up to the last instant; there was a huge amount of risk. At the same time, your victim was within inches of you, not dozens or hundreds of feet away. You were as close as if you were making love.

Amanda managed to get her foot up against the desk, but Ball realized what she was trying to do just in time. He pushed off to the right and pulled back, dragging her across the floor before she could throw herself back into him. The chair slid across the room. Ball threw his knee against her back, leveraging it against her as they twisted down to the floor. She was desperate now, her oxygen-deprived brain realizing that it didn't have long to live.

Ball was desperate as well. Adrenaline surged in his arms as he pulled against the wire. He pushed his knee hard against her back, harder and harder, pressing as she continued to struggle. His body began to swim with sweat. A metallic, musky scent rose to his nose. He slipped down to the floor with her but hung on.

Amanda Rauci dug her elbow into his gut. Ball clamped his teeth together and held on.

And then it was done.

Ball didn't realize it at first, and when he did realize it, he didn't trust it. He kept his arms taut, his knee braced. He lay on top of his victim, his clothes soaked in perspiration, his lungs venting like an overworked blow furnace.

THE LAST THING she thought was how unjust it was. Not this, not the attack or her death, but for the boys. They'd be haunted by something they had no control over for the rest of their lives.

BALL GOT TO his knees, still holding the garrote. Amanda Rauci's lifeless body followed, her head bobbing to the side. The wire had gone deep into her neck, and in fact had cut into his own hands; their blood mixed together on her shirt.

Blood.

There wasn't much of it, but there was more than he wanted. The floor would be easy to clean, but he'd have to move quickly.

The chief's fingers trembled as he unwound the wire. Damn bitch. What'd she make him kill her for? Why the hell didn't she just mind her own business? Why didn't they all mind their own business?

It was Gordon's fault. He'd set Forester on Ball. The funny thing was, he had convinced Forester that evening when he stopped him on the road in the car. Ball knew he had. He could tell by the Secret Service agent's face.

"I wasn't even in that unit," Ball had told him. "I knew who McSweeney was, but he wasn't my CO. Just dig up my military record. Come by tomorrow and I'll help if you want."

And Forester had nodded. Then he'd gone off and killed himself.

Jerk.

Ball got to his feet. There was too much to be done now to waste time cursing his rotten luck.

IT DIDN'T TAKE nearly as long as Gallo had feared for the information about Amanda Rauci's request to be forwarded to the NSA. It turned out that the credit-checking company staffed its computer center around the clock. Gallo talked directly to a tech there, explaining that they were trying to figure out whether a Secret Service guy had killed himself or not; the tech cut through the red tape and gave him the details he wanted.

In the meantime, he'd done a search and discovered that Christopher Ball was the police chief in Pine Plains—one town over from the library where Amanda Rauci had used the computer.

"Why would she be checking out the police chief?" Gallo asked Rubens when he found him in the Art Room a short while later.

"A very good question, Mr. Gallo. Let us see if Ms. De-Francesca can supply an answer."

RUBENS WAS JUST about to talk to Lia when one of the Art Room communications specialists told him that National Security Advisor Donna Bing was calling for him. Rubens told Marie Telach to brief Lia on what Gallo had found, then went to the empty stations toward the back of the Art Room to talk to Bing.

He glanced at the clock on the console as he sat down. It was five past nine. Bing didn't skimp on her hours.

Unfortunately.

Rubens pressed the connect button on the communications control clipped to his belt. The unit connected to his headset via an encrypted very short-range frequency (E-VSRF). "This is Bill."

"Billy, how are we doing on Vietnam?"

"I'm about to roll up the operation there. As I told you earlier, we're confident that there is no connection."

"And I told you to work harder. You're obviously missing key information."

Rubens considered how to respond. The U.S. Citizenship and Immigration Services had already been briefed on Thao Duong's organization; Tommy Karr had installed permanent listening devices in Thao Duong's house and the digital records would be forwarded to the Citizenship and Immigration Services and the FBI for their use. There was simply nothing else for Deep Black to do in Vietnam. Even if the President wanted them to continue investigating the attack on Senator McSweeney—as the National Security finding directed them to do—it was senseless and expensive to keep Karr and Dean in Vietnam.

"Are you still there, Billy?"

"I am still here," said Rubens. "And personally, I prefer to be called Bill."

"Have you proved that Vietnam was not behind the attempted assassination of Senator McSweeney?" said Bing, ignoring Rubens's remark about his name.

"It will be hard to prove a negative."

"Why do you always give me such a hard time? Is it because I beat you out for this job?"

"I am not giving you a hard time, Madam Advisor."

"Have a full report on the situation to me by noon tomorrow," said Bing, hanging up.

"THIS TIME OF night, where you're going to find the chief is in bed," said the Pine Plains assessor, who was the only one in the village hall when Lia got there. "He hits the hay around nine, nine thirty. Doesn't like to be bothered, either. Comes in at five, though. Sometimes earlier."

The assessor smiled and raised the cup of coffee to his lips. His small office was in the front of the building; the police department was in the back.

"How come you work so late?" Lia asked.

"First of all, job's part-time. I have a real job in Poughkeepsie nine to five. Second of all, gets me out of the house." He smiled, then glanced at the clock. "I usually leave by midnight, though. Another half hour."

"I have something to talk to him about that's pretty important," said Lia. "Where does he live?"

"You're going to wake him up?"

"Why not?"

The assessor smirked.

"The chief lives right around from the station, on Church Street. Number Eleven. It's just the next block over—right at the end here, then another right. Third house on the right. Do me a favor though, OK? Don't tell him I told you."

"THE BODY, MUCH as you expect," Dr. Vuong told Dean, recalling the state of Sergeant Tolong's body when he'd been exhumed. "Bones. Much decay. You can see by the photos."

Dean nodded but didn't bother reopening the file on his lap. The sergeant had been reduced to cloth and bones by the time he was dug up.

Dr. Vuong spoke decent English, far better than Dean had expected. Roughly sixty, the doctor was ethnic Chinese and had lived in the north during the war. He was short and energetic, and the whole room seemed to move as he spoke.

"So, the commission take control of the body. I examine. We do the paperwork. Many forms to complete." The doctor's tone sounded almost triumphant. "The commission stay several days, then return."

The doctor did not remember whether bullets had been recovered with the body, but there were chips and breaks on the rib cage—multiple gunshots, he thought, the sign of death from an automatic weapon. The locals had lacked the facilities for a complete autopsy under the circumstances, and in any event were more concerned with "preserving dignity of corpse," as Dr. Vuong put it.

"How difficult was it to locate the body?" Dean asked.

"I am not sure. I do not believe hard. The commission had directions. Many details. He was near a road."

"Near a road?" asked Dean. "How would I say that in Vietnamese? Let me think."

The translator in the Art Room gave him the words.

Vuong said again, Tolong's body had been found very close to the road.

"Why wasn't he found soon after he died?" asked Dean. "During the war?"

The doctor shrugged.

"There were landmarks," suggested Dean.

"Memory is the problem. It was said a friend bury," noted Dr. Vuong. "Descriptions, jungle, war." He finished his thought in Vietnamese.

"The war shook many memories," said the translator, explaining. "It took some away, and it changed others. Some things I cannot explain. He was near the road, you have a point, but . . ."

"Anything is possible, huh?" suggested Dean.

Dr. Vuong nodded.

"I know this is an odd question," said Dean, "but was any money found with the body?"

"Money?"

"American dollars?"

The doctor shook his head. Dean repeated the question in Vietnamese to make sure he understood.

"You have a good vocabulary," said the doctor. "With more practice, you could speak very well."

"Thank you," said Dean. "Could you locate the spot where he was found on a map for me? I'd like to take a look."

He ignored Rockman when the runner told him it wasn't necessary.

DEAN STUDIED THE map as Qui drove, comparing the terrain and twists in the road to the paper as they made their way to the spot where Tolong's body had been dug up. Dean had an extra advantage—the exact spot where the dead Marine had been recovered was recorded by a GPS reading, and the Art Room told him when he was getting close.

"Pull over there," said Dean as they came over a rise in the road. "It was to our right."

Fallow fields lay on both sides of the road. Dean got out of the car and began walking in the direction of the grave site.

"A little more to your left," counseled Rockman. "You got it."

Dean wouldn't have needed Rockman's guidance. Though the vegetation had reclaimed the land, the ground was indented where the recovery team had dug two years before. Dean turned around. It was only ten yards from the road, if that.

"I didn't think you were a fortune hunter, Mr. Dean," said Qui.

"How's that?"

"You came to Vietnam for lost treasure?"

"No." He smiled faintly, then began walking around the edge of the area where the body had been found. There were several other excavations, all farther from the road.

The body should have been easy to find.

Dean glanced back toward the car and saw that Qui wasn't there. He found her a short distance down the hill, standing next to fallen tree limbs.

"There was a village here during the war," said Qui. "It's gone. It must have been Catholic."

"How do you know?"

She pointed to some rocks a short distance away. They were the foundation of a small building. Beyond it, Dean found several stones laid flat—gravestones. There were other signs—an overgrown path that went to the road, scattered pieces of wood and branches, worked stones that would never have appeared here randomly.

"When the VC took over, some loyal villages were razed," said Qui. "I would imagine this was one."

"That's a shame."

"The whole war was a shame," said Qui. "To the victors, the spoils. To the losers, death."

"We fought very hard," said Dean, suddenly feeling that he had let her down by not saving her country.

"I'm sure you did. But someone always loses."

94

CHIEF BALL'S HOUSE was dark when Lia got there. She got out of her car and walked toward the front door, not quite sure what she was going to say to him until she pressed the doorbell.

She rang twice before she saw a light flick on inside and heard footsteps.

A short, frumpy middle-aged woman dressed in a red terry-cloth robe opened the door. She stood behind the screen door, eying Lia warily.

"Yes?"

"I'm looking for Chief Ball," said Lia.

"The chief isn't here right now."

"He's not here?" said Lia. "Where would he be?"

"I don't know," said the woman, eying her up and down. "Who are you?"

"Lia DeFrancesca. I'm with the federal marshals."

"Is there trouble?"

"I have to discuss something with him, about a case."

"I can have him call you in the morning."

"I'm here, Elizabeth," said a voice behind her. "Thank you. Go back to bed now."

The chief appeared behind his wife. She glanced at him as if she was going to say something, then moved away. Ball opened the door and stepped outside. He'd taken the time to dress, even putting on his shoes.

"What is it you want?" he asked Lia.

"Amanda Rauci. She's disappeared. We're hoping to track her down."

"Rauci is who?"

Lia's explanation leaned fairly heavily on the possibility that Amanda might have run away because she was somehow involved in murdering Forester, and hinted that she might have retrieved some evidence from the area. Lia left out the fact that Rauci had done a credit check on Ball roughly six hours before.

"Rauci." Ball squirreled up his face. "Was she the one in my office this afternoon?"

"Was she?"

"Well, it was someone. She was a Secret Service agent, right? Wouldn't tell me what the hell it was about."

"Did she have a notebook with her?"

"Notebook. Maybe. The one you asked about?"

"Did she have it?" Lia asked.

"She might have. I didn't take inventory."

"What did she want?"

"She asked whether I'd spoken to Forester before he died. I told her the same thing I've told everyone else. No. You people don't seem to take no for an answer."

"Do you?"

Ball frowned. "You telling me she's missing?"

"She's in this area."

"How do you know?"

"She used her credit card locally."

"So why do you think she's missing?" asked Ball.

"No one's seen or heard from her in days."

"That doesn't mean she's missing. Maybe she doesn't feel like talking to anyone."

"But she did talk to you."

"If she comes back, I'll be sure to tell her to call home," said Ball. He started to open the door and go back in, but Lia held it closed.

"What exactly was she asking about?"

"Besides looking for the notebook," said Ball, "she asked me about Forester's wife, whether I'd seen her in town. Pretty ridiculous. She showed some picture that probably fits half the people in town."

"Forester's wife?"

"You know, I've never seen so much damn fuss about a jerk who killed himself before," said Ball. "Waking people up in the middle of the night—can't this wait until morning?"

"Can you think of anything else she might have said?"

Ball shrugged. "We only talked a few minutes. I got the impression she was on her way somewhere."

"Where?"

Ball shrugged. "She went down One Ninety-Nine after she left the office. Could be going anywhere."

95

CHIEF BALL WATCHED the federal agent back out of the driveway and onto the road.

These people were worse than cockroaches. Blind, but persistent.

He was all right for now. This changed his plans for the morning, though. He had to move Rauci's car tonight—right now, if possible.

Drive it over to Rhinecliff and leave it near the train station. That part was easy. Getting back without a car wouldn't be.

He could go down to Poughkeepsie, take a train to the city, then another over to Harlem Valley.

Too much. And he had too much to do anyway.

His wife was waiting upstairs, just as he knew she would be.

"What's going on?" she asked, her voice halfway between whining and pleading.

"I'm working on something with the *federales*," he said, opening his bureau drawer.

"Is that where you were all night?"

Ball sighed. There were times when her voice drove him completely up the wall. Yelling at her would shut her up, but in the long run it was counterproductive. He looked at her and shrugged. "I'm not supposed to say."

"Not even to your wife?"

"It has to do with a Secret Service agent."

"Not the suicide."

"Yes. The suicide. It's complicated, Elizabeth. Please

don't go blabbing." He took two pairs of socks from the drawer.

"What are you doing?"

"I'm going to be doing a little legwork over the next few days. I won't be around. I'll check in from time to time."

"Leg work? With female marshals?"

"I don't go for those Asian chicks, especially when they're teenagers," he said. He turned around and gave his wife a kiss on the cheek. "But thank you for thinking she'd be attracted to me. Now get some rest, all right? And don't go blabbing, all right? This is an important case we're dealing with. The wrong word in the wrong place, and some murderer goes free."

"Murder?"

"Forget I said that, and keep your mouth shut. Please."

96

ABOUT HALFWAY BACK to Saigon, Qui turned to Dean and asked again if he had been in the Marines.

"Yes, I was."

She asked which unit. He hesitated a moment, wondering if somehow she knew of the ambush against Phuc Dinh. But she had a different motive.

"I met a young man, a Marine, from First Division," she began. "It must have been 1966. This was before I married, very much before. I was such a younger woman."

Dean glanced at the side of her face. The memory or the telling of it seemed to make her very old, drawing deep lines at the corners of her eyes and furrows above her brow.

"He was a good young man. We met in Saigon while he was on leave or furlough; I forget the word. He spoke French—he'd studied it in school, and was not very good."

Qui smiled at Dean.

"He tried very hard. It was charming. And he was handsome. Like you were, I'd imagine." Qui turned back to look at the road. "When he died, they didn't allow me to go to the funeral. One of his friends came to our house and told me. He died while on patrol. Three other men were wounded taking back his body."

Not knowing what to say, Dean said nothing.

"It seems odd that they would bury a Marine here," said Qui. "Even in haste. If they knew where the body was."

"I agree."

"You aren't with the Monetary Fund," said Qui.

"No," said Dean. He imagined Rockman wincing back at the Art Room.

Qui reached over and tapped his hand. "Good luck."

Dean caught her fingers, and held them for a moment. "Thank you," he said. "Good luck to you."

They drove the next hour in silence.

DEAN NOTICED THE car following them when they stopped for gas about ten miles outside Saigon. A white Toyota pickup pulled past as the attendant filled up the truck and two jerry cans Qui kept in the trunk; Dean noticed the truck again as soon as they were back on the road.

He reached to the back of his belt to make sure his com system was on, then pointed out the truck to Qui.

"Are you sure he's following us?" she asked.

"Pretty sure," Dean said. "White Toyota pickup, two middle-aged guys in it," he added, describing the truck for the Art Room, though of course Qui thought he was talking to her.

"Maybe someone became interested in you in Quang Nam," said Qui. "Or maybe it's a coincidence."

"I don't believe in coincidences."

The Art Room asked Dean if he could get the license plate numbers of the truck, but the sun was starting to fade and the vehicle wasn't quite close enough for him to do that while they were driving.

"Charlie, Tommy Karr is about ten minutes away," said Rockman a short while later. "He'll get a look at who's following you and we can decide what to do then."

"Stay on the highway," Dean told Qui. "I want to figure out what's going on here."

"We're almost in the city. If it's the security forces, they'll follow us everywhere."

"Let's just keep going for now."

Dean slid lower in his seat, trying to see the driver and passenger of the other car in the side mirror. The passenger seemed to be frowning. Dean leaned over, trying to get a better view into the cab of the truck.

Qui suddenly veered sharply to the left. Before Dean knew what was happening, she had crossed over the center meridian and was heading in the other direction. She veered far to the right and got off the exit, pulling another sharp turn at the end of the ramp and sliding onto a road going under the highway.

"What are you doing?" Dean said.

"I don't care to be followed."

"That's just going to tip them off that we made them," said Dean.

"So?"

"If there's a whole team, the other cars will move in. We won't shake them."

Qui took a quick succession of turns and ended up on another highway.

"We're not being followed now," she told him as she accelerated. "If we were being followed earlier."

"We were," said Dean.

"I'll take your word for it."

TOMMY KARR HAD just started looking for the white pickup truck when Rockman told him to stand by.

"Kinda hard to stand by when you're driving a motorcycle," said Karr.

"Dean's off the road. I don't know what's going on."

"Which way?"

"North of you. A mile."

Karr leaned down close to his handlebars, urging the bike to go a little faster. He tucked past a pair of tractor-trailers and neatly bisected a pair of sedans.

"They went off that exit that's coming up on your left," said Rockman. "His driver is trying to shake them. Find a place to turn around."

No place better than right in front of him, thought Karr. He hit his brakes and skidded across the narrow meridian strip, power-gliding in the new direction. The bike wasn't that familiar and his timing was off; he nearly went under the wheels of a large bus. But Karr managed to flick away at the last moment, squeezing between the bus and a van. He missed the exit but got off on the shoulder just beyond it, bumping down the rocky slope to the pavement.

"So I'm looking for a Toyota pickup?" he asked, following Rockman's directions to the highway Dean and Qui had just gotten onto.

"White Toyota. That's right."

"Don't see it."

"They must have lost him."

"Too bad," said Karr.

DEAN TOLD QUI to drop him off at the riverfront. He didn't want her going anywhere near the hotel—whoever was following them might be waiting for him there. As Qui wended her way around toward the water, she told him that they were being followed again.

"Big guy on a motorcycle," she said. "He has a helmet with a dark visor."

"Yeah, I know him," said Dean. "He's on my side."

Qui glanced at Dean but said nothing.

"You can pull in over there," he told her.

"What is your real name?" Qui asked when she stopped the car.

"Charlie Dean."

"Well, good luck, Mr. Dean."

Dean grabbed his bag and began walking, looking for a place where he could plant a video bug to make sure he wasn't being followed. Karr, meanwhile, had taken a turn behind him and was circling around, also checking for surveillance.

It took them nearly twenty minutes to make sure no one had followed. Karr drove up to Dean as he stood watching some small boats unload.

"Man, I'm starving," said Karr. "Let's go get some noodles."

"Our hotel's probably being watched," Dean told Karr and the Art Room. "We can't go back there."

"Agreed," said Telach. The Art Room theorized that the security people had been sent by Cam Tre Luc, who had made inquiries about Dean following their "meeting" at

Saigon Rouge. "He may just want to keep an eye on you, but there's no sense finding out."

"You want us to get new digs, or are we bugging out?" said Karr.

"Probably leaving, but that's Mr. Rubens' call. Lay low for a few hours. Avoid the police."

"Let's go get some food," suggested Dean, worried about Qui though he wasn't sure exactly what to do.

"Now there you go," said Karr. "For once, you've got your priorities straight."

97

AS HE WALKED up the path to the tidy brick Georgian, Rubens nodded at the plainclothes guard. Dressed in a black suit despite the prospects of a blisteringly hot day, the man was the only visible component of an elaborate security team and system covering the upscale suburban Maryland home. Without him, the house would have appeared completely unremarkable, little different from the cardiac specialist's home next door or the upper-level manager's across the street.

That was the idea, though as Rubens rang the bell to Admiral Devlon Brown's house, the thought occurred to him that it was perhaps slightly galling that the man responsible for the NSA should live in a house that symbolized only a moderate amount of achievement. Architecture reflected a man's worth, at least in Rubens' opinion, and while one might choose to be subtle, even subtlety showed.

Admiral Brown apparently did not share that opinion. He was waiting for Rubens inside the family room off the kitchen, sitting on a couch with his legs propped up on a nearby ottoman. He wore a blanket and his face was as white as the night Rubens had seen him in the hospital after the heart attack. But his voice was stronger.

"William, thanks for coming by. I hate doing business by telephone. I've come to hate it more and more," said Brown, motioning him to sit. "Breakfast?"

"I had a bagel earlier."

"Not with butter, I hope."

"As a matter of fact, no." Rubens chose a chair that had been borrowed from the dining room, pulling it close to the admiral's legs.

"I've been listening to my doctor's scoldings so much I'm becoming a scold myself," admitted the admiral. "Coffee?"

"I'm trying to cut back."

"Too bad. I'm not allowed any myself," said Brown. "I have to live vicariously, smelling the aroma."

Rubens had come to discuss several matters, the most important of which was the investigation into the Vietnamese assassination plot.

Or, more accurately, non-plot.

"Whether the CIA plot was a figment of an agent's imagination remains to be seen," said Rubens, who suspected as much, "but in any event, neither the attack on Senator Mc-Sweeney nor Special Agent Forester's death is related to it. What they may be related to, however, is the theft of government money some forty years ago."

Brown seemed to gain back some of his color as Rubens continued, briefly summarizing the story.

"Two suicides and an assassination attempt," said Brown. "They would all seem related somehow. But why is it coming to a head now?"

"I simply don't know. I assume there is much more here than we have uncovered. The question is whether to turn this over to the FBI or to continue investigating it ourselves. The NSC finding is open-ended," Rubens added. "It states that we should investigate the assassination attempt. But it was issued with the idea that a foreign government was behind the attempt. This would seem to be a domestic matter."

"Have you discussed this with the President?"

Rubens had a long-standing personal relationship with President Marcke. Nonetheless, Rubens felt slighted at the question, for it suggested that he might subvert his boss. It was the sort of thing that Bing would accuse him of.

"I don't see a need to go directly to the President," said Rubens. "I've briefed Ms. Bing, and as far as the missing money goes, there's no proof that it's a consideration here.

And in any event, I would come to you first before briefing the President," said Rubens.

"I appreciate that."

"I have another concern," added Rubens. "The National Security Advisor is trying to build a case against relations with Vietnam. She wants our operations there to continue, even though I've told her there is no point."

Brown put his fingers together in front of his chest, pushing them back and forth as if they were an old-fashioned bellows, generating air for a smith's forge.

"If Senator McSweeney stole the money, who would be trying to kill him? One of the Vietnamese who was supposed to get it?" Brown asked.

"Maybe someone who was double-crossed," said Rubens. "Or perhaps the person who is trying to kill him is worried that the senator will expose him in some way."

"Hmmm."

"There is also the possibility that it has nothing to do with the theft of the money. Both the FBI and the Secret Service say the attempt fits the profile of a disgruntled or disturbed individual."

"All assassins are disturbed, aren't they?" said Brown.

Unless they work for us, thought Rubens, though he didn't say it.

"Do you think McSweeney is a thief?" A sly smile broke across Brown's lips. "Any more than the average politician?"

"I'm afraid I don't know him well enough to judge," said Rubens.

"The NSC finding did not say you should stop if Vietnam was not involved. Close down whatever part of the operation isn't helping you."

"And Ms. Bing?"

"I'll deal with her when the time comes. A good wrassle will do me a world of good."

Rubens nodded, then moved to the next item he'd come to discuss.

98

"JIMMY FINGERS!"

James "Jimmy Fingers" Fahey turned to his left and spotted Eric Blica coming down the steps of the exposition hall. Jimmy Fingers immediately veered away from the campaign people he'd been walking with.

"Eric, howareya?" he said, pumping Blica's hand.

"Your nickname's a liability in a place like this," said Blica. "Looked to me like half a dozen people were ready to pull out handcuffs and arrest you."

"You'd like that, wouldn't you?" said Jimmy Fingers. "What are you doing here?"

"It's a law enforcement conference. FBI needs to be represented, right?" Blica was a deputy director at the agency; he ranked third or fifth in the hierarchy, depending on the whim of the director.

"The FBI is involved in law enforcement?"

"Yuck, yuck. What's your boss up to?"

"Sitting on a panel and hoping to get an endorsement from the sheriffs' association, among others. I think there's still time to work in something about the Bureau into the speech," added Jimmy Fingers. "How their budget ought to be cut."

"Hey, come on. We're working for you."

"You haven't found that shooter yet," said Jimmy Fingers.

"We're working on it," said Blica. "There's a theory that the Vietnamese are involved."

"The Vietnamese?"

"I don't have any details. I'm not in the working group."

"I thought you were in charge."

"That'll be the day."

"Well, if Bolso retires, you'll be a top candidate," said Jimmy Fingers. "And there's always the McSweeney administration."

"Give me a break. You guys have so many IOUs out, you're going to have to triple the size of the government to pay off."

There was actually a lot of truth in the remark, and Jimmy Fingers smirked good-naturedly. "So tell me more about this Vietnamese thing," he said.

"You didn't get it from me."

"You? I don't even know you."

THE CRAZY VIETNAMESE conspiracy theory was so good, so delicious, that Jimmy Fingers wasn't entirely sure it wasn't some sort of ruse. He decided to call Jed Frey, the head of the Secret Service, to see if he could smoke anything else out.

Frey had an assistant call him back. While technically that was the proper etiquette—aides dealt with aides—it still angered Jimmy Fingers.

"What's this rumor I hear that the Vietnamese were trying to assassinate my guy?" said Jimmy Fingers.

"I'm not prepared to discuss that," said the aide.

"Well, what the hell are you prepared to discuss?" said Jimmy Fingers, tongue-lashing the assistant. The senator deserved to know what was going on, the Service was not unassailable, the American public deserved better, blah blah blah. When he finished, Jimmy Fingers actually caught himself feeling sorry for the poor sap, who could only sit there and take it.

Having softened him up, Jimmy Fingers moved in for the kill.

"So, listen, between you and me," said Jimmy Fingers. "Is this thing true or not? Should I tell the security guys to screen out anyone from the hall with squinty eyes or not? I don't want to give this guy another chance, you know what I'm saying?"

"It is a valid theory that's being pursued," said the aide. "But it's not the leading theory."

"What is the leading theory? The nut-job assassin?"

"I wouldn't quite put it that way."

"And you're still looking at those e-mails, right? You know we got that other one the other day. You never told us what came of it."

"We're definitely investigating. If you don't hear from us, it's only because we have nothing of interest to say."

By the time Jimmy Fingers hung up the phone, he was convinced that the Secret Service had no idea what was going on. He was also convinced that the Vietnamese theory, as off-the-wall as it was, would benefit McSweeney immensely.

Which reporters, Jimmy Fingers thought, thumbing his cell phone's phone book open, did he want owing him a big favor?

99

DEAN AND KARR were just finishing dinner when Telach told Dean to stand by for a communication from Rubens.

"Mr. Dean, Mr. Karr, it's time for you to leave Vietnam," Rubens told them.

"Aw, and I was just getting used to the place," said Karr.

"Please, Tommy, don't interrupt," said Rubens. "We believe the security forces are looking for you. Therefore, we have arranged alternate transportation. A boat will meet you in the Saigon harbor at one A.M., your time. It will take you to a rendezvous with a helicopter five miles off the coast. The helicopter will take you to Thailand, and from there you will use commercial transport."

"Commercial transport as in first class?" said Karr.

"I believe coach will suffice," said Rubens. "Do you have any other questions?"

"Don't you think that's a long flight for coach?" said Karr.

"Any serious questions."

"Who are these security people?" asked Dean. "Where are they?"

"Mr. Rockman can give you the details," said Rubens. "They appear to be working at Cam Tre Luc's behest. I would not take them too lightly."

"I'm not," said Dean.

They paid their bill and left, gassed up the motorbike, and then headed in the direction of the port. The damp night air was thick with fog, but the breeze from the back of the bike felt good as it rushed past. Because of the fog, Karr drove conservatively, at least for him; they stayed under the sound barrier.

The rendezvous spot was a short, bare pier. Even in the dark, it seemed to be falling apart.

"We can't wait out there," said Dean. "Anybody going by on the street, or even on one of those other piers, can see us."

They planted a pair of video bugs to cover the area and then drove a few blocks before settling on a secluded alley where they could wait. While Karr looked at the feed from the video bugs, Dean took out his sat phone and called Qui Lai Chu.

A man answered.

"Is Ms. Chu there?" said Dean.

"Who are you?" asked the man in Vietnamese.

"I'd like to speak to Ms. Chu," said Dean.

The man said something to a companion that Dean couldn't make out. Another man came on the line and asked in English whom he was speaking to.

Dean hung up.

"Rockman, can you track down the location of the phone I just called?" Dean asked.

"Why?"

"Because I think Qui Lai Chu is in trouble."

"Charlie, I don't think—"

"Track the phone for me, Rockman. Do it now."

There was a pause. Marie Telach came on the line.

"Mr. Rubens wanted you to come home as soon as possible," Telach told him.

"Then you'd better give me the location of that phone," said Dean. "Because we're not leaving here until that woman is safe."

100

QUI LAI CHU sat on the wooden chair with her legs pressed together, staring at the floor. It had been quite a long time since she had had trouble with the police, but remembering how to deal with them did not require any great effort. The most important things were to remain calm and to do nothing to provoke them.

The door opened. Two of her jailers and a short, older man entered the room. As usual in Vietnam, the older man was in charge. The others stepped back from him deferentially.

"You, Qui Lai Chu—what did you do in Quang Nam?" said the man. The words shot from his mouth like crisp gunshots; he had a slight frown on his face, as if already angry that she was wasting his time.

"Who are you?" Qui asked.

"You are not in a position to ask questions! What did you do in Quang Nam?"

"I accompanied a business tourist there. I am a licensed translator," Qui continued before the man could say anything else. "He was an American and he obviously felt war guilt. He spoke to several people and inquired about a dead man. He met with a government official. I assume it was an old enemy who had vanquished him, and he had come to make his respects."

"What official?"

"He did not take me inside," she said.

"Why bring a translator and not use her?"

"I cannot explain an American's whims."

"You were paid?"

"Yes."

Perhaps, thought Qui, he is looking for a bribe. But after several more questions about how she was paid—Qui knew better than to say that he had paid with American dollars, for that would have been a crime—her interrogator changed the subject.

"What was this man like?"

"An American. Stupid. Lazy. Fat." They were the stock answers one was expected to give.

"Don't lie."

"He was a typical American." Qui held out her hands. "He said he was with a relief organization. He seemed intelligent, but spoke little. Like all Americans, I assume he had more money than he knew what to do with."

Once again, the subject was changed, with Qui asked how the man had come to hire her. This was somewhat tricky ground. She was licensed by the government to translate, and driving Dean in her private car was, potentially, a crime if she charged for it, even though it was a common practice. With no way of knowing what her interrogator was after, Qui gave as little information as possible, leaving open the obvious but not stating it for the record.

"Do you still wish to know who I am?" asked the man finally.

"Yes."

"My name is Cam Tre Luc. I am the director of the Interior Ministry Southern Security District. Do you know what that means?"

"You are an important man," said Qui, lowering her gaze.

"It means that if I lift my fingers you will be reeducated in the countryside."

"Reeducation" essentially meant banishment to a poor area where, if one was lucky, he or she might be looked on as a community slave. Reeducation could last a year or two or ten, depending on a number of factors, including bureaucratic whim and the emotions of the village's headman.

"I wish to speak to this Mr. Dean," said Cam Tre Luc. "You will arrange it for me."

Qui had not given Dean's name, but she was not surprised that Cam Tre Luc knew it.

"I don't know how to contact him," said Qui.

"He called you a short while ago," said Cam Tre Luc. He gestured to one of the younger men, who produced Cam Tre Luc's cell phone. "Call him back. Tell him to meet you at the Inchine Hilton."

Qui took the phone, trying to think of how she could warn Dean while still appearing to do Cam Tre Luc's bidding. The phone provided its own answer—Dean's phone number had registered as gibberish on her directory.

"I don't have a way to contact him," Qui told Cam Tre Luc.

"You will find a way," he said, abruptly turning and leaving the room.

AS HE WALKED down the hall from the interrogation room, Cam Tre Luc reached into his pocket and retrieved a small lump of misshapen metal, turning it over in his fingers as he walked. It was an unconscious habit; he had had the metal for going on forty years, ever since it was pulled from the rib where it had lodged, a few inches from his heart.

"Without luck," the nurse who had pulled it from him said, "you would be a ghost."

Lieutenant Son, the head of the division that had detained Ms. Chu, was waiting at the end of the hall.

"Keep questioning her about this American, Charles Dean," Cam Tre Luc told him. "In the morning, I want her taken to his hotel."

"He has not gone back, or I would have been informed."

"My goal, comrade, is simple," said Cam Tre Luc. "I wish Mr. Dean to be brought to me. If you have a better way of achieving that goal, by all means proceed. Just do not fail in the end."

"What if this Dean has already left the country?"

"He would have been picked up at the airport. No, he is

still here. He hasn't checked out of his hotel. Detain him, take his passport, and alert me."

"Absolutely, Comrade Director."

Cam Tre Luc stepped out in the humid night air, still turning the metal lump between his fingers. The American would pay for his impertinence. They had not fought the war to be treated like peons.

101

LIA SLID THE small dongle into the computer's USB slot as the librarian approached. She sat straight up and clicked on the Web browser, quickly typing in the address.

"Got it?" she said in a stage whisper.

"We're in," said Telach back in the Art Room.

"Young woman," said the librarian. "That's the third computer you've been on."

"I couldn't get used to the keyboards on the others," Lia told her.

"They are all the same brand of computer!"

"But the keyboards are different. Here, look at this one." Lia pointed her to the computer at the next desk. "The support isn't quite level. It wobbles. Try it."

The librarian frowned and sat down. She typed a few sentences.

"It seems perfectly level to me."

"It felt odd to me," Lia insisted.

"Some people," muttered the librarian under her breath as she went back to the circulation desk.

"They need about ten more minutes," said Telach.

"Fine," said Lia, not bothering to keep her voice low. She checked the browser history on the top line; there were only two requests logged, both sites for free recipes.

"This one may have been it," said Telach, relaying information from the technical people. "It looks like files have been erased. The entire history file has been erased."

"Can you get it back?"

"They can get back whatever wasn't overwritten easily. As for the rest, I'll have to talk to Mr. Rubens to get approval to take their hard drive. Stand by."

Lia looked up from the screen and saw that the librarian was staring at her.

"Just talking to myself," said Lia.

"Well, please be considerate. Other people are trying to concentrate."

"Sure thing."

102

CHRISTOPHER BALL HAD killed at least three dozen people in his life. Most were in Vietnam, where as enemy soldiers or guerillas they had clearly deserved it. Most of the rest were criminals, or involved in criminal activity, generally with Ball during the five or six years after Vietnam when he had parlayed his portion of the Key Tiger money into a sizeable nest egg by selling Asian heroin. Their deaths were also easily rationalized, as was the revenge killing of Jason Evans, the developer who had robbed Ball of much of his money in the mid-1980s, squandering over a million dollars in a scheme to build condos outside of LA. And then there was Reggie Gordon, whose murder—disguised as a suicide—was an absolute necessity. Gordon had clearly been the one to tell Forester about the theft of the Vietnamese payoffs: the only other people alive who knew what had happened were McSweeney and Ball himself. Killing Gordon was easy, in fact, pleasurable, though it had been more than a decade since Ball had found it necessary to use the skills he had learned as a young Marine.

But Amanda Rauci was different, and Ball couldn't precisely say why. It wasn't just that she was a woman; he had killed two women in Vietnam, both guerilla leaders, at least according to the CIA. It wasn't just that she was a federal agent. He'd killed a DEA agent during his drug dealer days, albeit one who was dealing on both sides of the law.

Ball tried to parcel out the differences as he drove north on the Parkway toward Albany. The more he tried to define it, the more impossible it became.

And the more her death haunted him. He heard her again, felt the way she pushed against his arms, life ebbing from her.

He told himself not to think about it, but there was nothing to replace the thoughts. He glanced down at his speedometer and saw that he was pushing ninety. Ball immediately backed off the gas. He wasn't afraid of getting a ticket; if he was stopped, he'd casually show his badge while reaching for his license, mention that he was on official business, and out of professional courtesy the trooper would let him go. But then someone would know where he was.

When Forester didn't keep his appointment that day, Ball had feared the worst—that the Secret Service agent had seen through his smile and his bs, and realized that he did know Gordon. Then, when he heard the news that Forester had killed himself, Chief Ball thought that God Himself had intervened.

There was a certain logic and even rough justice to the thought. All of the money he had gotten was gone, long gone, most of it stolen by that crook Evans. Ball had paid the price for his moment of weakness in many ways, and had done good work besides.

But now he saw that was simply wishful thinking. Clearly, these people weren't going to stop until they caught him. It occurred to Ball that Forester's suicide was a setup—they were eventually going to blame him for the death, and put him away for life.

They wouldn't give him the chair, because of the way the law read in Connecticut. Which was probably why they chose to do it there, rather than in New York—they wanted to torture him for the rest of his life.

Would he have to kill them all? DeFrancesca next? Then the FBI agent, and the other Secret Service agent—he couldn't even remember their damn names.

Could he kill them all?

He'd have to.

Not if it meant choking them. Amanda Rauci's eyes loomed in front of him.

Why were they after him now? Was it Gordon's fault? Or was McSweeney pulling the strings?

It couldn't be McSweeney. He had too much to lose.

God, the way Rauci shook when she died.

Ball felt her pushing against his arms. He saw her face when he picked her up.

Ball's stomach began to react. He made it to the side of the road just in time.

103

TELACH CAME DOWN to the briefing room to personally tell Rubens that they had located the computer the Secret Service agent had used the night before.

"It looks like she erased and overwrote what she had been doing," Telach told him. "We may be able to recover the information if we retrieve the drive."

"Then let's do that. Have Lia explain what is going on," said Rubens. "But only as much as is absolutely necessary."

"They'll probably ask for a subpoena."

"Of course."

Rubens nodded to Jackson as Telach left the room. Jackson continued updating the others.

"Tolong is the obvious suspect," Jackson said. "He and the other Marine on the patrol. He was immediately suspected. But then he goes on patrol and dies. So if I were to suspect someone, it would be Gordon. Anyone could have found the money if Tolong had kept it among his personal things. We have to check the unit where he was, and any other unit that could have come in contact with him."

Most of the analysts were actually computer scientists or cryptologists, but if someone had walked in off the street he would probably have thought he had stumbled into an artists' convention. There were tie-died sixties-style T-shirts, torn jeans, a leather-fringe jacket, and what appeared to Rubens to be a full baseball uniform. Body piercings made dealing with the security protocols a major daily hassle, so aside from a few earrings—on the men, for the most part—there were none. Tattoos were also covered, though Rubens suspected there were a good variety under the shirts and other clothing.

Hairstyles were a different matter. Desk Three's best cryptologist, a young woman two years out of Princeton, sported a green Mohawk. The team's resident weapons expert, a thirtysomething Marine sergeant on semi-permanent loan to the agency, had a shoulder-length ponytail.

"What about Gordon?" asked Angela DiGiacomo. "Maybe Tolong told him where the money was before he died."

"Good point." Jackson beamed at the young woman.

"There must have been one other person involved in the conspiracy," said Rubens. "That person feels cheated somehow, and is now out for revenge."

"Or wants all the money to himself," said Jackson. "But if that's our working theory, then we have to assume that Senator McSweeney was involved in the original theft. He's the one who made the assignments. He controlled the initial investigation, at least from the Marines' side. He's got to be involved up to his neck."

"Appearances *deceive*!" said Johnny Bib.

Everyone, including Rubens, turned to Johnny Bib, awaiting an explanation for his outburst. But none was forthcoming.

"Are you reminding us to keep an open mind?" Rubens asked. "Or have you thought of something specific?"

"Open mind." Johnny Bib grinned, then leaned back in the chair and stretched his legs. "What if Forester and Gordon really did commit suicide? What if the assassin has nothing to do with the theft of money? Two equations— common algebra."

"Mr. Bibleria is quite right," said Rubens, glancing at Jackson. "It is possible that these things are not related, and that in fact we do not have all the information here."

"We are missing critical information," added Johnny Bib. "The addition of a variable may change our answer set entirely."

Rubens listened as Johnny Bib divvied up new assignments, most of which involved searching records thirty and forty years old for possible clues and connections. The session over, the analysts filed out. They were a noisy bunch, talking and joking and in one or two cases even singing.

"Thank you for translating," Jackson told Rubens.

"Yes. Mr. Bibleria occasionally gets carried away with his metaphors."

Marie Telach was just coming down the hall as Rubens stepped out.

"Come with me to the Art Room," she said. "You won't believe what's on Fox."

104

THE ASSAULT BEGAN with a rocket attack, quickly followed by an infiltration on an unguarded flank. Before the enemy realized it, their perimeter had been compromised and the guerillas were already streaking toward their objective.

It was a classic VC raid, except that the attackers were not Vietcong. And the rocket attack actually consisted of two flash-bang grenades detonated by remote control. They had the desired effect, however; the security officers rallied toward the explosion, guns drawn.

Charlie Dean followed Karr as he leapt over the four-foot wall around the compound and ran toward the small building identified as a power shed by the Art Room, which was watching them via an infrared camera in the small "Crow" unmanned aerial vehicle they had launched twenty minutes before. The shotgun Dean had in his hands seemed to gain weight with each step until it felt like a howitzer. Dean threw himself against the side of the building, breathing harder than he thought he should be.

Karr was already kneeling next to him, attaching a block of plastic explosive to the conduit where the power line came out of the building. Dean checked the gear in his tactical vest, patting himself down to make sure he hadn't lost anything important in the dash. Two canisters of shotgun shells packed with disabling pellets and gas were tucked into each of the large front pockets; exchanging them with a blank magazine in the gun took about three seconds. The gun was based on a Pancor Jackhammer and looked like a cross between a cut-down Franchi SPAS-12 and an old-fashioned tommy gun. Its ammunition was designed to be nonfatal and meant for close-quarters combat; Dean had a Colt automatic in his belt as a backup weapon.

Karr had an MP5 machine gun. Like Dean's pistol, they'd only use it if things got hairy.

Dean readjusted his night glasses, pushing them back up the bridge of his nose and tightening the clasp on the strap at the back of his head. Though they looked like oversized sunglasses, they were more powerful than the Gen 3 night monocles used by the American Army. Then he pulled on the respirator, so any stray tear gas wouldn't disable him.

"Ready?" Karr asked, standing. The microphone in Karr's mask gave his voice a hollow sound.

"Ready," said Dean.

"We see two guards standing at the front of the building," said Rockman. "That leaves three unaccounted for, somewhere inside."

"Pot luck," said Karr. "You got point, Charlie."

Dean pushed off from the shack and ran toward the back corner of the police building, about thirty yards away. Once again he threw himself against the wall, pushing the nose of his gun level as he triple-checked his position. He was between the corner of the building and one of the large windows on the first floor.

Karr slid in on the other side of the window. He already had two flash-bang grenades in his hands.

"Ten seconds," said Karr. He wasn't even breathing hard. "Rockman?"

"Same as before."

Dean leaned toward the end of the building, then peeked around the corner. A basement entrance sat six feet away.

"Five seconds," said Karr. "Four, three, two—"

Dean stood back upright. As Karr said, "One," Dean swung the metal butt of the shotgun up toward the glass.

The sound of the glass shattering was drowned out by the explosion of the power shack.

"Clear," said Karr, glancing in the window. "Go!"

Dean grabbed the ledge of the window and jumped into the room. He stumbled as he landed, falling to his left. He rolled through the shards of broken glass, crushing it into tiny pieces with his shoulder, before jumping back to his feet. Huffing again, he raced to the open door of the room, reaching it a few seconds after Karr.

"Clear," said Karr, and they ran into the hallway.

Using infrared images from the Crow, the Art Room had pinpointed a room on the first floor where they thought Qui was being held. Karr sent his foot crashing against the door. The thin jamb gave way instantly. Karr tossed one of his grenades inside. As the room erupted with a flash, Dean followed inside.

The room was empty.

"Shit," cursed Dean.

"Coming in the front!" warned Rockman.

Karr threw a grenade down the hallway as one of the guards began to shout. Dean leapt into the hallway behind the explosion and pumped two shells into the three figures at the far end. The men went down immediately, their bodies pelted by oversized plastic BBs and soaked in synthetic cayenne.

"Has to be downstairs," said Karr, racing toward the back stairwell.

"Rockman?" said Dean, pausing to smash the emergency lights on the battery backup at the end of the hallway.

"She's definitely not on the second floor. It's unoccupied."

"This way, Charlie," said Karr, pulling open the door to the stairs. "And relax."

"I am relaxed."

"That why you're still cursing?"

WHEN SHE HEARD the first series of explosions, Qui Lai Chu began shaking uncontrollably. There was no furniture in the room where she was being held; she had nothing to hide behind or under except for the wooden chair where she'd been sitting. Trembling, she slipped off the chair, falling to her knees as she pulled the chair toward her.

The ground shook and the lights went out. Qui Lai Chu's mind fled from the present to her childhood, to the early days when French was the only language she spoke. She was back in Hanoi, in the large house her father had built, cowering in the basement with her mother as Communist fanatics hurled grenades at the decadent bourgeois imperialists. Qui didn't understand what the slogans meant, but she did know that the grenades were aimed at her family and friends.

There were fresh explosions above her. Now she was back in Saigon, during the eerie days just before the capital fell, just before history's overwhelming momentum crushed the last bits of the life her mother had built for the family here.

Before Qui's mother, seeing that she would lose everything a second time, threw herself in front of a Communist truck, so she might meet her husband and ancestors.

"Stay away from the door!" shouted a voice.

Qui didn't recognize it at first. It was amplified in an odd way, and she thought it was a hallucination from the past.

The front of the room exploded with light. Blinded, she pushed her face close to the ground.

"Got her, Charlie!" yelled someone nearby. "Go; let's go!"

A BEAM OF light appeared in the stairwell as Dean reached the door. Dean waved at Karr to stay back, then waited a few seconds until the circle of light came closer. When it hit the wall opposite him, he lifted his shotgun and leapt past the stairs, firing two rounds upward at the light's source. It was a flashlight, and as the bulb exploded, the man who was holding it toppled down the staircase.

Dean got back up and ran to a door at the side of the basement that led to the outside. The stench of cayenne pepper filled the small space; even though he had a respirator on, Dean began coughing as he pushed down on the crash bar.

The door didn't give.

Karr, carrying Qui over his shoulder, ducked next to Dean.

There were shouts above. Three or four bullets crashed against the sides of the stairwell. Karr lobbed a tear gas canister toward the first floor, then ran to Dean.

Dean pulled the pistol out of his belt and fired twice point-blank into the lock. He pounded against the door. The mangled metal gave slightly but didn't break.

"Together," said Karr, putting down Qui.

Automatic rifle fire sounded behind them. The stairwell magnified the sound of the AK-47, so that it seemed as if it were coming from inside Dean's skull.

"Now," said Dean.

They rammed their shoulders together. The lock gave way and Dean sprawled into the cement stairwell.

Karr tossed a grenade behind him and then rushed past carrying Qui. Dean followed, stumbling up the wide concrete ramp that led to the yard at the side of the building.

Rockman was yelling at him. Dean couldn't understand what it was, but he guessed it might be a warning. As soon as he saw something moving on his left, Dean lowered the shotgun and fired from his hip.

The pellets sailed wide right without hitting the figure. But the shadow collapsed anyway, its owner flattening himself on the ground to avoid a second shot.

"To the wall, Charlie, let's go!" yelled Karr.

"Two more, coming from the right side of the building," warned Rockman.

Dean stopped and dropped to his knee, waiting for the men to appear. They stepped out from a line of tree trunks at about thirty feet. Dean fired two shots, both times hitting home.

By now his lungs felt as if they were going to explode. He ran as fast as he could for the wall. Just as he reached it, a thousand firecrackers began exploding in the courtyard—another of Karr's diversions.

As Dean put his hand on the top of the wall, he heard an AK-47 firing somewhere nearby. He lost his balance in the haste, slipping all the way back to the ground. Chips flew from the wall.

I'm not going to die here, he thought. And he leapt to his feet and jumped headfirst over the wall.

THE MOTORBIKE BEGAN to move.

"Hang on," said the man who had carried Qui from the building.

Within a minute, they were on a highway, driving to the west. Qui felt as if she were riding on a thin stick and that any false move would send them over to the side.

Ten minutes later, they stopped. Qui's eyes still stung from the odor of the pepper gas.

"Why?" she demanded. "Why did you do this to me?"

The man laughed.

"Come on and get into the truck."

"Are you kidnapping me?"

He laughed again. "We're rescuing you. Come on. Get into the truck. We have a plane to catch."

He started to let the bike slide out from under him to the ground. Qui stepped away.

Dean drove up a few seconds later.

"Mr. Dean," she said after he hopped off his own bike. "Why did you do this to me?"

"What do you mean?" asked Dean.

"Why did you do this?"

"Rescue you?"

"I didn't need to be rescued."

"Hey, lady, are you serious?" said the other man.

"I am very serious. I could have handled this."

"They would have put you in jail."

"It's all right, Tommy," said Dean. "I'll talk to her. Go get the truck ready."

Karr walked away, chuckling to himself.

"I'm glad your friend is so amused," Qui told Dean.

"Tommy thinks the world's a sitcom. He's always laughing at something."

"You've given me a great many problems, Mr. Dean."

"No." Dean shook his head. "You're going to come with us. We'll be in America tomorrow."

"I don't want to go to America." Qui felt her body begin to tremble once again. "Who asked you to rescue me? Who? Why did you have to interfere?"

DEAN PERSUADED QUI to sit in the back of the truck while he talked over the situation with Karr.

"We can't take her back if she doesn't want to go," Dean told Karr.

"Gotta do something, Charlie. And we only have about a half hour to meet that boat. Telach said he'd only wait two hours."

Dean paced back and forth along the side of the van. Karr was right. But taking Qui away against her will didn't seem right, either.

How did you save people who didn't want to be saved? Or rather, who *did* want to be saved but didn't want your solution?

Vietnam, all over again.

"All right, come on," Dean said finally. "Hop in the truck."

"We going to the docks?"

"No. Plan B."

RUBENS WAS NOT a television aficionado and watched news shows only when absolutely forced to. But Marie Telach was right—he did want to see what was on Fox.

Not that he liked it very much.

The cable network was airing a noon press conference with Senator McSweeney in California.

"This is the first I heard about it," said McSweeney.

"So you can't confirm that the Secret Service is investigating whether the government of Vietnam tried to have you assassinated?" asked the reporter.

"You're going to have to ask either the Secret Service or, I guess, the government of Vietnam." The senator smiled as the reporters snickered. "Can we move on?"

"You weren't even notified?" asked another reporter.

"Guys, this sounds to me like an off-the-wall rumor. Really," said McSweeney.

More reporters pressed with questions.

"This is a replay," said Rockman. "It aired live about ten minutes ago."

"Why did the Secret Service tell McSweeney about the Vietnamese connection?" asked Telach.

"I don't know," said Rubens, turning to go back to his office and find out.

"HOW THE *HELL* did that get into the media?" roared Gideon McSweeney as he walked down the hallway after the press conference. Aides scattered; two hotel workers froze, sure that he was going to punch them in his fury. "And why the *hell* didn't they tell me! Jesus H. Christ."

"Relax, Senator," said Jimmy Fingers. "I told you. It's not going to hurt you."

"The hell, says you. 'Elect this man and start a war with Vietnam!' There's a slogan for you."

"You're overthinking it," said Jimmy Fingers. "People are going to admire you. For one thing, it reminds them you were a war hero—"

"Don't give me that war-hero crap, Fingers." McSweeney pointed his finger at his aide, waving it as if it were a stick. "You know how something like that can backfire. And I was *not* a hero. Heroes died. Those guys were heroes."

"You're being too hard on yourself, Gideon. Relax. This will blow over."

McSweeney grabbed Jimmy Fingers by the arm. "Don't tell me to relax."

The look in Jimmy Fingers' eyes was as sharp as a slap in the face. McSweeney let go of him, then exhaled slowly.

"I'm sorry, Jim. You're right. I'm overreacting. I'm not sure why."

"Pressure of the campaign. You'll get over it."

"Thanks." McSweeney tapped his aide and began walking again. "You've been working out?"

"Not really."

"Has Frey called you back?"

"I haven't spoken to anyone except his aide. He wouldn't confirm or deny."

"You get me Frey. Make sure it's him. I want to give him a piece of my mind."

"I put the call in as soon as I heard the first question."

FREY DIDN'T CALL back for another half hour. By then, Mc-Sweeney had sat down for dinner with a group of county party leaders. Jimmy Fingers sent someone to get the senator and in the meantime spoke to Frey himself.

"Let me give you a heads-up here," he told the head of the Secret Service. "The senator is really, really hot about the leak."

"I'm not too happy about it myself."

"I calmed him down. I told him it wouldn't have come from you. I am right, ain't I?"

"Of course I didn't leak it. Did you?"

"Me?"

"My aide Paul Quantril says you were asking about rumors."

"Why would I leak it?"

"Where did you hear the rumors?" Frey's voice still had enough of an edge to it to tell Jimmy Fingers that he thought it had come from him.

"A reporter. I don't know what his source was, but I can guess it was the White House."

"The White House?"

"There are people there trying to make the Vietnamese look bad," said Jimmy Fingers. "I assume this was part of their agenda. They don't like Senator McSweeney, either, but I don't think that entered into their calculations."

Jimmy Fingers looked up and saw Senator McSweeney striding across the suite room. The aide he'd sent to fetch McSweeney was nowhere in sight, clearly having been left in the dust.

"Brace yourself," Jimmy Fingers told Frey before handing over the phone.

107

"THE LEAK DID *not* come from us," Frey told Rubens. "Less than a dozen people are even aware of that theory."

"Where do you think it came from?"

"I'm not sure. James Fahey, McSweeney's ferret-faced right-hand man, thinks someone in the White House leaked it, trying to make points against Vietnam. Personally, I think he said that to keep suspicion off himself. He called my office saying he'd heard rumors a few hours before this came out. They call Fahey Jimmy Fingers because he's got his fingers in everything," added Frey. "He's always playing some angle."

"I would not necessarily rule Mr. Fahey's theory out," said Rubens.

"Who?"

"Without evidence, I would hesitate to accuse anyone," said Rubens, though he had an obvious candidate: Bing. "There are some agendas there that this would play into."

"If I find the person, I'll break them in two." Most people grew calmer as they talked; Frey seemed to do the opposite. "If they leaked this, what else did they leak? And what will they leak tomorrow?"

"Yes," said Rubens.

After they exchanged some calmer details of the investigation, Rubens hung up and walked to the center of his office. His back was knotted in a dozen places, and he could feel a headache coming on. His yoga teacher had suggested a routine to loosen his spine and help him relax.

Obviously, the leak had come from Bing, thought Rubens as he slipped off his shoes. Bing was the only person who had anything to gain from it. She'd do it cleverly, of course—an aide would have lunch with a reporter, drop a strategic comment, and that would be that. Plausible denial intact.

Rubens was just beginning a tiger pose when his phone rang. He got up slowly, and saw that it was Bing.

"Senator McSweeney was just asked at a press conference about the possibility that the Vietnamese government wants to kill him," she told Rubens when he picked up.

"Yes, I saw a tape of the press conference," said Rubens. "I have been wondering who alerted the media."

"Was it you?"

Rubens' back muscles immediately spasmed.

"I can't even see the logic of asking me that question," said Rubens, his tone nearly as stiff as his back. "Unless you're trying to turn suspicion away from yourself."

Bing was silent.

"Is there anything else?" said Rubens finally.

"I'm still waiting for the Vietnam report."

"There is nothing to report. As I told you the other day, there is no connection between the assassination attempt and the Vietnam government."

"That's all you have?" Bing asked.

"Nothing more."

She hung up. Less than thirty seconds later, Rubens got a call from the White House.

"The President wants to see you," said Ted Cohen, the chief of staff. "And he wants to see you *now*."

"Yes," said Rubens. "I suspected he might."

108

THE NEWS OF the attack on the station where he had ordered the woman held reassured Cam Tre Luc in an odd way. It confirmed that the man who had surprised him in the bordello was an American spy. This restored some of Cam Tre Luc's dignity; it would have been unbearable if the man had been simply a businessman or private citizen, as the official entry records and his sources at the hotel suggested.

Not that he was going to let Mr. Dean get away with it.

On the contrary.

Cam Tre Luc spent several hours checking personally with the officials who oversaw the immigration checks at all of the country's airports, not just Saigon. He called the chief of the local police and gave him a full description of the man, adding that his apprehension would be rewarded in meaningful ways. Finally, exhausted, Cam Tre Luc went to bed.

His eyes began to close even before his head slipped back on the pillow.

Cam Tre Luc realized that he was becoming an old man. This was a good thing in Vietnam; people respected a man with silver hair, appreciating his wisdom and making allowances for his failings. How much better would that aura seem, he mused, when he apprehended an American spy ring?

Very possibly he could move up to a national position. He saw himself in Hanoi—then his vision dimmed completely as he fell asleep.

The next thing Cam Tre Luc knew, a hand was pressed over his mouth and he was being hauled upright in the bed.

Light shined in his eyes.

Charles Dean stood before him. Cam Tre Luc tried to yell for his bodyguards, but the hand clamped over his mouth would emit no noise.

"Your bodyguards are tied up," said Dean. He repeated what he had said in roughly accented Vietnamese. "I want to talk to you."

Cam Tre Luc shook his head.

"All you have to do is listen," said Dean. He pointed at whoever was holding Cam Tre Luc, and the hand slipped from his mouth.

Cam Tre Luc yelled for his men.

"They're not going to come," Dean said in English. "I told you. They're tied up."

"I understand your English better than your Vietnamese," Cam Tre Luc told Dean as he started to repeat himself in Vietnamese. "Your accent is horrible."

"Why did you arrest Qui Lai Chu?" asked Dean.

"She is an enemy of the people."

"She's a translator. She has nothing to do with me."

"You are a spy."

"I came to your country to solve a murder. You helped me."

"I helped you?"

"You did," said Dean. "And I'm grateful."

Cam Tre Luc asked the American what he wanted.

Instead of answering, Dean told him that he wanted a guarantee that Qui Lai Chu would not be harmed. Cam Tre Luc made a face.

"Do you have a fax machine?" Dean asked.

"Fax?"

"A facsimile. It makes an image on paper and transmits over a telephone line."

"I know what a fax is," said Cam Tre Luc.

"Do you have one?"

"In my office downstairs."

"Let's go."

* * *

DEAN WAITED AS the machine beeped and began to whir. The machine was at least twenty years old and used thermal imaging paper instead of inkjets or a laser. But the image that came through was clear and legible. Dean took the first sheet as the cutter slid across and deposited it on the tray.

"This is a CIA pay list, from 1966," said Dean. "If you read English as well as you speak it, you can figure out the rest."

Cam Tre Luc's face turned pale as he looked at the paper.

"If I find out that Qui Lai Chu is hurt, the entire file will be sent to Hanoi," said Dean. "I don't think that will do much for your career."

Dean nodded to Karr, who let Cam Tre Luc go.

"Maybe you ought to call off the dogs at the airport," Dean added, grabbing the other two pages as they came through the fax machine. "I'd hate to think how they might interpret these pages if I have to hand them over at the airport."

109

"I DON'T CARE who you are," said the librarian. "I'm not going to allow you to take the hard drive."

"What's your fax number?" Lia said.

"Our fax?"

"I'll have a subpoena faxed right to you."

The librarian frowned, then took another tack.

"If I let you have the hard drive, which I'm not saying I'm going to do, that means my patrons are out a computer," she told Lia. "What am I going to tell them?"

"What if I got you a new hard drive?" said Lia.

"And you set it up? The network administrator spent two whole days getting one of our machines to work the last time we had a crash."

"I guarantee we can do it faster," said Lia.

The nearby fax machine rang and then began to print. The librarian went over to the machine.

"How did you do that?" asked the librarian. "I thought you didn't know our number."

Lia shrugged. "I have friends in high places."

"Let me call the town attorney and make sure this is legal."

"Please do," said Lia.

TWO HOURS LATER, Lia cradled her sat phone to her ear, pretending to use it as Robert Gallo talked her through the installation process. Gallo had already made a copy of the working data on the original drive; once Lia was ready, he downloaded a compressed version to the drive. As she was waiting for the files to reconstitute themselves, Lia handed off the original drive to a state trooper who had promised to take it to the airport, where a courier would pick it up and fly it to Crypto City.

"Done," Lia told the Art Room as the library's card catalog appeared on the screen. She hung up the phone and got up from the computer.

"You better go tell Chief Ball that you took the drive," suggested Telach. "He's bound to find out."

"Should I ask him why Amanda ran the credit check?"

"Hold that back. Maybe there's something on the drive that will make it obvious."

"Gotcha."

"Are you talking to me?" asked the librarian, who had come over without Lia noticing her.

"Just to myself," said Lia.

"Sounded like some conversation."

"You should hear when I disagree."

"HE DIDN'T SAY when he would be back. Gone a few days. That was the message he left."

"And he didn't say where he was going?"

"Uh-uh."

Lia stared at the Pine Plains police dispatcher, trying to figure out if the blank look on her face was real or phony. It was hard to tell.

The phone rang before Lia decided. The Pine Plains police dispatcher pulled her thick-framed eyeglasses up off the bridge of her nose, then turned and answered the phone, preening her frosted curls as she picked up the receiver. Lia felt as if she'd been dropped into the middle of a *Mayberry RFD* rerun on Nick at Nite.

"Pine Plains PD. Dispatch speaking. . . . No, I'm afraid he's not. . . . Yes, Marge, I recognized your voice. I'm sure we could get one of the part-timers over to direct traffic when you have your bake sale. When is it?"

"Lia, can you talk?" asked Telach.

"Excuse me a second," Lia said to the dispatcher. She

took out her sat phone and walked out into the hallway. "Marie?"

"The state police found Amanda Rauci's car at the Rhinecliff train station, about a half hour from where you are," said Telach. "They just called the Secret Service, and the liaison passed the information over to us. What's up with Ball?"

"Doesn't seem to be in."

The dispatcher was just hanging up when Lia returned.

"This is a number where the chief can reach me," said Lia, writing it on a pad. Anyone calling the number would be forwarded to her sat phone. "Can you give me directions to the train station?"

"Which one?"

"How many are there?"

"Well, if you're going to New York, there's Millerton and Poughkeepsie."

"Actually, I want the Rhinecliff station," said Lia. "Where do those trains go?"

"Oh, that's an Amtrak station. That goes north. You can go south to New York from there, too, I guess, but it's more expensive, and not as close as Millerton."

THE RHINECLIFF TRAIN station was a small, quaint little stop within a stone's throw of the Hudson River. It had a tiny parking lot at the side, tucked around a curve in the road. Amanda Rauci's car was parked in a spot close to the walk that led to the station entrance.

A tow truck was hooking up the car's bumper when Lia arrived. A small knot of troopers stood near the entrance, talking baseball. Trent Madden, the Secret Service agent who was following up on the Forester case, was with them.

"What's the story?" Lia asked.

"Yanks beat Boston, nineteen to three," said one of the troopers.

"Real funny."

"Rauci must've taken the train this morning," said Madden. "Engine's cold. Train goes north to Albany and Canada, or west through Buffalo, and south to New York City. We're checking all the stations."

"She got a really good spot," said Lia, looking at the rest of the lot. There were places for only twenty cars in the gravel lot; the overflow filled the nearby street and a church parking lot across the way. "Must've been here before everyone else."

TRUE TO HER word, Qui had remained at the small club where Dean had left her. She sat alone at a table toward the back, smoking a cigarette. The dim light softened the effects of age on her face; she looked twenty years younger. If rock and roll rather than Asian pop were blaring in the background, Dean might even have been convinced it was 1972 again.

"You're back," said Qui as he sat down.

"The business is all taken care of."

A waitress came over. Qui pointed at her empty glass. "For my friend, a Scotch," she added in Vietnamese.

"I don't want a drink," said Dean.

Qui patted his hand, and he acquiesced, though whether out of politeness or some sense that she needed to share something with him, he couldn't say.

"What did you do?" she asked in English when the server had gone.

"I threatened to reveal that Cam Tre Luc was on the CIA payroll during the war."

"Was he?"

"He was."

"I guess it's not surprising," she said. "People pretend to be pure, but they're not."

"You know Cam Tre Luc?"

"No. But his kind is very familiar. The leaders of the country. They claim purity." She smiled wistfully. "But so do we all, don't we?"

The waitress came with their drinks. Qui took a sip of hers; Dean did not.

"We cannot go against our nature," said Qui. "You couldn't. I should have realized when he told me that you called that you would come to rescue me."

"You're not implying that I'm pure, are you?" asked Dean.

"Not pure, Mr. Dean. Just that it is in your nature to try to fix things. You think it is a good trait, but it can cause much harm as well. Good and evil, at the same time. Thank you for trying to fix things with Cam Tre Luc."

Dean took the faxed pages from his pocket and slid them across the table to her. "If he bothers you, show him a copy of this."

Qui left the papers untouched on the table. Neither she nor Dean said anything for a full minute. Finally Dean rose to go.

"Thank you, Charlie Dean. I see what my future might have been. Now, I no longer have to mourn for it."

"WHAT THE *HELL* is going on, Billy?" demanded President Marcke as Rubens entered the Oval Office. "Why are the details of a top-secret mission being broadcast on national television?"

Bing was sitting next to the President. Her gaze was directed at the floor.

"I'm not sure, Mr. President," said Rubens. He braced himself. The entire trip down—he'd decided he better use the helicopter—he'd gone over different scenarios, different plans for what to say and do depending on what the President and, more important, Bing said. But they fled in the face of Marcke's anger.

Marcke's desk was littered with twisted paper clips—not a good sign.

"Are the Vietnamese involved in this, or what?" demanded the President.

"No, sir," answered Rubens. "There's no evidence of it at all."

"Who is?"

"I'm not sure. To this point, the investigation—"

Rubens stopped speaking as Marcke dropped the paper clip he'd been twisting in his fingers and rose. Rubens had often watched the President pace in his office before, but never like this. He nearly speed walked from side to side.

"McSweeney called me, you know," he told Rubens. "We were senators together. I always thought the man was a jerk, though we did manage to work together when necessary. We actually got a few good bills passed into law. But regardless."

The President stopped his pacing and glanced over at Bing. "You can go, Donna."

The President's glare made it clear there was no point in protesting.

"Yes, Mr. President," she said, her voice barely a whisper as she made her escape.

Marcke waited for Bing to leave.

"Who shot at McSweeney?"

"I only know for certain that the Vietnamese government was not involved," said Rubens.

"I want this figured out," said Marcke, cutting him off. "Do you understand?"

"The Secret Service and FBI—"

"Aren't getting squat done. That was a U.S. senator who was shot at, Bill. A presidential candidate," said Marcke.

"I'm working on it, Mr. President."

"Good. You can go."

"There's one thing that you should be aware of," said Rubens, deciding he'd better tell Marcke everything he knew about the situation. "We're still working on this, but there's a possibility that the attempt was connected with the theft of money in Vietnam during the war there. Senator McSweeney was an officer there at the time."

Rubens explained what they had found, carefully noting that there was no proof that McSweeney had taken the money, or that any American had.

"When did you find this out?" asked the President.

"Within the last twenty-four hours."

"Why haven't you been briefing me on this yourself, Bill?" Rather than angry, the President seemed almost hurt—or, more accurately, disappointed.

"You told me to report to you through Ms. Bing."

Marcke furled his arms in front of his chest. "Get to the bottom of this. I don't want any elected officials assassinated— even if they're running against me. Especially then."

"Yes, sir." Rubens waited a half second, then turned to leave.

"And Billy—you talk to me directly from now on when the matter concerns Deep Black. Everything else can go through channels, up the ladder with Admiral Brown when he gets back, Ms. Bing, and so on. But not Desk Three. Do you understand?"

"Yes, sir," said Rubens.

112

EVEN THOUGH CAM Tre Luc had reversed the order directing that Dean be apprehended, the Art Room arranged another pickup for them. A speedboat picked them up at the harbor just before dawn; a half hour later they were climbing into the belly of a helicopter whose owner made good money transporting roustabouts to the oil derricks off the South Vietnamese shore. The chopper took them to an airstrip, where they'd caught a plane to Thailand and then boarded a commercial airliner for home.

On the flight from Bangkok to LA—first class, arranged by Rubens despite his earlier comment—Dean thought of Qui. He remembered her face and voice, the easy way she had, how even when addressing him very formally and keeping him at a distance, she seemed intimate, more than a friend.

He tried but could not explain to himself what the attraction was. It wasn't physical, he didn't think; Qui was past the age where she might be called pretty, and in any event he hadn't felt sexually aroused by her. If he had represented an alternate future to her—what she must have meant when they said good-bye in the bar—she must have represented something different to him. But what exactly that was wouldn't fit into a neat equation.

"I see what my future might have been. Now, I no longer have to mourn for it."

Dean thought back to the mountain lion, to his shot then, and to the mission with Longbow. Every moment held a fork or a bridge in the road—a different direction based on a decision you made, often without knowing it. Some of the possibilities lived on, like ghosts haunting a future they couldn't have, or a past they'd come to regret.

Then Dean thought of Lia, longed to hold her, and drifted off to sleep.

113

"THE SENATOR IS in LA, not Albany," the secretary told Chief Ball. "I'm sorry."

"Give me that number then."

"I'm afraid—"

"Just give me the general number for the campaign there. No, wait," said Ball. "Give me Jimmy Fingers' cell phone."

"Mr. Fahey does not give out his cell phone number."

"Baloney. Every stinkin' politician on the East Coast has it."

"Sir, if you care to leave a number, I'm sure that Mr. Fahey will call you back when they return east."

"That's too long to wait." Ball turned around from the phone, glancing down the long, narrow barroom. He was being paranoid, he knew, but he was afraid someone was tracing the call and would send the police here any moment.

Ridiculous.

But if it *did* happen, what would he do?

"That's the best I can do," said the secretary. "It's almost five and we're on our way out. Do you want to leave your name and a message or not?"

"Not," said Ball. He hung up, then got the number for the LA campaign office from information. When he called it, he tried a different tack.

"This is Christopher Ball. I do security for the senator back east in New York. I need to talk to either him or James Fahey. If Jimmy's around, he'd be fine. I'm not sure where they are and I happen to be in the field at the moment, without my Rolodex. Can you get me in touch with them?"

The volunteer who'd answered put Ball on hold. He came back in a few minutes with Jimmy Fingers' cell phone number.

Ball punched it in quickly, afraid that he would forget it. Waiting for the number to connect, he glanced down at the silver coiled wire holding the receiver to the phone. It reminded him of the wire he'd used to kill Rauci.

"This is Jimmy. Who is this?"

"Jimmy, this is Christopher Ball."

"Chris Ball—hello, Chief," said Jimmy Fingers. His voice boomed over the phone. "What can we do for you?"

"I have to talk to the senator about something."

"Gee, that's going to be rough today, Chief. Problem is, these damn campaign people have him double-booked, wall-to-wall, the whole time we're out here. Dumbest thing I've ever seen, but that's national politics, I guess. They don't do it like we do it at home."

Ball recognized the aw-shucks tactic; it was standard operating procedure when Jimmy Fingers didn't want McSweeney to talk to someone.

"Listen, Jimmy, I need to talk to him. It's about a personal matter that involves both of us."

"Well, listen, Chief, you tell me and I'll pass it along."

"No. I *want* to talk to him."

"A lot of people want to talk to him right now." Jimmy Fingers' voice was starting to get an edge. "Let me help you out."

"This is personal, damn it." Ball felt the back of his neck getting hot.

"You have something I can deal with, you let me know," answered Jimmy Fingers. The phone went dead.

"You can't hang up on me. Jimmy. Jimmy!"

But Jimmy Fingers had hung up. Ball's anger wrenched out of control, his body wet with it. He slammed the phone back onto the receiver and slapped open the door to the phone booth.

There were only two other people in the bar besides the bartender; both were looking in the other direction, doing their best to avoid Ball's gaze. He made his hands into fists and rubbed his fingers with his thumbs, trying to control his emotions. He walked to the bar, pulled out a stool, and sat down.

"Just a Budweiser, please," he said softly.

The bartender came right over with it. Ball slid a five-dollar bill onto the bar, then took a long sip from the beer.

He felt as if the ground beneath him had given way. He couldn't stop himself from falling.

"Bad day?" asked the bartender gently.

"Bad lifetime," snapped Ball, taking a sip of his beer. He couldn't quite understand why all of this was happening. A few months ago he'd been completely in control, never thinking at all about Vietnam, about the money, his days selling drugs as John Hart, his life before all that. Now it was all he thought about.

He shouldn't have killed Rauci. She wasn't that smart.

Maybe not, but sooner or later she would have figured it out. Sooner or later someone was going to go back far enough, back beyond Vietnam, and find out who he really was. A DNA test would do it. And then everything would unravel.

Ball's fingers were trembling.

Could you lose everything like that, in a flash, by *one* wrong decision?

It wasn't even a question. Here he was, falling.

Ball took another sip of beer.

McSweeney had clearly decided to cut him off. Jimmy Fingers wouldn't dare to do that on his own. Ball thought back to the last time he'd spoken to the senator, to his one-time captain.

"We have to do something about Gordon."

"Mmmm-hmmmm."

Mmmm-hmmmm . . . that was all McSweeney had said. Ball knew exactly what it meant, but no one else would.

Pretty clever. Maybe McSweeney had set the whole thing in motion.

Of course he had. Ball and Gordon were the only connection to McSweeney and the money. Now it was just him.

His word against a senator's—against a man who would be President of the United States? Who would people believe?

Especially if they found out about Rauci. Who would trust the word of a murderer?

Ball stared at the pockmarks in the copper-topped bar. McSweeney was a genius. He'd set the whole thing up beautifully. Twice—once at the start, and now.

If it hadn't been for him, Ball's life would have been perfect. He could have come home as the man he was, Robert Tolong—Marine Sergeant Robert Tolong. A good, solid record, killing enemy guerillas who had to be killed.

"An audacious record."

McSweeney had said that, the first time he broached the idea.

"An audacious record, and yet you have nothing to show for it. You deserve more."

If it hadn't been for that conversation, Robert Tolong would have rotated home in a few weeks. He would have knocked around for a month, maybe two, then gone into the state troopers, like he planned. Become a police chief in Georgia, just like in New York, but without ever having to look over his shoulder.

McSweeney had stolen that from Tolong. And now the son of a bitch was going to be President of the United States.

"You OK?" asked the bartender.

"I'm getting there." Ball forced a smile. "What are you gonna do, right?"

"Laid off?"

"Nah, nothing like that. Friend screwed me, that's all."

"Over a woman?"

"A woman was involved."

"Bitch."

"I don't really feel like talking," said Ball sharply.

The bartender backed away. Ball tried to smile apologetically, but it was a halfhearted attempt. He picked up his beer, his hands trembling even more than before.

He was falling down a hole. He'd felt like this before, in Nam, when he'd killed the real Christopher Ball, the man whose identity he'd adopted, abandoned, and then adopted again.

God, he'd forgotten that. Buried it. He saw Ball's face again, the stunned look in his eyes.

Like Amanda Rauci's.

He'd almost killed himself that night. That was the way he felt now.

"It's all right, Sarge. I owed you one for that time you got the gook on the highway, remember?"

Ball turned to his right. The real Ball sat next to him on the stool, dressed in his class A uniform. He smelled of Old Spice aftershave.

"You had to kill me, too."

Amanda Rauci was on his left.

Ball turned around. The entire bar was filled with the people he'd killed—gooks, drug dealers, the *federales*. They were all in their best clothes, as if attending a wedding or a reception. Or a funeral.

I'm in hell, Ball realized. McSweeney put me here.

The bastard is going to pay.

"I think you already paid," said the bartender. He pointed at the beer glass, now three-quarters empty. "You need a refill?"

"I gotta go," said Ball, getting up from the stool and forcing himself to walk through the crowd of well-dressed ghosts.

114

JASON RICHARDS HAD been a corporal in Vietnam at the time Sergeant Tolong had been killed, and was a member of the unit sent out to locate and recover the body. More than thirty-five years had passed, but his anger and frustration were still so palpable that Hernes Jackson had to hold his phone away from his ear as Richards recounted what had happened that day.

"We should've gone out right away. That was the first screwup," said Richards. An air-conditioning installer, Richards had just come home for dinner when Jackson tracked him down by phone in Oklahoma. "They kept us at the base three or four days while they figured out what to do."

"Was that normal?" asked Jackson.

"What the hell was normal?" Richards took a sip of something—beer, Jackson guessed. "But waiting three or four days—wasn't a good thing, right?"

"Unless there was a reason."

"No reason except incompetence, general incompetence."

Richards had more complaints about the mission, which was led by a nugget lieutenant—"the newest one at the base." The intelligence was terrible, they were airlifted fifteen miles from where the grave was supposed to be, and the man who'd buried Tolong wasn't with them.

"Wasn't he hurt, too?" asked Jackson.

"Nah. He came through without a scratch. Maybe he lost his nerve. He was in Da Nang—he could have come out with us easy. From what I heard, he just sat in a bunker for the next month, until it was time for him to rotate back to the States."

"Do you remember his name?"

"Nah. Wait. Maybe Gordy or something."

"Gordon?"

"Yeah, something like that."

"Reginald Gordon?" asked Jackson.

"Maybe. Reggie? I don't know. Gordy, though. Definitely. How the hell do you leave your buddy? How do you do that?"

Richards continued to lace away at the mission, which was eventually cut short by a VC ambush. According to Richards, the ambush consisted of a few rounds in the distance; as soon as the lieutenant heard them, he called for an evacuation.

"Worst operation I was ever on in the Marines," said Richards. "Maybe the Army did crap that way, but we didn't. And you know who I blame? Captain Gideon McSweeney. He sent us out. He handpicked that sucker of a lieutenant and got the worst guys to go. It was his fault. You know who he is, right?"

"Senator McSweeney?"

"That's right. Running for President. He screwed up when he picked the mission."

"Was McSweeney a poor leader?" asked Jackson.

"No. Actually, he was pretty damn good. Usually, he was. I'll vote for him. I heard a lot of good stories about him, especially when he was a lieutenant. Had balls. But this time, I don't know. He didn't even push it when we came back empty-handed. To a man, we would have gone back out in the field. We were proud to be Marines, you know what I'm saying? We were proud. And we did a crap job here."

"So he didn't push?"

"No. I mean, probably there was a colonel above him telling him to lay off and everything, but Tolong was one of his guys. He should've. You want to believe that your CO is going to come for you; you know what I mean? If he's a Marine, he ought to."

"How well did you know Tolong?" asked Jackson.

"I didn't. This is just stuff I heard about him. You know, they'd been around, those guys. I was what, maybe ten days in-country? I'd just gotten there."

"Were Tolong and McSweeney friends?"

"Friends? I don't know, but I kind of doubt it, you know? Even then, especially then, officers and enlisted, they didn't really mix in a friend kind of way. Sometimes. But Tolong was in the villages program," added Richards, using a slang term for the combined pacification program Jackson had come across earlier. "And McSweeney ran the Corps part of it. From what I know, Tolong was a troubleshooter. The guy was pretty amazing—he'd been a sniper, but he was better than most of those guys. They used him to assassinate people."

"That's not in his personnel records."

Richards laughed, and took a long swig of whatever he was drinking. "There's gonna be a lot of stuff missing from those records, Mr. Jackson, if you know what I mean."

115

WHILE AMANDA RAUCI'S car was towed to a nearby state troopers' barracks to await an FBI forensic team, Lia drove back over to Pine Plains to see if the police chief had returned. The drive took about twenty minutes, on a twisting but scenic road. The bucolic surroundings seemed to make crime and intrigue impossible, the kind of countryside people would flee to so they could raise their children. An old farmhouse loomed over a rock wall at the edge of a curve about halfway to the village. It was a beautiful old house, freshly painted.

Too close to the road though, Lia thought. Not a good place for kids.

"I told you I would call, hon," the police dispatcher said when Lia entered the police station. "I won't forget."

"So he's not back."

"No."

"It's just very important that I talk to him."

"I know; I know. People have to talk to the chief all the time. I never lose their messages. If you're looking for a place to eat dinner, try the Stissing Bakery," added the dispatcher. "Sandwich and soup, three dollars. Can't beat it. Great blueberry pie, and the strawberry-rhubarb isn't bad, either. Everything's homemade."

"Thanks," said Lia, stifling an urge to ask if Aunt Bee from *Mayberry R.F.D.* was around somewhere.

Lia decided to take the dispatcher's advice and walked over to the bakery, which turned out to be a café whose ambiance straddled country quaint and urban sophisticate, with a strong whiff of fresh-baked desserts to hold it all together. On her way in, Rockman started giving her an update; Lia pulled out her phone as she sat down.

A security camera at Penn Station in New York City had picked up a woman who looked like Amanda Rauci near the platform where the Rhinecliff train had stopped that morning. She had gone to the ticket counter and bought a ticket to Baltimore.

"Paid cash. No luggage," added Rockman. "We're waiting to check the tapes from the Baltimore station. We've already alerted the FBI and Secret Service."

"Why would she go to Baltimore?"

"You tell me."

"The people around here say that if you're going to New York, the train from Poughkeepsie is cheaper. It also runs more often."

"Rauci wasn't from around there, was she?" said Rockman, who seemed annoyed that Lia was questioning him.

"Was Chief Ball with her in the video?"

"Ball?"

"They're both gone." Lia frowned at the approaching waitress. "Ball left before the police dispatcher got in, which means no later than eight A.M. Amanda Rauci's car was at the Rhinecliff train station early enough to get the best spot in the lot. So maybe they left together."

"Are you sure he's gone? Maybe he just took a mental health day?"

"This doesn't look like a place where you'd need mental health days," answered Lia. The waitress was standing over her. There were no menus here; customers ordered from the blackboard, or maybe memory. "I'll get back to you," Lia told Rockman, pretending to turn off the phone.

Dinner over—the soup and sandwich were good, and the chocolate ganache cake to die for—Lia went over to the chief's house to see if Rockman was right; maybe Ball was just blowing off the day.

Not that he seemed the type.

If Pine Plains as a whole reminded Lia of the old television series *Mayberry R.F.D.*, Mrs. Ball's expression when she opened the door came straight out of *The Addams Family*.

"I was wondering if Chief Ball was here," said Lia. "Or when he would be back?"

Mrs. Ball stared at Lia, then shook her head and started back inside, walking as if in a daze. Lia followed her inside to a paisley-covered couch in the living room. The decor was American colonial circa 1976, so out of fashion it looked hip.

"Are you all right?" Lia asked.

"I thought. Oh. I thought you were coming to tell me that the chief had been, had been—"

"Killed?"

Mrs. Ball nodded.

"Where is he?" asked Lia.

"Don't you know?"

"Why would I know?"

"He said he was on a case. That I couldn't talk about it. He told me right after you came last night. I thought he was working with you."

Lia began drawing out as much as she could from Mrs. Ball. Being gentle was difficult, not so much because it meant being nice, but because it meant being patient, asking small questions that led to other small ones. Being patient had always been extremely difficult for Lia; her first-grade report card had complained that she always wanted to rush to the next thing.

"Has the chief helped out on big cases before?" Lia asked.

"About a month ago. Otherwise, not in a long, long time. He's needed here."

"Who did he work with?"

"I don't know. He's very . . . tight." Mrs. Ball shook her head.

"Did he say where he went?"

She shook her head again. Lia came back to the question several times, tacking back and forth. Finally convinced that Mrs. Ball simply didn't know, Lia changed her tactics.

"Where did he go the last time?" she asked. "Maybe that will help."

"I don't know."

"Did he use credit cards, or take a plane, anything like that? The receipts would tell us."

Tears puckered in Mrs. Ball's eyes. "There's something here you're not telling me. He's hurt, isn't he?"

"I don't know," said Lia. "But I am a little concerned. I *was* hoping that he would help me, and it sounds like he was going to, but he hasn't called me today. I expected him to check in—if he was going to help. And another person I'm looking for is missing. A federal agent."

"He said he was working with the *federales*," said Mrs. Ball, who was struggling not to show her concern. "That's what he calls you people. But I thought it was you."

"Do you know this woman?"

Lia took out her PDA and brought up a photo of Amanda Rauci. Mrs. Ball shook her head.

"How about this man?" asked Lia, showing her a picture of Forester.

"No."

"This was a Secret Service agent who wanted to talk to your husband about something, but he died first."

"That's the man who killed himself?" said Mrs. Ball.

"Yes."

"What a shame. Why would he do that?"

"I don't know. Did your husband have any theories?"

"You'd have to ask him. I'm not a policeman."

"But maybe he had an idea."

Mrs. Ball shook her head. "He was surprised, too. He read the story a couple of times, so I know he was surprised. Usually, he doesn't even bother with the paper, except to skim it. And for sports."

"Lia," said Rubens, popping in on the Desk Three network. "Mention Vietnam. See if he discussed a connection there. It was on the news last night—mention it."

Lia did so, asking Mrs. Ball if she had seen the stories

about Vietnam being implicated in a possible attempt on Senator McSweeney. Of course she had, she answered.

And then Mrs. Ball's face grew pale.

"Are they after my husband?"

"I don't know," said Lia.

"He was in Vietnam."

"Did he serve with Senator McSweeney?"

"No, but he knew who he was."

"Does your husband know him now?"

"Oh yes. Everyone knows Senator McSweeney."

"Real well?"

"Well, he likes to pretend he does. But you know. The senator is a senator, and a police chief is just a police chief."

Lia let the matter drop, and went back to trying to find a clue about where the chief might have gone. It took a few more minutes, but Mrs. Ball agreed to let Lia look at the credit card statements.

"Use the camera attachment on the PDA," said Rockman as Lia followed Mrs. Ball to the spare bedroom they used as a home office. "Get pictures of everything."

No kidding, thought Lia.

"This was my son's room," said Mrs. Ball. "We felt terrible redecorating. I did. The chief just said, 'He's out of the house now, dear; let him be his own man.'"

"How old is your son?"

"He died in a car accident two years ago," said Mrs. Ball. Her lower lip quivered. "The chief never really was the same person after that. It was a terrible blow. I—"

The tears welled up and she couldn't finish. She pointed to a filing cabinet, then left the room.

Lia found the folder and began taking pictures of the statements.

"Flights to Atlanta and D.C.," said Rockman. "Ask her about that. What he did."

Lia finished with the credit cards. The wall was covered with citations and plaques. There were a few photos as well—the chief and his wife with various local officials.

"As you can see, the chief is very well liked," said Mrs. Ball. Her eyes were red, but she'd restored her composure.

"What's that?" Lia asked, pointing at a framed medal.

"That's the Navy Cross. The chief won that during the war. For bravery."

"He does seems like the hero type."

"You should have seen him when he was younger," said Mrs. Ball, smiling broadly. "He looked just like a Hollywood star. All the girls wanted him."

"But you got him."

"Wasn't easy."

Lia started to follow her out of the room. "Why did the chief go to Atlanta?"

"I don't know. When was it?"

"A few weeks back."

"Was it the case he was working on? That must be it."

"Ask her if he knew someone named Gordon," said Rubens.

Lia did, but Mrs. Ball had never heard the name.

"Lia, Ball never won the Navy Cross," said Rubens. "That's a pretty rare medal. Can you tell if it's authentic?"

How can I do that? Lia wondered. Before she could ask, Rockman practically shouted.

"Ball didn't get the medal," said Rockman, "but Tolong did. Six months before he died."

"Lia, please ask Mrs. Ball if she's ever heard of a Sergeant Tolong," said Rubens calmly. "And then see if she would agree to let us monitor her credit card and cell phone accounts to help us find him."

116

THE DIFFICULTY WITH a campaign strategy, especially a successful one, was knowing when to end it. You wanted to cut it off just as it peaked, though that could be difficult to determine.

Not in this case. The news media reverberated with the Vietnamese connection to the attempted assassination. The administration's denials were fanning the frenzy. With everyone screaming, it was surely time to move on.

"I HAVE A problem with my mother's aunt that I have to take care of," Jimmy Fingers told McSweeney as the senator waited to go on the radio with a local Rush Limbaugh wannabe. "I'm going to have to fly to Ohio tonight."

"You have a mother?" said McSweeney.

"She denies it. I'll be back in time for tomorrow night's receptions."

Jimmy Fingers started for the door.

"Jimmy?"

He turned around. McSweeney had a worried look on his face.

"Good luck with your aunt."

"Thanks, Senator."

"And listen—take as much time as you need. Don't rush back. It'll be OK."

McSweeney's expression gave his true feelings away—he was worried that he'd be lost without his aide. Jimmy Fingers didn't know which he liked McSweeney more for: needing him, or lying and telling him to go ahead and do what he had to do.

"I'll be back. Maybe even by the morning."

117

"THE CONNECTIONS ARE entirely circumstantial," Rubens told the President. "Captain McSweeney was in charge of assigning the men who escorted the courier. He assigned Tolong and Malinowski. The courier disappears with the money. Malinowski dies. The CIA begins to investigate. Tolong volunteers to go on a patrol. He's allowed to go, apparently because McSweeney OK'd it. During the patrol, he and a man named Gordon are separated from the rest of the men. He is killed, according to Gordon. Gordon buries him, and comes back with one of his dog tags. McSweeney sends out a mission to recover the body. The body is not recovered. Twenty-some years later, the body is recovered."

Rubens glanced across his office, looking at Ambassador Jackson. The former diplomat nodded grimly, a folder of his notes on his lap.

"Then there is Chris Ball," continued Rubens. "He's a Marine from Georgia who is about to go home. He doesn't have much family; both of his parents are dead. His only close relation is a half sister who lives just outside Athens, Georgia. We tracked her down, and she tells us that, aside from a few postcards, he never bothered to talk to her after the war. Ball completely disappeared, in fact, until 1978, when he became a part-time patrolman in upstate New York."

"And you think Ball is Tolong," said the President. He was using his speakerphone, pacing around as they talked.

"We've done a computer rendering that shows how both men would have aged," said Rubens. "Chief Ball and Tolong match precisely. The young Ball and the chief do not come close."

"A computer program hardly seems definitive."

"If we could exhume the remains of Tolong's body, we might have definitive proof," said Rubens. "We're working on tracking down some of Tolong's relatives."

"We should have a call back in a few hours," said Jackson.

Rubens repeated the information for the President. "There's no smoking gun in the records," Rubens added. "But if we were to prove Ball was Tolong, perhaps he would tell us what happened."

"If you can find him," said the President.

"We are working on that, along with the FBI."

"Why would he try to kill McSweeney?"

"Honestly, I'm not sure why Ball would want to kill McSweeney," said Rubens. "If it's related to the money, though, perhaps there was a double cross somewhere. He was in Washington when Gordon killed himself. And the investigator there thinks it's possible it wasn't suicide."

Rubens saw Jackson wince.

"I may be overstating the case on that," Rubens added. "He has agreed to revisit it, however."

"As much as I don't like Senator McSweeney, I have a hard time seeing him as a thief," said the President. "Go ahead and exhume the body. Let me know what comes of the DNA tests. By the way, Billy."

"Sir?"

"I'm going to be out in California myself the day after tomorrow. Senator McSweeney and I will be sharing a podium. I'd like to have something specific to tell him when he asks who's trying to kill him."

"Understood."

118

AS SOON AS he was out of the jetway, Jimmy Fingers increased his pace, striding quickly in the direction of the exit. Las Vegas' McCarran International Airport had never seemed so immense. Fortunately, he'd only taken a carry-on, so there was no need to wait with the others in the luggage-receiving areas. Jimmy Fingers joined the queue at the taxi stand; it moved briskly, and he soon found himself in a cab.

"The Strip," said Jimmy. He reached into his briefcase and pulled out the secondhand laptop he'd brought along.

"Which hotel?"

"I'm not going to a hotel," said Jimmy Fingers, turning the laptop on.

"Hoo-kay," said the driver.

What Jimmy Fingers wanted to do was find a wireless network where he could connect and send the e-mail—from the cab, if possible. But the radio waves didn't seem to want to cooperate, and the driver seemed nosey besides, checking his mirror every few minutes to see what was going on.

"You know where there's a Starbucks?" Jimmy Fingers said finally.

"Starbucks. Coffee?"

"Yeah, that's right."

"Expensive place for coffee. I know a place—"

"Starbucks is where I want to go."

"Hoo-kay."

* * *

JIMMY FINGERS ORDERED a tall decaf, then went and sat outside in the small fenced-in area at the side of the Starbucks at Centennial and I-95. He connected to the Internet and, with cars whizzing back and forth, sent what he knew would be the last e-mail of the campaign, this one threatening Congressman Mark Dalton of Florida, whose status as a veteran had not helped him break into double digits in any of the primaries so far, and whose campaign was all but finished.

After he signed off, Jimmy Fingers walked to the back of the store, toward a row of Dumpsters. He was just about to throw the laptop into the nearest one when a soft moan caught him off guard. Two teenagers were making out in the scrubby bushes nearby.

Cursing silently to himself, Jimmy Fingers immediately whirled around and began walking in the opposite direction. His heart double pumped, and his hands became clammy. A bus was just pulling up; Jimmy Fingers got on it. He realized it was a mistake but felt trapped; when the bus driver told him he needed exact change, Jimmy Fingers blinked at him for a second before recovering and reaching into his pocket for the right coins.

By the time he gathered himself, the bus was moving. Jimmy Fingers realized he now had a bigger problem than getting rid of the laptop in his briefcase—he had no idea where the hell he was.

Jimmy Fingers stayed on until he came to the Cannery Hotel. Still feeling disoriented, he went inside and found a bar—the Pin-Ups Lounge. He ordered himself a beer, and drank it greedily. When he was done, he simply got up, leaving the briefcase with the computer.

He was about halfway to the door when a woman in her late sixties called after him, telling him he had forgotten his bag.

I'm never going to get rid of the damn thing, Jimmy Fingers thought to himself, pretending relief as he thanked her and tucked the briefcase under his arm.

He made his way to the men's room, where he flushed his face with cold water. It was the heat that was getting to him, he told himself, not the pressure. There was no pressure—he was within a few months of achieving everything he'd ever dreamed of achieving. McSweeney would be President; Jimmy Fingers would take a job as special assistant to the President, and hold a post in the party as well.

Scores would be settled, friends rewarded.

And they would achieve a great deal. Jimmy Fingers had been a believer in democracy and the little man when he started out, and as cynical as he had become, deep down he still believed that an elected official could do some good. If the right people were guiding him.

Jimmy Fingers caught sight of his face in the mirror. He looked a lot paler, and a lot older, than he had thought.

As he reached for the paper towels, he realized the solution to his laptop problem stood right before him.

With a quick shove, the laptop fell from the briefcase into the wastebasket. Jimmy Fingers rolled out a fistful of paper and threw it on top. He washed and dried his hands again, adding still more paper to make sure the laptop couldn't be easily seen. Hands dry, he went to find out how to get a cab to pick him up.

119

"IT'S ONLY IN the last ten years that this has become practical. The exact methods we use weren't even around then, I don't think," said the FBI specialist as she scraped the inside of Jason Cedarhouse's mouth. "You'd be amazed at what the scientists can do."

"I am amazed," said Ambassador Jackson. He guessed that the technician had been in middle school a decade before.

"Mummm, too," said Jason.

"Hold on, sweetie," said the FBI technician. "Almost done with you. Have to be very careful about contamination with these tests."

She slipped the probe—it looked like a Q-tip that retracted into a pen case—into a small plastic container, screwing it closed. She'd taken a dozen samples.

"All done. That wasn't so bad, was it?"

"Uhhh-uh," said Jason.

"What we're going to do with this is a Short Tandem Repeats test. STR. It's a kind of PCR protocol, where the DNA replicates itself. Of course, we may have to fall back on the mitochondrial test. We'll do a whole series. Not likely to get an error—unless there was contamination."

"Yeah, but, uh, this is going to prove my uncle is the one that's buried in Arlington National Cemetery, right?" said Cedarhouse. "Because my mom would want to be sure. She's a little concerned since you called," he added, turning to Jackson.

"It should be able to confirm it," said Jackson.

"Every family has a certain amount of DNA that they share," said the FBI expert. "And they inherit it. Now let's say Robert Tolong was your father rather than your uncle. Then the odds that a match was a coincidence would be one in a quintillion, assuming we were using STR. In this case, the odds will be a little less, but they're still way up there."

"Quintillion is one with eighteen zeroes," said Jackson, who had heard the entire lecture on the way over.

"It will take us roughly six hours to pull the results together," added the technician. "The actual DNA cycling is three hours; that's where the time is, because you need enough strands to do the actual test."

"Cool. Can I have dinner now?" asked Cedarhouse.

CHIEF BALL HAD a cover story all ready, but the clerk at the car rental counter didn't even bother looking at the name as Amanda Rauci's credit card cleared the scan. He was too busy selling the optional insurance.

"I guess I'll take it," said Ball as soon as the man glanced at the card. "The insurance."

"Can't be too careful," said the clerk happily. He slapped the card through the reader and handed it back to Ball without checking the name.

In the old days, the days when he was back from Vietnam, Ball would have immediately driven down to the worst ghetto in the city and sold the car for cash and, with luck, a new ID. He'd quickly acquire a whole set of phony identification— license, credit cards, Social Security number, anything and everything he needed.

But he was too old for that, and not "hip" to the local scene. He didn't know where the chop shops were, and certainly wouldn't have known who to trust. He didn't even know if you could make money doing that anymore.

Looking tough when you were sixty wasn't nearly as easy as when you were twenty. If he looked like anything now, it was probably a cop: an old, has-been cop.

He'd fallen down a rat hole. Plunged down.

He'd never felt like this, not even in Vietnam.

He thought of Amanda Rauci, and his hands started to tremble.

Just drive, he told himself. Just drive.

RUBENS WAITED UNTIL he had reached his office to call the President. Even so, it was only just 6:00 A.M. The switchboard operator gave him Mark Kimbel, the most junior aide to the chief of staff.

"Mr. Rubens, what can we do for you?"

"I have important information for the President," said Rubens.

"Important enough to wake him up?"

"No," said Rubens. "But he should call at his earliest convenience."

President Marcke called Rubens back an hour later.

"What's going on, Billy?"

"The man who was identified as Sergeant Tolong and buried at Arlington National Cemetery is not Sergeant Tolong," said Rubens.

"Is it Ball?"

"We're working on that," said Rubens. The FBI had been unable to obtain DNA samples to match relatives; tracking them down, obtaining and testing samples, and most of all doing it with the legal paperwork necessary to be used in court would take some time.

"Assuming you're right, linking this Chief Ball and Tolong won't actually prove that McSweeney was involved in the theft of the money, will it?" asked Marcke.

"No, sir. As I said, there may in fact be no link."

"Which would mean he would get away with it, wouldn't it?"

"Yes."

"What do you think the senator's reaction would be if someone told him what you know now? In other words," explained the President, "if you said that the attempt on his life may have had something to do with the theft of money in Vietnam, and that we think he's being pursued by one of the men."

"I don't know."

"As we saw with the Vietnam information, word will leak at some point," explained the President. "Let's see if it will give us some advantage. Don't mention that we suspect he may have ended up with the loot, or is otherwise involved."

122

THE CUSTOMS AGENT came up to Tommy Karr's belt.

"Could you and Mr. Dean come with me, Mr. Karr?" she asked.

"Now how do you know I'm Tommy Karr?" said Karr, suppressing a laugh.

"I was told to look for the biggest man on the plane."

"Got you there," said Dean, shouldering his carry-on bag.

The diminutive customs agent led them around the side of the row of customs stations, through a door, and into a hallway that was part of a secure area at Los Angeles International Airport. Another customs agent met them and asked to see their passports.

"Gee, I don't know if I have mine," said Karr, before handing over his brown diplomatic passport.

"Plane ride put you in a goofy mood?" asked Dean as they were led down the hall.

"No—twenty-something hours of Abbott and Costello did. I have the 'Who's on First' routine memorized. Want to hear it?"

Dean declined.

They were shown into a conference room used by the customs agents for briefings and updates. When the agents left, Dean asked the Art Room what was going on.

"We think Tolong's death was staged," said Sandy Chafetz, who'd taken over as their runner while Rockman got some rest. She explained that DNA evidence had proven that the remains that were brought back weren't Tolong's.

"Our working theory is that McSweeney, Gordon, and Ball were involved in taking the money during Vietnam," said Chafetz. "And for some reason they had a falling-out. The FBI and the local police are reinvestigating Gordon's death; it's very possible he was pushed rather than jumped from that window."

"So you think Ball was the one who tried to kill McSweeney?"

"We're not sure," said Chafetz. "It looks from his credit cards that he was there. But we can't find him now to verify that. There may be another player—it's possible someone killed him, or he's just hiding out. Everyone's looking for him—FBI, Secret Service, and us. Tommy, they want you to join the press corps covering McSweeney. Stay undercover and see if you spot Ball or pick up anything else suspicious. We've uploaded photos and other information for you, along with credentials."

"I always wanted to be a reporter," said Karr.

"What am I doing?" Dean asked.

"Mr. Rubens wants to talk to you about your assignment himself."

123

AMANDA RAUCI'S CREDIT card had been used the day before to rent a car in Buffalo, NewYork; the information was flagged and passed along to the Desk Three analysts as soon as it reached the credit card company from the processing firm, roughly eight hours after the transaction itself. The information led the analysts to request the tapes from video surveillance cameras at the two train stations that served Buffalo, Exchange Street and Depew. Neither station was very large, nor did many trains stop there. But Amanda Rauci had not been spotted.

A man who *might* have been Chief Ball, however, had gotten off at Depew, a suburban stop within a few miles of the rental outlet and the Buffalo Niagara International Airport.

"Why would they be traveling together?" Lia asked Rockman when he briefed her after she got up.

"No idea. There's a slight possibility that they're working together to solve this."

"I doubt it," said Lia. "What about the rental place? Did they have a video?"

"Don't you think that was the first thing we checked?" said Rockman testily. "Clerk doesn't remember her. Probably didn't even look at the card. We're checking to see if there are other video cameras in the area."

"Did the FBI forensic team find anything in her car? Like blood?"

"Nothing. The car was vacuumed recently; that was about it. You can interpret that any way you want."

Lia thought back to Amanda Rauci's condo. She hadn't struck Lia as a neat freak. Then again, maybe Amanda had cleaned the car before leaving on a long trip. Some people were like that—they wanted to start fresh.

Amanda checks out the police chief; then she leaves her car at a train station.

Maybe she didn't leave it there—maybe Ball left it there after he got rid of her.

"You with me?" asked Rockman.

"Yeah, I'm with you," said Lia.

"We're going to send the clerk an e-mail with Amanda Rauci's photo and see if he can remember her. You may have to go up there and talk to him. We'll let you know later."

"Peachy."

"In the meantime, do you think you could get a sample of Chief Ball's DNA?"

"As soon as I see him I'll ask him to spit into a cup."

"A few strands of hair would do it," said Rockman. "Ask his wife."

"You think she keeps it in a locket?"

"Hair in a comb. Listen, even a sweaty shirt will do."

"All right." Lia dreaded going back to the house and talking to Mrs. Ball; the woman's pain registered transparently on her face. Whatever the truth, this was going to end very badly for her. Lia, so stoic about pain when it came to herself or the sort of enemies she usually dealt with, suddenly found she had no stomach for inflicting it on a bystander.

"Check in every hour," said Rockman. "We'll call you if there's anything new."

"Fine," said Lia. She pretended to turn off the sat phone, then signaled the waiter for another cup of coffee.

124

SOME GUYS WORE the fact that they had served in the Marines on their bodies—literally with tattoos and more figuratively in the way they spoke and thought and acted. They were lifers, and proud of it, and went out of their way to make sure everyone knew they were *Marines.*

Capital *M.*

Charlie Dean wasn't one of them. He'd been an active Marine for a substantial portion of his life—but being a Marine wasn't *all* of his life. If the service had helped define him, the key word was "helped." Charles Dean was a good Marine, but he'd also been more than that. He'd been a successful—and unsuccessful—small businessman, a private investigator and bodyguard, a clandestine employee of the government, a hunter and outdoorsman. While there was a great deal of truth in the old adage that a Marine never became an "ex-Marine," from his earliest days in the Corps Charlie Dean had known there was more to the world than his drill sergeant would have had him believe.

And yet if there was one thing that Dean believed in deeply—believed in so firmly that it was rooted to his soul—it was the values that the Corps preached. Some of them had a way of sounding trite or even shallow when explained to someone else, but then, simple things often did. That didn't make them any less important.

So the idea that a Marine had stolen from the government and betrayed, maybe even killed, a fellow Marine hit Dean like a blow to the chest. As he thought about Senator McSweeney,

Dean recalled the first time he'd been shot, an AK bullet going through the fleshy part of his calf. It had burned like all hell, and sent his body into shock, but the thing he remembered now, the bit of the experience that remained vividly with him, was the disbelief, the sheer wonderment at the wound—the realization that he wasn't invincible, or charmed, or special, or above the action, or any of the other white lies a man might believe when he went into combat the first time.

A Marine could betray his fellow Marines and his country. It didn't seem possible.

Dean was not naïve. He'd seen plenty of poor Marines and a few out-and-out cowards, not only in Vietnam but also afterward. He'd seen, and at times had to deal with, terrible officers. But this was magnitudes worse. It seemed a product of evil, rather than weakness.

"You're not to accuse him of any wrongdoing, or involvement," Rubens told Dean, instructing him on how to deal with McSweeney. "Simply let him know about Tolong. Study his reaction, but nothing more."

Senator McSweeney was now the leading candidate for President in his party; it was very possible that he would beat Marcke in the next election.

A traitor as President.

Maybe the assassin felt the same way. Maybe that was why he wanted to kill McSweeney.

"Mr. Dean, are you still with me?" Rubens asked.

"Yes, sir."

"Charlie, can you do this? Can you talk to him?"

"Absolutely."

It was the same word he'd said when he'd been given the mission to assassinate Phuc Dinh. It was the thing he'd always said, as a Marine.

"I NEED PICTURE ID for the plane ticket," said the attendant. "Rules."

"Oh yeah, right." Ball reached into his pocket for his wallet. He'd tried to think of a way around using his actual ID but just couldn't come up with one. His only solution was to buy tickets to other destinations with the hope of throwing anyone looking for him off the trail.

"Here you go," said Ball, pushing his license forward on the counter.

He hoped they weren't looking for him yet. Or if they were, that the usual efficiencies of government bureaucracies would mean they wouldn't find him until it was too late.

DEAN WONDERED WHETHER Senator McSweeney might recognize him from Vietnam somehow, and vice versa. But there were many captains and many, many more privates, and nothing registered in McSweeney's face as he shook Dean's hand and gestured for him to take a seat in the hotel room.

Nothing clicked for Dean, either. He'd seen McSweeney so many times now in the briefings that it was impossible to visualize him as he was thirty-some years ago. And this was a good thing—insulation from his emotions.

"I'm supposed to give you the update alone," Dean told the senator. More than a dozen people were milling around the room.

"Oh, that's all right. These people know just about everything about me anyway, right down to the color of my underwear."

McSweeney turned to one of his aides and examined the clipboard in her hand. Dean waited until he had McSweeney's attention again before answering him.

"I'm afraid my orders were pretty specific."

The senator frowned. "This is a pretty busy day."

"Yes, sir."

McSweeney turned to another aide, who had questions about how to deal with the local press. Dean folded his arms and scanned the room. The Secret Service had blocked off the entire floor of the hotel as well as the one below it, and it was impossible for anyone who didn't have a confirmed appointment to get up here. The curtains were drawn and the furniture had been rearranged to make it almost impossible for a sniper to get a good shot from the only building in range.

But that wouldn't keep a truly devoted assassin from making an attempt on the senator's life. The easiest thing to do, thought Dean morbidly, was to blow up the whole damn suite—fire a mortar or rocket round point-blank from across the way and everyone in the room would be fried, Dean included.

"How long will this take?" McSweeney asked.

"A few minutes," said Dean.

"Let's go into the bedroom then," said McSweeney, leading the way.

Dean closed the door behind him.

"The President sent you?" said McSweeney.

"The President ordered the briefing," said Dean.

"Well, shoot."

"Do you remember Vietnam very well, Senator?"

THE QUESTION CAUGHT McSweeney completely by surprise. He tried to cover it by seeming annoyed.

"Of course I remember Vietnam," he told the NSA agent. "Do you?"

"As a matter of fact, I do very well."

Something about Dean's manner and appearance—perhaps his erect stance, or maybe his buzz cut—told McSweeney that he was a fellow Marine.

"Where'd you serve?" McSweeney asked him.

"I was a Marine Corps sniper," said Dean, adding some of the details of his tour.

"Jesus, we were in-country at the same time," said McSweeney, relaxing. He patted Dean on the shoulder and pulled over the chair in the corner to sit down. "Have a seat. Sit on the bed; go ahead. I didn't know you were a Marine. I should have known. I apologize."

"You don't have to apologize, Senator."

"You know, I went back to An Hoa a few years ago. Has to be one of the most beautiful places on earth."

"I imagine you're right," said Dean.

"You've seen some shit, I bet," said McSweeney.

"Absolutely."

"So what's going on? Are the Vietnamese really targeting me, or is that all bullshit?"

"You're definitely being targeted, but the information about the Vietnamese being behind it is wrong," said Dean.

"Good. Surprised?" added McSweeney. "That I think it's good?"

Dean shrugged.

"I don't want to be an international incident," McSweeney told him. He started to get up.

"How well do you remember Vietnam?" Dean asked again.

McSweeney gave Dean a puzzled look, then suddenly realized he knew everything.

DEAN CAREFULLY REPEATED what Rubens had told him to say, highlighting the missing money and the suspicion that Tolong had arranged to fake his own death. He didn't mention Gordon by name; Rubens wanted Dean to listen for the name, to see if the senator volunteered it. They weren't sure if McSweeney knew he was dead or not.

"One theory is that Tolong, or whatever he calls himself now, is the person who's hunting you," said Dean.

McSweeney's face had remained placid as Dean spoke; nothing seemed to have registered. He spoke without emotion now, without even the mild excitement he'd displayed earlier when Dean told him he was a fellow Marine.

"What's the other theory?"

"That whoever shot at you got Ball."

"I see. So, what does he want? Revenge?"

"We're still trying to figure everything out."

"I knew Tolong," said McSweeney. "I sent one of my aides when his body was recovered. I don't see how his death could have been faked. Are you sure about this?"

Dean nodded.

"Have you done DNA testing?" asked McSweeney.

"Yes."

McSweeney made a face, then rose. "All right," he said. "Thank you. I assume you or someone else will keep me updated."

"Yes, sir."

Dean knew he was getting a performance, but he wasn't exactly sure how to interpret it. The senator seemed disturbed and concerned, but no more than anyone might be.

Maybe he wasn't involved. Maybe Tolong or whoever was trying to kill him had other reasons, and McSweeney was innocent.

"You're welcome to stay, Mr. Dean," said the senator, opening the door to the suite room.

"I have to check back with my boss," Dean told him. "I'll be around."

"Good."

127

JIMMY FINGERS ENTERED the suite at his usual gallop, and was nearly flattened by one of the Secret Service agents.

"Careful there, big guy," Jimmy Fingers told the agent, barely squeezing out of the way.

"You're back," said Senator McSweeney, appearing behind the bodyguard. "And before eight."

"Told you, Senator. Early bird gets the worm."

"How's the uncle?"

"Great-aunt. Not so great. I'm the closest relative," added Jimmy Fingers.

"I hope she's loaded."

"Wouldn't that be great?" Jimmy Fingers could tell that something was bothering McSweeney, but there were too many people around to ask what it was. He fell in beside the senator as he and his entourage made their way back to the elevator.

"Secret Service people have a new theory about the assassin," said McSweeney. "They've gotten the NSA involved as well."

"Vietnam?"

"Yes, but not what you expect. It's a whacked-out theory."

"How whacked-out?" Jimmy Fingers tried to smile, but he knew his effort fell far short.

"Has to do with a Marine that worked for me and now supposedly wants revenge. Pretty whacked-out."

Relief ran through Jimmy Fingers' body like the rush from a descending roller coaster.

"It would have to be whacked-out," said Jimmy Fingers. "Assassins aren't sane people. Smart, but not sane."

"Good point," said McSweeney, stepping into the elevator.

128

TOMMY KARR HELD up the laminated press card for the Secret Service agent in charge of screening the press horde covering McSweeney. The agent squinted, frowned, then consulted his list of reporters.

"If I'm not on there, can I take the rest of the day off?" Karr joked.

Secret Service agents were not known for their sense of humor, and this one was not an exception. He scowled at Karr, frowned at his list, and then told him to go ahead.

Karr tucked his new reporter's notebook into his back pocket and ambled past the checkpoint and down the hall of the hotel. He'd pulled a sport coat over his jeans so he'd have enough pockets for his PDA and phone; the jacket placed him in the upper percentile of better-dressed journalists, at least in the room set up for the press conference. About fifty reporters were milling about, most of them hovering near the carts where coffee and donuts had been set out.

"Hey ya," Karr said to no one in particular as he walked over. "Is this stuff free or do we have to pay?"

A few of the others laughed, thinking he was joking. Karr didn't see anyone taking money, so he helped himself to a coffee and a pair of Boston creams, which he stacked on top of each other chocolate to chocolate.

"Nothing like a sugar rush first thing in the morning, huh?" said one of the reporters nearby. She gave him a smile almost as sweet as the custard filling in the donut.

"Have to eat the whole table to get a sugar high going," said Karr, his mouth full of donut.

"Theresa Seelbach, *Newsweek*," said the reporter, sticking out her hand. "You local?"

"No, actually, I just came out from back east," said Karr. He held up his credentials, from the *Daily Record.* The paper was legitimate, though tiny. Telach had actually arranged for Karr to work for them as an unpaid freelancer with the help of an intermediary. "Editors finally decided McSweeney's the real deal. I'm doing a feature."

Karr wasn't exactly sure what a feature was, but the reporter seemed to be satisfied. She smiled at him.

"Been a reporter long?"

"Just about a year," said Karr.

"First campaign, huh?"

"First big story," said Karr.

"Your first story?"

"Oh, nah, nah," said Karr. "Mostly I've covered like police stuff. And a fight in the city council. That was cool. Mayor got decked."

The other reporter laughed.

"When does McSweeney get here?" Karr asked finally.

"Oh, not for an hour or so. He's out watering the money tree. Come on, the real coffee is in the lounge around the side. I'll buy you one."

129

"WHY WOULD THEY need DNA?" Mrs. Ball asked Lia. Her lip trembled. "Is he . . . did they find him . . . is he . . .?"

"He's still missing, Mrs. Ball. It's just a general precaution." Lia struggled to find the magic formula that would get the DNA sample she needed voluntarily, without having to take out the warrant. Doing so would surely tip Ball off, if he wasn't tipped off already.

"It's how they identify bodies."

"They can also use traces to see if someone was at a certain place," said Lia. "You'd be surprised—sweat from a finger on an elevator button. I don't think they have anything specific, but they want to be prepared."

"Maybe in his comb," said Mrs. Ball finally. She led Lia upstairs to the bedroom.

"Does he have any places he liked to go to be alone?" Lia asked. "A place people might not think of, a park or something? Somewhere he might be contemplative?"

Some place where he might bring a nosey investigator, Lia thought, though she didn't say.

"I don't know. He wasn't—he didn't contemplate." Mrs. Ball went into the bathroom and returned with a comb. Lia took out the plastic Baggie she'd bought at the supermarket and put the comb inside. Then she pointed to the medal she'd spotted yesterday and asked about it again.

Mrs. Ball shrugged. Her head was drooping. Lia thought she was resigning herself to her husband's death. She probably thought Lia was lying to protect her, and that he really had been found and they wanted to cinch the identification before telling her.

Lia turned to another photo on the wall, one that showed Ball about twenty years younger, a rifle in his hand and a deer at his feet.

"Does he like to hunt?" Lia asked.

"Oh yes, of course. Every year he gets his deer. After a few weeks I'm quite sick of venison." Mrs. Ball smiled, her mood lifting slightly.

"Where does he hunt?"

"A few places. The Castro farm down in Clinton. Then there's Irv Burdick's property along Stissing Mountain. That's pretty good. Irv keeps one of the old farmhouses in decent shape up there for some hunting friends, and the chief used to spend the night for a very early start. Car noise spooked the deer. Hasn't had to do that in a while, though— more deer than he can shoot. Plus, I think his back bothers him if he doesn't sleep on a thick mattress. Irv was a little cheap about that."

"Could you point out those properties on a map for me?" Lia asked.

"He wouldn't be hunting this time of year."

"Probably not," said Lia. "But maybe he's up there thinking."

130

BALL LEANED FORWARD from the taxi's rear seat.

"Could you turn that up, please?" he asked the cabdriver.

The man, a dark-skinned Latino, flicked the radio's volume up a notch.

". . . the President is expected to meet the governor tomorrow evening. The next day, he'll attend ceremonies at the Ronald Reagan Library, where among other guests at the nonpartisan event will be the man the opposition party seems to be leaning toward as his next opponent, Senator Gideon McSweeney. . . ."

"That's fine," said Ball, leaning back in the seat.

At least he knew where McSweeney would be tomorrow. There was no question of getting him there, though; the security around the President would be too great.

When would he do it?

As soon as possible. The longer he waited, the better the odds would be that they would get him before he got McSweeney.

And he was going to get McSweeney.

CHECKING INTO THE hotel presented Ball with another dilemma. He'd need a credit card. He didn't want to use his own, and was leery about using Amanda Rauci's as well. Someone was bound to be looking for her by now.

The fact that Ball had arrived before the hotel's 4:00 P.M. check-in time gave him a brief reprieve. He told the young woman that he would check in later if he could leave his bag. After she took it he walked back out into the lobby lounge area and sat down to think.

There were Web sites and criminal rings where you could buy credit card numbers, but obtaining the cards themselves required you to meet someone in person. There must be a hundred black-market dealers in LA, but they'd never trust him enough to deal with him, not quickly anyway. And finding them would be next to impossible: if he went down to South Central and just started asking around, he'd be rolled inside of an hour.

Maybe the solution wasn't to stay anywhere. He needed to use a computer, and there was a business center in the hotel; he'd give them a false room number. Beyond that, what did he need?

A shower would be nice.

And sleep.

There was too much to do to sleep.

Ball had just decided to use Amanda Rauci's credit card again when a better solution fell literally into his lap—a woman passing nearby dropped her purse on the floor. Ball got up and gave it up for her. There wasn't time to take the card from her wallet—she would have seen—but now that he had the idea, all he to do was find the opportunity.

Opportunity presented itself about a half hour later, at a hotel restaurant across the street. Ball positioned himself in the bar near the cash register, planning to swipe a card off an unattended tray after the cashier had run up the charges. But as Ball ordered a beer he noticed that the bartender and some of the waitstaff stowed their pocketbooks on a shelf next to the bar. He slipped his hand down and took out the bartender's wallet as she poured the beer at the far end of the bar.

Ball slid a ten across the bar and smiled at the woman's joke about it being a little early for anything stronger. Then he went to the men's room. The purse he'd picked had six different credit cards; he took the one that looked least worn

from swipe machines. Returning the wallet was easy; the bartender had gone into the other room to help set up for dinner.

Ball sat down and finished his drink, sipping slowly as he
planned out what he needed to do next.

131

IT WAS ALL about patterns, Johnny Bib liked to say; the universe had a certain order to it, and anything that violated that order did so for a reason. Anomalies were as informative as symmetry, many times more so.

Which made the unsuccessful attempt on Senator Mc-Sweeney's life stand out.

"It's the gas," Gallo told Rubens. "Ball normally buys gas every two to three days when he's in Pine Plains. It's always twenty dollars. Clockwork. Habit. He never tanks up—except for the day before Gordon killed himself. Then there's no activity on his card during the three days around the time Gordon dies."

"He used cash," interrupted Johnny Bib. "And probably someone else's credit card."

"Whose?" asked Rubens, looking at Gallo rather than Johnny Bib.

"Haven't figured that out," said Gallo. "But getting back to the pattern, there's a gap around the time when Gordon dies, but no gap when someone shoots at McSweeney. And it's not because his wife was using his card—she uses a Discover Card, and the charge pattern is consistent."

"It is consistent with what the wife told the op," added Johnny Bib. "He was only away that time."

"He wasn't the shooter," said Gallo. "Maybe he killed Gordon, but he didn't shoot at McSweeney."

Rubens looked at the billing information. It would have been much, much better to find positive evidence—a trail of receipts that would have put Ball in a specific place at a specific time. But real life was messier than that—or maybe Ball was simply very clever.

"Keep working on it, Mr. Gallo," said Rubens. "Continue gathering as much information as you can about the police chief. There's no such thing as too much information."

That wasn't entirely correct, but neither man pointed that out as they left his office.

132

BY THE TIME Lia made the connections with the courier at the county airport and shipped Chief Ball's hair off, it was already after six. Lia tracked down the properties the chief's wife had mentioned, and though it was dark she checked them as best she could, driving as much as she could through them and then walking around with her flashlight and even checking on an old building at the Burdick farm. Lia kept calling Amanda's name, though she had long ago concluded she wasn't going to find her alive.

Lia had no evidence, but she did have a theory: Amanda Rauci had found something in Forester's car, maybe one of his notebooks or something else the state police had missed. That led her to investigate the chief and then confront him. He'd killed her and then run away.

Or maybe not. Cold and tired, Lia went back to the hotel, had a quick meal, and fell asleep facedown on her bed without bothering to change. When she woke, it was two hours or so before dawn. Lia got up and went straight to the Castro property, not even stopping for coffee.

The place looked even more forbidding during the day. Dominated by an old gravel mine, it consisted of roughly a thousand acres. Large clumps of rocks and deep gouges in the earth made the landscape look like the back side of the moon. A stream ran through the middle of the property, bisecting a spider's web of dirt trails before disappearing in the woods.

Lia drove her rental car to the edge of the widest trail,

looking for signs that someone else had been through recently. She got out and walked up the narrower paths. But she saw nothing suspicious.

The old Burdick farm was several times the size of the Castro property, with even more places to dispose of a body. Besides the standing farmhouse that she had checked the night before, six or seven other buildings stood at the far end of the property, obscured by rows of bushes and young trees. They were all in various stages of disrepair, moldy, their thin walls bereft of siding and pockmarked with bullet holes.

Lia checked them all, without finding a body. It was a long, hot day, and even though she'd spent it entirely outdoors, Lia didn't feel particularly close to nature when she gave up looking for Amanda late in the afternoon.

133

TIMOTHY O'ROURKE HAD worked for Senator McSweeney for several years, as a combination chauffeur-bodyguard. When the senator had geared up for the presidential campaign, he had been switched to a full-time security officer. But he'd been pushed aside even before the arrival of the Secret Service and the redoubling of the Service's efforts following the attempt on McSweeney's life. O'Rourke was considered a bit too old and too rough around the edges to really fit in.

Though that wasn't his interpretation of what had happened.

"These young guys and their BlackBerry thingers," O'Rourke had told Ball bitterly several weeks before, when he had effectively been demoted to the status of an advance flunky. "They don't understand the importance of experience. What experience do they have, anyway? None."

Ball remembered the conversation as he waited for O'Rourke to answer his cell phone. It was shameful how they pushed older guys out, he thought, though he knew in this case there was probably a bit more to the story than O'Rourke let on. The retired trooper was several years older than Ball, and not nearly in as good physical shape. And he'd never been as smart.

"O'Rourke."

"Hello, Tim, how are you?"

"Chief?"

They exchanged greetings and caught up briefly, enabling Ball to ascertain that O'Rourke was in fact on the West

Coast. While he'd had a backup plan in case O'Rourke wasn't, things would be considerably easier this way.

"I wonder if you could do me a favor," said Ball.

"A favor? What do you need, Chris?"

"I'd like to talk to you in person, if you don't mind. I'm in town, actually."

"LA?"

"It's kind of important. I know you're busy."

"Busy." O'Rourke made a derisive sound as if he were spitting into the phone. "They're humoring me here, Chris. I could go away for a month and they'd never miss me."

"I doubt that's true."

"Close."

"Want to have dinner?"

"Already ate."

"Let's grab a drink then," said Ball. "I know a place."

THEY MET AT a small bar Ball had picked out before making the phone call. O'Rourke had retired as a zone sergeant for the New York State Troopers before signing on with Mc-Sweeney, and like most of their conversations, this one began with him recalling a minor incident they'd watched unfold in the local court, where the citizen judge had actually fallen asleep several times during the proceedings. Ball chuckled, though he felt bad for the judge. They were on their second beers before O'Rourke asked what he had wanted.

"I need a job, actually," Ball told him. "I was wondering if there might be something on the senator's staff."

He wove a story of political intrigue, claiming that his foes in the village had finally outmaneuvered him.

"Well, I'm sure Senator McSweeney would help. Somehow. There isn't much to do now. I mean, there are plenty of things to do, but the Secret Service takes care of most of it."

"You're not involved at all?"

"Of course I'm involved."

Ball bought another round, encouraging O'Rourke to talk. He picked up as much information as he could about the security arrangements, pulling out names and data about the routines.

By the time they were done, O'Rourke had convinced himself that he was going to get his old friend a job. They were going to have a great time together.

O'Rourke had also had quite a bit to drink, more than enough to make him tipsy.

"I think I better drive you home," said Ball.

"Nonsense. I'm sober."

"If you get stopped, it'll look very bad for the campaign. And I won't get my job."

It took another round to convince him.

KILLING AMANDA RAUCI had taken so much out of Ball that he decided he wasn't going to kill O'Rourke; instead, he'd leave him locked in the trunk of the rental car and park it somewhere no one would find it for a day or two. But when Ball pulled off the road and got out of the car, pretending that he was going to relieve himself, the sleeping O'Rourke suddenly stirred.

"Where you goin', Chris?"

"Gotta take a leak."

"Where the hell are we?"

"Damned if I know," lied Ball.

And then suddenly O'Rourke became belligerent, pointing out that they should have been back at his hotel by now.

"Look, I don't know the damn state," said Ball. He had already taken O'Rourke's pistol; he put his hand on it as he walked around the car toward the field.

"We're out in the middle of nowhere," said O'Rourke, getting out of the car. "Hey, where's my gun?"

"Here," said Ball, and he killed O'Rourke with a single shot to the head.

A sharp edge of panic struck Ball in the ribs as O'Rourke fell. Had someone seen him stop? Was he close enough to the nearby houses to be heard?

He'd checked the place carefully, he reminded himself, but his paranoia continued to grow. He picked O'Rourke up and put him in the trunk, then took off his shirt, worried about bloodstains. Ball went to the ground and kicked at the dirt.

Get out of here, he told himself. Go! Take the car and go.

He felt better as he drove. By the time he left the car in the long-term parking lot at LAX and queued up for a cab to take him back to his hotel, he was back to his old self.

Not the police chief self, but the man who'd lived on his wits in the city years before, the man who knew how the night worked, and how to take advantage of it.

The man he needed to be for the next twenty-four hours.

134

RUBENS STOOD AT the back of the Art Room, surveying the room. It was nearly empty, with only two runners and the supervisor, Chris Farlekas, on duty. It had been a long, fruitless day, and Desk Three's center of operations was eerily quiet—never a good sign.

"Nothing?" said Rubens when Farlekas glanced up at him.

"A few things. The analysis of the DNA sample from Chief Ball should be available soon. Ambassador Jackson checked in from Secret Service headquarters. There was a threat against another candidate. The Service isn't sure if it was a copycat or not. It was sent by e-mail and they know where it originated. They're in the process of seizing the computers. I volunteered our help, but they said it was under control. The network is in Las Vegas, and they have plenty of agents there. It was sent from a Starbucks," added Farlekas. "A little different than the others."

"The President?"

"Due in LA around five A.M. tomorrow. The Service is confident they can protect him."

"Have Mr. Dean wait for him at the airport. He wants to be briefed personally."

"I already told him."

Rubens glanced around the room. There was nothing for him to do here, and he had more than enough work waiting back upstairs. Still, he wanted to stay.

No, what he wanted to do was solve this, apprehend Chief Ball, and find out who was trying to assassinate

McSweeney—assuming Gallo was right and it wasn't the police chief.

"I'll be in my office. Let me know if anything develops overnight."

"You're going back to your office?" asked Farlekas. "It's past seven."

"I have a few things to wrap up," said Rubens. "Thank you for your concern."

135

DEAN HAD NEVER been in the presidential limo before, and his first impression was one of disappointment. He wasn't sure what he'd been expecting, but the reality seemed almost disappointing. The back consisted of two bench seats facing each other. The leather seats were plush, but otherwise the interior seemed no more luxurious than what you would find in a standard Mercedes S. There was a bit more room, but still, Dean's knees nearly touched the President's.

"And what did Senator McSweeney say when you told him about the money?" asked President Marcke.

"Not much. He just took it in."

"Did he react when you mentioned Tolong?"

"Not that I saw."

Marcke nodded. The two men were alone; the President had pointedly asked his aides to stand outside the car while Dean briefed him at the airport.

"George Hadash used to speak very highly of you, Mr. Dean," said Marcke. "He was the reason you came to Deep Black."

"Dr. Hadash was a very good man," said Dean.

"A straight shooter," agreed the President. "Rare for an academic, don't you think?"

Dean nodded.

"Marines have a reputation for straight shooting," added Marcke. "And I'd like you to do that now. What's your impression of McSweeney—do you think he took the money?"

"Hard to say. The evidence seems to point that way."

"If he did take the money, he's responsible for another man's death," said Marcke. "At least one."

"It's possible he didn't know anything about it," said Dean. "He might have been oblivious. Maybe one of the noncommissioned officers in his unit really ran things."

A faint smile appeared on the President's lips. "You're trying hard not to jump to any conclusions, aren't you, Mr. Dean?"

"Yes, sir."

"Because he's a fellow Marine, or because that's the way you are?"

"Probably a little of both."

Marcke nodded, then reached for the button to lower his window. "Stay with me today, Mr. Dean. If you can."

"Yes, sir."

136

TWO THINGS WERE important—the faked credentials Chief Ball waved in his hand and the strut of his body as he entered the Paley house. He wouldn't have been able to say which was more persuasive.

"The first thing we need are two people at the top of the driveway, next to the gate," he said, to no one and everyone as he flipped his wallet closed. "And there's no one on the back fence—I could have hopped it and climbed up on the patio and no one would have noticed."

"Who the hell are you?"

"Chris Stevens," said Ball, using the name on the ID. "Who the hell are you?"

"It's twelve hours before the reception," said one of the men standing in the foyer.

"Who are you?" asked Ball.

The man identified himself as a member of the sheriff's department. Ball frowned for just a moment, then made a show of becoming more conciliatory, his voice hinting at forced congeniality. "I don't want to bust your chops. I'm just doing my job."

"What is your job?" asked a woman, appearing from the top of the steps.

"Christopher Stevens, ma'am."

"You're from LAPD?"

Ball smiled without answering.

"Who are you with?" she asked again, coming down the stairs. Two other agents, both male, followed her down. Ball could tell they were Secret Service by their lapel pins, but they didn't identify themselves.

"I work for the senator," Ball told the woman. "Tim O'Rourke sent me over."

She smirked. "Let's see some ID."

"Sure."

Ball pulled out the campaign ID he had made a few hours before at the campaign headquarters.

"Driver's license," said the woman.

Ball reached into his pocket and took out the license. The agent held it sideways, making sure it contained the holographic imprint used by New York State. Then she studied the ID number.

"Run this," she told one of the men. Her eyes still locked on Ball's, she asked for his Social Security number.

Ball repeated the memorized number. The man who had taken the license nodded, then retreated to another room inside the house.

"He's going to remember that?" Ball asked the woman.

"He's good with numbers."

The Social Security number and the ID on the license belonged to the real Christopher Stevens, who was in O'Rourke's files as a backup driver and occasional extra "suit" for work in the district. Ball had met Stevens a few times. He was a few years younger and two inches taller, but otherwise the general description was close enough that the scant information on the license matched.

Ball stood quietly, waiting while the information was checked against the criminal and Secret Service databases. He knew the criminal check would come clean, and as long as Stevens hadn't made any threats against the President in the last few weeks, the Secret Service files should have nothing against him, either.

The female agent stared at him the whole time. Ball stared back. The last thing he wanted to do was seem weak. Finally, the man returned with Ball's license. The agent handed it to the woman, nodding almost imperceptibly. She took it, looked at it again, flipped it over in her hand, then handed it back.

"So who did I just give my credit report to?" asked Ball, taking the license. "I want to know who to call when the phony charges hit my account."

One of the male agents smirked. The others didn't.

"Lucinda Silvestri," said the woman.

Ball extended his hand. Silvestri looked at it a moment, then finally shook it. Ball had expected a crusher grip, and he got one.

"Where's O'Rourke?" said the man who had smirked.

"I don't know whether he's under the weather or what. He told me a couple of days ago to come out in case I was needed. Called me this morning, told me to be here."

"He didn't have you shovel him off a barroom floor last night?"

"That's enough," snapped Silvestri. "Mr. Stevens, stay out of our way."

"I'm only here to help," said Ball, holding his arms out in protest. "I'm just doing what I'm supposed to do."

Silvestri frowned, and went back to the stairs.

"O'Rourke's a bit of a joke," said the agent who'd spoken earlier. "No offense to you."

"Look, the guy's my boss. I can't bad-mouth him," said Ball. "I know you guys run the show."

"Preston Dell," said the agent, extending his hand. "You come from New York?"

"Yeah, upstate. I was a cop in New York for twenty years. Took retirement. Have a little security firm. They call me mostly when the senator's back home, you know? I first met him when he was a congressman."

"You like Rockland?"

"That's the next county down," said Ball, not sure if the agent had made an honest mistake or was testing him. "I live in Goshen. That's Orange County. Not much difference, I guess, except for the house prices. Damn hard to afford anything now."

"I have a cousin in Pearl River."

"I don't know Rockland too well," said Ball, "but that's pretty close to the city, right?"

They traded geographical references for a few minutes. Ball had been to Goshen many times over the years—the Orange County Jail was there—but he didn't know it like he knew Pine Plains or the towns around it.

"County building is a crazy jumble," he told the agent. "I get lost every time I go to get my license renewed or for jury duty."

"They let you serve?"

"Well, funny thing—they won't automatically dismiss you in New York, but most of the lawyers won't let you on a jury. So you go through a big rigamarole. Earn forty bucks for the day, though. Pays for lunch over at the Orange Inn."

"Yeah," said the agent. "Listen, stay away from Lucinda, all right? She and O'Rourke have had some words. And stay away from the bar."

"Absolutely," said Ball.

"Things won't really get rolling until after lunch."

"I'll fade into the background until then."

"Good," said the agent, turning to go.

137

LIA REALIZED SHE'D been mistaken when she looked for Amanda Rauci outside of Pine Plains. The police chief wouldn't want her body discovered, certainly—but if it were, he'd want to be the one to control any investigation. So surely he would have found a hiding place in his own village.

Pine Plains had been settled in the late seventeenth century, its main streets and principal boundaries laid out well before the country gained its independence. Because of that, there was relatively little undeveloped land in the village. The biggest parcel, about two acres, was behind the old grocery store at the edge of town. The store, shuttered for several years, had a back lot overgrown with weeds and small trees. Trash dotted the area. But there was no body, or signs that the ground had been disturbed.

Next, Lia looked at some wooded lots near the school. It surprised her to find that these were spotless, without litter or even cigarette butts; either students in general had changed since she was a kid, or they were much more conscientious about trash in Pine Plains.

Finally, she scoured the creek bed that ran through the southwest corner of town. All she got for her effort was wet sneakers.

By three o'clock, she decided that it was useless. She checked in with the Art Room, then went over to the police station to see if Chief Ball had called in.

"Now, hon, I told you I would call," said the dispatcher. "Did I call?"

"My phone's been off." Lia glanced around the station. There ought to be something here, she thought, some sign she should be able to interpret. "So he hasn't come in?"

"Haven't heard a peep."

"That's unusual, right?"

"Very." The dispatcher lowered her voice. "Chief Ball is working with you? His wife said—"

"No."

"And you really don't know where he is? He's not . . ." She let her voice trail off.

"No," said Lia. "But the longer he's gone, the worse it looks. Is there anyone you can think of who might not like him?"

"I know what you're thinking," said the dispatcher. Her face reddened slightly. She pressed her lips together and shook her head. "I called in Sergeant Snow to cover things. He'll be in around four, if you want to talk to him."

Lia nodded. "If you were going to hide something big— the size of a large suitcase or trunk, say—where would you hide it? It would be around town somewhere, somewhere most people wouldn't look."

"Is that what the chief is looking for?"

"No. It has nothing to do with him." Lia leaned down on the dispatcher's desk, as if she were truly contemplating an impossible question. "Can't be in your house. It's not in your office—"

Lia stopped herself. Why not in his office?

Or rather, his building.

"Can I use your bathroom?" Lia asked.

"Down the hall, near the stairs."

AS SOON AS Lia saw the freezer at the bottom of the steps, she knew she'd found Amanda Rauci. Lia pulled the lock pick set out of her belt and went to work on the lock. She had it open within thirty seconds. Taking a breath, she closed her eyes and pulled open the door to the freezer.

A stack of ice pops, covered with frost, sat on one side.

Opposite it was a small aluminum foil–wrapped package with a handwritten label that read: "Venison, '06."

Otherwise the freezer was empty.

"WHERE DO YOU keep the deer meat that the chief butchers?" Lia asked Mrs. Ball a short time later.

"The meat's long gone now," said the chief's wife. "We had the last of it in February. I made venison steak for Valentine's Day."

"But until it's all eaten?"

"Well, in the garage. We have a freezer."

"Do you mind if I take a look?"

Confused, Mrs. Ball started to leave the house to show her the way.

"I think I want to do this alone," Lia told her.

Mrs. Ball started to tremble. Lia thought she might collapse. But a policeman's wife had to have a reserve of strength to survive, and she called on it now, pulling herself together.

"You'll need the key," she told Lia, going to the kitchen to get it.

WHEN THE KEY that the chief's wife gave Lia didn't work, Lia knew she was finally right. She forced her emotions away as she picked the lock.

A pair of ice trays sat over a black garbage bag at the top of the chest.

Amanda Rauci lay beneath the bag.

138

GETTING TO THE Paley house so early allowed Ball to seem like part of the furniture as the day went on; each arriving wave of agents and security personnel found him already ensconced. But he couldn't escape scrutiny entirely, and he had to leave the house with the others when the Service conducted two separate sweeps for bombs and hidden weapons.

After the second sweep, the security teams were issued fresh ID tags. Ball knew from experience that the tags would be used to segregate the teams into different zones and assignments, and that in order to stay in the house at night he would have to be with the senator's personal staff.

But when Ball got to the table, he saw that his tag was coded for access to the external areas only.

"Hey, you made a mistake here," said Ball, pointing at the badge. "I'm with the senator."

"You have to take that up with Lucinda."

"I'm not moving until I get the right badge. This is my job you're talking about. My neck."

"Look—"

"Hey, I'm with the senator's staff, all right? Now come on. I know you guys are in charge, but let's be realistic."

Lucinda Silvestri, in charge of the house team, appeared in one of the doorways.

"What seems to be your problem, Mr. Stevens?"

"My problem is, you guys don't want me to do my job."

Silvestri walked over to the table and bent close to the agent who was handling the passes. Ball leaned closer to listen.

"Excuse us, please," snapped Silvestri.

"Maybe I should call the senator."

"You can call the President for all I care," said Silvestri.

Ball clamped his mouth shut, though he continued to seethe. He could accomplish what he wanted to accomplish outside, but that wasn't the point—the senator's security was supposed to be inside the room when the senator arrived. Not protesting would be extremely suspicious.

But Ball didn't want to call the campaign if he didn't have to. He'd already checked in with the coordinator O'Rourke normally reported to, who had been in the middle of a million things and seemed to barely hear him when he asked where O'Rourke was. The person he'd have to talk to to get anything done was Jimmy Fingers—and he feared the weasel would recognize his voice.

The agent who'd been talking to him about Rockland County earlier was standing near the stove, going over a map of the exterior grounds. Ball walked over to him, reintroduced himself, and asked if he could plead his case.

"It's my job, you know?" said Ball. "And you've seen for yourself, I'm not getting in the Service's way. You guys are running the show, but I'm here. I have to do my job."

The agent shrugged but then went over to Silvestri.

"At least he's an upgrade over O'Rourke," Ball heard him say.

"All right. We'll give you the proper tag," said Silvestri finally. "Stay awake, though."

"With the coffee you guys brew, I'll be awake for the next ten years," answered Ball.

139

THE MCSWEENEY CAMPAIGN made a bus available for the reporters covering the senator during his appearances. The bus
tooled along at the end of a procession of vehicles that included the senator and his aides in a pair of Ford sedans,
bodyguards in a Chevy SUV, and various hangers-on in a
Chrysler minivan. While strictly speaking there were no assigned seats in the bus, a caste system generally dictated
who sat where. The best seats were in the back, where the
big dailies and newsmagazine people sat; smaller papers and
freelancers got the middle; and newcomers got everything
else. Karr found this out by accident, plopping down next to
Theresa Seelbach, the *Newsweek* writer he'd met the day before. She smirked and started to laugh, then explained how it
worked.

"It's like junior high," she told him.

Karr had skipped much of junior high, but he started to
get up anyway.

"Oh, don't worry," she said. "Sit down. You're kind of
cute, and so big I don't think anyone will ask you to move."

Karr smiled, though he felt himself blushing.

"Got anything useful for your story yet?"

"Not much," said Karr. "We don't actually see McSweeney
too much, do we?"

"Not really. Ten minutes here, five minutes there."

"Maybe I can write about the food. Breakfast was OK."

"God, I couldn't stomach anything," said Seelbach. "Going

to be another boring day today. A million stops. We'll hear the same speech and step over the same drunks."

"Maybe somebody will take a shot at him again," said the reporter sitting behind them.

"You think?" said Karr.

The others nearby laughed, but the reporter who had said it turned serious. "Gallows humor, son."

"Who do you think shot at him?"

"One of his campaign people, I'd bet," said Seelbach. "Why do you think he started listening to them?"

The others started making similar jokes. It was clear that the reporters had no serious theories, or at least weren't sharing them.

"What about the Vietnamese thing?" asked Karr as the jokes petered out.

"Oh, that's a crock," said Seelbach. "The Secret Service and the FBI say there's no evidence. McSweeney probably made the whole thing up to draw attention to the fact that he served there. He never does or says anything without an agenda."

"Whoever did it, it was great for his campaign," said the reporter behind Karr. "He was fading before then. Look at him now. He's on top of the world. If I were him, I'd put that sniper on the payroll."

"As long as he continues to miss," said Karr.

This time, the others laughed with him, rather than at him.

140

DISCOVERING AMANDA RAUCI'S body in Chief Ball's freezer changed everything. Ball was now formally a murder suspect, and obtaining warrants to gather information about him would be child's play.

Which bummed Gallo big-time. He would have much more enjoyed hacking into the different databases and taking what he needed, rather than having to deal with the bureaucracy.

Still, there was something to be said for the bureaucracy. A search of FAA flight records showed that a C. Ball had purchased tickets in Cleveland for Chicago and Houston, in Chicago for LA and New York, and in LA for Pittsburgh and Miami. The car that Amanda Rauci's credit card had been used to rent was found at the Cleveland airport after the plane manifests were checked, so it was a pretty good bet that C. Ball was the police chief.

The question was where was he now?

"These are only the lists of the people who bought tickets," Gallo told Johnny Bib. "We're still working on the final lists, the people who actually showed up. Those come from the airlines themselves. My bet is on Pittsburgh," he added. "It's the smallest city—doesn't really go with the others."

"Ha!" said Johnny Bib. His voice was shrill enough to echo off the noise-dampening ceiling of the computer lab.

"Ha?" asked Gallo.

"Ha!" repeated Johnny Bib.

"Each time he lands, he buys two tickets," said Gallo.

"When he reaches his final destination, he doesn't buy any. Both the Miami and the Pittsburgh plane landed yesterday afternoon. So he's in one of those cities—Pittsburgh, I think."

"Why does he buy two tickets?" Johnny Bib asked. He sounded like a philosophy professor lecturing a freshman class on Plato and the Socratic method.

"He doesn't want us to know where he's going," said Gallo.

"*Ha!*" said Johnny Bib.

"Maybe Pittsburgh is too close to Cleveland," Gallo said. "If he was going there, he could have driven. That would be harder to trace."

"Ha!" said Johnny Bib.

"I give up," said Gallo, completely baffled by his boss.

"He . . . knows . . . we . . . are . . . watching," said Johnny Bib, pausing between each word.

"He never left LA!" said Gallo, finally getting it. "He just wants us to think he did."

"*Ha!*"

RUBENS LISTENED QUIETLY as Gallo laid out what he had found and surmised from the FAA passenger lists. The security tapes at Los Angeles International Airport were being scrutinized; Chief Ball had not been spotted yet.

"It's possible that we're overthinking this," Telach said. "One of the other candidates is in Florida this weekend. I think it's Winkler."

"No, it's Dalton," said Gallo. "And, like, there hasn't been one attempt on another candidate, despite the threats."

"Maybe Ball made the threats to throw us off the trail," said Jackson over the phone speaker. He was with the FBI liaison in Washington.

"I very much doubt that it was Ball who made the threats," said Rubens. "I don't believe Ball had anything to do with the assassination attempt, either."

"It doesn't fit the pattern," explained Gallo. "It's an anomaly."

"You mean there's another killer?" said Jackson.

"A would-be killer, Mr. Ambassador," said Rubens. "The question is whether he will attempt to improve on that status."

"Ball may know who it is," said Gallo.

"Yes," said Rubens. "Unfortunately, we're going to have to find Chief Ball before we can find out."

"WHAT DO YOU think, Jimmy Fingers? Can we blow off Paley?"

"Sure, if you'd like to kiss off about $350,000 worth of donations. That's what he'll be worth in general."

"All right," said McSweeney wearily. "All right. And who's after the Paleys?"

"That would be Mr. and Mrs. Davis. They gave a lot of money to the last campaign. They're going to try talking you out of going to the Getty tomorrow."

"Why would they care? No, wait, that's fine. I don't really need to know. Tell me again what movies Paley has produced."

LIA HAD JUST turned into the parking lot at LaGuardia Airport in New York City when her sat phone rang. It was Sandy Chafetz, confirming that they had reserved her flight to Baltimore/Washington International Airport. A car would meet her there and take her back to Crypto City to be debriefed. Rubens hadn't decided whether she should join the search for Ball—or, if she did, what she would do.

"Great," said Lia. "I'll talk to you after I clear security."

"There's one other thing I think you'd like to know," said Chafetz. "Gerald Forester's divorce attorney got a letter from him a few days after he died. The attorney had it authenticated before contacting the Service and sending a copy to his ex-wife. It's an apology—a suicide note. He explained that he just couldn't go on."

Lia fought back an urge to argue. Instead, she pushed the button on her phone to kill the transmission, and felt a tear run down the side of her cheek. Wondering why she felt so bad about Forester's death, she locked the rental car and walked into the terminal to find her flight.

SHADOWING THE PRESIDENT was a revelation for Dean. He'd never imagined that so many people would want—*need*—to talk to Marcke in the course of an hour, let alone twenty-four. Aides constantly vied for attention. There were phone calls and e-mail messages, forwarded BlackBerry alerts. Briefing papers piled up; summaries and reports were passed from assistant to assistant. Ted Cohen, the chief of staff, had two telephones constantly pressed to his ear, and more often than not was speaking to someone nearby as well.

Marcke seemed unfazed by it all. He seemed to give whomever he was speaking to at the moment his undivided attention, and it was only after they had moved on that Dean realized the President must have been thinking about a dozen other things. If anything, Marcke seemed to want *more* to do: in his few moments of peace he fidgeted, habitually bending paper clips with his fingers and spinning them into knots and odd shapes. He ordered the car stopped several times, and, to the visible discomfort of the Secret Service detail, insisted on shaking the hands of some of whatever bystanders happened to be there.

Every so often, President Marcke glanced over and found Dean. Marcke smirked at him, as if they were co-conspirators on a private joke.

"So, Mr. Dean, enjoying yourself?" asked the President as they rode to his next stop, a new biology lab four miles south of the city.

"It's interesting."

"Boring as hell, huh?" Marcke smiled at him. "George Hadash used to call these sorts of swings 'orchestrated time chewers.' He hated traveling with me, but he did have a way with words."

"Yup."

"You never took one of his classes, did you?"

"No, sir." Dean had met Hadash in Vietnam when he'd been detailed to give the then-congressional aide a "ground–level" view of Vietnam. Hadash had impressed him not so much because he insisted on going into the field—plenty of civilian suits from the States did that—but because he actually listened to what Dean said.

"He was a good teacher. And a friend. I miss him." The President paused. "He was working on a new theory of the Vietnam War when he died, you know. He was writing a book. He thought the war was due a reevaluation. He was going to call the book *A Necessary War*."

"Really?" Dean had never heard anyone say that Vietnam was anything but a waste.

"He thought if it hadn't been for Vietnam, the rapprochement with China would have been delayed at least ten years. And he believed there would have been another armed clash between the Soviets and ourselves, perhaps in the Middle East. We might never have become involved in helping the Afghan rebels, which at least indirectly led to the end of the Soviet Union. I doubt I'm doing his ideas justice," added the President. "They were quite extensive."

Dean nodded.

"What do you think, Mr. Dean?"

"A lot of good people died," said Dean.

"True. It's a difficult thing, sending people to die. But that's not really the question."

"Vietnam shaped my life," said Dean. It was a statement he wouldn't have made before going back, as true as it was, because he hadn't realized it.

"It shaped mine as well," said Marcke. "But again, that wasn't the question."

The car stopped. The Secret Service agents began to swarm outside.

"I think it was an important event," said Dean. "But I don't know if it was necessary. Most things that happen, we don't have the luxury of knowing if they're necessary or not. Even for ourselves."

"Well put, Mr. Dean," said the President, pulling himself out of the car.

144

THERE WERE MANY more Secret Service agents at the Paley house than Chief Ball thought there would be. They were a humorless bunch, for the most part not given to chitchat, but that was just as well—Ball worried that saying too much to the wrong person might inadvertently give him away. He spent most of his time sitting in the den with one of the liaisons to the federal marshal detail—brought in for extra coverage and mostly assigned to the grounds—watching a soccer match on television. Ball had no interest in soccer, but the marshal was far and away the most amiable of the feds inside the house.

An agent stuck his head through the door.

"Hey, emergency services briefings. Let's go."

Chief Ball got up, then fell in behind the marshal as they walked to the kitchen. Two ambulances from a local company had been retained to provide coverage if any guests or staff members got sick. The Service itself would handle getting the senator to the hospital if necessary, using a special SUV and following a pre-scouted route.

"Who's Stevens?" asked a pug-nosed, light-skinned black Secret Service agent, entering the room at full gallop.

"That would be me," said Ball.

The agent looked at him as if he'd just ruined his day. "Call your office. Now."

"All right." Ball started toward the nearby wall phone.

"Not on that line," hissed the man.

A titter of barely suppressed laughter ran through the room.

Ball went outside and found a sympathetic sheriff's deputy to lend him a phone.

"I'm supposed to call in," he told the woman who answered at campaign headquarters.

"Bruce Chazin wants to talk to you."

Chazin was O'Rourke's nominal supervisor.

"This is Stevens," said Ball when he came on the line. "You wanted to talk to me?"

"Where the hell is O'Rourke?"

"Uh, I don't know. I kind of assumed he was there."

"When did you last talk to him?"

"Well, he called around noon to check on me," said Ball. "Sounded like he was having lunch."

He answered the rest of Chazin's questions as vaguely as possible. The deputy campaign manager needed someone to review the arrangements at the next day's events.

"I'd be glad to do that for you, but they have us in a lock-down situation here," said Ball. "Can't go in or out."

"I don't want you. I want O'Rourke. I need someone at the meeting."

Chazin fumed some more, and seemed on the verge of ordering Ball to check on O'Rourke's hotel—and the bar in the lobby. But finally Chazin just hung up.

Ball realized as he went back into the kitchen that being yelled at had transformed his status. Before, everyone had stared at him, trying to figure out who he was. Now, they smirked.

That was a lot better. Having a role to play—even as the butt of everyone's jokes—meant he belonged. He took a bottle of water from the cooler on the floor, opened it, and leaned against the sink.

The nearby clock said it was ten minutes past five. Guests wouldn't be arriving until seven; the senator was expected around nine.

Just a few hours to go, Ball told himself, taking a long slug from the bottle.

145

THERE WAS A perceptible uptick in the energy level of the President's aides as Marcke entered the back of the banquet hall where he was to give the keynote address to a group of entertainment executives. The number of BlackBerries being consulted at any one moment doubled; men and women tilted their heads forward ever so slightly as they walked. The chief of staff veered to the side of the bubble to take a phone call.

The President, though he couldn't have helped but notice, continued into the reception area, shaking hands and smiling as he greeted the guests. Dean glanced at the Secret Service agents fanned out around Marcke. They watched the crowd warily, eyes sweeping indiscriminately, checking and rechecking. A few of the guests pulled back under their stare, but the President seemed not to notice his bodyguards or their concerns, plunging deeper into the crowd.

"Hard to watch what's going on in a place like this," Dean said to a Secret Service agent he'd been introduced to earlier. The man, concentrating on a nearby doorway, grunted.

As the President reached the entrance to the main reception hall, his chief of staff, Ted Cohen, approached from his left and touched his elbow. Marcke bent toward Cohen, listened to a whisper, and then nodded before continuing into the hall. Dean followed along, now at the back edge of the bubble. The buzz in the room grew louder. All eyes except the Secret Service agents' either were on the President or were trying to get there. There was wonder and awe in people's faces; Dean realized he must have looked that way, too, when he first met Marcke.

"Charlie, we're going to go back to Washington after this," said Cohen, sidling up next to him. "The President has a problem to deal with. Are you coming with us or staying here?"

"I don't know," said Dean. "I'll have to check in and find out."

"There's food in the room there for staff," Cohen added. "The President wants you to stay close. Is that all right?"

"Of course."

Dean found a quiet spot in the hallway. Pretending to use his sat phone, he turned his com system on.

"This is Dean."

"Hey, Charlie, how's it going?" said Rockman in the Art Room.

"I'm all right. The President is cutting short his trip and flying back to D.C. tonight. What am I supposed to do?"

"Stand by."

Dean glanced down the hall. Beside the Secret Service agents, there were men from the LA Police Department and two federal marshals who'd been called in for extra protection.

"Charlie, this is Chris Farlekas. How are you?"

"I'm fine, Chris."

"If the President doesn't need you, we'd like you to stay in LA and help look for Ball. We're pretty sure he's in Los Angeles. We're supposed to get an update from the research people and the FBI people at ten P.M. Ambassador Jackson will be on the conference call. A Secret Service agent named John Mandarin will be in charge. He's traveling with the McSweeney campaign but will be back at the local office by then. We'll plug you into the circuit."

"The President still may want to talk to me," said Dean.

"Why?"

"He didn't say."

"He's the boss," said Farlekas. "Let us know when you're free."

* * *

THE APPLAUSE THAT greeted the end of the President's speech was polite but not particularly enthusiastic. The President had told the movie and television moguls how important their industry was to the country and in the course noted several times how profitable it was. They—rightly—interpreted that to mean they weren't getting the production tax breaks they'd been lobbying for. He could have suggested government censorship and received a more enthusiastic response.

One of the chief of staff's aides gave Dean the heads-up, and Dean went with her to the presidential limo.

"Mr. Dean, I hope you had a good meal," said the President when Dean reached the car. "Ted got me a doggie bag. Come on and ride with me. We're going to visit Senator McSweeney."

Dean realized he must have looked surprised, because the President laughed.

"I hope he's as surprised as you are," said Marcke. "I planned on doing this tomorrow, but this is even better. I want to see if what he tells me is any different from what he told you."

146

MCSWEENEY ENGAGED IN his pre–meet and greet ritual—he took a quick shot of bourbon from an ancient metal flask, then washed it down with a squirt of mouthwash. He peeled off a Wint-O-Green mint from his roll of Life Savers and popped it in his mouth, reaching for the door of the car.

Jimmy Fingers met him outside the car. "You're not going to believe this," said Jimmy. "The President wants to talk to you tonight."

"What, does he want to make sure we don't wear the same dress tomorrow?" snapped McSweeney sarcastically.

"He didn't say. It may have to do with Iran—there was just an assassination attempt on the prime minister. It's just hitting the Internet now."

"Oh," said McSweeney. He couldn't decide whether to feel flattered or to suspect a trick.

Being from New York, McSweeney had a significant number of Jewish constituents and was considered close to Israel; ironically, he also represented a substantial number of Iranian-Americans and had twice spoken to pro-reform groups.

Before becoming President, Marcke had spoken with him regularly about the Middle East. Now that there was a crisis, McSweeney thought, he had no choice.

"Where does he want to meet?" McSweeney asked Jimmy Fingers.

"At the Paley house. It's on his way to the airport, or so he says."

"The Paley house? He's up to something."

McSweeney considered what that something might be. While the President changed his schedule the way some politicians changed their socks, this was the sort of deviation the press couldn't miss. Why go out of his way not just to meet McSweeney but also to do it on what was metaphorically his turf?

"Marcke is always up to something," said Jimmy Fingers. "The question is what."

McSweeney thought back to the meeting with Dean—was that what this was about?

Jesus.

"Should we put him off?" said McSweeney.

"We don't want to look like we're ducking him. He is the President." Jimmy Fingers rubbed his knuckle along his lower lip. "He wants to get you on the record."

"What if I don't want to go on the record?"

"It's a no-brainer. You back Israel. Be very strong."

"I can't take the meeting."

Jimmy Fingers gave him a look McSweeney hadn't seen in years.

"What do you mean?" said the aide.

"It's some sort of trap. It's got to be."

Jimmy Fingers shrugged. "Marcke coming here—frankly, even if you didn't give him a commitment, you'll still look good."

McSweeney thought about the man who had confronted him the day before—Dean, clearly sent by the President. After dissecting the meeting, McSweeney had decided that Dean didn't know everything, and that he certainly couldn't tie him to the money. But maybe he'd been wrong—maybe the President could.

If that was what the President wanted to see him about, then he couldn't run away, could he? Marcke might be hoping he would.

It would be just like Marcke to get on his high horse, to try to confront him—try to trick him—to get sanctimonious with him.

Let him. He'd find a way to turn it around.

He would. And in any event, it was too late to run away.

"Maybe this has to do with the whacky Vietnam theory," Jimmy Fingers suggested. "Maybe he wants to tell you personally."

"Maybe."

McSweeney teetered on the brink of telling Jimmy Fingers the entire truth, but he pulled back. It would be a mistake, a bad mistake. He had to tough it out.

"Do you want to take the meeting or not?" asked Jimmy Fingers.

"Yes," said McSweeney quickly. "I have nothing to fear. Bring him on. It makes me look good, right?"

Jimmy Fingers studied him for a moment. Should they call it off? McSweeney wondered. Would that make it look worse?

He was being paranoid, he told himself. This certainly had to be about Israel and Iran.

"It'll make you look good," agreed Jimmy Fingers finally. "Very good."

147

TOMMY KARR WHISTLED as he walked through the foyer of the Paley house.

"Nice digs," he said. "You could build a cathedral with all this marble."

"What makes you think this isn't a cathedral?" said Theresa Seelbach, the *Newsweek* reporter.

"It's a shrine," said another. "To cheap Arizona real estate and slasher movies."

"To *once*-cheap Arizona real estate," said Seelbach.

"I didn't realize Paley was backing McSweeney. Didn't he give money to Marcke last time?"

"It's the wife," said Seelbach. "Besides, all these people hedge their bets."

Karr continued into the large great room. It was easy to tell who was a newsperson and who wasn't; the guests were several times better dressed and lacked the cynical masks that were part of the journalists' uniform. Security people were scattered around the edges of the room, trying to look as unobtrusive as possible. It was a small gathering—only about seventy-five people had been invited—but the net worth in the house rivaled that of several Third World countries.

"Tommy, are you listening?" asked Rockman from the Art Room.

"Always," said Karr, walking toward the jazz combo set up near the indoor fountain.

"Can you talk?"

"Only with my mouth."

Karr glanced at the fountain, wondering if it would be tacky to throw a coin in and make a wish.

"President Marcke is on his way over to the Paleys'."

"That's nice."

"You see Chief Ball there?"

"Lots of policemen. And even more Secret Service people—I bet there's more of them than squirrels outside. But I haven't seen Ball yet."

"Is McSweeney there yet?"

"Nah. Supposed to be here soon, though. They send the press ahead. You know these mansions get bigger and bigger as the night goes on?"

"Keep an eye out for Ball."

"Now there's something I hadn't thought of myself," said Karr, smiling at the band member who had started to stare because he was talking to himself.

"Excuse me, sir," said a Secret Service agent, easily identifiable by his lapel pin, radio earbud, and bad haircut. "But we're asking everyone to go outside so we can sweep the building again."

"What are you sweeping it for? Dirt?" joked Karr.

"Weapons, sir," said the man. His utter lack of humor made Karr laugh even harder.

148

THE PRESIDENTIAL CAVALCADE whipped through the Paleys'
gates, sweeping by the armed Secret Service agents and their
black SUVs flanking the road and driveway. The President's
car was admitted past a small barricade formed by police
cars and Secret Service vehicles to a courtyard in front of
the house. The rest of the fleet had to park on the driveway,
aides and then reporters disgorging through a gauntlet of security people as they were shuffled toward the house.

Dean, sitting with the President in his car, could tell the
aides were baffled by his decision to talk to the senator. It
was obvious that, with the exception of Cohen, they didn't
know Marcke's real reason for coming.

They probably wouldn't have approved even if they did,
Dean realized. They looked at things from a political point
of view; it was their job, after all. But having spent his time
watching Marcke, Dean had come to believe that the President wanted to confront McSweeney not because he was a
political rival, but because Marcke was personally outraged
that a senator could have betrayed his trust as an officer and
a Marine during the war. He was going to call McSweeney
on it.

It was, Dean thought, an overly idealistic, perhaps even
naïve idea. And yet he completely agreed.

A pair of helicopters whipped overhead. While the Secret
Service had already secured the house for McSweeney, they
had redoubled their efforts because of Marcke. Agents armed
with high-powered rifles with night scopes stood nearby.

While they were always present when the President traveled, generally they were a bit more subtle.

The head of the Secret Service detail came to the President's car. Marcke, talking to a donor on the phone whom he was disappointing by changing his schedule, raised his finger for the agent to wait. The agent glanced at Dean wistfully, as if to say, *Does he do this to you, too?*

"What do we have?" Marcke asked when he got off the phone.

"Senator McSweeney is at the gate."

"Well, let him through. He's why we're here."

The President made another call. By the time he was done, McSweeney's car was parked a short distance away.

"Stay close, but in the background," Marcke told Dean. Then he got out and went to meet the senator.

"Senator, looks like we beat you here!" shouted Marcke.

"Mr. President," said McSweeney, leaving his aides and bodyguards in the dust.

"Gideon, you're looking very well," said the President. "Campaigning agrees with you."

"It does, Jeff. As with you."

The two men shook hands.

"I understand you're not going to make the dedication tomorrow," said McSweeney.

"No, the attempt on the Iranian prime minister has complicated the situation out there immensely. The Israelis are being blamed and they're bracing for an attack."

"Were they behind it?"

"Not that we know."

"Obviously, we have to support the Israelis," said McSweeney.

"I'm glad you feel that way."

"Come on in," said McSweeney. "Have a drink."

"Aren't you afraid I'll steal your thunder?"

"Ah. I already have their checks. Come on," added McSweeney. "We can talk about this some more."

"I do want to talk to you, yes," said Marcke. He turned and motioned to Dean. "Charlie, come along with us."

* * *

MCSWEENEY FROZE FOR a second as soon as he saw Charles
Dean step out of the shadows.

Good God, he thought to himself, Marcke knows
everything.

Does he? Or was this some sort of bluff, designed to un-
nerve him?

McSweeney glanced to his right, looking for Jimmy
Fingers.

"I'm here," said the aide.

"Actually, I think this would be better discussed between
you and I," said Marcke.

"Well you have your aide," said McSweeney, smiling
tightly. "I don't want to be outnumbered."

"Mr. Dean is along for informational purposes only."

"I have a few things to do inside the house," said Jimmy
Fingers.

"Thank you, Jimmy," said the President.

Jimmy Fingers, his back toward Marcke, rolled his eyes.

"Go ahead," said McSweeney.

Maybe it was better that it was just him, he thought.

"So what's this about, Jeff?" he asked the President. "Iran
and Israel?"

"I wanted to talk to you about a couple of things," said
Marcke, starting toward the house.

When in doubt, deny, deny, deny, McSweeney told himself, hustling to keep up.

149

BALL RETREATED TO the kitchen as soon as he spotted the reporters getting off their bus. McSweeney would be here in moments.

Was he doing this?

Ball thought about the village—*his* village—of Pine Plains. Over the years he'd occasionally chafed at its small size and, much more often, the political bs that was a necessary part of small-town government. But by and large he had had a good life there—an excellent one, one that commanded respect and attention.

That was gone now. Even if he didn't shoot McSweeney, he was doomed. Gordon and his big mouth had begun the unraveling. Gordon and his greed—trying to get McSweeney to go along with something he'd never go along with, certainly not at a time when he was trying to become President. Gordon had been a fool, even coming to Ball—tracking him down after all of these years!—and asking him to talk to McSweeney. As if he had any real influence at all.

What Ball didn't know was whether Gordon had gone to the Secret Service, or they had merely stumbled upon him somehow. From the questions that Forester and then the others had asked, it appeared that someone had made threats against the senator, and the Secret Service had then begun trying to figure out who had made the threats. Maybe they'd gotten a list of disgruntled constituents and others. Gordon would have been on the list. A routine check, a hint or two from Gordon, and it mushroomed. Forester's suicide—legitimate, as far as Ball knew—must have provided the catalyst. Ball realized now that at some point they must have suspected it wasn't suicide, and that he was involved.

Or McSweeney set it all up. It played out that way as well. Ball just couldn't decide which it was. McSweeney was devious enough to try to kill him, but Ball didn't think he was smart enough.

He should have done Gordon in Vietnam. That would have been the sensible thing to do.

Voices began to murmur in the other room. The reporters were snapping to. McSweeney would be there any second.

Ball took a deep breath, then turned around.

TOMMY KARR CONTINUED his seemingly casual tour of the house, methodically checking each room while planting video flies.

"Oh, so there's the food," said Karr, spotting a server leaving the kitchen with a tray of hors d'oeuvres. "What are these?"

"Liver pâté on herbed crackers," said the man.

Karr took one and plopped it in his mouth.

"Tastes like liverwurst," said Karr.

The man made a face and started to walk off.

"Hey, I like liverwurst," said Karr.

Just as he grabbed two more crackers, a tall, balding man walked from the kitchen past him.

Ball. And he hadn't even bothered to don a disguise.

SENATOR MCSWEENEY SWEPT into the house with a surge of energy, leading the President as if he were the host.

"Ladies and gentlemen, the President of the United States!" announced McSweeney, injecting as much bravado into his voice as he could muster.

The crowd parted. McSweeney raised his hand.

I'll get through this easily, he thought to himself. I've been in much worse situations. It happened a million years ago, and they can't prove a thing.

* * *

TOMMY KARR PUSHED the waiter to the side and started after Ball. But Ball was already going through the door, three or four steps ahead of him.

THERE HE WAS; there was the bastard right in front of him, raising his hand, waving as if he were the King and everyone else peasants.

Ball knew he'd made the right decision. He pulled the gun out.

Someone yelled. Someone started to duck. Someone dove at him.

There were others—the President and his bodyguards.

Where the hell had they come from?

Ball pushed the gun forward and squeezed the trigger.

CHARLIE DEAN DIDN'T realize what was happening at first. He saw a blond flash of hair flying out of the other room and realized it was Tommy Karr.

The Secret Service people grabbed at Marcke.

What's going on? wondered Dean.

And then he knew.

JIMMY FINGERS SAW it from the side of the room, saw the man coming from the crowd. He recognized him, knew exactly who he was: Christopher Ball, small-town police chief from Pine Plains. The bastard had once threatened to lock him up during a particularly nasty committee fight years ago.

What the hell was he doing here, and with a gun?

MCSWEENEY SAW SERGEANT Tolong in front of him, just to the side of his Secret Service bodyguard. McSweeney blinked, thinking it must be an apparition, a vision brought on by his unsettled nerves.

The vision didn't disappear. It was Tolong, not as he'd known him in Vietnam, but as Ball. He'd helped him settle years and years ago when the former sergeant hit rock bottom.

McSweeney, then a county legislator, had felt sorry for him—and guilty as well.

Plus, Ball had hinted that he might talk about what they had done if he had no other choice.

There was anger in Ball's eyes, anger that McSweeney hadn't seen since Vietnam.

He had a gun.

Something popped, and McSweeney felt a pain in his side.

TOMMY KARR THREW himself forward. He grabbed Ball's back just as he fired the gun. Karr's momentum sent them both crashing to the floor.

Ball had more energy in him than Karr expected. The chief squirmed to his left, and worked his elbow up into Karr's ribs. Karr grunted with pain—he'd broken the ribs a few months back and they were still tender—then leveled a fist into the side of Ball's face.

"Secret Service!" yelled Karr. "I'm with the Secret Service! He's down! He's down!"

His cry was too late to stop the three burly agents from jumping on top of him, squeezing him against Ball, who still had his elbow in Karr's ribs.

"Just get the gun," said Karr, fishing under Ball for his arm and the pistol. As he grabbed it, there was a muffled shot and a shudder beneath him.

JIMMY FINGERS CAUGHT himself as he fell back against the table, propping himself against one of the dishes of fancy desserts.

McSweeney was down. Chief Ball was down. The President was being hustled from the house.

It was like a dream, a very, very bad dream.

But it was happening, right in front of him.

All Jimmy Fingers could think of was that the President had set this all up.

Of course he had. If Jimmy Fingers could arrange a mock assassination attempt, then it would be child's play for the President to arrange the real thing.

Someone with a tackle box came from outside.

A paramedic. The President had sent one of his Secret Service paramedics.

Jimmy Fingers pushed himself forward toward McSweeney. His legs were so rubbery that he nearly tripped, and after three steps he collapsed to his knees, right over the senator. The paramedic had pulled away part of his shirt and had what looked like a large towel pressed against the side of his stomach.

"Jimmy Fingers," said McSweeney.

"Are you all right, Senator?"

"I know him," said McSweeney. "Tolong."

"No, it's Chief Ball," said Jimmy Fingers. "I can't believe it. A police chief? You'll be OK."

As the words left his mouth, he glanced up at the paramedic. The man grimaced and continued to work.

"I'm not going to run," whispered McSweeney.

"Why?"

"I can't."

"Did Marcke set this up? Did the President set you up?"

"The President has it all figured out."

"You're going to be OK. You'll *be* OK," Jimmy insisted.

"It's over."

KARR FINALLY MANAGED to convince the men on top of him that it was safe to get off his back. He slid his feet to the right of Ball's prostrate body and then, still holding Ball's arms, pulled him up.

"Still breathing," said Karr.

"He shot himself in the chest," said one of the Secret Service agents who'd jumped on Karr.

"We need another paramedic," said another of the agents, talking into the mouthpiece at his sleeve. "Stat."

Karr rolled Ball onto his back, and pulled away his blood-soaked shirt. The bullet had made a large hole in his chest, though there was so much blood it was hard to tell where exactly the gunshot was.

Ball blinked his eyes.

"Mr. Karr, this is Rubens. Is Mr. Ball conscious?"

"Barely."

"Please ask him if he took the shot on the senator at the hotel in Washington."

"Did you try to kill McSweeney before?" Karr asked.

"What?"

Rubens gave him the date and hotel.

Ball gave him a confused look. "No," he said finally.

"Paramedic's here," announced the Secret Service agent behind Karr, tapping him to make way.

150

THE E-MAILED THREATS had several things in common: they'd all been sent by e-mails, they had all come from e-mail accounts created only a few minutes before they were sent, and they had all been sent over the Internet by a user who had found an unprotected wireless network.

And that was about it, at least as far as Gallo could determine. He sent a number of e-mail messages to the addresses used to send the messages; each contained tracers that would have helped him track down the sender's "true" address. Not one was opened. The e-mail services that provided the accounts were of little help, since the information that had been provided was quickly shown to be fake.

What else did he know? Gallo got up from his computer to give his eyes and neck a break. He started doing push-ups on the floor.

The sender had oldish laptops; the working theory was that they were secondhand and disposed of after being used.

The sender knew at least a little bit about computer networks.

The sender moved around a lot. A message had been sent from Washington, D.C., one from suburban New York, and one from Las Vegas.

Gallo was on push-up seventy-three when his phone rang. Usually the phone meant trouble, but he was getting winded and decided to answer it anyway.

"Robby, this is Hernes Jackson. The Secret Service has

been looking at the last of the threatening e-mails, the one sent to Dalton."

"No kidding. I'm, like, working that thing right now."

"That's why I'm calling, Robby," said Jackson. "A custodian found the laptop in Las Vegas, and the police tracked the owner to the Washington, D.C., area. He said he'd sold it at a used-computer meet in Washington several months ago. When the Secret Service showed up looking for the e-mail sender, the police told them about the notebook."

"Um, the thing is, Hernes, there aren't going to be records of the same, right?" said Gallo. "I'm going to guess it was a consignment thing."

"I know, but I thought you'd like to know."

"Yeah."

"I did have another idea."

"Fire away."

"You compared the e-mails to make sure they had the same author, right?"

"Sure. Didn't really need the text compare, but I did anyway."

Text compare was a software tool that took two or more pieces of prose and examined them for "commonalities"; it could tell whether they were written by the same person or not. In this case, the messages were so similar, the tool was superfluous.

"The constituents whom McSweeney had trouble with— can we compare those letters to the e-mails?"

"Yeah," said Gallo. "On it."

151

THE PRESIDENTIAL LIMO and the caravan of agents and aides traveling with it followed a preplanned exit strategy, racing to the highway in the direction of the airport. Though by now the Secret Service not only was in control of the situation there, but also understood exactly what had happened, they were taking no chances with the President's life. Feeder roads were shut down, and even traffic in the opposite directions was stopped. The airport itself was locked down. Air Force One was reported to be ready to leave as soon as the President went up the stairs.

President Marcke, however, had other ideas.

"In this political climate, leaving like this will make it look exactly like I'm running away," he told Vince Freehan, the head of his Secret Service detail, as the limo headed for the airport.

"Please, Mr. President. We really do know what's best."

"No, I'm afraid you don't," snapped Marcke angrily. "I am the President. Your job is to do what I say. Not the other way around."

It was the first time Dean had ever seen the President mad. It was more than the natural reaction of a headstrong leader when an underling tried to tell him what to do. Marcke was angry that McSweeney had been shot; it had been his responsibility to keep the senator safe, and he felt he had personally failed.

Dean guessed that the President was carefully considering his next move, thinking not about his own safety but of the effect of the incident on the country. While the chief of staff and the head of the Secret Service detail spoke excitedly to a variety of people outside the limo, Marcke switched on the live television feed and watched the initial reports of the incident on the local news stations.

He remained silent until the motorcade pulled onto the airport grounds.

"Find out where Senator McSweeney has been taken," he told the chief of staff.

"Pardon me, sir, but it's Sisters of Mercy Hospital," said Vince Freehan. "We have secured the hospital."

"Good. We're going to visit him."

"Jeez, Jeff, that's not a good idea," said Cohen.

"Bullshit it's not," the President told his chief of staff.

"Listen, if this is a conspiracy, if the Vietnamese are involved, there could be other shooters."

Marcke turned to Dean. "Are the Vietnamese involved?"

"Not that I know of, sir."

If Cohen's eyes had been daggers, Dean would have bled to death. Freehan began making logistical arguments about why the President should stay away from the hospital.

"I am the President of the United States," said Marcke finally, his voice calmer than before. "The President goes where the President has to. What if an enemy thinks he can scare me into running away?"

"There's a difference between running away and showing prudence, Mr. President," said Cohen.

"If that hospital is secure enough for Senator McSweeney, it's secure enough for me," said the President.

"You still have to be in D.C. for the Iranian-Israeli crisis," said Cohen. He was still arguing, but he had the tone of a defeated man.

"We'll get there," said Marcke.

Then he turned to Dean.

"Do you know what the most important moment of the Reagan presidency was, Mr. Dean?" asked the President.

"No, sir, I don't."

"The moment he joked with his doctors after being shot.

Now most of the accounts of that are apocryphal, but even so, it was the sign of strength and vitality that the country needed. They rallied to him. His approval ratings soared after that, and his image was sealed forever. It allowed him to accomplish a great deal."

Dean nodded.

"People want to believe in their leaders," said Marcke. He turned back to Cohen and Freehan. "Let's get this show back on the road."

"Give us a few minutes, Mr. President," said Freehan.

152

THE FIRST TEN thousand or so letters were a little interesting, but even with the computer doing 99.9 percent of the work, Gallo found the comparisons beyond boring. He had to mechanically queue each batched correspondence file with the e-mailed threats so the computer could compare them. An hour into the project and he was falling over the keyboard, half-asleep. He tried drinking a Coke, standing rather than sitting, kneeling rather than standing, punching things in with his left hand rather than his right. But it was still dreadfully dull and routine.

His work was made harder by the fact that the files that the FBI had created during its investigation of the threat occasionally contained mistakes, like adding correspondence and in several cases memos from the senator's office, which threw off the analysis. Gallo had to inspect each file and strip that material out. Fortunately, he quickly learned that the files that were most likely to be "polluted" were large ones, and he zeroed in on those, stripping out the correspondence and memos, then resaving the file and running it through the tool.

He had just found a particularly large file, complete with several letters and three staff memos, when an instant message blipped on his computer screen from Angela DiGiacomo asking if he wanted to have dinner.

Well, yeah!

Whoa.

But how did he feel about a woman taking the initiative? Like he should've said something himself weeks ago.

He shot back a message, asking when she wanted to go. Waiting for her reply and seriously distracted, he managed to delete the wrong material from the file before inserting it into the tool.

The funny thing was, the tool came back with an 87 percent match—the best hit of the night, by far.

"*SAME PERSON!*" YELPED Johnny Bib.

And it really was a yelp. Rubens thought Johnny looked as if he was in physical pain, his hands twisting together.

"Read the memos!" said Johnny. "Note: uses colon. E-mail threat: uses colon. Likes to use the word 'now.' No serial comma. Perfect spelling."

"Well, that could be spell-check," said Gallo.

Rubens studied the documents and the report from the textual analysis tool, which purported to have discovered the author of the death threats among McSweeney's staff. While in general Rubens was a big believer in technology, he had his doubts about this tool—there were too many vicissitudes involved in writing even something as simple as an e-mail note or memo.

He turned to Gallo. "What do you think, Mr. Gallo?"

"Looks like it's a match," said Gallo. "But the guy is on the senator's staff."

Rubens turned toward the front of the Art Room. "Ms. Telach, where is Mr. Karr at the moment?"

"He's at the house where Senator McSweeney was shot, talking to the Secret Service people."

"Tell him to locate James Fahey. Tell him to watch him carefully."

"Fahey is with his boss," said Telach. "At the hospital."

"Charlie Dean's on his way there with the President," said Rockman. "They're just pulling up."

153

JIMMY FINGERS SANK into the steel hospital chair, his body deflating into a worthless pile of skin and bones.

McSweeney lay a few feet away, recovering from emergency surgery. The doctors had removed the bullet swiftly and without major complications; the prognosis for recovery was excellent.

But McSweeney wasn't going to run. Jimmy Fingers didn't know exactly what had been dragged out of his closet but knew it was serious. According to one of the campaign people, Ball had been ranting in the ambulance, going on and on about how McSweeney had cost him his life in Vietnam. McSweeney, he said, had made him steal government money in Vietnam.

A nut job, obviously. But one who wasn't going to be easily dismissed.

Especially since what he said tracked with what Dean had told McSweeney.

The ambulance people had heard it, and Jimmy Fingers would just bet one or both of them were on the phone right now with some reporter somewhere, selling tomorrow's headlines.

The Secret Service agent who had headed the investigation into the threats, John Mandarin, had come to the hospital but wouldn't talk to Jimmy Fingers at all. That, the aide concluded, was the worst sign of all.

I oughta blow the bastard's head off, Jimmy Fingers thought to himself. He wasn't sure which bastard he meant, though—Mandarin, Ball, McSweeney, or Marcke.

* * *

POLICE LINES HAD been set up blocks from the hospital, blockading traffic, but several television crews and a number of reporters had been allowed through and were camped about a block from the front entrance. The Secret Service brought the President to a side entrance near the laundry, blocking off access from the rest of the complex and getting Marcke in before the reporters knew what was going on.

A detail of Secret Service agents, along with backups from the federal marshals' service and the Drug Enforcement Agency, had effectively taken over the hospital. Armed federal agents stood at every hallway intersection, stairway, and elevator. Dean stayed close to the President, who, despite the pleas from his security detail, kept stopping to shake hands with nurses, aides, and doctors—and their accompanying Secret Service escort—as he made his way around to the emergency surgical center where Senator McSweeney had been taken.

JIMMY FINGERS DUG his hand deep into his pans pocket, fingering the trigger of his pistol.

All the years he'd spent getting McSweeney ready to run, then pulling off the masterstroke—the genius stroke, unprecedented in American history—that brought the senator from underdog to front-runner in one quick shot.

How was he ever going to find someone else to hitch his wagon to?

The short answer was, he wouldn't. He was too close to McSweeney. If the senator went down, he went down.

Poof.

McSweeney gurgled something. One of the nurses jumped over, checking the monitors.

"Where am I?" muttered the senator.

"You're at the hospital," said Jimmy Fingers.

"What the hell are you doing here?" McSweeney asked.

"What am I doing?" Jimmy Fingers felt his anger rise. "I'm watching out for you, the way I always do."

McSweeney shook his head.

I ought to kill you right now and be done with it, thought Jimmy Fingers.

Two large men in suits, obviously members of the Secret Service, parted the curtains at the front of the room.

"You're Fahey?" one asked.

"I am," said Jimmy Fingers. "What's up?"

"The President is on his way."

"What the hell is he doing here?" said Jimmy Fingers.

The agent couldn't have looked more shocked if Jimmy Fingers had turned into a butterfly.

"We don't want the President here," said Jimmy Fingers.

"What are you saying, Jimmy?" asked McSweeney.

"Senator, the President is on his way," said the Secret Service agent. "One of the chief of staff's assistants should be here momentarily. The President will be along right after that."

"We don't want him here, Gideon," Jimmy Fingers told the senator. "He's using this for political gain."

"The President can go anywhere he wants," said McSweeney. "I'm touched that he's concerned."

"He's *not* concerned," snapped Jimmy Fingers. "Not about you. This is all part of some setup."

"My God, Jimmy, give it a rest. Let the President come if he wants. I'm dying here."

THE PRESIDENT'S CHIEF of staff had located the head of the surgical team that had operated on McSweeney. The doctor and two of his assistants were standing in a small waiting area just outside the recovery room.

"Mr. President, this is an honor," said the surgeon. "I wish it were under different circumstances."

"How's your patient?"

"Doing very well, considering the circumstances," said the doctor. "He's conscious. Some of his people are with him."

"Can I speak with him?"

"By all means."

They started walking down the hall. Dean stayed close to the President, buttressed by two burly Secret Service agents.

There were armed federal marshals on both ends of the hall, and all the rooms in between had been vacated.

"Charlie, can you talk?" asked Rubens in his ear.

Dean took a few steps away and pulled out his sat phone, pretending to use it.

"Dean."

"There's a possibility that the person who set up the assassination on McSweeney was a member of his staff," said Rubens. "It may have been his aide, James Fahey, also known as Jimmy Fingers. We're in the process of informing the Secret Service right now. Fahey may be at the hospital. If so, it would be a good idea to apprehend him there now. He needs to be questioned."

"All right," said Dean, noticing that the President was heading into the recovery room.

JIMMY FINGERS HAD always prided himself on his ability to keep cool under difficult circumstances, but this moment was more trying than most. It wasn't bad enough that Marcke had ended McSweeney's career; now he was going to rub it in by using the assassination attempt to bolster his own image.

It was almost too much to handle. It *was* too much to handle, but Jimmy Fingers couldn't do anything about it. He was trapped in the room as the President came in, surrounded by his bodyguards and aides.

Damn all these bastards, thought Jimmy Fingers. Damn them all.

DEAN PULLED ASIDE Freehan, the Secret Service agent in charge of the presidential detail.

"Which one of these guys is James Fahey?" Dean asked.

"The senator's aide?"

"We have to talk to him."

"What?" Freehan put his hand to his ear, listening to a message. Then he looked back at Dean. "You sure about this, Dean?"

"Yeah."

The Secret Service agent turned abruptly and strode into the recovery room. Dean followed. A short, wiry man stood near the senator's bedside, glaring at the President, who was just bending over at the right side of the bed.

"Down!" shouted Freehan.

JIMMY FINGERS REALIZED the moment he saw the Secret Service agent's glower that they had figured it all out.

Somehow, they had figured it all out.

And then they were rushing at him, and he did the only thing he could do under the circumstances—he pulled his pistol from his pocket.

CHARLIE DEAN SAW Jimmy Fingers start to pull something from his pocket. He launched himself at the man, flying through the air like a guided missile.

Something cracked below Dean about midway across the room, but he continued onward, elbow and forearm up. He caught Jimmy Fingers in the neck and they fell back toward the wall. There were two more loud cracks, and Dean felt incredible pain.

He flailed, unable for some reason to form his fingers into fists, unable to kick with his legs or do anything else but grind his upper body into the other man's. There were shouts all around him, and another crack. Jimmy Fingers pushed up, and then his face exploded, a few inches from Dean's.

"He's down!"

"Go!"

"Go!"

"Dean? Dean? . . . Dean?"

THE PAIN WAS SO intense that it was impossible to tell exactly where it came from. It surged like a tsunami over Dean, pushing him beneath itself. Then suddenly he lifted free, spinning in a slow circle in the middle of the room.

Everyone was watching.

Not the Secret Service agents. Not the President. Not the senator or his aide. But everyone else.

Everyone. People he hadn't seen in thirty years, back in the Marine Corps. His first business partner. Sal, the gas station owner who'd given him his first job.

Longbow stood silently next to him, his bolt gun over his shoulder.

"I missed you, Charlie," said Longbow.

Dean couldn't answer. The room filled quickly. He didn't recognize many of the faces. Phuc Dinh was there—or rather, the man Dean had killed thinking he was Phuc Dinh.

Oh, thought Dean. Oh.

AS SOON AS the Art Room told Tommy Karr what had happened, he commandeered one of the Secret Service cars and drove to the hospital. He knew the general location, if not the address, but he didn't have to ask the Art Room for directions; half the city seemed to have turned out, trying to find out what was going on.

Helicopter gunships circled overhead and every police officer who lived within a hundred miles of LA had been called in to work. Even with his credentials out, Karr had a difficult time negotiating the roadblocks and the traffic; finally, with the hospital in sight, he abandoned the car and began jogging toward Dean.

Dean was still in intensive care when Karr arrived.

"Better get Lia here right away, whatever it takes," Karr told the Art Room.

"HOW MANY THINGS would you change?" asked Longbow.

"I don't know," said Dean. "Maybe nothing important."

"Interesting," said his old friend. "You mean you've made no mistakes?"

"No, that's not what I mean. Of course I made mistakes. But how do you separate them from everything else?"

"Interesting."

"You know we killed the wrong guy in Quang Nam," said Dean. "It was his brother. He sent him as a decoy. Must suck to live with that."

"*You* killed the wrong guy."

"Yeah. He'd been tipped off somehow. But he was only on the list in the first place because the Americans who were paying him off stole his money and they were afraid he'd squeal."

"Did he?"

"Eventually."

"So that was one mistake you'd take back."

"I don't know. No. His brother was VC, too. Well, one thing I'd do differently—I wouldn't let you go to fill the canteens."

Longbow smiled. "Well, I wouldn't have let you go in my place. The man who got me had circled below the ridge. I shouldn't have been surprised. I even saw him before he fired. But I slipped a little—I missed my shot, Charlie Dean. Isn't that crazy? Whoever heard of a sniper missing his shot?"

"It happens."

Dean thought of the mountain lion, the sudden surge of adrenaline. A moment that could have gone either way.

How many moments were like that, when you could change things? How many would he change, if he really had the power to do so?

Maybe he did have the power. Maybe that was what happened—maybe you got another shot at doing things right when you died.

LIA'S LEGS TREMBLED fiercely as she walked down the hall of the hospital. Tommy Karr walked beside her. For the very first time since she'd known him, he didn't crack a joke; he didn't chuckle; he didn't laugh; he didn't even smile.

"This way, ma'am," said the aide who was leading them. They passed through a double set of doors into a large room. Hospital beds were clustered around the room, each one surrounded by several carts of medical equipment. Monitors beeped; displays burned green; vital signs charted into undulating hills on the black screens.

Charles Dean lay in a bed next to the nurses' station, surrounded by machines. Tubes ran to his face and arms. He'd been hit by three bullets. One had punctured his lung; one had severed an artery; a third had slipped against the outer wall of his heart.

"Charlie Dean," gasped Lia. "Oh, Charlie."

A WOMAN PARTED from the crowd. It was Qui Lai Chu, the woman who had been his guide and translator in Vietnam.

"You've come back, Mr. Dean," said Qui. "Why?"

"It was my assignment. I didn't come on my own."

"You came to see the road you might have taken."

"No," said Dean. "You're wrong."

"Where will you go now?" asked Qui.

"I'm not sure."

"Are you ready to die?"

Dean thought about the question for a long time. Finally, he said that he didn't think it was up to him.

"No," said Qui. "But you should know that you won't be forgotten. You will not turn into a hungry ghost."

For some reason, that comforted him.

LIA GRIPPED DEAN's hand and leaned close to his ear.

"Charlie? Charlie? Can you hear me?"

He turned his head toward her. The nurse behind her waved to one of the doctors, motioning him over.

"Lia," Dean said, without opening his eyes.

"Charlie?"

"I'd do it all again. Everything. Us."

Lia sank to the floor. "Oh, God," she prayed.

"It's all right," said Dean, opening his eyes. "I'm going to be OK."

"Charlie."

"I'm going to be OK."

"You want kids?" she asked.

"Yeah. Do you?"

"Yes."

Dean smiled, then closed his eyes. "I'm tired. Real tired."

Lia looked up and saw the doctor staring down. "Is he going to be OK?" she asked.

"I'm going to be OK," Dean said to her. "I'll be walking out of here tomorrow."

"You're not walking out of here tomorrow," said the doctor sharply.

"But he will be OK," said Lia.

The doctor paused for what seemed the longest time, then nodded slowly.

"He'll recover. But he has to take it slow. Very slow."

"That word's not in my vocabulary," said Dean.

Lia put her hand against his cheek. "It is now," she told him. "It is."

Turn the page for an excerpt from the next
book by Stephen Coonts

THE ASSASSIN

Coming soon in hardcover from
St. Martin's Press

Prologue

Ragheads dragged the driver out of the vehicle and took him away," the sergeant told the lieutenant, who was sitting in a Humvee. "They shot the woman in the car. She's still in it. Iraqi grunt says she's alive but the assholes put a bomb in the car. They're using her as cheese in the trap."

"Shit," said the lieutenant and rubbed the stubble on his chin.

The day was hot, and the chatter of automatic weapons firing bursts was the musical background. The column of vehicles had ground to a halt in a cloud of dust, and since there was no wind, the dust sifted softly down, blanketing equipment and men and making breathing difficult.

U.S. Navy Petty Officer Third Class Owen Winchester moved closer to the lead vehicle so that he could hear the lieutenant and sergeant better.

He could see the back end of an old sedan with faded, peeling paint sitting motionless alongside the road about fifty yards ahead. Three Marines and three Iraqi soldiers were huddled in an irrigation ditch fifty feet to the right of the road. On the left was a block of houses.

"Let me go take a look," Winchester said to the lieutenant.

"Listen, doc," the sergeant said, glancing at Winchester. "The ragheads would love to do you same as they would us."

"I want to take a look," Winchester insisted. "If she can

be saved . . ." He left it hanging there as distant small-arms fire rattled randomly.

The place was a sun-baked hellhole; it made Juarez look like Paris on the Rio Bravo. The tragedy was that real humans tried to live here . . . and were murdered here by rats with guns who wanted to rule the dungheap in the name of a vengeful, merciless god, one who demanded human sacrifice as a ticket to Paradise.

The lieutenant had been in Iraq for six months and was approaching burnout. The wanton, savage cruelty of the true believers no longer appalled him—he accepted it, just as he did the heat and dirt and human misery he saw everywhere he looked. He forced himself to think about the situation. A woman. Shot. She would probably die unless something was done. So what? *No, no, don't think like that,* he thought. *That's the way they think, which is why the Devil lives here.* After a few seconds, he said, "Okay. Take a look. And watch your ass."

The sergeant didn't say another word, merely began trotting ahead in that bent-over combat trot of soldiers the world over. With his first-aid bag over his shoulder, Winchester followed.

They flopped into the irrigation ditch directly opposite the car, where they could see into the passenger compartment. There was a woman in there, all right, slumped over. She wasn't wearing a head scarf. They could see her dark hair.

Fifteen feet from them was the rotting carcass of a dog. In this heat, the stench was awe-inspiring.

An Iraqi soldier joined them. "She has been shot," he said in heavily accented English. "Stomach. I get close, see her and bomb."

"How are they going to detonate it, you think?" Winchester asked, looking around, trying to spot the triggerman. He saw no one but the Iraqi soldiers and Marines lying on their stomachs in the irrigation ditch, away from the dog. The mud-walled and brick buildings across the way looked empty, abandoned, their windows blank and dark.

"Cell phone, most likely," the sergeant said sourly. "From

somewhere over there, in one of those apartments. Or a garage door opener."

"Saving lives is my job," the corpsman said. "I want to take a look."

"You're an idiot."

"Probably." Winchester grinned. He had a good grin.

"Jesus! Don't do nothin' stupid."

With that admonition ringing in his ears, Winchester ditched the first-aid bag and trotted toward the car. From ten feet away he could see the woman's head slumped over, see that the door was ajar. He closed to five feet.

She wasn't wearing a seat belt, and a bomb was lying on the driver's seat. Looked like four sticks of dynamite, fused, with a black box taped to the bundle. The woman moved her head slightly, and he heard a low moan.

Winchester ran back to the ditch, holding his helmet in place, and flopped down beside the sergeant.

"There's a bomb on the driver's seat," he told the sergeant, whose name was Joe Martinez. "And she's still alive. I think I can get her out of there before they blow it. Takes time to dial a phone, time for the network to make the phone you called ring. Might be enough time."

"Might be just enough to kill you, you silly son of a bitch."

"The door is ajar and she isn't wearing a seat belt. I can do this. Open the door and grab her and run like hell."

"You're an idiot," Sergeant Martinez repeated.

"Would you try it if she was your sister?"

"She ain't my sister," the sergeant said with feeling as he scanned the buildings across the road. "What do they say? No good deed goes unpunished?"

"I will go," the Iraqi soldier said. He laid his weapon on the edge of the ditch, began taking off his web belt. "Two men, one on each arm."

"She's *my* sister, Joe," Owen Winchester said to Martinez. He grinned again, broadly.

The sergeant watched as Winchester and the Iraqi soldier took off all their gear and their helmets, so they could run faster.

"You fuckin' swabbie! You got balls as big as pumpkins. How do you carry them around?" Martinez laid down his rifle, took off his web belt and tossed his helmet beside the rifle. "I'll get the door. You two get her." He took a deep breath and exhaled explosively. "Okay, on three. One, two, threeeeee!"

They vaulted from the ditch and sprinted toward the car. The sergeant jerked the door open. The other two men reached in, Winchester grabbing one arm and the Iraqi the other, and pulled the wounded woman from the car, then hooked an arm under each armpit. Joe Martinez picked up her feet, and they began to run.

They were ten feet from the car when the bomb exploded.